the Viper & the Urchin

NO. 3

the
SLAVE
CITY

CELINE JEANJEAN

Cover design by Oli Price
www.capuchincreative.com

Want to find out how Rory became a pickpocket and how she met Jake?

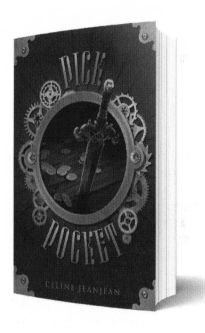

Then *The Pickpocket* is for you. You can get this book for free, exclusively, by going to:

For Oli.
My stories wouldn't be the same
Without the adventures we share.

CHAPTER 1

Cruikshank watched the tattoo gun trace a delicate black line on her abdomen. The teeth of a cog slowly came into being—a simple outline.

"I thought you were done with going overseas," Liv said without looking up from her work. The tattoo gun whirred in her hand, the little magnet at the top spinning back and forth, moving the needle up and down. A thin tube pushed pressurised steam through the gun, while another tube allowed it to escape at a safe distance with a faint hiss.

Cruikshank had designed the gun herself—a fun, neat little invention but one that carried a lot of weight and meaning despite its diminutive size. This was its fifth iteration, and this time she had built it using mementos from her life. The little knob that controlled the steam pressure, and therefore the speed at which the needle moved, was a coin from a mission in Aalergia. The handle was wrapped in the leather from her very first vest as a machinist. The ink was stored in a small crystal vial, one of the many gifts she had received to celebrate the completion of Damsport's Enclosed Docks. The vial was, in fact, the smallest and least valuable of the gifts, but it had come from a poor merchant who was thanking her for the opportunity the docks would bring to him and his family.

Cruikshank had made the vial part of her tattoo gun because the knowledge that her docks helped poor Damsians prosper meant more to her than all the other accolades she had received.

"I thought I was done going overseas too," Cruikshank said. "But I guess I was wrong."

"Will it be dangerous?"

"Would I be getting a cog if it wasn't?"

Liv nodded, her gaze never leaving the cog outline she was drawing.

Cruikshank looked away, letting her gaze drift aimlessly over the innumerable sketches, drawings, and plans that papered the walls of Liv's studio. The air even smelt of paper and ink—a familiar, comforting smell. It seemed every important event in her life since the Three-Day Battle had either begun or ended in Liv's studio, with Liv tattooing a cog on Cruikshank's skin.

The Three-Day Battle had won Damsport its independence from the Airnian Empire and had made it the city it was today. Cruikshank had been organising the city's defences the night before the battle. As a young machinist, she was woefully underqualified for the job, but there was no one else. An impulse made her pull Liv, a timid teenager apprenticing in technical drawing, away from her task. Out

2

of a bit of copper tubing, some thread, and a needle, Cruikshank fashioned a tool that could serve to draw a tattoo. Liv had tattooed the outline of the very first cog on Cruikshank's right wrist.

Cruikshank still couldn't explain the impulse, but she knew that it had been the right thing to do. Liv had completed the tattoo once the battle was finished, and over the years, Cruikshank had added another cog for every important event and person in her life since then. The tattoo now covered her right arm and shoulder as well as her back. The bottom of the tattoo was gradually extending around her waist and across her stomach.

Some cogs represented people Cruikshank had lost, others people she had met. Some were situations she had survived or challenges she had overcome. She knew what each and every cog represented. Together, they were a physical manifestation of her memories, which made her as surely as cogs made up the inner workings of a machine.

Liv, however, was the only one who knew the meaning of the tattoos. To everyone else, they were simply the quirk of a machine-obsessed woman. The tattoos bound them in a friendship that had spanned decades.

Cruikshank let her gaze trail over her right arm. A number of the cogs there represented missions she had carried out for the Marchioness when she'd been younger. It was a rocky period, during which Damsport struggled to establish itself. Short of people she could trust, the Marchioness entrusted Cruikshank with a number of diplomatic and covert missions as well as having her design

Damsport's defences. Once Damsport's position was secure, Cruikshank had asked to retire, preferring to return to a life of machine work.

It seemed the time had come for her to come out of her retirement. She looked at the partial cog outline Liv was still drawing to represent this event. She felt a thrill of trepidation. Cog outlines were only ever drawn when she was embarking on something potentially dangerous, and it had been a long time since she'd needed one.

Ever since that first tattoo before the Three-Day Battle, which was completed after the battle had been won, Cruikshank hadn't been able to shake off the superstition that she needed an incomplete tattoo to ensure her safe return from whatever she was embarking on.

"Azyr," she whispered softly to herself, feeling the word on her tongue.

Lady Martha had only told her it would be a rescue mission. The full briefing would be later that day. Cruikshank had prepared by researching all she could about the distant city state.

Liv finished the cog outline. "There."

It was flawless, as expected—precise, neat, and fitting perfectly within the wider tattoo.

"You'll come back to complete it?" Liv asked, glancing at Cruikshank's face and then away again.

Cruikshank smiled. Even after decades of close friendship, Liv's crushing shyness and extreme introversion made expressing emotion difficult for her.

"Absolutely. And soon."

"Good." The word was curt, but it was accompanied by a small, warm smile. That was as close as Liv would get to expressing that she cared and would worry.

"Thanks, Liv."

Liv nodded and gave another quick smile.

Cruikshank stood up and let loose the oversized white shirt she'd held bunched up to her chest.

She said a quick goodbye to Liv and stepped out into the sunshine, heading for the mansion. She took a deep breath, the old, familiar feeling in the pit of her stomach. Now that she had the tattoo, the mission finally felt real.

***

Lady Martha was the very picture of efficient confidence, perfectly fitting in her role as acting Marchioness. Her mother had retired while she mourned the loss of her old lover, Mizria, and until the Old Girl returned to power, Lady Martha held the reins of the city.

Cruikshank occasionally found herself wanting to impart advice or guidance. She had known Lady Martha since she was a baby, but Lady Martha had long ago stopped being a young girl, and she'd been helping to rule Damsport for a long time. And Cruikshank had to admit that she was doing a stand-up job of stepping into her mother's shoes.

Lady Martha's office was all bright light and pale tones, a comfortable space designed to put people at ease. Cruikshank knew from experience that while Lady Martha didn't use intimidation as a tactic, she could be every bit as formidable as the Old Girl.

"You know Samuell Kadelta?" Lady Martha asked.

"Yes, he's a Damsian machinist," Cruikshank replied. "I worked with him for a time. He had some good ideas and considerable skill, but he was obsessed with the idea of creating a submersible. The problem is that a steam engine requires air, and it requires an exhaust. You can make a ship that sails just beneath the water, with air pipes and exhausts breaking the surface, but all it takes is a large wave, and the engine floods. Kadelta's last attempt at solving that problem resulted in an explosion that severely injured his assistant, and he fled the city in disgrace."

Cruikshank didn't add that while he had talent, Kadelta was arrogant to a fault and headstrong. They had collaborated on a couple of projects, but despite his skill and the potential of the machine he wanted to build, she had found him too unpleasant to work with and refused to collaborate further.

Lady Martha nodded. "It seems he has solved that problem."

Cruikshank raised both eyebrows, intrigued.

"I've been in communication with Reheeme, an Azyrian woman and the Head Alchemist out there. Her parents knew my mother well. They were reformists, and they were killed during the Seneschal's cleansing of the opposition during his rise to power."

Cruikshank knew about Azyr's troubled history. The Prelate was Azyr's leader, a title passed down in his family over generations. He was mostly a figurehead—the reports Cruikshank had read said he was more interested in eating, drinking, and watching pit fights than in ruling his city-state.

Meanwhile, the Seneschal was his chief advisor and the head of the Council—and therefore the true leader of Azyr.

The Prelate had raised his childhood friend to the position of Seneschal of Azyr the day he inherited his title, and the Seneschal had then meticulously cleansed the city of any opposition, dissolving the old Council and setting up a new one made up of only his strongest supporters.

"It appears that Kadelta has washed up in Azyr," Lady Martha continued. "And he has been made a slave by the Seneschal."

"How on earth did that happen?" Cruikshank asked.

"I don't know. But I want you to head up a rescue mission to get him and his machine out of Azyr. I'd be lying if I told you I was only looking to save a Damsian from a life of slavery, as abhorrent as the practice is. That machine of his—his ship that can sail under the sea—could mean that Damsport dominates all sea trade."

"That's *if* his machine works," Cruikshank pointed out. "He might only be making out that it's finished as an enticement for a rescue mission."

"Possibly. But it's a chance I'm willing to take. There's another reason why I'd like to send a team into Azyr. Reheeme is heading a rebellion against the Seneschal and the Prelate. She's looking to continue what her parents started, seeking fairer representation for the poorer parts of Azyr and an end to slavery. I've brokered a deal with her in which she will smuggle you and your team into the palace to help you rescue Kadelta. In exchange, I will provide you with documents confirming that Damsport will officially recognise Azyr's new government, once the rebellion has happened, and negotiate trade deals and alliances, with the proviso that slavery be abolished and the poorer areas of Azyr have both representation and fair access to water."

"They don't have access to water?" Cruikshank asked incredulously. She knew, of course, that not every part of the world experienced the kind of rainfall found in Damsport, but for her, ready water access was such a basic right, like access to air, that she couldn't imagine life without it.

"No, they don't," Lady Martha replied. "The wealthier part of the city controls all the water, and the people there use it as a way to keep the poorer parts in check."

Cruikshank nodded. "So we'd also be there to provide support to the rebellion."

"Exactly. And hopefully to provide a powerful incentive for everyone to play fair. When the Seneschal re-established the old slavery laws, Azyr lost a lot of its alliances and trade deals because very few countries want to be seen endorsing slavery. Damsport, for example, does no trade with Azyr. Having a trade deal with us should help as a motivation for the new government to be as fair as possible."

Lady Martha leaned forward intently. "If this mission fails, if the rebellion fails, the Seneschal would be left with the submersible, which would make it very easy for him to engage in slave smuggling. Azyr needs more foreign trade, and that is how he will obtain it. I can't stand by and allow slavery to come back. It was only abolished two generations ago, and there are many who would be happy to see the return of a lucrative source of income."

Cruikshank knew Lady Martha was right. Just off the top of her head, she could name a number of countries that would be happy to see international slave trade return.

"What will be our official reason for visiting Azyr?" she asked.

"An exchange of alchemical knowledge."

Cruikshank gave a wry smile. She had arranged mechanical exchanges between Damsport and other countries in the past, believing in the importance of spreading knowledge. The Marchioness had initially used some of those exchanges as fronts for covert missions. When Cruikshank had retired, she had categorically refused to let the knowledge exchanges continue to act as a front for spying and other such work.

"There won't really be an exchange of alchemical knowledge," Lady Martha explained. "I know you don't agree with using a real knowledge exchange as a front for a mission, but this will purely be a front. That will explain Reheeme hosting you all as Head Alchemist as well as the presence of Longinus—who will be posing as Damsport's Head Alchemist. Rory will be his assistant, you will be there to share your knowledge on how to run these types of exchanges, Adelma will captain the ship taking you there, and Rafe will pose as Longinus's bodyguard. A man of status in Azyr is expected to have a retinue and at least a couple of bodyguards, so this way, no one present will attract any suspicion."

Cruikshank nodded thoughtfully. It was a clever setup. She looked Lady Martha over. Her speech had contained no doubt—no search for reassurance or approval from an older, more experienced woman—even though this was the first mission she was setting up. Cruikshank respected that. It was the way a leader should be.

"It will be good to have a proper fighter with us too," Cruikshank said, "should anything go wrong. I've heard Adelma can be quite formidable, but having a Varanguard on our team should be an added asset."

Cruikshank had a lot of respect for the Varanguards, the elite fighters that formed the Marchioness's personal guards. She didn't know Rafe very well, but she knew he was well regarded as a Varanguard, and that counted for a lot.

"Adelma can have her ship ready to sail in three weeks," Lady Martha continued. "That should leave you enough time to get ready. Be careful out there. By all accounts, Azyr is a dangerous place. The Prelate is volatile and the Seneschal completely ruthless."

She stood to signal the end of the meeting. She and Cruikshank shook hands, and Cruikshank headed out to begin the necessary preparations for the mission.

Once she was back outside, the adrenaline finally began spreading through her like a red flower slowly unfurling. She would be leading a rescue mission in the far-off and dangerous city of Azyr. She pulled out a cigar, inhaled the smell of the tobacco, and lit it. She exhaled the smooth smoke with a smile.

It was crunch time.

CHAPTER

2

The Damsian docks were as busy as ever, an assault to the senses. Shouts rang out across the water, bells clanged, and metal grated as chains were used to lift heavy cargo. The air was thick with the smells of spices being brought to shore, mixing with the stink of livestock, old fish, rotten food, and the slimy green algae that clung to the stone of the docks. The day's heat was almost at full blast, the sun baking the docks and intensifying the stench.

Cruikshank loved the Enclosed Docks of Damsport. She had designed the complex system of locks that allowed the water level in the docks to be controlled and maintained, as well as the steam-powered cranes that swung up ahead to load and unload heavy cargo. In fact, she had been involved in every part of the creation of the docks.

They felt like more than just another of her creations. The enclosed docks felt like her children, and now that they were fully grown, they had taken on a life of their own—a noisy, stinking, hectic life. Cruikshank could never have predicted just how central to Damsport the docks would become, and every time she stood amid the chaotic sensory overload of the docks, she felt proud.

Adelma, the smuggler who would be captaining the ship taking them to Azyr, was doing her bit to add to the din. She stomped around the deck of her ship, the *Slippery Eel*, bellowing orders. Every so often, she paused to swing her five-year-old son, Tommy, up into her arms and carry him around with her for a time before placing him back down.

She was a massive woman, like a slab of muscle turned human, large enough to dwarf Cruikshank. The sides of her head were shaved, leaving only a thick plait of black hair along the back that swung all the way down to her waist. Her skin, which was dark even for a Damsian, spoke of years lived at sea.

Cruikshank hadn't yet decided what she thought of the woman. She liked her directness and the fact that she clearly knew what she was about, but Adelma also struck Cruikshank as a bit of a loose cannon, and that was never good when it came to a mission. And then, of course, there was the fact that Adelma liked to drink.

"Drunks can't be relied on," she muttered to herself.

"You do know talking to yourself's the first sign of senility?" a voice at her elbow said.

Cruikshank turned to find Rory grinning at her.

"You do know that eavesdropping is rude?" Cruikshank replied with a wry smile.

Rory's grin widened. "Just practicing ahead of our mission. Spying needs good eavesdropping skills, right?"

Cruikshank gave the girl an amused look. Rory was fond of "practicing" eavesdropping—almost as fond as she was of "practicing" stealing and picking pockets.

She was so slight that she looked as though a breath of wind might knock her over. She had put some weight on since her days as a scrawny street urchin, but no matter how much Rory ate—and she ate quite a lot—she didn't seem to get any bigger.

Her small frame looked all the smaller for the masses of hair that dwarfed her. It was matted and clumped in thick segments that looked more like rope than hair, trailing down her back. She had taken to wearing small copper rings and tubes in it, slipping them up some of the ropelike segments.

But Rory's most unusual trait was her eye color: they were blue. Damsians were a dark people—dark of skin, dark of eye, and black of hair. Rory had the dark skin of a Damsian, and at a glance, she could pass for one. But her blue eyes marked her out as having foreign blood too.

Growing up abandoned on the Damsian streets, she had no idea of her parentage, and Cruikshank often wondered what had happened to her parents. Her rough childhood never seemed to hold Rory back, though. She was one of the most positive and enthusiastic people Cruikshank knew.

"If you ask me," Rory said, "it's worth the journey to Azyr just to help them Azyrian rebels get their revolution underway. No person's got the right to take away someone's freedom and make a slave of them. That just ain't right."

"Don't forget that's the *unofficial* part of our mission," Cruikshank said. "We can't be seen to interfere with the way

13

other countries or cities are run. That would put Damsport in a very tricky position politically."

Rory tapped her nose. "Me and *unofficial* missions are like kin. It's like picking pockets—you don't go around advertising you're a thief." She gave a little laugh. "Or an assassin, for that matter."

Cruikshank followed her gaze to where Longinus was fussing over the porters carrying one of his trunks.

"Careful, careful!" he called. "This contains priceless alchemical equipment. Gently, *gently.*"

The porters inched the trunk down to the ground, following Longinus's instructions. Cruikshank was amused to notice that Longinus had them wearing gloves. They were burly men, dark-skinned and sweaty, and their ragged, dirty trousers were incongruous next to the clean white gloves Longinus had given them.

Longinus opened the trunk and inspected the contents. "Good, good. You may continue. And remember, if you drop the trunk, the wrong liquids might mix together and cause you to die a most agonising death."

Cruikshank frowned. "That's not true, is it?"

"Nah," Rory replied with a smile. "Just something to scare people into doing things the Longinus way. One of Adelma's sailors were gonna load his stuff on the ship for him, and Longinus nearly bust a vein when the sailor picked up his clothing trunk and threw it onto the deck. He's hired his own porters now and is paying them extra to do it all the way he wants. The time it's taking him, I hope he'll be done before the ship's ready to cast off."

Cruikshank shook her head. "He's an odd one, that boy."

Everything about Longinus was conspicuous, from the way he spoke to the way he dressed. Right now he stuck out like a whore in a convent, with his teal silk shirt, burnt-orange trousers, and hat with an elaborate teal-and-orange feather arrangement.

He wore his hair almost down to his shoulders, and somehow, it always looked as though he had just stepped out of the barber's. With his thin moustache and elegant, jewel-encrusted sword at his hip, he looked as though he belonged to a bygone era, not to the fast-developing industrial city of Damsport.

The porters picked up the trunk again, under a constant stream of warnings from Longinus.

"He ain't happy to be bringing his precious alchemical equipment," Rory said.

"You're telling me. I've had to listen to his endless complaining ever since he found out the official purpose of our mission." Cruikshank turned to Rory. "What about you? Are you ready?"

"Cruikshank, I own, like, five things. 'Course I'm ready."

Cruikshank slung an arm around Rory's neck and pulled out a cigar. "Well, lovey, in that case, we're not far off ready to leave. Rafe's already on board, checking on supplies, and Longinus should hopefully be finished with his fussing in an hour or so. We'd best get ourselves on the ship and get ready to cast off. You excited? I remember when I was sent on my first mission. I could barely sleep the night before."

"Am I excited? Going to a far-off city? Adventuring, thieving, and spying? Nah. Actually, you know what? It all sounds duller than ditchwater. I reckon I'll just stay here." Rory winked.

Cruikshank grinned back at her.

CHAPTER
3

It had never occurred to Longinus that he might not be a good sailor. The excellent curvature of his calves should, at the very least, have guaranteed him good sea legs, but it seemed to be part of the sea's idiosyncrasies not to take such information into account, and he had been seasick with a steadfastness that, in other circumstances, would have been admirable.

He gripped the cold metal railing of the ship's port side with both hands, steadying himself, as he felt yet another wave of nausea rise up within him. To add insult to injury, the sea that would soon be the recipient of his breakfast was animated by only the most gentle of swells, rolling contently beneath a blue sky scattered with fluffy white clouds.

The wind was so weak, in fact, that the ship had to rely on its small steam engine rather than its sails to propel it forward. If Longinus had to be stomach churningly sick, at least let it be on a stormy sea with lashing rain, howling wind, and cracking lightning! Was it really too much to ask for suitable levels of drama to accompany his dreadful ordeal?

Apparently so.

His head pounded, and his stomach lurched as if directly attached to every movement of the ship. The slightest sway sent his stomach roiling, and he was so sick and miserable that he had barely thought of Lady Martha or even taken the time to write her a single poem. A shame, as there was some beauty to be found on the ship, such as the diamond sparkle of sea spray in the sunlight. Longinus could have used that as a line for a poem, but he was too weak, too tired, and too sick to think about writing.

A seagull passed overhead, letting out a screech of mirth. Longinus glanced up at it, cursing the animal beneath his breath. He managed to briefly distract himself from his sickness by trying to come up with a poison that could kill seagulls midflight. It didn't last long, and soon enough, the metal railing was digging into his stomach as he leaned over it, his breakfast coming back up for a revisit.

At this rate, I'll lose so much weight that none of my clothes will fit by the time I get to Azyr.

As if the ordeal of seasickness weren't bad enough, he was also potentially facing a sartorial crisis.

"How's it?" Rory asked, walking up to his side. She clapped a hand on his shoulder.

"Soon I'll have nothing to wear," he replied miserably.

"What?"

Longinus didn't have it in him to explain. He straightened up, closed his eyes, and let the faint breeze flutter over his face.

"You no better, then?" Rory asked with concern. "I thought maybe when we stopped at that last port—"

"Getting off the ship just seemed to have made it worse since I got back on. Next time we stop, I'll think I'll stay on board."

"I'll stay with you, then. Although I don't think we got another stop now until Azyr."

Longinus turned to look at her. "Honestly, this time aboard the ship is enough to make me a religious man. I'd be tempted to take up orders if there was one god in this world that could make us arrive quicker."

Rory scratched her head, fingers disappearing into her mass of hair. "I dunno what god has to do with the sea. There's one what does the winds, I think. Anyway, they're all arseholes up there. They just do what they like, right, and then laugh at us when we fall. Like the wind god is probably making the wind weak so we go slow, because it's fun to watch you be sick. Like children picking the wings off a fly, the gods. I wouldn't count on them."

"If that's true about the wind god, I'll make a poison to kill him," Longinus croaked, feeling the beginnings of a new wave of nausea.

Rory grinned. "You go right ahead. If you can make a god-killin' poison, I bet there's some serious money to be made in that. We could set up a side business venture. I reckon Lady Martha wouldn't mind too much, so long as we complete our work for her."

Longinus groaned but didn't reply. He couldn't care less about money right now. What he cared about was the awful feeling in the pit of his stomach.

Rory had taken to ship life as easily as a seagull took to defecating on the ship's deck. She'd removed those god-awful boots and stored them below decks, so she could crawl up and down the rigging barefoot like a little monkey. She'd also swapped her leathers for linen trousers cut to a ragged hem below her knees—at the time of departure, nothing could be found that was small enough to fit her. A linen tunic, also too big but lashed to her waist with her plaited leather belt, fluttered in the breeze. Her skin had gone a shade or two darker since she'd been at sea, and it suited her. Her unusual blue eyes sparkled in the sunshine.

"I have a new sword-fighting move to tell you about," Longinus said, hoping to distract himself from his nausea again. He had planned to spend the journey continuing Rory's training, but the seasickness had prevented him from doing even that.

"Oh yes?" Rory asked immediately, giving him her full attention.

He began explaining the move, knowing Rory would appreciate it. He wasn't a fan of it himself, but then, he didn't like any form of attack that wasn't poisoning. The move consisted of throwing oneself forwards, legs first, using the momentum to slide past an opponent's legs, then slashing them at the right time with a sword or long knife and catching the tendons at the back of the ankles. It was downright crude compared to the subtle art of poisoning, but there was a certain showmanship to it that he knew Rory would like.

But before he could get into much detail, nausea gripped him again, and he fell silent, breathing heavily against it.

"The sword's not the right weapon for you," Rafe called from a little farther down the deck.

Rory glared at him but didn't answer.

Longinus didn't like Rafe very much. The lad's only response to things seemed to be sardonic amusement, a trait Longinus found thoroughly irritating. And worse, he had hurt Rory's feelings, which for Longinus was unforgivable.

But he had to admit that he agreed with Rafe—he simply didn't have the heart to tell Rory. She was too slight, too small for the sword, and although she was making progress, he thought she would be better suited to something like matched long daggers.

Longinus knew how much Rory wanted to be a swordswoman, so he kept quiet for the moment, not wanting to crush her dream. The girl was smart enough— she'd come to the right conclusion in her own time. So having Rafe stomp over this delicate matter with all the tact of a pig in an alchemical workshop was infuriating.

Rafe smiled at Longinus, as if oblivious to Longinus's glower. He had taken to ship life as well as Rory had. He too went around barefoot and in loose linen clothing. He was whip lean but without Rory's skinniness. Instead, he looked like he was made of pure muscle, an impression compounded by the economic yet graceful way he moved, each motion perfectly controlled and deliberate. His jet-black hair was blown about eyes that always danced with amusement.

"Nobody asked your opinion," Rory told him stiffly.

Longinus felt too nauseous to trust himself with speech.

"I know nobody asked me," Rafe said, making and unmaking various knots with a length of rope. "Doesn't change the fact that it's true." He looked up at Rory and Longinus through the strands of hair blowing in his eyes.

Rory glared at him. Longinus vainly tried to find some cutting remark to put the lad back in his place before he did something stupid like damage Rory's confidence. He had just come up with a suitable response when a resounding crash interrupted him.

CHAPTER 4

Cruikshank was climbing up from below decks, and she looked furious. If Longinus hadn't already been acquainted with Adelma, he would have described Cruikshank as fearsome. The machinist was dwarfed by the smuggler, but she was still an impressive sight, especially when angry. She wore a sleeveless linen shirt that fluttered around her, lashed to her waist by a leather girdle. Her arms were roped with muscles, the enormous tattoo of cogs on her right arm seeming to come to life as she moved.

She normally liked dyeing her hair russet, but she hadn't bothered of late, and her black Damsian roots gleamed darkly at the top of her head, streaked with silver, while the rest of her hair was a red, messy pile from which thick curls escaped. Her hands were as square as her jaw, and both were marred by soot, her fingernails rimmed with mechanical grease.

Cruikshank heaved a crate up from below decks, and it rattled with glass bottles. Her jaw was set in a determined line. A very nervous-looking ship's boy followed her soon after. He heaved one crate out and went back below decks, soon returning with another.

"There was a fourth crate, I think," Cruikshank told him. "In her cabin, under her desk."

The boy paled.

"You... you expect me to go into her *cabin*?"

"Yes. I'll stay here with this lot."

The boy looked around him anxiously, licking his lips.

Cruikshank put a hand on his shoulder. "That's a direct order, son," she said, not unkindly. "Adelma understands how the chain of command works. Any issue she has will be with me and not with you."

The boy looked miserable, but he nodded.

"Shit, she's actually doing it," Rory breathed.

"Doing what?" Longinus asked.

"Hey!" Came a small voice from the crow's nest. "Put my mum's rum back!" Tommy leaned over the edge of the crow's nest, watching the scene below.

A resounding crash below decks made Longinus jump.

"Where is she?" Adelma bellowed from below decks. "Where is that damned prig-faced harpy?"

"I taught her the word *harpy*," Longinus told Rory with a note of pride. Adelma's insults had always been colourful, but they were crude, and he felt that they could do with a little more panache, which he had been more than happy to supply.

The ship's boy backed away from the trapdoor leading below decks, as if some dangerous wild animal might spring out of there.

Which, on reflection, isn't far removed from facing an angry Adelma.

Cruikshank calmly lit a cigar and, clamping it between her teeth, hefted one of the crates. "Grab one of the crates and follow me," she told the boy.

The boy looked from her to the trapdoor, uncertainty and fear written all over his face.

"She won't do anything to you," Cruikshank added.

Longinus wasn't so sure, because what Cruikshank was doing was entirely inconsistent with the maintenance of health and life. Coming between Adelma and her rum was barely safer than coming between her and her son.

Adelma's head suddenly poked out of the trapdoor.

Rory laughed. "She looks like a hippo that's had nettles shoved up its arse."

Rafe snorted. "You tell her that to her face."

"You crazy? I ain't got no death wish."

Adelma heaved herself clumsily on deck, looking more like a beached whale than her usual strong and intimidating self. "Put that down," she bellowed as she picked herself up. She was a towering, walking slab of muscle, a woman so huge and strong that Longinus still sometimes had trouble believing she belonged to what he had once thought of as "the gentler sex." Cruikshank and Rory had done much to prove that the expression had no basis in reality, and Adelma had hammered the nail into the concept's coffin.

Cruikshank ignored Adelma and continued carrying her crate of bottles towards the ship's railing.

"Get back here!" Adelma rushed after her, lurching wildly as if the ship was rolling on a heavy swell. Her voice sounded thick with alcohol.

With a grunt, Cruikshank threw the crate overboard.

"No!" Adelma reached Cruikshank and swung a meaty fist.

Longinus winced, but Cruikshank ducked deftly and swung a leg out, kicking one of Adelma's legs out from under her.

Adelma staggered back, arms flailing, but she managed to regain her balance. "Dammit, woman! Having you on board's worse than having rot!" Her gaze alighted on the ship's boy, who stood slack jawed, still holding a crate. She growled, "You put that down, boy, or you're goin' overboard with it."

The boy dropped the crate as if it had turned into molten iron.

"Don't threaten the boy," Cruikshank said calmly. "He's acting under my orders."

"I'm the captain of this damned ship." Adelma marched up to Cruikshank. She was a good head taller than the machinist, who had to crane her neck to keep making eye contact.

"And I'm the leader of this damned mission," Cruikshank replied calmly. "My authority extends over *you* as well as everyone else on board."

"Not while we're at sea!" Adelma yelled, spraying Cruikshank with spittle.

Cruikshank wiped her cheek impassively with one hand. "At all times while the mission is underway. And I'll have no one getting drunk during this mission."

"Dammit, woman, look! Look at the damned sails." Adelma pointed up overhead. "Flatter than a flounder's tit! Ain't nothing to do but wait for the wind to return. And when the wind is weak, we drink and have a good time."

"It's tradition," one of the crew members added.

"Not while under my orders," Cruikshank snapped. "If you're thirsty, drink water."

"Ha! I'll drink water when the fish climb out of the sea to take a piss," Adelma replied.

Longinus frowned. *That makes no sense. I'll have to spend some more time on Adelma's insults.*

"Fine, then go thirsty," Cruikshank said. "The steam engine still needs tending to—"

"And it *is* being tended to," Adelma replied.

"It's nowhere near satisfactory. If you'd let me alter it before we left like I wanted—"

"I ain't letting nobody mess around with my ship before a long trip, alright? I'm responsible for all lives aboard the *Slippery Eel*, so I ain't having no unknown machinery."

"Responsible? *Responsible?*" Cruikshank laughed incredulously. "Look at you. You're not even capable of being responsible for yourself."

Adelma's expression changed to that slightly sly, slightly surprised look drunks took when they found themselves with an idea. "Well, I don't recognise your authority, and you can't make me." She pulled out one of her battle-axes.

"Whoa, whoa," Rory said, heading over. "Adelma, hey. Don't do nothing stupid, alright? We can figure something out, and…"

Adelma walked over to the crate the boy had abandoned and, with a grunt, moved it next to the main mast. She dragged the other crate next to it, smashed the lid open with her axe, and pulled out a bottle of rum.

"You want my rum, come and get it." And she sat heavily on the intact crate, plonking first one boot, then the other on the open crate. She uncorked the bottle with her teeth, spitting the cork across the deck. Her battle-axe gleamed nastily, lying across her lap.

"If you don't stop that right now," Cruikshank said, "I'll have you arrested."

Adelma grinned. "By who? Huh? I'm too big for you to move me alone, even if I get so drunk that I pass out. And let me tell you, ain't nobody on this damned ship stupid enough to move me without my permission."

Longinus glanced around at the ship's crew, who were watching the scene with amused interest. What he saw on their faces confirmed what Adelma had said: not one of them would cross their captain, irrespective of what Cruikshank said.

Cruikshank seemed to realise that too, and her face darkened.

Adelma burst out laughing. "Face it, you whey-faced, sour old shrew. You've lost this one. I'm staying right here, and me and my crew are gonna have a good time, enjoying the fine weather. And there ain't a damned thing you can do about it." She grinned, and true to her word, she began to glug down the rum like it was water.

Cruikshank's face looked like thunder. She turned to the first mate, a small, wiry man who stood at the ship's wheel. His bare chest was corded with sinew and muscle beneath his dark skin. He was as quiet and calm as Adelma was loud and mercurial.

"You agree with this?" Cruikshank asked him.

He nodded silently. "We only need a skeleton crew on a day like today. Sails don't need tending, and steam engine doesn't require much."

Adelma crowed with laughter, half choking on her rum. "Come on, boys and girls. You know the drill! Skeleton crew until the wind returns. Rum all around!" She hooted before returning to her bottle.

With unspoken agreement, the crew rearranged itself, most of them abandoning their tasks so that only a few still manned the ship. The rest either sat down to talk and laugh and drink with Adelma or brought rations of rum to those still working.

Cruikshank gave the crew a disgusted look before heading back below decks. Soon, lewd songs were being sung, each crew member taking it in turn to invent new, more disgusting verses. Rory seemed to hesitate at first, but she slowly drifted towards the group, smiling, drawn in by the laughter and the fun. Longinus was far too sick to partake. He breathed deeply instead, hoping the seasickness would soon pass.

"Sometimes I wonder if this is Lady Martha's idea of a joke," Rafe said.

Longinus turned to look at him.

"On the positive side of things," Rafe said, "the drunker they get now, the better the chance they'll finish all the rum before we reach Azyr."

He slapped Longinus on the shoulder in a gesture that felt far too friendly for Longinus's taste. Before he could tell the boy not to trespass into the territory of familiarity, his stomach found some remnants of breakfast.

Rafe made a derisory sound and walked away as Longinus whipped around and leaned once more over the ship's rail.

CHAPTER
5

Rory lay in her hammock, wide-awake, listening to the sounds of the ship at night. The rigging creaked, and the wood of the hull stretched and contracted, groaning softly. She could barely make the sounds out over the snoring that whistled from left and right.

The afternoon's shenanigans had been good fun, and now most of the crew were sleeping off the rum. The ship had sailed smoothly to the sound of raucous laughter and drunken singing, the crew evidently used to operating in that manner. Rory had joined in—it had looked like too much fun not to, no matter what Cruikshank said.

She felt a pinch of guilt remembering the disappointment on Cruikshank's face.

Now, though, she was regretting how enthusiastically she had taken part. Her head was pounding, and her poor, shrivelled brain felt like it had shrunk to the size of a raisin. The rocking of her hammock, normally comforting, was making her feel queasy. That was the problem when you were half the size of everyone else: even drinking half as much as the others resulted in her feeling sick.

Rory turned in her hammock. It was too hot down here, too close. The air was heavy with the breath and sweat of all those sleeping around her, and it stank of stale alcohol as if the stuff was leeching out of everyone's pores.

She tried to find a position that relieved her headache while blotting out the snoring. She felt a bit foolish and a far cry from the confident adventurer she had imagined herself to be as a kid. Still, she had done it: she had learnt to fight with a sword, and she had left Damsport to go to a far-off and exotic city.

Unbidden, thoughts of an old friend came to her. Daria.

She'd been Rory's first friend, the girl who had taught her pickpocketing. Rory turned in her hammock, shutting the thoughts away. She didn't like thinking of Daria. The sadness that came with those memories was suffocating.

Rory had been very efficient in keeping thoughts of her friend at bay for the last few years, carefully tucked away in a box that she didn't like to open.

But try as she might she couldn't stop the box from opening now. Maybe it was the alcohol, or maybe it was being on a ship—after all she had thought she'd leave on adventures with Daria, all those years ago.

Images kept flashing through her mind. She and Daria laughing as they pelted through the Damsian lanes, having just fleeced an old codger... the way Daria would sling her arm around Rory's neck... the way she would talk, so loud and brash.

Rory tossed and turned, doing her best to shut the box again.

It didn't work.

The sadness started to rise up. The sense of loss, because all she had left of Daria were those steel-tipped boots.

Rory huffed and tossed to her other side. Her hammock swayed, and she almost fell out. She rubbed both hands over her face. There was no point fighting it. For tonight, and only for tonight, she'd sit with her loss. After that, the box would be shut tight once more.

She sat up and winced at the thumping in her head. "I ain't never getting that drunk again, and no mistake," she muttered.

Clambering down from her hammock felt clumsy, her movements awkward and disjointed. She made noise, but the snoring continued, uninterrupted. She padded over to the barrel full of freshwater, grabbed the cup floating at the surface, and dunked it. The water was cool and fresh, and she fancied it soothed her head a little. She gulped down a second cup and wiped her mouth on her sleeve.

Then she went back to her hammock and crouched down beneath it to retrieve her boots from the box that held her few possessions. As she stood up, she found that she was desperate to get outside. She was having difficulty breathing down here. It was too hot, too close. Too crowded.

Fresh air was what she needed. Fresh air and time to sit with Daria's memory. She cradled the boots to her chest and headed to the ladder that led up to the deck.

"Tonight only," she whispered.

***

The starry night sky stretched out, limitless, overhead. Silver moonlight bathed the deck. The wind had picked up a bit, and the ship was making good progress. Rory took a deep breath and closed her eyes, revelling in the wind in her hair. The night was cool and crisp, and it felt good against her skin after the thick, fusty air below decks.

A glance over her shoulder told her the first mate still helmed the ship. He stood at the wheel, a storm lantern at his feet next to a cup of coffee from which rose a curl of steam. His face was hidden in the shadows, but Rory knew he would have seen her, and she gave him a small wave. He nodded back.

There was a skeleton crew silently manning the ship that night. Rory managed to pick out a couple of faces, and she recognised them as being some of the quieter members of Adelma's crew, the ones who hadn't taken much part in the afternoon's revelry.

A large, dark shape at the base of the main mast showed that Adelma hadn't budged. Rory wondered if Cruikshank had tried to move the smuggler. She felt a little bad for Cruikshank—but then again it had been a good laugh watching Adelma stand up to her. Rory shrugged to herself. All that would work itself out when they arrived in Azyr.

She padded past Adelma on silent feet, not wanting to wake her up. The smuggler shifted and grunted as Rory walked past.

"Radish," Adelma muttered. She made incoherent sounds. "Radish…" Her voice was thick with longing. "Where are you?"

Rory moved on quickly, not wanting to eavesdrop on Adelma's pain, even if the woman was asleep. Radish had been Adelma's man, and a good man he had been too. He'd deserved better than to have his brains turned to mush. Much better.

Radish had been made into a mindless zombie and then sent to murder Rory as part of a ploy to kill the Marchioness of Damsport. Adelma had killed him while trying to stop him.

"Radish, Radish," Adelma muttered.

Rory decided she would talk to Cruikshank in the morning. She wasn't sure if the machinist knew the full story about Radish, but surely, that would be reason enough to let Adelma get drunk in peace. Adelma wasn't the kind of person to whine or show weakness—she was more the kind to drown her grief in alcohol. Luckily for her, the sailor manning the crow's nest sometimes doubled as a nanny for Tommy, and the boy was kept away from the worst of his mother's drunkenness.

Rory climbed up towards the ship's prow, one of her favourite spots. She could sit right at the front, watching the horizon, or even lean over the side, watching the ship's hull slice through the water. It was the best spot for being bowled over by the sheer vastness of the sea, a feeling Rory still experienced every time she sat there. She often went up there when she couldn't sleep, sometimes even spending the night curled up on the deck, waking up with the sunrise.

It was a good place to sit and be with Daria's memory. Rory cradled the boots tighter. She opened her mouth and was about to whisper something to Daria's shade, when she realised that someone was already sitting in her spot, hidden in the shadows.

"Who's there?" she whispered.

The figure turned around with a start, face moving into the moonlight. Rafe.

Rory's stomach did a funny jolt. "What you doing here?" she hissed.

He raised an eyebrow at her. "Feels like we've been in this situation before," he said, quirking a smile. "You going to tell me that this is your spot, Mistress Magnate?"

Rafe hadn't called her that for a while. It was a nickname he had come up with when they'd first met, when he'd been seated in her spot atop a derelict house in Damsport. He had a habit of stumbling across the places where she liked to be.

"This *is* my spot, actually," Rory whispered. "So move."

Rafe shrugged and turned back to the sea. "It's my spot also. I've been coming here quite a bit. I was here first. There's no reason for me to move." He looked back over his shoulder. "But since I'm a generous man, far more generous than you, I'll allow you to sit down. See, it's called sharing."

Rory hesitated. She didn't want to sit next to Rafe, especially not when she had planned to spend time with

Daria's memory. But she also didn't want to turn tail and head back below decks. Daria deserved to feel the wind and see the sea and the night sky, and this was the best place to do it. And Rory really didn't want to go back below decks with the heat and the smell and the snoring.

"You better keep quiet," she whispered.

Rafe shrugged again. "Suits me. I didn't come here for conversation." He kept his face turned away from her and stared out at the sea.

Rory hesitated then sat down next to him. He faced a little to port side and she a little to starboard, the ship's prow between them. She couldn't actually see him, although all the little hairs on her arms were aware that he was nearby.

They sat in silence, the ship sliding swiftly through the sea beneath them, and Rory's discomfort soon ebbed away as she lost herself to the moment and the wind. She held the boots to her, and for a time, she felt like Daria was with her. Her sadness welled up again, and it was bittersweet to feel faint echoes of the connection she'd shared with her friend.

Rory still missed her, even after all these years, even though she conscientiously avoided thinking of her. Even now that she had Longinus, Cruikshank, and Adelma in her life.

"See, I told you we'd make it as adventurers," she whispered softly. She leaned her chin down against the cracked leather at the top of the boots. "We'll do good, you and I."

"You've lost someone?" Rafe asked in a voice so low that at first Rory wasn't sure he had spoken. He didn't sound like himself either. His voice had none of its usual sardonic drawl.

Rory frowned, annoyed that she'd forgotten about him and spoken out loud. "Yeah. Everyone's lost someone."

"I guess so."

They sat in silence for a time, and Rory found herself a bit sorry that he had stopped talking.

"My sister was a kid," Rafe said at last. "Just a little kid."

Rory looked over at him, surprised. She had never considered that Rafe might also have painful memories. He always seemed amused, sarcastic, like he didn't have any cares, and it felt odd to think of him as carrying the pain of loss.

She hesitated. "Daria was older. But I ain't sure that makes it any easier." She thought of Adelma, speaking Radish's name into the night.

"No, I don't think it does," Rafe replied.

They fell silent again. Rory watched the sea, her eyes catching on the small sprays of white foam as the wind blew off the top of the low swell. The soft rocking of the ship was soothing. She found she didn't mind so much that Rafe sat next to her. She was beginning to feel weirdly comfortable with it.

"I'm sorry I threw your bracelet at you," she said at last, surprised to hear the words coming out, despite them being true. Rafe had given her a bracelet back at Cruikshank's workshop just after they had finished unravelling the mystery of the Black Orchid. Rory had flung it back at him in a knee-jerk reaction to the panic and fear she had felt at the thought of having a man in her life who bought her bracelets and kissed her.

Rafe shrugged. "I'm sorry I bought it for you." His voice sounded different from earlier. "And I'm sorry for messing with you. I like to go slumming from time to time—it infuriates my father. The more inappropriate, the better, and you are by far the most inappropriate girl I've found." His voice had relaxed back into the sardonic drawl Rory was used to.

At first, Rory was stung, and then she found that she was relieved. This was far, far less frightening than the thought he had been genuine in wanting something from her. Deep down, she had known there was no way anything between them was real. His family was one of the oldest and wealthiest in Damsport, and she had grown up a street rat.

He turned to her. "You're a great girl, and I feel bad for messing with you, especially now that we're working on this mission together. So let's draw a line in the sand. Truce?" His eyes were dark and serious in the moonlight.

"Truce." She smiled, feeling like a tension had been lifted. She could stop feeling so nervous around him now and focus on the important things: the mission, her first adventure, and getting better with a sword.

They lapsed back into a comfortable silence.

The next thing Rory knew, she was blinking groggily into light that felt as piercing against her eyes as shards of glass.

She winced and closed them again, feeling as if the sun had drilled right through to her brain.

Rafe was gone. Maybe he had gone in the night, and she had fallen asleep alone—she couldn't remember. But their conversation came back to her, and she felt pleased. It no longer mattered whether Rafe had slept next to her or not.

And the box of Daria's memories felt securely shut again.

Didn't that just make life easier.

CHAPTER 6

Standing at the prow of the ship, Cruikshank watched as Azyr drew nearer. The sky was almost preternaturally blue, the sun beating down with the all the force of a smith hammering an anvil. The wind had picked up, the ship slicing gracefully through the small waves like a razor-sharp knife through jelly.

Cruikshank felt knots forming along her upper back, and she rolled her shoulders, cocking her head left and right to crack some of the tension out of her neck. They weren't yet in Azyrian waters, but soon they would be, and then they would have passed the point of no return.

The city gleamed ahead on the horizon. Cruikshank's research had revealed that Azyr was a city of two halves. One half sat atop vertiginous white cliffs that were streaked with red and black. The colours were caused by an unusual geological phenomenon, but legend had it that years of violent oppression had created them, with blood and ash pouring down the white cliffs. The second half of the city clung to the base of the cliffs, considered inferior to its higher counterpart.

All that Cruikshank could make out were the cliffs with a vague outline of the city atop them and, at the bottom, a grey mass that had to be Azyr the Lower. The ship seemed to take an age to approach Azyr, and for the umpteenth time, Cruikshank wished she had been able to tinker with the steam engine to improve its speed and efficiency. It wasn't a bad effort, but it was far from what a machinist of Cruikshank's calibre could produce. They could be pulling up into the Azyrian port by now, rather than crawling along out at sea. If only Adelma weren't so bloody stubborn about it all.

The thought of Adelma had Cruikshank frowning. The smuggler seemed sober enough now that they were drawing near to Azyr, but Cruikshank was all too aware of how good drunks were at hiding their drunkenness. She also knew from experience that when it really came down to it, you couldn't trust a drunk. Her father had been as boisterous and entertaining as Adelma, and he had been unreliable right up until the end.

Rory had tried to intercede for Adelma, explaining about her recent loss. Cruikshank felt sympathetic, of course, but not to the point that she would allow Adelma to endanger the mission.

As if she had heard Cruikshank's thoughts, Adelma shouted out orders that were neatly echoed back to her by her crew as they set to work. The ship sailed on smoothly. There was a good wind, the sails whipping as they caught it, propelling the ship forward, the steam engine now silent, slowly cooling.

Tommy stood next to his mother, gazing at her with the kind of adoration only found in young children. At times, Adelma whispered instructions in his ear, which he shouted back down the speaking tube for the crew below, a big grin on his face.

Cruikshank remembered feeling that way about her father before she grew up enough to realise his antics weren't funny, they were downright dangerous. She hoped Tommy wouldn't have to go through that. Caring for a drunken parent was no task for a little boy.

The wind played with a taut rope that ran along the length of the metal central mast. The rope thrummed against the mast, making a regular rhythm that seemed to measure the ship's approach to Azyr, like the beating of a drum.

As they got closer to the city, another thudding could be heard, like a deep heartbeat. It took Cruikshank a moment to realise that the sound was coming from Azyr.

The lower part of the city was gradually becoming visible, and it seemed to be coated in a grey haze. In front of the cliffs was a collection of large machines too far away for Cruikshank to identify. She could vaguely make out enormous pistons swinging, and the movements matched the booming that echoed over the water. They probably had something to do with the mining of beranthium, a precious mineral that was Azyr's greatest and most valuable resource.

The booming grew louder as the ship sailed forward, until Cruikshank could feel it reverberating in her chest. What must it be like for those working in the mines?

The higher part of the city was hidden behind high walls, with only the palace protruding over the top, dazzling white and winking in the sun like a great eye watching over the ship's arrival.

Cruikshank blinked, shielding her eyes from the sun as she looked up. Kadelta would be in there—probably deep within the palace walls. Her eyes roamed over the city. They would have to break into the palace somehow, find Kadelta, then get him out, through Azyr the Higher, down the cliffs, through Azyr the Lower, and onto the ship—and of course, all of that without being caught or killed.

A walk in the park, then. Cruikshank grinned to herself as she pulled out a cigar and lit it. Let it not be said that she didn't enjoy a challenge.

The city slowly grew in size, the grey mass of Azyr the Lower coming into focus. It was made up of ramshackle shacks leaning one against the other. More crude dwellings reached out into the sea on either side of the port, balanced on stilts, while yet more floated on rafts tethered to the stilts. All of it was caked in grey dust.

The effect was that of a set of greying, diseased arms opening up to welcome the ship and enfold it into the city.

The booming of the mines was like a heavy, steady heartbeat. Cruikshank could smell something acrid on the air. She sniffed, trying to identify what it was.

Rory walked up next to her. "Not a joyful sight, is it? Reckon that smell is coming from the mines?"

"Probably."

The booming grew louder, reverberating in Cruikshank's rib cage. The floating shacks bobbed on the swell, seeming to curl in behind the ship while the palace winked harshly overhead beneath the beating sun.

"Welcome to Azyr, I guess," Rory muttered, gaze fixed on the palace.

Cruikshank nodded. "Welcome to Azyr."

CHAPTER

7

The arrival in the Azyrian port was smooth as silk—not that Rory was surprised. You didn't gain a reputation like Adelma's without being able to back it up with some serious skill.

Adelma yelled more commands, her voice mostly drowned out by the low booming coming from the Azyrian mines. Even without fully hearing her orders, the crew moved with the efficiency of a well-oiled machine. Tommy stood next to her, holding onto her leggings and watching the approaching city with curiosity.

In no time at all, the ship had pulled up to the docks and into the available slot the dockmaster indicated for them. He shouted orders at the dockworkers in Azyrian, a language rougher than a cat's tongue, but he spoke in Airnian when dealing with the Damsians. The Airnian Empire had once engulfed over half the world, and its language, also spoken in Damsport, had remained the universal trading tongue.

The crew got busy tethering the ship, throwing fat coils of rope to the waiting dockworkers, who secured them to metal rings the thickness of Adelma's wrists—and she had some big wrists on her.

Adelma grabbed Tommy, balancing him on one hip before heading below decks. Tommy wasn't to come to the city with them. He would stay on board with the crew.

Rory turned away from Adelma, gazing at the docks, trying to take it all in. She stared at the Azyrians, full of curiosity and excitement.

Azyrians had skin as black as coals, their hair cropped so close to their heads that it was barely more than fuzz. They were a slight people, slimmer and more fine-boned than Damsians and their features were a little different, too. Their noses were wider and their lips fuller, while their eyes were a little slanted.

Everyone on the dock was clearly Azyrian, and it was an odd feeling for Rory to realise that for the first time in her life, *she* was a foreigner. A thrill ran down her spine.

The Azyrian dock was very different from the Damsian docks. There wasn't the same sense of hectic urgency or the chaos of people, goods, and animals that reigned in Damsport. It was still a busy port, but the Azyrians working the dock plodded along in a sullen, resigned way. Nobody shouted, other than the orders from the various supervisors and dockmasters. Rory heard no laughing, no insults, no conversation—just silence punctuated by the booming of the great mining machines of Azyr the Lower.

Now that the ship was sheltered from the sea wind, the heat intensified, and between that and the grey dust, the inside of Rory's mouth was rapidly growing dry. She ignored her thirst, not wanting to miss anything while she fetched water. Behind her, the sailors were securing the rigging.

The dockmaster who had indicated the slot they should occupy was busy scribbling on a clipboard. Whereas all the dockworkers were covered in a thin layer of grey dust, the dockmaster's skin and clothes were clean. The men and women who unloaded the cargo from ships perspired, their sweat carving tracks through the dust that covered their bodies.

The grey dust collected everywhere—in the cracks between the flagstones, at the corner of windows, on hair, faces, and clothes. It gave the scene a blurred, almost hazy look.

Beyond the docks, Azyr the Lower stretched off towards the cliff in a uniform grey mass. The dust covered everything there, too, so that the buildings all seemed to blend into one, as though the dust was slowly absorbing the structures until, in the distance, all that could be seen was a grey haze out of which poked the great mining machines.

Dust blew into Rory's nose, and she sneezed. It occurred to her then that there was no smell beyond that acrid one that had wafted out on the sea to greet them. She had grown up on the Damsian docks—you could call the place a *riot of smells* if you were being generous and poetic. The reality was that the Damsian docks reeked worse than week-old fish. She wasn't naive enough to expect every dock to be the same as Damsport, but the lack of smells, the deadened attitude of the dockworkers, and the grey dust made the place seem ghostly, not quite alive.

As the dockmaster turned to talk to someone, Rory saw the sun catching on something at his eyebrows. Some kind of jewel?

Rory noticed that the dockworkers also had objects at their eyebrows, although they didn't glitter like the dockmaster's jewels. A man passed close enough to the ship for Rory to get a good look at his face. Just above his eyebrows was a set of studs made of a material that looked like carved bone.

She caught sight of a woman with metal studs. The Azyrians all had studs at their eyebrows, though none gleamed like the dockmaster's, and she wondered if it was a display of wealth.

Longinus came up to her. "How much longer do you think it will be until we disembark? I tried to ask Adelma, but she was apparently too busy to answer." He looked at the dock with yearning. "So close yet so far away," he added miserably to himself. "Oh, gods alive, make it end." He clutched his stomach.

Rory looked up at the sails, which were being lashed to the yard arms. "Not too long, I expect," she told him, rubbing his shoulder in a lame attempt to comfort him. Poor Longinus. He had been sick for weeks. The whole journey had been an ordeal for him.

"Prepare the gangplank!" Adelma shouted.

Longinus straightened up. "Finally!" he said, hurrying over to where the sailors were extending the gangplank over the water. They protested as he climbed on before they had even finished tethering it.

Rory felt a surge of nerves and excitement knot her stomach. This was it, her first time in a foreign city—and on a mission for the Marchioness of Damsport, no less.

She followed after Longinus. He gave a strangled cry of relief on reaching the dock, but his cry soon turned to dismay as he lurched as if on board a rolling ship.

Adelma, who had followed behind them, grabbed him by the arm to steady him, laughing. "He needs to find his land legs."

"But I never found my sea legs," Longinus protested. "*How* could I have lost my land legs? The curvature of my calves…"

A louder boom than the rest rang out, startling everyone and drowning out whatever was important about the curvature of Longinus's calves.

"You'll be fine," Adelma said.

Sailors began to unload the trunks and equipment that were to go with Rory and the others into Azyr. At that moment, a complement of guards arrived on the docks, heaving their way through and pushing workers aside as if they were inanimate objects. One woman fell over, dropping her load. She didn't react, her face keeping a bland expression, but the worker who came to help her up shot a vicious look at the guard. He didn't seem to notice or care.

The guards wore sapphire-blue uniforms beneath burnished golden breastplates, and they each held a long spear. Rory gaped. They had to be cooking inside the metal, but their faces showed no hint of discomfort. They were completely free of dust, and their blue uniforms stood out garishly against the dull grey of Azyr the Lower.

The guards fanned out along the docks, and among them, an Azyrian woman appeared. She was as beautiful and vibrant as the dockworkers were dull and worn. Her skin was as smooth as black velvet, her eyes were wide and bright, and unlike everyone around her, her hair was long, teased out into a thick halo around her head. Fiery orange stripes had been dyed throughout her hair, giving it the appearance of a tiger's fur. Her clothing seemed to be made of many gossamer-thin pieces of fabric overlapping each other and rippling with every movement. They were the colour of fire, so that with her hair, she looked like a flame turned human.

And she looked furious.

Cruikshank stepped off the gangplank, frowning. "Reheeme, I presume?"

The woman glared at Cruikshank, whose frown deepened at the intensity of the animosity levelled at her.

"Arrest the foreign scum," Reheeme snapped.

CHAPTER

8

Before anyone could move, the guards had rushed on board the ship, while those remaining on the docks pointed their spears at Cruikshank, Rory, Longinus, and Adelma.

"Stop right there," someone shouted, and Cruikshank saw four spears pointed at Rafe, who had already drawn his knives and fallen into a fighting stance. His eyes moved quickly, scanning each of his opponents, but he stayed still.

"Tommy!" Adelma roared.

The boy must have come back on deck to see what was going on. Luckily, a sailor had swept him up in his arms. Spears were pointed at the two of them, and Tommy burst into tears, calling for his mother.

"Tommy-Boy," Adelma shouted, "you be a good boy, now, and don't you move an inch."

"What the hell is going on?" Cruikshank called to Reheeme.

She was supposed to be an ally. She was supposed to be their contact in Azyr, the one who would help smuggle them into the palace in exchange for their support for her rebellion.

The docks seemed to have gone perfectly silent save for the pounding of the mines that measured the seconds as they trickled past. The dockworkers watched dully, some with vague curiosity.

Cruikshank felt like a cord about to snap. "I said, what the hell is going on?"

The woman sneered. "What is going on is—"

"Reheeme, Reheeme, wait, wait!" More guards arrived, accompanying a small Azyrian man. His arms and legs were long and skinny, but he had a taut, round belly, making him look a little like a spider. He had expensive studs, the same as Reheeme's, and Cruikshank guessed that this made him her social equal. His hair was cropped to a fuzz, but unlike the men on the docks, he wore a small, square fabric hat, and his loose robes were made of expensive material. A great many bracelets crusted with gems jangled at his wrists.

Reheeme whirled on the man, shaking with rage. "How *dare* you! How dare you write to that woman in my name?"

Cruikshank's stomach sank. This was bad, bad news.

"Now, Reheeme, be reasonable," the man said, making placating gestures with his hands. "We can talk about all of this back up in the Higher like civilised—"

"Civilised?" Reheeme spat. "*Civilised* doesn't include forging my handwriting and signature!"

The man gave her a pointed look. "Witnesses," he said in a low voice.

At that, Reheeme seemed to get control of herself, albeit with some difficulty. Her face settled into a blank expression, but fury still burned in her eyes.

"This is all well and good," Rory said, "but it's hot here, and we been on a long journey to come all this way. So can you two sort out your argument somewhere else and let us get on with unloading the ship?"

Cruikshank stifled a smile. She had to give it to Rory— the girl had nerve, even when facing the wrong end of a spear.

"Yes, yes, of course," the man said hurriedly. "I do apologise for all the confusion. I am Jabir, Reheeme's husband. You are, of course, all free to continue with your unloading." He snapped an order at the guards, who glanced uncertainly between him and Reheeme then lifted their spears.

The moment the spear at Adelma's neck was gone, she charged on board the ship like a bull seeing red. She rammed into the guard who had threatened Tommy, dealing him a massive punch that cracked so loudly that Cruikshank winced. The man crumpled like a rag doll, while all the other guards shouted, turning their spears towards her.

"Stand down," Jabir yelled. "Stand down."

The sailor holding Tommy passed him to Adelma. She swept the boy up in her arms, and he wailed loudly, clinging to her.

"Anyone go near my son again, and I won't just knock you out," she growled, glaring at all the other guards aboard the ship.

"Your son is safe," Jabir called out. "I give you my word. Everyone off the ship *now*."

The guards disembarked quickly, going to stand in formation behind their master.

Cruikshank stepped up close enough to speak to Jabir and Reheeme in a low voice. "You both had better have a good explanation for threatening my team," she said in a low, tense voice. "And I second what Adelma said. Do Azyrian manners include threatening the children of your guests?"

"Reheeme didn't mean to threaten her son," Jabir said at once.

Reheeme had the decency to show a flicker of remorse. "Of course I hadn't meant to threaten the boy."

"I'm glad to hear it," Cruikshank said coldly. "And I look forward to an explanation of this… *regretful* situation. I am Eleanor Cruikshank, by the way. Head Machinist of Damsport."

"Ah yes. Your reputation precedes you," Jabir said with a tilt of the head and a smile. "I've heard you prefer to go by Cruikshank?"

Cruikshank nodded. The Azyrians spoke in a lilting accent with so many *r*s that their voices sounded as if they'd been roughened with sandpaper, but their command of Airnian was very good.

"I'm sorry our acquaintance started on such poor terms," Jabir continued. "I was looking forward to this meeting."

His wife gave him a venomous look, and he fell silent. Cruikshank looked from husband to wife, wondering what was going on. There could be no explanations out in the open—that much was obvious.

"I suggest we proceed to our quarters," Jabir said, "where we will be able to explain everything. You needn't worry about your things either. I have arranged for them to be lifted up to the Higher and carried to our home. Reheeme and I will escort you up."

Cruikshank turned back to the others, looking at them with a question in her eyes to see if they were comfortable with this plan. Rafe nodded, as did Rory. Longinus didn't look happy, but he too nodded.

"Fine," Adelma said. "But I got a couple of things to take care of first." She leaned over to her first mate and gave a few quick orders in a voice too low for Cruikshank to hear. Her sailors sprang to action, moving swiftly about the deck.

Then Adelma dipped her head down to Tommy, whispering. The little boy clung to her fiercely, but she gently removed his arms. His chin trembled, and he looked like he would cry again.

"Now, come on. Where's my brave boy?" Adelma said, ruffling his hair. "I'll be back soon."

She handed him to the first mate, and this time, Tommy let her. Adelma grinned at him. "Just think of all them stories I'll have for you when I get back, my boy!"

Tommy nodded wordlessly.

Adelma returned to the docks. "Alright. I'm ready. Just so we're clear, the *Slippery Eel* will be leaving the port."

Jabir made a surprised noise, and Adelma turned to him. "If you think I'm gonna leave my ship sitting in a dock with my son on board when you've just shown you're willing to point a weapon at him and my crew, you must think I'm as dumb as a bag of whelks. The *Eel* will be out at sea, and she ain't coming back to port without my signal. We don't return safe and sound to them, they're going straight back to Damsport with word of what happened here."

And Adelma will keep control of our ability to depart the city, Cruikshank added internally. It was a smart move. The ship couldn't be attacked while they were up in the city, nor could the crew or her son be used as hostages.

"Of course," Jabir said. "As I said, neither Reheeme nor I had any designs on your son. It was just a misunderstanding. But if you feel more comfortable with the ship at sea, we completely understand. So, shall we?"

The guards immediately stepped into a different formation so they would be framing the whole party. Cruikshank noticed how Rafe tensed the moment they moved. He had a pack strapped to his back with his helmet inside—the fighting gear Varanguards were famed for. They wore helmets with long horsehair ponytails amongst which were tied razor-sharp knives. That enabled them to fight even when outnumbered and surrounded. Every movement Rafe made seemed calculated, and his eyes scanned the guards, planning possible attacks and defences.

Cruikshank looked at the guards with worry. If it came down to a fight, the chances of all five of them making it out alive were slim. The numbers they were facing were too great. But the only options they had were to either trust Jabir or turn back to Damsport. She hoped she wasn't making a terrible mistake.

"Lead the way," she said to Jabir.

CHAPTER 9

Entering the streets of Azyr the Lower was like stepping into a world of grey. Dust covered every surface, every window, every face. It collected up along the edges of the streets and gathered in front of doors. Some people swept their doorways and cleaned their windows, leaving only a thin dusting for that day, but most places were thick with it. The dust was a kind of equaliser, coating everyone so that you couldn't tell the difference between rich and poor—or rather, between poor and poorer.

Longinus had always like the colour grey. Back in Damsport, grey was elegant and dignified, but in Azyr, it was synonymous with poverty and despair.

The Lower Azyrians slunk past the guards, staring pointedly at the floor. A few flicked venomous glances at the shiny uniforms. Their skin looked even greyer in this part of Azyr the Lower than it had on the docks, the ramshackle buildings providing some shelter so that the wind didn't displace the dust. The studs at their eyebrows were made of simple materials—bone, wood, or iron. A few people were missing studs, and the holes gaped like missing teeth. Longinus found the sight of those gaps almost painful to behold. It made him feel nauseous.

A small child ran out into the street they were all on, crying. It was ragged and dirty, and Longinus couldn't tell if it was a boy or a girl. The child stopped with an abrupt hiccup when it caught sight of the guards. One of its eyebrows was swollen, the skin around the studs crusty with infection. Longinus winced at the sight.

A woman who had to be the child's mother appeared behind, gasped, swept it up in her arms, and hurried away. The guards, Reheeme, and Jabir didn't seem to have noticed the little scene. Compared to the woman and her child, they glittered garishly.

Longinus had certainly never been one to judge an ostentatious sartorial display, but even by his standards, such colour and wealth, paraded among such drab poverty, was obscene.

There weren't even any shops in this part of Azyr, or if there were any, they were kept hidden behind closed doors and grimy windows. There were no eateries, no drinking taverns—and of course, there was no sign of a decent coffee house.

"I never thought I'd ever utter the words 'Rookery' and 'civilised' in the same breath," Longinus said to Rory in a low voice, "but compared to this, the Rookery is a beacon of civilisation, charm, and comfort."

Rory nodded. "Yeah. I mean, where I grew up was proper poor, but at least it's alive. This feels like a ghost town."

Eventually, they stepped out of the narrow streets and into a wide-open space. The booming from the mines grew so loud that it was almost painful, reverberating inside Longinus's rib cage.

"Bloody hell," Rory muttered. "Feels like my insides are being rattled like dice inside a cup."

The machines that were creating the noise were finally fully visible. Enormous pistons swung back and forth, smashing enormous pieces of rock. Each impact was so massive that the vibrations shook the ground. The engines powering them belched out towers of black smoke into the sky, darkening the cliffs behind them.

Farther along, large metal frames supported cog-driven conveyor belts powered by more engines spouting out coal smoke. Some of the frames holding the conveyor belts had started to rust from the sea air, and the cogs squeaked—a low, constant whine beneath the booming. They carried fragments of rocks along some kind of system, Longinus guessed.

The whole mining complex looked like an enormous, hellish insect, its many legs working up and down as if it was readying itself to rush over Azyr the Lower and crush the city beneath its massive pistons.

Beneath the machinery were thousands of Azyrians squatting on the ground and sifting through the smashed rock. Others crawled in and out of mining shafts, like so many ants. Each one carried a basket on his or her back, with straps that ran from the handles up and over their foreheads. The ones coming out of the tunnels strained obviously under the weight they carried.

Longinus could see his shock reflected in Cruikshank's expression. "The mining is done by hand?" she asked Jabir, shouting to be heard over the pistons.

"We don't have any machine as effective or precise as human fingers," Reheeme replied loudly.

"Slaves?" Rory asked coldly.

"Oh, no. They're perfectly free," Reheeme replied. "They could go work somewhere else if they preferred."

Longinus looked back at the grey ghost town behind them. Work where, and on what? Even a decent assassin would struggle to make a living in Azyr the Lower.

He looked back at Reheeme. She was supposed to be the leader of a rebellion attempting to change things in Azyr. That had better include better prospects for the Lower Azyrians. It wouldn't take much to train them in the basics of poisoning or the sartorial arts, for example, thereby giving them a chance at some dignity.

Reheeme and Jabir led the way forward. There was no shade from buildings in this part of the Azyr the Lower, and the sun beat down even more mercilessly than before with no wind to reduce the heat that burned hot as a furnace.

"Burn my body, it's hot enough to drown a woman in her own sweat," Adelma said.

Longinus didn't like to acknowledge that he sweated, but he had to agree with her.

"There is a decent establishment not far from here where we can obtain refreshment before we begin the climb up," Jabir shouted in response.

Sure enough, they soon stopped outside a stall sheltered beneath an awning. The space was as close to dust free as anything was ever going to get in Azyr the Lower, and the owner fretted anxiously over her wares, while a young girl—her daughter probably—waved a fan in an attempt to keep the dust at bay.

"Quince wine," Reheeme said, pointing at a glass bottle full of a golden liquid. The stall owner immediately began pulling out glasses, inspecting each one carefully for dust, and blowing on the ones that didn't quite pass muster. She poured out the quince wine, passed the glasses around, and waited, scanning their faces anxiously as they drank, her mouth working the whole time.

It was, in fact, highly refreshing, and Longinus emptied his glass with relish.

"Very good," Rory said with a smile and a thumbs-up as the booming of the mine covered the sound of her voice. The owner broke into a relieved smile and hurried to top up Rory's glass and then Longinus's.

"It's better than good," Adelma said. "More, please." She gestured with her glass, and the owner got her meaning, refilling it. Adelma downed it in one draught and held her glass out again. "Another."

Cruikshank glared at her, but Adelma seemed utterly indifferent. Cruikshank was fighting a losing battle—she'd have a better chance of parting Longinus from his silks, and that would *never* happen.

"We should go," Jabir said. "We have a long climb, but don't worry. There will be plenty of opportunity to buy refreshment on the way."

CHAPTER
10

Rory had been so absorbed by the mines and by Azyr the Lower that she hadn't given any thought as to how they would be getting up to Azyr the Higher. For the first time, she looked up, and she was shocked to see an enormous staircase that slithered up the cliff like a great snake. It curved back and forth endlessly on itself from the ground all the way to the top. The lower part of the staircase was carved directly into the cliff, but a little more than halfway up, the stone stairs switched to wooden ones that clung to the rock all the way to the top.

The lower part of the staircase was wide and looked secure, but the wooden part looked narrow and rickety. And yet the stairs were heaving with people moving up and down quickly like an efficient colony of ants, the wooden part clearly able to deal with the weight and activity of heavy traffic.

"We're going first, before the guards," Rafe said in a tone that brooked no arguments. "Jabir and Reheeme can lead the way, then Cruikshank and Longinus, then Rory, and Adelma and I will bring up the rear."

Jabir frowned. "It is customary to have guards at the front to clear the way."

"It is also both easier to defend and attack from a higher position," Rafe replied curtly. "After the incident at the docks, I won't have your guards above us where they could once again attack."

Reheeme looked like she was about to argue, but Jabir quickly stepped in. "Of course, I completely understand your reluctance to put yourself in a vulnerable position. The guards will bring up the rear, as you say."

They all slowly filed up the stairs in the order Rafe had specified. He was last, after Adelma. At first, Rory tried to keep an eye on the guards as Rafe was doing, but she quickly became distracted by the sheer number and variety of stalls set up right on the edge of the steps, going as far up as she could see.

The stalls were small but ingenious, set up like stacks of shelves behind which the owners peeked out. They sold light fare: food and drink as well as trinkets and amulets carved from driftwood and seashells.

"Take whatever grabs your fancy," Jabir told them. "One of my guards will settle all the bills."

Under the booming of the mines, the transactions took place without a single word exchanged. People gestured to each other instead, communicating in signs. As Rory watched, she was impressed to see just how intricate this makeshift language was. People weren't simply pointing at things and showing fingers for prices—they were talking in complicated symbols.

She also realised, with an amused start, that all the coins exchanged were whole. Damsport had the practice of using the weights of copper, silver, and gold coin to deal with the sheer number of currencies that flowed through the city. Coins could therefore be cut into halves or quarters in order to make change.

It was a small difference to see only whole coins used, but it was yet another reminder that Rory was in a distant, foreign land, and it sent a thrill of excitement down her back.

Stall owners called out as Rory and the others began to climb past. They weren't saying words but were simply shouting and waving to attract attention. They looked cheerful enough, but Rory wasn't fooled. Their smiles were brittle, a thin veneer. She felt eyes following them as they climbed up the stairs.

As she took in more and more of the stalls, she forgot about the strained faces of the vendors, astounded by the variety and weirdness of the food on offer. Her stomach began to rumble in reaction to the smells, which managed to drown out the acrid smoke smell from the mines.

There were sea crickets dried and salted to a crunch, seahorses on skewers, fried spiders, dried starfish, large millipedes that were lowered, still wriggling, on top of hot coals to the order of a customer. Rory tried not to think what would happen if coals were knocked out of the brazier and burned someone—they were already high enough that anyone who slipped and fell from the stairs would be seriously injured.

Cured rat meat was sold in little paper bags, snakes were stuffed with seaweed, and pickled cod eyes looked out of large glass jars. There were seagull eggs preserved in ash and salt, tiny iridescent beetles drowned in fish broth, and scorpions fried living in the tiniest hint of scorpion poison, Jabir explained, for those who liked a kick with their food.

Rory bought herself a bag of skewered seahorses. They were delicious and crunchy. She offered one to Longinus, but he declined.

"Still feeling green about the gills?" she asked him. The booming had begun to recede enough that she only needed to talk loudly rather than shout to be heard.

He nodded.

Behind them, Adelma had stopped to purchase a bottle of purple liquid. The seller made some gesture at her, and she nodded, thanking him, although Rory was pretty sure she had no idea what the seller had said.

They continued to climb, and Adelma uncorked the bottle. Rory looked back in time to see Adelma try the drink. She spluttered, looking shocked and then impressed. "Burn my body, but they make it strong here—whatever that is. Nice almond aftertaste, though."

The climb continued, and the stairs began to narrow. The stalls narrowed as well, the sellers hanging off the edge, tethered precariously to their stalls, which were screwed into the rock. The sellers were strapped into makeshift harnesses of well-worn rope and cracked leather, and Rory prayed the harnesses were more solid than they looked. The drop to the ground below would be enough to turn anyone into a smashed porcelain doll.

A faint wind picked up, but it blew so hot it felt like the gusts from a smith's bellows. Rory could feel the grit from the dust against her cheeks.

Up ahead, Longinus grumbled about unsightly sweat patches. "What kind of city expects a gentleman to climb so many stairs in this heat? I mean, really. It borders on the barbaric. Look at this. Look at my clothes."

Rory grinned. "Could be you're the first gent to set foot in this place," she joked.

"You know, you might be right," Longinus replied seriously. "Which then bodes the question: what kind of city is devoid of gentlemen? I tell you what kind—the barbaric kind."

"Alright, ease up on the *barbaric* talk," Rory muttered, glancing about her. Nobody seemed to have picked up on the comment, but she didn't really want to start offending Azyrians when only a shove was needed to send someone careening over the edge.

They finally reached the point where the stairs turned from stone to wood. As she stepped onto the first wooden step, a drop of sweat trickled into her eye, causing her to blink against the stinging saltiness. She rubbed her eye and continued to climb. The stairs were narrower here, and everyone had to continue in single file.

Rory would never have voiced a complaint—reputation to uphold and all that—but her legs were starting to grow tired. There was a dull ache in her calves and a burn in her thighs. Longinus didn't seem to be faring much better, and Adelma was sweating profusely and swearing openly. Up ahead, Cruikshank's breath wheezed heavily with each step she took.

In fact, the only one in their little group who seemed to be faring well was Rafe. He seemed as fresh and alert as when they'd first set off. He glanced back, and Rory realised with a guilty shock that he was checking on the guards, while she had completely forgotten about them. His face was serious and focused, and when he looked at the vendors around them, it wasn't with Rory's curiosity and wonder but with a calm, calculating stare that seemed to be evaluating everything and everyone. He showed no signs of tiredness. Worse, the guards in the back seemed no more bothered than if they were out on a pleasant stroll, in spite of their heavy armour and weapons.

Rory gritted her teeth and continued to climb. She'd be damned if she was going to slow down or show any more discomfort than the Azyrians. She tried to look back and stay aware of the guards, but she quickly found that she was too tired to be of much use.

Now that they were on the wooden stairs, the stalls had disappeared, and instead, the sellers hung from beneath the stairs higher up, dangling at the end of ropes like puppets. Buckets filled with sand dangled next to them, with skewers of insects and seafood stabbed in like incense sticks. A surprisingly lively trade took place here, with buckets lowered to collect money and deliver food or drink. With the booming reduced to a low thudding, voices could easily be heard, and negotiations took place swiftly while the buckets moved up and down. The sellers reminded Rory of Damsian seagulls, the way they hovered overhead, calling to the traffic beneath and watching with beady, interested eyes.

"What happens when they need to take a piss?" Rory asked in a low wheeze, too out of breath and hot to bother trying to hide her breathlessness.

"Do you... really... have to go there?" Longinus wheezed back.

"Ever heard the expression, when the gods take a piss, it rains on Damsport?" Adelma asked. She was out of breath too, but not as badly as Rory or Longinus. "Well, I guess in Azyr when the stair merchants piss, it rains on Azyr the Lower." She laughed and took a careful swig from her bottle, wincing.

"What the hell is it?" Rory asked, dreading to think how strong the drink would have to be to make Adelma wince.

"Beats me. It's seriously strong, but it's starting to grow on me."

The procession continued upward. By the time they were almost at the top of the cliff, Rory was fast running out of steam. The muscles in her legs were aching, and for the first time in her life, her skin felt like it was growing sunburnt—something she had assumed only happened to milk skins.

Still, neither Jabir, Reheeme, or the guards seemed bothered by the climb. Their endurance was astounding.

CHAPTER
11

At the top of the stairs was a massive iron-and-stone gate. It was little more than a crude arch spotted with murder holes. On either side, walls stretched along the cliff's edge, spiked with guards.

There wasn't a single detail or decoration, nothing other than the cold, brutal purpose of the structure: to kill people. The message of the arch was painfully clear: Attempt to rise up and force your way to the Higher city, and you will be crushed. It would be the easiest thing in the world to destroy the top of the wooden staircase, cutting the lower city off from the higher.

In spite of the ugliness of the gate and how unpleasant it would be to pass under murder holes, Cruikshank melted with relief at the sight of it. She had always thought of herself as being tough as old boots, but after all those stairs, her leg muscles were on fire, and her knees felt like jelly. That rankled, and the sting to her pride burnt far more than the soreness in her thighs.

Greased gears, she wanted a cigar. And a beer. Preferably together, preferably somewhere cool and quiet. At least that awful booming had stopped.

She plodded up the last few steps, her joints protesting with each one, thighs and calves on fire. The arch was two yards thick, and passing beneath it meant a brief relief from the burning sun.

Cruikshank craned her neck, looking up into those murder holes, wondering if whoever was inside the arch would be looking back down at her. She had never seen such crude methods of defence before—it was like something from the dark ages. Thick walls, rocks ready to be dropped on assailants, almost as if steam power hadn't been invented. And yet she knew Azyr was quite developed technologically.

She and the rest of the group were ushered through with Jabir and Reheeme, but others weren't so lucky. She saw a number of Azyrians in poor clothing, showing papers and pleading with what looked like the city Watch to be let through. She saw one Watchman push a civilian back with a categorical shake of the head. Cruikshank wondered just how few Lower Azyrians ever managed to make it through to the Higher.

She was so absorbed in her observations that she didn't realise the others had continued on without her.

"Please follow us, Cruikshank," Jabir called. "I know it's been a long and difficult climb for you all, but we're nearly done walking."

Neither Jabir nor Reheeme was showing any strain from the climb. It was infuriating. Reheeme in particular looked as fresh as a flower. There wasn't so much as a single bead of sweat on that perfect brow.

"If you need assistance for the last distance," Reheeme called loudly, "one of my guards can carry—"

"I'm fine," Cruikshank cut in sharply. She'd sooner crawl over hot coals than have someone assist her like an old woman. She caught up to the others, letting out a stream of insults and curses under her breath as she walked.

"My thoughts exactly," Adelma muttered as Cruikshank reached level with her. "I want to hit something and drink my own body weight in beer." She looked up. "There better be beer where you're taking us," she called to Reheeme. "I'm planning to drown in it."

Reheeme looked back over her shoulder with ill-concealed distaste. "You Damsians clearly have an unusual concept of hospitality—of course there will be all you want to drink."

Rory gave an incredulous laugh. "Back in Damsport, we're stingy on drink but generous when it comes to not threatening our guests."

"Now, now," Jabir said at once, "that was just a misunderstanding. If we could *just* make it back to our home, all will be explained."

They turned a corner, and when Cruikshank saw the transport that awaited them, she had to admit she was impressed. Standing placidly in the sun was a larger-than-life-sized steam-powered mechanical elephant. The sun winked off the polished steel, making it gleam. It had articulated legs, an articulated trunk, and from what Cruikshank could tell at a glance, even articulated ears, although that was likely for effect. A faint plume of smoke escaped the trunk, and Cruikshank guessed that the engine would be lodged in the rib cage, the trunk serving as an exhaust.

A litter was set up on the elephant's back, lined in rich red fabric, with awnings and mechanical fans. More red fabric was draped over the elephant's back, keeping most of the metal out of the sun's glare. The pilot was seated just behind the head. He was an Azyrian man, wearing only loose green trousers tucked into boots, his features hidden behind a wide set of goggles. His chest was bare, and Cruikshank felt an absurd prick of satisfaction to see that it glowed with a sheen of sweat. At last, *someone* who felt the heat. Then she realised that he would likely be dealing with the heat generated by the steam engine and the sun, and her satisfaction quickly faded.

They reached the elephant, and the pilot moved a couple of levers at the back of its head. Panels along the rib cage opened in a hiss of steam, rearranging themselves into a neat set of steps.

"Transportation to our quarters," Jabir said with small bow, gesturing for them to climb up.

Cruikshank was the first to climb on. She didn't even feel the soreness in her legs at the steps, too interested in the machine beneath her to care about physical discomfort. As she had hoped, the stair panel left a gap in the elephant's rib cage, allowing a glimpse of the machinery below, between the metal slats that acted as ribs to give the elephant's body its shape. Unfortunately, the harsh sunlight was blinding compared to the gloom within the elephant's rib cage, and she couldn't see much.

She climbed the steps slowly, squinting at the machinery beneath.

"Cruikshank, you can look at cogs to your heart's content later," Longinus said behind her. "There are more pressing things to attend to right now, such as getting out of this blasted sun and to a place where I can get a bath."

Regretfully, Cruikshank continued the climb at a more normal pace and reached the litter, which was made of wood secured to the elephant's back. There were benches covered with plush red cushions, a red awning stretching across four poles, and flaps that could be released to provide total cover from the sun. Small fans that seemed powered by the main engine blew a cooling breeze across the seats. Cruikshank let out a grateful groan as she sank into the cushions.

Longinus came next. He hesitated before sitting down. "I always hate dirtying silk," he explained, still a little breathless from the climb. "Dirt's impossible to get out, and this is a divine colour. But needs must."

Soon they were all packed into the elephant. Rafe didn't seem to have relaxed his watchfulness for a moment, still evaluating everything around him. His hands never strayed from his throwing knives.

It was reassuring to know he was keeping a close eye on things, although Cruikshank didn't think there would be an attack—not when there had been ample opportunity when going up the stairs.

Jabir's gaze caught the bottle of purple liquid Adelma had bought. "Ah, I see you have made a very wise purchase," he said with a smile. "This is an extremely effective disinfectant. Always very handy to have."

Adelma's eyebrows shot up. "Ahhh, that explains why it tastes so strong."

Cruikshank shook her head in disbelief.

Down below, the guards fanned out around the elephant's legs in a diamond formation. The pilot got up and began undoing the flaps to lower them.

"I'd rather stay in the sun and see the city," Rory told him.

"Yes, and me," Cruikshank said.

The pilot gave Reheeme a questioning look, which she answered with a nod.

"There won't be much to see for a while," Reheeme warned as the pilot returned to the elephant's controls. "Not until we get to Tarwa, the *decent* part of Azyr the Higher."

Cruikshank raised her eyebrows but held her tongue. Nothing about Reheeme matched her expectation of a rebel leader seeking to end repression in Azyr.

The elephant set off in a hiss of steam.

CHAPTER
12

If Azyr the Lower had been a grey slum, this part of Azyr the Higher, called Maksur, was uniformly the colour of sand. The ground, baked by the sun, was a honeycomb of cracks that forked out in every direction as if searching for water. The buildings were simple, made of mud bricks so that they seemed to have risen up from the earth itself, and they were little more than cubes with holes for doorways and windows.

A hodgepodge of receptacles and buckets was lashed to the roofs, probably to capture rainwater, although Cruikshank couldn't imagine it rained very often. She knew that a big part of the division between the two main areas of Azyr the Higher centred on water. An underground river ran beneath Tarwa, the wealthy part of the higher city, so its residents had access to all the water they wanted. The poorer area of Maksur had to rely on Tarwa drawing water from the river and selling it to them. This kept Maksur poor and at the mercy and control of Tarwa.

Cruikshank looked around. Although Maksur was clearly poor and parched, it was at least very much alive compared to Azyr the Lower. The streets were busy, with people walking by briskly, carrying out trade and conversations. Some cast looks towards the elephant, oftentimes dark looks, but their attitude was different from the deadened resignation of the Lower Azyrians. Some people seemed cheerful as they went about their day, chatting and calling out greetings.

They passed an actual elephant far smaller than the steam-powered version, but it was a sad, shrivelled thing, its skin loose, its trunk drooping. The beast was pale—not the grey Cruikshank had heard of but, rather, a dirty pale yellow.

"Everything's the colour of old underwear," Rory murmured. "Even the elephant. Old underwear left too long without washing."

"Ugh," Longinus replied. "Rory! I always enjoy a good simile, but really? That's disgusting."

Rafe laughed. "Well, at least it paints a vivid picture. A pretty disgusting one but a vivid picture all the same."

"It's true!" Rory protested. "I mean, even in the Rookery, where we're piss-poor, at least we got colour and stuff."

A ghost of a smile played on Reheeme's lips. "Wait until we reach Tarwa—you'll see colour like you've never seen before."

"Well, now that we are out of earshot," Cruikshank said to Jabir and Reheeme, "could you please explain what exactly is going on, because I am getting the feeling that we have been lured to Azyr under false pretences."

Reheeme shook her head. "We are not talking of this here," she said tightly. "Too much of a risk of being overheard."

"It would be best if we waited until we were inside," Jabir added with an apologetic smile. "I promise, all will be made clear."

After a time, they crossed a square that was little more than a wide-open space without anything to occupy the centre. People milled about the square or cut straight through, heading briskly towards their destinations. In one corner was a water seller, a large crowd gathered around him.

Straight in front of the elephant's path, two old Azyrian women were playing some kind of game with a chequered board and black and white counters. They sat on little three-legged stools, a low table between them.

One was a dried husk of a woman, her dark skin a collection of wrinkles. She examined the game, sucking on a long-stemmed pipe. But while everyone else got out of the elephant's way grudgingly, the two old women didn't move. The one with the pipe looked calmly up at the elephant, a faint challenge in her eyes.

To Cruikshank's surprise, Reheeme snapped a brief order at the pilot, who had the elephant veer around the two old women. The one with the pipe followed the elephant with her eyes for a moment then nodded to herself, as though satisfied, before returning to her game. Reheeme looked angry. Jabir placed a soothing hand on her arm, but she snatched it away, glowering at him.

Cruikshank wondered what that was about and who the woman was. Azyrian society seemed to be structured around the studs people wore—the more expensive and rare the material of the studs, the higher the social position. The old woman had worn simple metal studs, and Cruikshank guessed she should have deferred to Jabir and Reheeme and moved out of their way. She added that question to the many that already crowded her mind.

Soon enough, the elephant reached another heavily guarded wall. Cruikshank looked left and right—as far as she could see, this wall bisected the city.

"The Dividing Wall," Jabir said.

The books on Azyr had it wrong: it wasn't a city of two halves—it was a city split in three. They passed through a gate, the arch overhead revealing yet more murder holes. Cruikshank guessed that the people of Maksur had very little to do with the Great Gate at the top of the stairs and that the people of Tarwa were deeply afraid of the Azyrians who made up the other two thirds of the city.

The steam elephant plodded down a wide street and turned into a huge square, where a number of other steam-powered elephants were lined up. Some steam wagons were also parked there, and large silk awnings stretched over the edges of the square, keeping the various engines out of the merciless sun.

"We must get off the elephant here," Jabir said, rising. "The streets of Tarwa are too narrow for it. We are too many for palanquins, so we will continue by foot."

Cruikshank felt her impatience grow. How long was it going to be before they arrived and could get an explanation of what was going on?

With their armed escort, they continued on, and it was like they had stepped into a different world. Where before all had been dry and uniform, now all was lush with vegetation and bright with colour.

They made their way down narrow streets that were shaded by silk awnings or vine-covered pergolas, the flowers filling the air with a pleasant fragrance.

"Smells like a tart's handbag in here," Adelma muttered.

Rory snorted with laughter.

The buildings that lined the street were also square and built one against the other, the same as in Maksur, but there the resemblance ended. Each facade was brighter than the next, painted in colours and patterns, the window and door edges lined with gorgeous mosaics, the tiny tiles catching the sunlight. The doors themselves were carved, many of them displaying renditions of elephants. Potted palms on either side of doorways rippled in the breeze, and bright flowers filled the air with scent.

Like Reheeme and Jabir, the Azyrians in this part of town wore loose clothing all in bright colours and patterns. Yellows, pinks, greens, and purples clashed merrily with checks and swirls and more complicated abstract patterns. Jewels gleamed at eyebrows, ears, and fingers. A lot of the women wrapped their hair up in bright scarves, while the men tended to wear their hair cropped to a fuzz beneath square hats as Jabir did. Cruikshank was surprised to find that men wore bracelets in Azyr but women did not. They were similar to Jabir's—gold and copper and studded with gems.

For every Tarwanese, there was a retinue of bodyguards and slaves, the latter easily recognisable by their eyebrows devoid of studs and their dull clothing. The slaves carried bags or fans or simply walked a few paces behind their masters.

Cruikshank noticed with disgust that some Tarwanese even swanned about in steam-powered palanquins followed by slaves who were forced to trot in the blistering heat, holding fans. It would have been the easiest thing to add mechanised fans to the palanquins as had been done on the steam elephant. These slaves had to be a kind of show of status.

Every time Cruikshank and the others came across a palanquin, there had to be a whole kerfuffle relating to stud etiquette. There would be a brief standoff while Jabir, Reheeme, and the palanquin's owner would look each other over to establish whose studs were superior. The fact that after each examination the palanquin reversed back to the closest junction, tucking itself out of the way in a side street, spoke volumes as to how high up in Azyrian society Jabir and Reheeme were. During each interaction, pleasantries were exchanged with long, convoluted official greetings, although all of it was in Azyrian, so Cruikshank didn't understand a word.

Their progress took an age, and Cruikshank grew more and more impatient, almost to the point of being agitated.

When would they arrive? Eventually, they came to a halt in front of a yellow-and-green building. The entire facade was covered with mosaics, and some of the little tiles were mirrored, so they shimmered in the sunlight.

"We have arrived," Jabir said.

"Finally," Cruikshank blurted.

"I would ask you all to surrender your weapons before entering my house," Reheeme said.

"No bloody way!" Rory and Adelma exclaimed at the same time.

"You are not entering my home armed to the teeth," Reheeme replied coldly.

"*Our* home," Jabir interjected.

"Might I just point out," Longinus said, stepping forward, "that since our arrival in Azyr you have threatened us with your guards, going as far as to threaten Adelma's child. You have dragged us up those awful, endless steps, making us sweat. You have kept us completely in the dark about who actually wrote to us and why. And on top of it all, you have yet to extend us a single courtesy or comfort as your guests, in acknowledgement of the fact that we have all gone through a very long and tiring journey to get to Azyr. After all this *barbaric* treatment, do you really expect us to trust you with our weapons? Only a fool would think this a possibility, and you don't strike me as a fool, Reheeme. But then again, I have been known, in certain *extremely* rare circumstances, to be wrong. Am I wrong?" Longinus raised an eyebrow.

"You are absolutely right," Jabir said hurriedly, "and you are welcome into *our* home, including your weapons. We will offer you refreshments and answers to the many questions you must have."

Cruikshank let out a brief sigh of relief. She failed to see how anyone would have been able to part Adelma from her battle-axes without the effort turning into a bloodbath, and she was glad the conflict hadn't devolved into a full-on confrontation.

Reheeme looked at Jabir with incandescent anger. "Inside," she snapped. "Now."

CHAPTER 13

Jabir quickly gave orders to the relevant servants to settle the Damsians, while Reheeme dragged him into a nearby sitting room. He did his best to maintain his calm, almost placid exterior.

"How dare you," Reheeme hissed, turning on him as soon as the door closed. "Writing to them in my name—my name and the name of my parents? And asking for help?" She spat the word like an insult.

"Now, Reheeme, be reasonable," Jabir said in as calm and conciliatory a tone as he could manage.

He walked to a nearby sideboard, where a tray was laid out with various drinks in crystal bottles. There was a bottle of something to be found in every room in the house—his wife liked it that way because she drank quite a bit. Which of course did nothing for her already mercurial disposition.

"Drink?" he asked, pouring two glasses of amberyth liqueur without waiting for an answer.

Reheeme snatched her glass, downed it quickly, and slammed it back on down on the sideboard. "You had no right," she snapped. "No right to ask for help in my name. You made me look weak—and to that woman, that Damsian woman who never even came to my parents' aid when they needed it."

Jabir sighed, taking a sip of amberyth. It was like dealing with a child. Any mention of Damsport and Reheeme felt the need to rehash how her parents had been caught up in the Seneschal's cleaning out of his opposition and how the Marchioness of Damsport, a supposed ally to her parents, had failed to stop their execution.

"Reheeme, you know the Seneschal acted far too swiftly for any help to come from Damsport. It takes weeks to get here by ship, and the Seneschal had it all done in a few days. What could the Marchioness have done?"

Jabir wished Reheeme would let this go. He was tired of hearing the same nonsensical arguments over and over again. It achieved nothing. "And you didn't appear weak. You appeared like the leader of a rebellion in need of some assistance."

"I don't need help from anyone," she replied angrily, eyes blazing.

Reheeme really was quite magnificent when she was angry. It was a shame that she was so nasty with it. Otherwise, their marriage could have been fun.

"Right," he said. "So the stalemate that we find ourselves in is going to be resolved how?"

"Not by those Damsians out there, that's for sure."

"Think about it," Jabir said, putting on his most persuasive voice. "Damsport is known for the fact that it successfully rebelled against Airnia—the largest Empire in the world!"

"I doubt any of the people currently soiling our house with their dirty boots had anything to do with that," Reheeme sniffed.

"Actually, Cruikshank was involved," Jabir replied. "But more to the point, you know the stalemate we find ourselves in. Maksur doesn't trust Tarwa, and they won't rise up until they have written assurances that they will be given full access to water and representation in the Council for them and the Lower. Tarwa is too afraid of Maksur and the Lower to grant access to water and give them any kind of power. There is no way out of that stalemate short of bringing in an outside element, and that's what I've done. Don't you see? The Damsians are a pawn we can use to bring about what we want: Tarwa and Maksur working together to bring down the Seneschal."

Reheeme narrowed her eyes, but she didn't immediately contradict him, which was a very good sign.

"The Marchioness of Damsport is prepared to publicly support the rebellion against the Seneschal," he continued, injecting his speech with all the passion he could muster. "And she has offered to negotiate trade deals with Azyr, so long as slavery is abolished and Maksur and the Lower have been given full access to water and representation. Do you see? Tarwanese merchants are desperate for trade deals with Damsport—it's one of the busiest trading cities, and for now, they have no access to it because Damsport won't be associated with any country or city-state engaging in slavery. It would be a coup for them to have Damsport's support. But since Damsport's support is dependent on Tarwa giving Maksur water access, it also gives Maksur the reassurance they want."

Reheeme shook her head. "You're really expecting me to believe the Damsians would do all that just to help Azyr?"

"Well, no. They want something in exchange, of course," Jabir said.

"I knew it. I don't trust Damsians. They lie, they cheat—they'll do anything to get what they want."

Reheeme poured herself another drink. She didn't offer to top up Jabir's glass, and he ignored the slight. There were bigger things to fight over.

"What the Damsians want is to be smuggled into the palace so they can rescue that Damsian inventor, Kadelta. Which is perfect, since we need the Maksur rebels to get into the palace and open one of the gates anyway. It won't cost us anything, and we get our rebellion under way and trade deals with Damsport."

"It'll cost us controlling Kadelta's machine," Reheeme said at once.

"Sure. But the alternative is that we remain in this stalemate, with no rebellion and no opportunity to depose the Seneschal. He controls that machine anyway, not us. We're not actually losing anything."

Reheeme finished her drink. "I rose to this position on my own, without help from anyone," she said in a low voice.

Jabir resisted the urge to roll his eyes. How many times had she given him this little speech?

"I clawed my way up," Reheeme continued, "*alone* after my family lost everything. I will not now hand over all that I achieved to a bunch of dirty, stealing, lying foreigners— foreigners who didn't even help my parents in their darkest hour. I have gotten this far alone, and I will continue alone. I will rebuild everything my parents lost. I will regain every supporter, and then I will storm the palace and tear down the Seneschal."

Jabir sighed. His wife was intelligent, of that there was no doubt. She was Azyr's Head Alchemist, and it wasn't simply because of her wealth and connections, although of course that helped quite a bit. She also had the talent to justify her position. But when it came to the rebellion, she could be as stubborn and stupid as any common mule.

Jabir still failed to understand why everyone looked to her for leadership—or rather, he understood but couldn't quite believe it. People followed her because of her parents. Their legacy lived on, and the respect they'd commanded flowed naturally down to their only daughter.

A fact that made Jabir feel as bitter as an old gourd. He had no legacy from his parents to carry him forward. Reheeme liked to claim she'd done it all alone, but the truth was that she was one of the most privileged people he knew, for all her talk of hardship during her childhood. Unlike

Jabir. *He* had had to do it all himself. He had faced ridicule and been underestimated his whole life, and now he was one of the wealthiest and most respected men in Azyr.

Although that wasn't yet enough to sate his ambition. He wanted more.

Marrying Reheeme had seemed like such a coup, an opportunity to be there when the government was toppled and a new era was established, with all its opportunities for power.

Of course, things had worked out quite differently. His wife had proven to be a difficult, almost shrewish woman with a terrible temper. She was a poor leader, and she was so focused on winning back every person who had deserted her parents that she had completely lost sight of the rebellion itself.

Once he had realised that, Jabir decided that the only way forward was to take matters into his own hands. Left to Reheeme, the rebellion would slowly peter out and die. And Jabir was tired of being treated like an inferior by his wife. She made him run every decision by her, as if he wasn't capable enough on his own.

He'd had enough. It was time for things to get back to the way they were supposed to be. He had put plans into motion, and he would see them carried through. In the end, every Azyrian would look at him in wonder, and every person who had ever laughed at him or underestimated him would bitterly regret it.

He just needed Reheeme to go along with things.

"Look," he said to his wife in a conciliatory tone. "Talk to the Damsians. See what they have to say. If their involvement means Tarwa and Maksur see eye to eye, it might be worth allowing outsiders to get involved, just to see our goal realised. They might just be what we need to set the people of Azyr on fire."

Reheeme was fond of saying that she wanted to "set the people of Azyr on fire," and the phrase seemed to have the desired effect on her.

"Hmm," she said thoughtfully.

Jabir kept silent, not wanting to risk saying a wrong word and setting her temper off again.

"Fine," Reheeme said at last. "But if I decide the Damsians are of no use to me, they are gone."

Jabir nodded slowly, not wanting to disagree with her. "They might not take too kindly to being sent packing," he said cautiously.

"I don't care. They are here to serve me."

Us, Jabir corrected mentally. "Of course they are. They are here to serve the legacy of your parents."

"Exactly. If I decide I have no use for them, they have no say in the matter. I will march them off Azyr myself, and if they resist, I'll have them arrested and sink their ship."

Jabir gave as calm a smile as he could manage. "Anything you want."

CHAPTER
14

While Jabir and Reheeme went off to argue, Longinus and the others stepped into a magnificent interior courtyard of such taste and luxury that Longinus was annoyed to find himself impressed. He had firmly intended to dislike everything in Jabir and Reheeme's home, but he found that he couldn't.

Across the door's threshold was the cool green shade of a cloister made entirely of twisting, flowering vines that climbed up and across a wrought-iron frame. The green cloister lined all four sides of a square internal courtyard, with open spaces left for each doorway. A little sunlight slipped through the leaves, dappling the green shade with spots of gold, while the little white, bell-shaped flowers of the vine released a subtle but pleasant perfume.

In the centre of the courtyard were four square pools of water spread out around a star-shaped fountain from which water gurgled. The water shimmered in the sunlight, casting beautiful ripples of reflected light on the two upper floors.

The first upper floor was ringed with a white marble cloister and balustrade, both intricately carved. Each arch of the cloister was cut out in a fine, lacelike pattern. Potted palms, dotted along the cloister's edge, rippled in the soft breeze.

The topmost floor was walled, with only small windows looking out, and Longinus guessed this was where the servants' quarters were located.

As he stepped into the cool green gloom of the vine cloister, Longinus became aware of how exhausted he was. The long journey to Azyr had taken its toll, and the heat and climb up the steps had drained him. But rest would have to wait.

Understanding the situation they were all in was imperative, as was figuring how to best turn it to their advantage. The fact that Reheeme hadn't been the one to write to them was highly suspicious, and the brief—if aborted—threat they had all been under upon arriving at the city made it clear that they needed to be on their guard.

Which was why, much as Longinus yearned for a bath, he would remain in his travel-stained clothing for a while longer. In times of great need, gentlemen were forced to make sacrifices.

Servants ushered him and the others to a sitting room off the internal courtyard. It was a kind of informal lounge room that looked inviting and comfortable, scattered with sofas, plush chairs, and large cushions. A burnt-orange silk canopy draped down from the ceiling, and thick carpets covered the floor.

Longinus wished again that he'd had an opportunity to clean up before sitting down on the fine fabrics. Adelma had none of Longinus's compunction, and she dropped into a wide chair with all the grace of a cog falling off its axle. The chair creaked dangerously beneath her bulk.

"Burn my body, I'm bloody knackered," she groaned. "Them stairs were quite something."

The others took seats, Longinus selecting a chaise longue in an orange that matched the canopy.

"Keep your wits about you," Cruikshank said as soon as the servants had left the room. "I don't like the fact that we have been brought here under false pretences."

"We sure it's a good idea to keep on with the mission?" Adelma asked.

"Yes," Cruikshank replied. "For now. There's too much at stake. If what we're dealing with here is simply a case of Jabir having written in the guise of his wife, there might not be any threat to us. The key is to understand *why* he did that."

Longinus nodded. "And we should also bear in mind that he's a man who isn't averse to a little duplicity."

"Exactly," Cruikshank replied.

At that moment, slaves entered the room, bringing in refreshments and bowls of scented water along with towels to wash their hands. Longinus watched them file in, shocked. Jabir and Reheeme were supposed to be involved in a rebellion seeking, among other things, to end slavery in Azyr. Why on earth would they keep slaves?

***

Reheeme and Jabir reappeared just as the slaves were leaving with the bowls of now dirty water. Jabir looked calm, while Reheeme looked tense, though no longer as angry as she had been earlier. Longinus wondered what had calmed her down.

Slaves poured everyone glasses of cinnamon wine, delicious and fragrant.

"I would offer to take you to our underground baths," Jabir said, "but I'm sure you're all eager to talk."

"That's putting it mildly," Rafe said. "The word 'understatement' even comes to mind."

"There's nothing much to tell," Reheeme said. "My husband and I had a misunderstanding, as you saw down on the docks, but we've now resolved it."

"I'm sorry," Adelma said, leaning forward. "Do we look like farmers?"

"What?" Reheeme asked, taken aback.

"Farmers. Do we look like them?" Adelma looked around at Longinus and the others as though examining their appearance. "Or do we look like shit shovelers what move manure all day?"

Reheeme frowned, obviously nonplussed. "What are—"

"Then why are you trying to serve us up shit so fresh from a bull's arse it's still steaming?" Adelma snapped. "And more importantly, what makes you think we'd accept it?"

"What Adelma is trying to say," Longinus said, "is that your explanation is woefully inadequate. Please do not insult our intelligence by assuming we will be satisfied so easily.

You mentioned that your husband forged your handwriting and signature. We would all like to know why he felt compelled to do that and why exactly he wanted us here and you didn't. We came here under the expectation of a fair exchange, during which we would help spark your revolution in exchange for your assistance in getting our countryman, Kadelta, out of the palace. I'm sure I don't need to point out that all of this is highly sensitive and dangerous, and in order to successfully work together, there needs to be some degree of trust. I think I speak for us all when I say that right now, the amount of trust between us is as nonexistent as Rory's sense of style."

Rory let out a low laugh.

Jabir ordered drinks for himself and Reheeme from the slaves, his Azyrian commands as rough on the ear as sandpaper. "I think we owe them a full explanation. Dear."

Reheeme bristled at the endearment, while Jabir looked amused. Their marriage was clearly more a thing of convenience than a meeting of souls.

"My wife has achieved a lot…" Jabir began.

"Don't talk about me like I'm not here," Reheeme snapped. "If there's an explanation to give, *I* will give it."

Jabir raised his hands in a placating gesture.

Reheeme took a deep gulp of the liqueur a servant had brought her. "The thing is," she said, "that right now I—"

"We," Jabir interjected.

Reheeme shot him a look, but she corrected herself. "*We* find ourselves at a bit of an impasse. As Jabir explained in his letters, we are attempting to organise a rebellion against the Seneschal and his current government. My parents had organised a resistance against him back when I was a child, but they were betrayed, and the Seneschal had them executed." Reheeme's mouth twisted as she spoke the words. "As you noticed when we crossed the city, Azyr is a city split into two main areas."

"Three, isn't it?" Rafe interrupted. "Maksur, Tarwa, and Azyr the Lower."

Reheeme waved a dismissive hand. "Azyr the Lower cannot rise up, not with the current defences in place. For the purpose of the rebellion, they are of no use."

"Not if you tear down the defences from the top," Rafe replied. "Attack the Great Gate by the cliffs from the Maksurian side."

"And if we did that, we would get attacked from behind, either from the Dividing Wall or from the palace or both," Reheeme replied coldly. "We cannot afford to focus on Azyr the Lower until the revolution has happened and the palace is under control. Don't presume to tell me how best to manage *my* rebellion."

"The boy only means to help," Jabir said gently.

"That boy," Cruikshank said, "is a Varanguard, a highly trained warrior. I'd be a little more respectful if I were you."

"My apologies," Jabir said.

Longinus noticed that although Jabir still looked outwardly calm, he was starting to show some strain. The conversation was off to a pretty bad start.

"As I was saying," Reheeme said, "we are at an impasse. The Sons and Daughters of the Elephant represent the rebels in Tarwa, and the Risen are the rebels in Maksur. Neither party trusts each other. I'm trying to broker trust between them, to unite them in one rebellion, but I'm struggling to get the full support of the Sons and Daughters. The Risen don't really trust me either, because I'm from Tarwa. The Risen have a way of smuggling a small group of people into the palace, which we could use to open one of the palace gates to let the main force sweep in."

"Won't they be under heavy guard?" Rafe asked.

"Most of them are," Reheeme replied. "But large portions of the palace are empty. The Prelate spends money like he eats food: without limit. The palace treasury is almost drained—hence, the importance of that submersible. By establishing slave trade with other countries, the Seneschal is hoping to refill the coffers."

"And I'm guessing that since parts of the palace are empty, gates in those areas aren't too closely guarded?" Rafe asked.

Reheeme nodded. "There's a small gate in the east, which was once a trade gate. It has been barred and is no longer in use. It is guarded but not heavily. Normally, there are no more than six or seven guards."

Longinus waved his hand in the air as though at a trifle. "If I am given the element of surprise and the cover of night, I will be able to dispatch those guards before Adelma even has time to draw her battle-axes."

"Adelma might want to draw her battle-axes," Adelma growled, an amused glint in her eyes.

"There'll be plenty of opportunity for you to use your axes once the attack begins," Reheeme said with a cold smile. "There is communication between all the gates in the palace, so I expect that they will find out about the attack quickly, but by then, it will be too late."

Again, Longinus waved a hand. "You assume that the Watch there will realise that they are under attack and have a chance to sound the alarm. They won't. When you have a poisoner of my calibre in your team, you don't simply expect a regular attack with noise and all the problems that creates. The guards at the gate will die without the opportunity to raise any kind of alarm. There are times when you use fighters like Adelma, and then there are times when you use expert poisoners like myself. This is one of the latter."

"Has anyone told you how modest you are?" Rafe asked.

"Modesty, my dear boy, is for *amateurs*."

Rory snorted with laughter.

CHAPTER

15

"I have a question," Cruikshank said quickly before the conversation could move forward. "Why won't the Risen open that east trade gate? I understand that they don't trust the Sons and Daughters of the Elephant, but surely it's as much to their advantage as to yours. I can understand them not wanting to give their hand away, but why won't they open the gates so forces from both rebel factions can storm the palace together?"

"Because they want a written agreement that if they open the Eastern Trade Gate, the Sons and Daughters won't just seize power for themselves," Jabir explained. "The Risen also want an official document confirming water access once the rebellion goes ahead, and that document needs to be signed by every member of the Sons and Daughters to ensure that nobody can later deny having agreed to those terms."

"What about Azyr the Lower?" Rory asked.

"The underground river cascades farther down the cliff," Jabir replied. "They don't have much, but they don't lack water."

"I'm guessing," Rafe said, "that there are many Sons and Daughters who are against giving Maksur free access to water."

"Exactly," Jabir said. "It would take months to get all those signatures, if we could even get them all. Many of the Sons and Daughters fear that if they relinquish control of the water, they will have no way of controlling Maksur. They believe that limiting water access keeps Maksur in check."

"Why do the Sons and Daughters even want to depose the Seneschal?" Cruikshank asked. "People in Tarwa are clearly doing quite well under his regime."

"Because they remember the loyalty they pledged to my parents," Reheeme replied stoutly.

"And because the Seneschal keeps raising the taxes to cover the Prelate's astronomical spending," Jabir added.

Cruikshank guessed Jabir's answer was closer to the truth than Reheeme's.

"But they aren't so desperate as to trust the people of Maksur," Rafe said.

"Exactly." Jabir glanced over at Reheeme. "That is why I sought to bring in a neutral foreign force to try to force things to move."

"However," Reheeme said coldly, "I have no trust in you Damsians. I've heard enough of your reputation to know better."

"Our reputation?" Cruikshank asked.

"Yes. Doing business with a Damsian means getting robbed on the price and then robbed on your way home," Reheeme replied.

"Well, obviously," Rory said, unable to stifle a grin.

"Excuse me if I won't trust a nation of swindlers," Reheeme said stiffly.

"That ain't swindling," Rory said. "That's just having a good head for business, is all."

Longinus turned to her. "I'm not sure this is helping, Rory."

The girl shrugged, her dislike for Reheeme written all over her features. "I bet she don't like anyone what's not Azyrian. Probably don't matter to her what we're about— we're foreign, so she don't like us. I read that Azyrians don't like *any* foreigners."

"We don't dislike foreigners," Reheeme replied haughtily, "we simply pity them for not being Azyrian."

Cruikshank raised her eyes to the sky, shaking her head. She had read that Azyrians had strong xenophobic tendencies, and she had always found that kind of attitude to be shortsighted, narrow-minded, and, quite frankly, idiotic.

"And also," Reheeme continued, her voice rising, anger returning to her eyes. "This is *my* revolution. My parents' legacy. I won't have it spoiled by having foreigners meddle with it."

"Which is why I wrote to Lady Martha, posing as Reheeme," Jabir said. "I knew Reheeme would never agree to it, yet I also knew we needed help."

"I do not need help," Reheeme said through gritted teeth. "I don't need help from anyone. I got to where I am on my own. Where was the Marchioness of Damsport when my parents were arrested and dragged out of their home? Where was Damsport when I was left alone, a young girl, with only one friend in the whole of Azyr who would take me in after the Seneschal had singled out my family? I started with nothing, and I got myself here, the leader of the Sons and Daughters and Azyr's Head Alchemist. I did it through sheer will and determination, not by going begging to foreigners with no real interest in Azyr. I don't need *anyone*."

"Oh, please," Rory scoffed. "You want to compare rough childhoods? You think we're gonna feel sorry for you 'cause you didn't live in complete luxury as a child or because you only had one friend for a bit? Lady, unless you had to eat cockroaches to keep away starvation, you ain't got nothing on me as far as rough childhoods go, alright? You know what? I also had one friend in the world when I were young." Rory slowly stood up, her voice rising. "And she was murdered for no good reason. No good reason at all. And at least you knew who your parents were. I got no idea who mine are or what my name should be. I don't even know my real *age*.

"All of us here got scars," she continued, jabbing a finger at Reheeme. "All of us here, and we all lost people. D'you see us complaining about it? D'you hear Adelma walking around insulting people and treating them badly all because she lost her man? She ain't swanning about reminding everyone how tough she's had it. So stop whining, and stop using your past as an excuse to act like a spoiled girl who ain't getting her way!"

Rory sat back down with force.

There was a silent pause, everyone clearly a little taken aback by the violence of her outburst. Reheeme's face had gone from livid to unreadable as a stone. Cruikshank reached across and squeezed Rory's arm. She realised the girl had expressed real pain, especially when she spoke of not knowing her name or who her parents were. She wondered about the friend Rory had mentioned—whoever that was, it wasn't someone Rory had ever spoken about.

"To be fair," Adelma said, "I *do* tend to go around insulting people. But I get what you meant, and I agree."

"Look," Rafe said softly to Reheeme. "You don't like us—that much is clear. I think I speak for all of us when I say we don't like you either. But likes and dislikes don't matter here. We both have a goal, a mission that we're working towards, and as it happens, for now, our goals align. We can speak to the Sons and Daughters and give them the assurance from Lady Martha that they will be able to get trade deals with Damsport. We can speak to the Risen and confirm that those trade deals are conditioned on Maksur getting water access and the Lower and Maksur being represented in the Council. In short, we can help pull you out of your stalemate so your revolution can happen."

"What it boils down to," Adelma said, "is that everyone in this rooms needs your revolution to go ahead. We need it so we can get smuggled into the palace and free Kadelta. You need it—well, because you need it. We're already working together anyway, so arguing now is just stupid. We should be figuring out what the next step is so we all get what we want."

"I agree," Cruikshank said.

"The Damsians are right," Jabir said to Reheeme. "What matters is the revolution—ending the oppression of the Azyrian people and honouring your parents' legacy. The rest is details."

Reheeme's face remained stony. Cruikshank frowned. How stubborn could the woman be? Was she really going to choose doing it all alone and risk jeopardising the revolution?

The truth was that irrespective of her opinion of Reheeme and of their mission regarding Kadelta, Cruikshank wanted the revolt to go ahead. Just thinking of the people in Azyr the Lower—to say nothing of the barbaric practice of forcing people into slavery—made her clench her fists.

"If you turn us away," Longinus said casually, "we will find another way into the palace. Yes, our goals align for now, but we are not dependent on you. Between Rory, Adelma, and I, we have ample experience in slipping into places undetected. We'll find a way. But if you turn us away, and this causes your revolt to struggle or fail, you *will* regret it. And I doubt you'll have another chance to make it happen. From what I've read and heard of the Seneschal, he isn't a man to give an opponent a second chance."

Reheeme gave Longinus a searching look. "Are you really as good a poisoner as you say you are?"

"Absolutely," he replied.

"Can you make me a poison that will cause a slow and agonising death?"

Longinus narrowed his eyes at her.

"For the Seneschal," Reheeme said. "I want him to suffer. I want him to die slowly."

Longinus gave her a nod. "It would be my pleasure."

"Then we have a deal," Reheeme said. "We work together, for now, to bring the Seneschal down and get Kadelta back to Damsport."

CHAPTER

16

Rory was relieved when Jabir suggested the rest of the discussions take place over dinner, and her stomach grumbled its agreement loudly. Jabir led them all to a dining room richly decorated in red and burnt-gold tones. A huge, low ebony table inlaid with gold sat in the middle of the room, surrounded by enormous plush cushions. Alchemical globes cast a soft golden light on the room, and fragrant incense curled up into the air.

It was all ridiculously lavish, although Rory liked the idea of eating while sitting on the floor. She guessed that Longinus would approve of all the rich fabrics and gold inlay on the dining table, but all she could think about was how many families you could feed just on the value of the items in the room.

And of course, another part of her was already making calculations, seeing if there was anything she might steal and sell back in Damsport. Preferably something small and valuable. She'd keep an eye out.

"It is customary to dine barefoot," Jabir said, gesturing to a number of chairs that had been lined up against the wall. He sat on one of them and clapped his hands. Slaves trailed into the dining room, one of them stopping to crouch at Jabir's feet to remove his sandals. Feeling distinctly uncomfortable, Rory followed suit, along with the others, and sat on a chair.

The slave who crouched at her feet was a young boy. Rory knew a boy about his age back in Damsport, an urchin called Pip who sometimes did odd jobs for her or carried messages across the city. The boy at her feet, with his black skin and almond eyes, looked nothing like him, yet something about him reminded her of Pip.

It made the sight of the ugly holes at his eyebrows all the harder to take in and the fact that he was crouched at her feet, taking off her boots seem all the more wrong. Pip would never have done that, not in a million years. If someone had tried to force him, he'd have sworn at them and kicked and wriggled until he could run away, pelting down the streets. To see the Azyrian boy in front of her so docile as he removed her boots sent a pang to her stomach.

Once her boots were off, the boy reached behind her legs, under the chair, to retrieve a wide bowl of scented, petal-covered water. He placed her feet inside the bowl and, to Rory's increasing discomfort, washed them. All the other slaves were doing the same, and Reheeme and Jabir seemed perfectly at ease with this. Rory kept quiet for as long as she could, but as soon as the slaves had left, she had to say something.

"If you're wanting to end slavery in Azyr, why the hell you got slaves in your house?" she asked Reheeme and Jabir.

"It's expected," Jabir replied matter-of-factly. "People with our kind of studs without slaves would be worse than an anomaly, and we can't afford that kind of scrutiny."

Rory gave him a dubious nod. She hoped it was true, although even if it was, it did little to make her feel better.

They took their seats at the dining table. Rory slipped her legs beneath the table easily enough, sitting cross-legged. Adelma, however, had more trouble. She grumbled and swore under her breath as she struggled to find a comfortable position. If she sat cross-legged, she lacked too much flexibility to get her knees low enough to fit under the low table, and she also lacked the flexibility to sit with her legs out flat.

In the end, to Rory's amusement, Jabir had a separate table brought, high enough to accommodate Adelma's knees when she sat cross-legged. Adelma glowered at the room, daring anyone to laugh. Rory swallowed her laughter, and she exchanged a look with Rafe, who was also doing his best to keep a straight face.

Slaves went around the table, filling everyone's glasses with more cinnamon wine, then food was served in large chiselled copper bowls placed in the middle of the table. Mouth-watering smells wafted up from each one, full of fragrant herbs and spices.

Serving spoons stuck out of each dish, and Rory helped herself liberally to the food, her stomach grumbling for all it was worth. There were mountains of flatbreads in baskets—some plain, some with herbs, some with nuts and raisins, and some that bulged, stuffed with meats.

Rory was surprised to see Reheeme tear off a chunk of the bread and use it to pick up a piece of meat from her plate. That was when she noticed there was no cutlery. Jabir did the same. Not one to let something like getting her fingers dirty get in the way of a good meal, Rory gamely tore a chunk of flatbread and began devouring what was on her plate. It was spicy as sin but full of flavour, and she ate with gusto in spite of the fire that roared in her mouth.

"So," Cruikshank said, "what is the first step we need to accomplish to get us into the palace?"

"We should go there tomorrow," Jabir said to Reheeme, "so the Damsians can get a sense of the layout. The Prelate will have heard of their arrival, and no doubt, he will be curious to meet them. We can use that as a cover for a reconnaissance mission. We cannot go into the palace without it being cleared with the Seneschal first." He turned to Cruikshank. "So once we have introduced you to the Prelate, we probably won't get another chance for reconnaissance, and you will need to have some idea of the palace layout to reach Kadelta."

Reheeme shook her head. "First, we need to meet with Oma—that's the leader of the Risen—" she added to Cruikshank, "and make sure we can get an agreement with them to smuggle in the fighting force that will open the Eastern Gate. If that doesn't work, the whole thing falls apart."

111

Jabir frowned. "True, but all the same, we should first stake out the palace."

"No," Reheeme snapped. "We are speaking to the Risen first."

Jabir put his hands up in a placating gesture. There was sauce on his fingers, making him look like a child caught doing something naughty.

"Where do we meet the Risen?" Rafe asked.

"At the races," Reheeme replied. "I will send word, and we will meet them tomorrow evening."

"Well," Jabir said, "in the meantime, tomorrow during the day, we could go to the pa…" His voice faltered as Reheeme threw him a look that could have frozen the ocean.

Rory felt sorry for Jabir. He evidently meant well, and if not for him, Reheeme would still be stuck in her stalemate, while they wouldn't be in a position to save Kadelta and help Azyr with its rebellion. But it seemed that Reheeme didn't recognise her husband's contributions, and it was obvious from their interactions that she didn't treat him with any kindness or respect.

Rory's sympathy for Jabir wasn't enough to interfere with her appetite, though, and she soon finished her plate, wiping the sauce clean with her remaining piece of flatbread. She belched quietly behind her hand then hesitated, looking around her to determine if she would be offending anyone by going for seconds.

Rafe, who sat next to her, let out a low laugh. "Do you really care if anyone minds you going for more? I'm surprised you waited until your plate was finished—I don't think I've ever seen anyone eat so quickly."

"That were nothing," Rory said. "Wait till you see what I can do when food ain't so spicy it's burning holes in my stomach."

Rory eyed his plate, which was still half-full.

"You don't get mine," he said jokingly, making a mock show of sheltering his plate.

"Well, then, I guess that settles that. More it is, or I'll be going hungry." Rory reached forward for a nearby dish containing a delicious, but searingly spicy, goat curry.

**

"There's another issue we face," Reheeme said as Rory was reaching the end of her second plate. "The communication between the palace and the Dividing Wall."

"How does that work?" Cruikshank asked, leaning forward and setting her bread down.

"There are a number of long tubes just beneath the roads, and they connect the Dividing Wall and the palace. The tubes contain a special liquid—Sodiumate of Crianthum," Reheeme added to Longinus, who nodded with interest. "I can explain to Longinus in greater detail, but essentially, the liquid can be used to carry alchemical signals from one place to the other in a matter of seconds. The problem is that at either end, the readers are able to identify any kind of interference with the pipes. Any leak will trigger an alarm, and any attempt to interfere with the liquid alchemically will also immediately be registered.

"So far as we can tell, we cannot cut communication between the two sides without them both immediately realising it, which will warn them of the attack. So if we attack the Dividing Wall to let the Risen through, the palace will know what has happened. That means that timing will be absolutely crucial—we need to have forces from the Sons and Daughters ready to strike the palace and the Dividing Wall simultaneously."

Cruikshank frowned, and Rory could practically see the cogs of her brain turning. "Have you got a method for the various teams to communicate?"

"We can't get them to communicate now," Jabir muttered. "The gods only know how we'd manage it in the middle of a battle."

"We haven't yet solved that problem," Reheeme said stiffly, throwing Jabir another look.

"That's something I can look into," Cruikshank said. "I could maybe find a way to disrupt communications between the palace and the Wall without them catching wind of it."

"Don't take this the wrong way," Reheeme said, "but I know far more about alchemy than you do."

"Maybe I could take a look," Longinus said.

Reheeme frowned. "Are you implying that you are a better alchemist than me?" she asked coldly.

Rory braced herself. Longinus wasn't one to be economical with self-praise.

"I'm sure, Reheeme, that you've looked at every alchemical possibility," Cruikshank said quickly before Longinus could speak. "But that will have limited you to looking for a way to interfere with the solution inside the tubes. I'm not sure that another alchemist using the same approach would yield anything more, so there probably isn't much point Longinus looking at it. But maybe a machinist's eye could see something that you missed."

Reheeme shrugged, looking dubious.

"Her gratitude for Cruikshank's suggestion is overwhelming," Rafe murmured so low only Rory heard.

She quirked an eyebrow at him in agreement. She liked Reheeme less and less. Working with her was going to be trying.

"Do you know where the tubes are?" Cruikshank asked Reheeme.

Reheeme nodded. "Yes. We were able to obtain a copy of a map outlining the lines of communications."

"Good. I'll need to have a look at that map. If the tubes go over a hill, no matter how small, even a little rise will do, then I know how we can cut communications."

CHAPTER
17

After dinner, Cruikshank and the others were taken to the suite of rooms that had been prepared for them. They were also given directions to the set of private baths in the basement of the house, which Longinus took immediate advantage of. Despite her protests, he dragged Rory along with him.

Cruikshank was too interested in the problem of cutting the communications between the Dividing Wall and the palace to want to sit in a bath. And there was really no point in washing before work.

The room she had been given was overstuffed with cushions and drapes and rugs. Fortunately, her trunks had been brought in. She had even more trunks than Longinus, to fit all the things she might need. Her equipment was larger and heavier than Longinus's as well, but all the same, she was amused to think of Longinus as travelling light by comparison. Cruikshank even had a small travelling furnace fuelled by an alchemical solution that produced a good hot flame.

Cruikshank had gone over the map of the communication tubes with Reheeme, and they had indeed identified a couple of spots where the tubes went up and over a small rise. Reheeme and Longinus had then launched into a dreadfully dull conversation about the exact nature of the alchemical signals and the composition of the liquid inside the tubes. After much debate, they had finally reached an agreement on the single question that actually mattered: could the alchemical signal travel through air? And the answer, greased gears be kind, was no.

Which meant that Cruikshank's idea would work. She shoved her trunks aside, rolled the rug up and, after opening her door, threw it out into the communal sitting area she shared with the four others.

"Adelma, Rafe," she called, "would you mind coming to help me move something?"

It took the three of them a few tries before they managed to move her massive four-poster bed so that she was able to grab the rug beneath, roll it up, and throw it outside.

"Redecorating?" Rafe asked.

"I don't want anything flammable around me when I work." Cruikshank frowned, examining the walls, which were extravagantly painted in patterns of indigo and gold. "Not much I can do about the paint, though."

Once Adelma and Rafe had left, Cruikshank moved to the curtains on her window, unhooking them before throwing them out. The bed sheets received the same treatment, as did the mattress, the gauze canopy above the bed, the rich tapestry that covered one wall, and the sheaf of writing paper neatly stacked in a tray on the desk.

Once the room was suitably bare, she got to work setting up her temporary workshop. First, she checked on all the things she had brought with her to ensure nothing had gotten lost, stolen, or broken.

In the two largest trunks was her steam-powered spider, dismantled so that it could be transported more easily. She carefully checked each part, making sure nothing had been dented or otherwise damaged—later on, she would reattach the legs to the abdomen of the spider. She felt quite sure the spider would come in useful.

Once she had finished checking everything over, she got to work. She hummed to herself as she moved about the room, setting everything up. Nothing made her feel more satisfied or happy than starting a new project. She reckoned she should have her solution to the communications problem ready before the races the following day.

As Cruikshank fussed with her tools, she felt something on her right shoulder, a kind of itch. She scratched it absentmindedly, vaguely waving her hand in case there was an insect buzzing about. Then she got the furnace working and unpacked the delicate tools that would allow her to put together a drill's mechanism.

CHAPTER
18

Rory woke up with a start. Her room was dark and silent save for the ticking of the clock hanging on the wall. Before they'd all gone to sleep, Rory and the others had agreed to keep guard during the night, just to be safe. She'd left her shutters open so that moonlight could stream into the room, giving her a bit of light to see by.

Rory sat up, checking the time, and she nodded to herself. Her shift started in ten minutes. She stretched and rubbed her eyes, yawning. The rug on the floor was so thick and plush, it had been the softest, most comfortable night's sleep she'd ever had. The bed was too big, too high off the floor, too wide, too soft—in short, too bed-like for her tastes. The rug had been a much better choice.

Rory grabbed her sword, retrieved her dagger from under her pillow, and attached her grappling hook to her belt. Her door opened soundlessly, and she stepped into the communal sitting room, which was bathed in moonlight. The furniture had transformed into shadows that crouched in corners. All the things Cruikshank had thrown out of her room made a dark, lumpy shape, and someone had pushed the rest of the sitting-room furniture against the walls.

Rafe was on the current watch, and he was practicing fighting moves. Rory watched, mesmerised. He seemed to possess the fluidity of water. He held a pair of matched long daggers, moving them with a kind of deliberate slowness, and yet somehow, the overall effect was of speed and accuracy. He had stripped to the waist, his chest bathed in sweat so that it gleamed in the moonlight. His movements were more like a dance than a fighting sequence.

"Anybody tell you it's rude to stare?" he asked.

Rory snapped out of it, mortified that she had been caught watching. "Didn't want to disturb," she replied with a shrug, "but it's time for my shift."

Rafe threw a glance at a clock on the wall. "So it is." He slipped his daggers back into his belt. As he turned around to reach for a towel, Rory looked at the four smaller throwing knives nestled at the small of his back.

"Did you give any thought to what I said on the ship?" Rafe asked.

"About what?"

"About your sword."

"Oh, that."

Rafe had suggested that the sword might not be the right weapon for Rory. She had promptly dismissed the suggestion.

"I know it's probably not what you want to hear," Rafe continued.

120

Rory shrugged. She would be a swordswoman, and she didn't care what Rafe thought.

"I'm sure you have your reasons for favouring the sword," Rafe said, "but you'd do better with twin long knives like the ones I was using just now. Or even something like a chain whip."

"A chain whip?" Rory asked, curiosity getting the better of her.

"It's a long chain with a sharp spike at the end. The heavier version could have a spiked ball at the end, like a kind of morning star, but to be honest, I think the spike would be far better for you. I've seen fighters who wield them—they move with impressive speed, and they can be lethally effective."

"I wouldn't know where to start with a chain," Rory said.

"You're good with your grappling hook, so I reckon you'd be able to pick up the movements quickly. Or if not, try the twin daggers. I just think you'd be a better fit for something smaller and more agile."

Rory shook her head. She had no intention of abandoning the sword. She had dreamt of being a sword fighter since she was little. The sword still represented strength and independence for her, and she had no intention of putting it aside now—not after coming so far.

Rafe walked over to a table against the wall, and he picked up a bottle of oil and a rag. He pulled out one of his daggers and began oiling it with careful gestures. "I never told you the reason I became a Varanguard, did I?"

"No, you didn't." Rory perched herself on the arm of a deep armchair.

"It was my little sister's dream to be a Varanguard. When she was a kid, she was obsessed with them, talked of nothing else. She would make my father take her to the Mansion so she could see them. She even had a doll of a Varanguard—it was done very well, with real horsehair in the helmet and everything. I took it from her so many times, because that's what big brothers do, I guess. She'd threaten me by saying that when she was captain of the Varanguards, she'd beat me up for each time I'd taken her doll."

Rafe smiled to himself, and then his smile faded abruptly. "Anyway, there was... an accident, and she died when she was seven."

Rory remembered that night on the ship when Rafe had hinted at having lost a sister. It still felt odd to think of him as having experienced grief.

Rafe shrugged. "So I became a Varanguard because of her, because it had been her dream. I also worked like a dog to try to make captain as soon as possible. I was aggressive and driven to the point of being ruthless. I was good, but nobody on my team liked me—not that I cared. It was my captain who took me aside and spoke to me. He was captain before our current one. He told me that at some point you have to let go of the past. He knew my family's... situation, and he knew about my sister. His point was that although the memory of my sister had helped get me into the Varanguards, it was no longer helping. In fact, it was weighing me down and spoiling things for me. I could keep my sister's memory alive without letting it drive everything I did. Becoming the youngest captain wouldn't bring her back.

"Which is why when I see you insisting so hard on becoming a sword fighter, part of me wonders if you also have something driving you. Do you want to be a sword fighter because it's the best path for you or because you are holding on to something and refusing to let it go?"

Rory kept her expression cold and blank. A complex mix of emotions roiled inside her: sadness, anger, confusion, and a deep sense of discomfort. She could feel the box of her memories like a hot stone, lodged deep inside her, and she steeled herself, ignoring the sensation as she had so many times before.

She crossed her arms, and took a breath, feeling herself regain control again. She had no intention of letting Rafe tell her she had to give up her childhood dream. "Isn't time for your watch to end?" she said coldly.

Rafe looked surprised. "I'm only trying to help."

"Yeah, well, don't. I'm doing fine on my own."

The familiar sardonic expression returned on Rafe's face, and his eyes danced with amusement. "You know who you sound like? Reheeme."

"It really is time for your shift to end," Rory replied stiffly.

Rafe gave her an infuriating smile and a shrug. He grabbed his shirt and headed to his room. Rory stared impotently after him, furious yet unable to come up with a good answer to his suggestion that she was in any way like Reheeme.

Once she was alone, she paced the room to try to calm herself down, muttering angrily. The worse thing was that a small part of her couldn't help but wonder if he was right about the sword.

"No," Rory said aloud. "He's wrong."

She pushed all thoughts of Rafe out of her mind, drawing her sword to practice the moves Longinus had taught her. The steel gleamed brightly in the moonlight, beautiful and sharp. Rory moved comfortably with it, slashing through the air, parrying invisible attacks.

She smiled to herself. Rafe had just been trying to rattle her—another one of his stupid tricks. After all, he had messed her around before. He had even admitted to it on the ship. Maybe this was a way for him to amuse himself. She had no intention of letting it get to her.

No, Rory was quite happy with her decision. The sword was the weapon for her. She continued practicing her moves, although she couldn't help but notice that she didn't move with anything close to Rafe's fluidity and speed.

CHAPTER

19

Longinus awoke feeling refreshed. How wonderful to sleep in a proper bed that didn't sway beneath him. How delightful to get up and stand on dry, firm land, without the smell of the sea in his nostrils and the rising taste of nausea in his throat. Longinus smiled and stretched.

He mulled over the previous day's events, his mind fresh and alert. Something important had been missed during the discussions: for all the talk, no mention had been made of how exactly Jabir had come to get a letter from Kadelta to Lady Martha. He had alluded to not knowing Kadelta's exact location, which begged the question of how he had obtained the letter.

Longinus decided it would be best to wait to see if that information was freely offered. It was also odd that Reheeme had blocked the suggestion of them all going to the palace that day—they could have gone before the races, after all. What were her motives there?

Longinus stretched again and got up. His bedroom was all in pale greens and blues, everything decorated along a nature theme, which was a soothing contrast to the blasting heat and dust of the city. The furniture was clearly the product of highly skilled workers too—engraved ebony inlaid with silver. The walls were painted in rich patterns that stayed just clear of looking busy.

Although there was a lot to dislike about the two Azyrians who were their hosts, their taste in furnishings was one thing Longinus couldn't criticise.

He got up, casting a quick look over the trunks that contained his alchemical equipment. It had all arrived without a scratch, nothing broken or even cracked, which was a relief. If he had time, he might rustle up a poison or two during the day. He didn't like working in the same room that he slept in—even an alchemist of his calibre sometimes had a mishap. It was never a good idea to sleep among the residual fumes of a poison gone awry. He might have to ask Reheeme for a separate room to work in.

For now, he set about preparing for the day. He pulled out his travelling kit, a small cabinet that housed vials of each of his poisons. He also had a small amount of his Writing on the Wall poison, which he kept in its own box. It was a virulent poison that paralysed on instant contact with the skin, with death following just a few short moments after. There was no antidote, and the box was lined with a special fabric that was able to neutralise the poison, as any leak could be lethal.

Cruikshank had at first been deeply uncomfortable with the thought of him taking that poison with him, but she had come around and, not long before they left, had even designed a way for him to dispense it more efficiently. Up until that point, he had used it as a kind of ink, killing his targets by writing on their skin. Cruikshank had made him a contraption that strapped to his wrist. By flicking his wrist a certain way, he could send out a fine spray of poison.

It was far from precise, but if he ever faced a large number of opponents, he would be able to easily get the better of them.

Longinus had been able to make some aesthetic suggestions for the design of the contraption, too, so that it could look elegant enough to be camouflaged as an accessory.

He pulled out the box that housed the contraption, checking it over. It was attached to a glove made of the neutralising fabric. The poison vial was of deep sapphire-blue glass that looked like a jewel, and it was housed in a delicate copper filigree. The spraying mechanism was hidden beneath a fine casing, also covered in filigree, and only a tiny tip of nozzle protruded.

In all, it looked like an elaborate glove reaching to midforearm, with a fake sapphire and fine copper filigree—perfectly fitting for someone of his tastes and style. He'd had a matching glove made up, but without the poison, to help with the camouflage.

Longinus had also asked Cruikshank to build a safety catch into the mechanism so he couldn't accidentally discharge the spitter. He left the box open, debating whether to bring out his weapon.

He decided it might be wiser to keep it as an element of surprise. Not only that, but the clothes that matched his weapon probably wouldn't be suitable for the races.

Longinus first picked a couple of versatile poisons for the day—he liked to be prepared for any eventuality—then he threw his wardrobe open, scanning his clothes to pick an outfit to match. He selected a salmon shirt, which would go divinely with his chosen poisons. He smiled and congratulated himself on his effortless style.

It comes so naturally to me.

He was about to lay the shirt out on the bed when he had the uncomfortable sensation that someone was watching him. He paused, holding out the shirt in front of him.

Longinus was too old a hand at stalking targets to fall into the trap of looking around him and giving his suspicion away. Instead, he examined the shirt, moving this way and that so the light caught it at different angles. As he did, he glanced around the room. He couldn't see anything, and yet the feeling only intensified, the little hairs at the back of his neck standing to attention.

He placed the shirt on the bed, smoothing the fabric with his hand.

The patterns on the wall are too complex for me to be able to detect a peephole, and if I walk up to the wall, whoever is watching will close it.

Longinus allowed himself a small smile—he would have to solve that little riddle alchemically.

First things first: he put the salmon shirt back in the wardrobe and was careful to ensure that the doors were fully closed, the clothes within protected by the wood.

Still clad in his silk dressing gown, he began pulling out his alchemical equipment from the trunks, humming to himself. The humming was more for the watcher than anything else. Longinus could still feel eyes on him.

It will be a shame to ruin the dressing gown but worth it if I can find the peephole.

Longinus quickly got to work. Cruikshank had made him a replica of her travel furnace, smaller than the original but large enough that he could heat up a solution quickly if he needed to.

It didn't take him long to obtain the mix he was after. A final few drops of sublimate of milkweed flower, and the potion began to emit a thick smoke.

"Oh dear. Oh *no*," Longinus exclaimed, picking up the smoking beaker. Acting like a man clumsily trying to dispel the smoke, he moved about the room, the beaker spreading its smoke. It had an unpleasant, bitter smell, but there was no sting to it or nefarious effects.

The smoke built up in the room, turning unpleasant. Longinus coughed for effect, and when he decided there was enough smoke, he put the beaker down and threw open the shutters.

By the time the smoke had cleared, a grey residue covered everything in the room, including the wall. At a quick glance, Longinus couldn't see anything that might give away the peephole's location. Whoever had been watching had probably closed it.

He walked along each wall slowly, scanning the patterns etched in the paint. Eventually, he found it: a circular spot where the residue was much fainter. Whoever had been watching must have closed the peephole once the smoke had begun filling the room, so only a little stained the hole. The circle was perfectly integrated within the pattern around it, making it almost impossible to detect, but the residue gave it away.

Feeling with his fingers, he found a fine crack lining the edge of the circle. He smiled and nodded to himself, satisfied. He made a small mark above the circle as a reminder before checking the rest of the walls to ensure that there wasn't another peephole.

He'd begun wiping the walls down to remove the residue when there was a knock at the door.

"Can I come in?" It was Rory.

"By all means, although I'm still in my dressing gown." Longinus wasn't sure why he had bothered to inform her of that fact, seeing how little the girl cared about basic etiquette.

"Sleep well?" she asked, walking in. "Whoa, what happened here?"

"Experiment gone wrong," he replied, putting a finger to his lips as he spoke. He gestured at the air around them, then at his ear. Just because the peephole was closed didn't mean there might not be a way for someone to listen to their conversation. "I need your help with something. I can't seem to decide what shirt would be best for today."

He gestured for her to follow him, and together they stood in front of the wardrobe as Longinus opened it. Their backs were to the peephole so nobody would see their lips move.

Longinus had barely pulled out his salmon shirt when he again felt the skin-crawling sensation of eyes on him.

"There—I was initially thinking of this one," he said then added in a low whisper, "We're being watched."

"Oh, I'm not a huge fan of it," Rory replied in her normal voice then whispered, "How? Who?"

"Hmm. Then that is a significant point in this shirt's favour." Longinus's voice dropped to a whisper. "I found a peephole in the wall. I think we're being watched right now. Here is the other one I was considering," he added more loudly, pulling out another shirt. This one was indigo and completely wrong for the poisons he had selected.

"Better," Rory said. She dropped her voice to a whisper. "Who d'you reckon it is?"

"Right. So salmon it is," Longinus replied then whispered, "No idea. I'd lean towards Reheeme."

Rory nodded. "Yep, I agree," she said out loud.

Longinus understood that she was referring to Reheeme. He sighed, as though she had only talked about the shirt.

"Well, now you've ruined the whole decision process. If you agree on the salmon shirt, then I need to cast it aside. I can't wear something that you approve of, given your nonexistent sense of style."

Rory rolled her eyes. "I should probably leave you to it, then. I'll go see how the others are doing."

Longinus nodded. A good idea. She could warn them. There were likely to be peepholes in the other rooms too.

CHAPTER

20

The races during which Rory and the others would meet the
Risen started late in the afternoon, when the sun was low
enough to have lost the most unbearable part of its heat.
They had to walk back to the place where the mechanised
elephant was parked. From there, they would ride to the
racetrack.

"Why don't we just walk to the racetrack?" Rory asked as
they set off. "I had a look at a map. Going back to the
elephant makes us go in the wrong direction."

"Because," Reheeme replied, "people with our studs can't
be seen to arrive at the races on foot."

Rory turned to Adelma and rolled her eyes. Azyrians did
seem to be quite taken with all that stud nonsense. Who
cared about a piece of metal or stone at the eyebrows? That
didn't say anything about a person's character or skill.

They set off with a large retainer of guards, the streets
pleasantly cool as the sun hid behind buildings. The vines

133

and awnings overhead provided deepening shade on the streets below.

Once again, a whole palaver ensued every time they crossed paths with anyone in the narrow streets, the superiority of one person's studs needing to be established before the other person would give way. It was ridiculous, and Rory found herself getting frustrated as they made slow progress.

Finally, they reached the open square where the steam-powered elephants were kept. Reheeme and Jabir's pilot was already waiting for them atop their elephant. Rory was about to climb on when she heard a cry of pain intersected with a sharp smacking noise.

She turned to see a man beating a young boy with his cane. The boy had no studs at his eyebrows, and Rory recognised him at once: it was the boy who had washed her feet the night before, the one who had reminded her of Pip.

Anger flooded her, and before she could think, she rushed over. "Hey, you there! Stop that! Stop that at once!"

The man raised his cane again, polished wood gleaming in the late afternoon sun. He was shouting at the boy in Azyrian.

Rory lunged for the cane. She missed and, instead of deflecting it, received a sharp blow on her forearm. She hissed in surprise at the pain. The boy took the opportunity to scramble out of the way.

The man shouted at her in Azyrian.

Rory lunged at him again and this time managed to grab his cane. The man wrestled her for it, but Rory wouldn't let go, her fury lending her strength.

"Stop this at once," a voice shouted behind her.

The man was startled enough to loosen his grip, and Rory yanked the cane out of his hands, flinging it aside. She was breathing hard. Jabir walked up to them, followed by his guards, his face livid with anger.

He spoke angrily at the man, who was at first defensive, then apologetic.

Rory looked down at the boy, wincing at the sight of him. "Are you alright?" she whispered.

It was a stupid question. His face was swollen where the cane had hit him, including a nasty lump on his forehead. Welts had also begun to appear on his arms, showing where he was struck as he had tried to defend himself.

Sleeping that night was going to be painful for him. Rory crouched down and helped him up to his feet. He kept his gaze trained on the ground, and Rory could see he was shaking with fear.

The man bowed stiffly to Jabir and retrieved his cane before walking away.

Jabir sighed. "Terrell apparently accidentally stepped on his robes and dirtied them." He shook his head. "Most Azyrians don't believe in treating slaves with kindness." He turned to the lad. "It's alright, Terrell. You haven't done anything wrong. No need to be afraid." He called for one of his guards. "Take Terrell back home, and see that his wounds are properly seen to."

The guard looked surprised but didn't argue. He gestured for Terrell to go with him. The boy hurried away, never once looking up at any of the faces around him.

Rory watched him leave, guessing that most people didn't bother to tend to a slave's wounds. She was still shaking with anger at what she had seen. Beating a young boy senseless over something as insignificant as dirtying a robe was disgusting.

"Does this sort of thing happen often?" she asked Jabir.

"Sadly, yes," Jabir replied.

He and Rory returned to the elephant. "I'm sorry you all had to witness that," he said to the others as he and Rory joined them on board the elephant. "Such a display doesn't put my people forward in the best of lights."

Rory looked at Jabir again. She had been quite sure that his excuse of owning slaves to keep up appearances was just that: an excuse. Now she wasn't so sure.

"Oh, enough with the theatrics," Reheeme said. "We have important things to tend to, so let's go."

Rory hadn't thought it was possible to dislike Reheeme any more than she already did, but lo and behold, it had happened. If Reheeme hadn't been the leader of a rebellion seeking to end slavery, there really wouldn't be anything to redeem her. Not only that, but Rory was also growing more and more sure that Reheeme didn't care a button for the fate of the Azyrian slaves—or of the people from Maksur, for that matter. Her focus on the revolution seemed little more than a vainglorious attempt to replicate her parents' legacy.

Rory thought back to that morning, when Longinus had caught someone watching him. She felt quite sure it had been Reheeme. They would need to be very careful with her.

***

Once they were all on board the elephant, they set off. As they made their way to the racetrack, Rory found her excitement growing again at the thought of attending a race. She had never been to the races before—or rather, never to a proper one. The makeshift races set up in the Rookery ranged from having cockroaches race against each other to having larger animals, like rats, compete. It was nothing like what they would see at the Azyrian races, she felt quite sure.

She had also never been to a secret meeting with the leaders of rebel factions, and if truth be told, Rory wasn't sure which she was more excited about witnessing—the race or the secret meeting.

"What kind of race will it be?" she asked Jabir.

He shuddered. "Lizards."

"Oh." Rory tried to hide her disappointment. They had lizards in Damsport—tiny pale, spotted creatures that lived in the corners of houses and ate flies. Azyrian races didn't sound much different from Damsian races after all.

Still, she reminded herself, the most important thing was that they would meet with the leader of the Risen. That would provide more than enough excitement, and it was far, far more important than watching a few lizards running around.

The elephant plodded on while the light around them turned to gold as the sun began to dip on the horizon, turning a deep orange, like a fat yolk in the sky.

The racetrack was right at the border between Tarwa and Maksur, at the westernmost point of the city. The racetrack itself was apparently integrated within the Dividing Wall.

The closer they got to the races, the thicker the stream of traffic—clearly, the races were popular in Azyr.

Not everyone had mechanised elephants. Some came in steam palanquins or even regular litters carried by six bearers. Rory was growing used to the stud system in Azyr already, and she noticed that the studs of the ones in the old-fashioned litters carried by slaves were significantly inferior to the studs on the passengers of steam elephants or palanquins.

Finally, their group turned a corner and reached the racetrack.

It was an enormous pale stone building that towered several stories overhead. The Dividing Wall ran right up to it, and in the distance, Rory could see it continue from where the track ended.

"Tarwa has an entrance," Reheeme explained, "and Maksur has its own entrance the other side of the wall."

Rory nodded. She had thought that maybe the races were an old tradition that transcended things like studs, one of the few occasions where the people of Azyr mixed together, but that was evidently not the case.

"There is a space where we can meet people from Maksur discreetly," Reheeme added.

"Ah," Rory said, understanding. "A place where Azyrian toffs go slumming, eh?" She shook her head. "Toffs are all the same, no matter where you go—all snobby in public, but beneath it, you all love a bit of filth."

Rafe laughed.

"Some of us don't sink to that kind of debauchery," Longinus said primly.

"Ha," Adelma said. "Or you go far worse."

Reheeme shot Rory a contemptuous look. "Don't forget that while in Azyr, you're one of the 'toffs,' as you put it."

A point that made Rory feel distinctly ill at ease.

"Wait," she said, frowning as something occurred to her. "How the hell does anyone see the lizards in such a big building? Is it lots of little races?"

"You'll see," Reheeme said smugly, and Jabir shuddered again.

Rory began to wonder just what kind of lizards they would be watching.

The elephant joined a queue of palanquins and mechanised elephants disgorging their passengers into the racecourse entrance. Rory watched, astounded, as an old Azyrian woman stepped down from a steam palanquin. She wore a huge golden headdress shaped like a large fan. Little bells and jewels the size of eggs dangled from the edges. Fine gold chains twisted along the front of the headdress, curling around strips of fabric among which nestled more jewels.

But what astounded Rory was that the headdress was so heavy that the old woman had to have slaves walk on either side of her, propping it up. The woman moved in a slow, stately fashion, obviously used to walking this way.

Blue-gold stones gleamed at her eyebrows, standing out among the seams of wrinkles on her face. She reached the city Watch at the entrance to the races, surrounded by her own heavily armed retinue of guards.

"When you're so big-headed you need people to help you carry it," Rafe murmured to Rory.

She stifled a laugh as they followed through the entrance.

CHAPTER

21

Inside the racecourse, it was dark and so choked with incense that taking a breath was like inhaling perfume. Longinus grimaced and held his handkerchief to his nose to try to mitigate the smell.

In all other ways, however, the building surrounding the racetrack was surprisingly bare. Having seen the rest of Tarwa, Longinus would have expected an important building such as this to be richly and brightly decorated. Instead, it was all of pale stone cut in huge blocks. There were no paintings on the walls, no wallpaper, and no rugs on the floor—nothing but smooth, bare stone. The building felt old, as though it had been there since the birth of Azyr.

Jabir led them all up a flight of stairs, turning his head to speak to them over his shoulder. "I have a box in an excellent location. Only one level up, and about halfway down the arena."

"Don't tell me," Rory said. "You don't even like the races, but you have the box because it's expected of someone with your studs?"

"Well, yes," Jabir said a little sheepishly.

Adelma snorted. "Burn my body, but you Azyrians do the stupidest things in the name of your studs. I've always thought that too much money rots the brain, but in your case, too-expensive studs cause even more stupidity."

"Adelma, maybe this is not the best time for this kind of speech," Cruikshank said in a low, deliberate voice, making a small gesture to encompass the space around them, which was full of wealthy Tarwanese with expensive studs. A few were already giving the Damsians pronounced looks.

Longinus had to admit that while he understood the importance of appearances better than most, he couldn't condone the way Jabir and Reheeme behaved. After all, a gentleman should be as punctilious about his principles as about his clothes, and displaying poor morals was as much in poor taste as having a soiled cravat.

They reached the first floor, and Jabir led them down a long stone corridor as bare as the entrance level. The shadows were thick, made even thicker by all the incense. Enormous coils hung from the ceiling, plates dangling beneath them to catch the ashes. Their smoke curled out, thickening the shadows with haze.

Longinus coughed and blinked. The smoke was making his eyes itch.

To the left of the corridor were passageways that led to the boxes. The bright sunlight shone through, cutting golden rectangles out of the thick gloom. People milled about, the hallway as full with Azyrians as it was with smoke. They passed through the light and the shadows, their jewels glittering hard one moment and fading to dullness the next. The stone passageway hummed with hushed conversation, the whispers bouncing off the walls so that they seemed to be coming out of the stones.

"Rafe, Adelma, and Rory," Reheeme murmured, "would you please stay behind the others? Bodyguards and staff are expected to always walk a step behind."

"Staff?" Adelma asked coldly.

"That's how a ship captain would be considered," Reheeme replied. "And the people here would think it an insult if I let you too close to them or, worse, if I were to introduce you."

Before Adelma could reply, Jabir was greeting an Azyrian man with a deep bow. Reheeme did the same before introducing Longinus and Cruikshank. Longinus matched Jabir's bow, as did Cruikshank. He didn't understand a word of Azyrian, but the introductions and greetings seemed to last a long time. The Azyrian man looked the Damsians over with dislike and suspicion. Eventually, he bowed again, and Longinus again matched Jabir's bow. Then the man and his retinue were on their way. Longinus watched him go, wondering what was behind his suspicion. Simple dislike of foreigners or something more?

They continued on.

As Longinus's eyes adjusted to the gloom, he noticed that alcoves had been cut into the rock, and the one nearest to him housed two Azyrian men, deep in hushed conversation. Their clothes were dark, and with their black skin, they almost blended into the shadows, making them look mysterious. They shook hands briefly, and Longinus guessed a lot of deals were made in the shadows of the racecourse.

Reheeme and Jabir went through a formal introduction with another Azyrian, this time a young woman who couldn't have been much older than Rory. She looked as cold as the man from earlier, giving the Damsians the same oddly suspicious, appraising glance.

Longinus wondered if their group had crossed paths with any members of the Sons and Daughters. The rebels would still be attending events like these, to keep appearances up, if nothing else. But if there were any signs that identified them, Longinus hadn't yet picked up on them.

The progress through the passageway was slow as Jabir and Reheeme stopped to greet people every few steps. There was a complicated hierarchy of greetings, no doubt based on the studs of each person, ranging from deep, elaborate bows to curt nods of the head, from lengthy introductions to vague greetings.

After one such meeting, Longinus heard a gasp from Rory, and he looked up to see an aberration walking towards them. It was a man covered head to toe in heavy leather. Even his face was masked with leather, dark goggles hiding his eyes and a breathing apparatus covering his mouth and nose. He had a heavy tank strapped to his back, from which protruded a thin hose that wound up over his shoulder. It was joined to a long pointed nozzle that he carried with both hands across his body.

In the gloom and the haze of the incense, he looked like some kind of hellish creature with enormous black eyes and a large metallic mouth.

"What is it?" Longinus whispered to Cruikshank, grimacing.

The crowds parted as the man passed through. Even the most heavily decorated Azyrians made room.

"That's a man carrying a steam gun," Cruikshank replied with obvious disgust. "That nozzle can deliver a burst of high-pressured steam, and with alchemical treatment, it can be made hot enough to melt the flesh off a person's bones."

Longinus shuddered. He was well aware of what alchemically treated steam could do. In some barbaric parts of the world, people were executed by steam guns as punishment for heinous crimes. Surely, Azyr didn't sink so low as to use such weapons on its people?

"In Damsport, we only have them as defences on the wall that separates us from Airnia," Cruikshank said.

"If you ask me," Adelma said, "someone's overcompensating for something. Look at the size of that nozzle. If that ain't a man what's feeling a little insecure, I don't know what is."

Longinus spluttered at this, although he had to admit Adelma had very effectively dealt with his unease—or if he was honest, fear—of the steam gun.

The man with the steam gun passed them without any trouble and continued on.

"Ah, there we go," Jabir called. "My box is just over there." He pointed ahead.

"Finally," Longinus said.

It would be a relief to step out of that incense-choked passage and into the golden evening light.

CHAPTER

22

Rory blinked in the sunlight as they stepped into Jabir's box. The stench of blood hit her in the face as hard as a brick. It was as thick as the smell of incense, and the two mixed in a cloying, sickening odour. She blinked again, her eyes slowly adjusting to the light.

"Oh, gods," Longinus groaned. "I feel sick."

The box was shaded by a large burnt-orange silk awning and contained two rows of plush seats in matching fabric. Longinus grabbed the back of one of the seats with one hand, his knuckles strained white.

"Are you alright?" Jabir asked, frowning.

"He's fine. He just needs to sit down," Cruikshank said, helping Longinus to a chair. He looked as if he had stepped right back onto the ship.

Rory looked around, but she couldn't see blood anywhere. The box was one level up from the arena—a deep rectangular stone pit, the bottom of which was covered in sand. They were about halfway down one of the long sides. A gate blocked one end of the arena, while the other end had no seating in it, just a stone wall with a palisade at the bottom that was made of planks of wood.

Everything looked clean, no blood—dried, old, or otherwise—to be seen.

Rory didn't ask Longinus if he was alright, knowing he would already be mortified by his queasiness. Any kind of attention or fuss would simply add to his ordeal. She knew how ashamed he was of his inability to withstand the sight or smell of blood and how hard he tried to keep it secret.

She wasn't sure what kind of race this was going to be, but if the smell was anything to go by, it was going to be bloody. She groped for an excuse that would allow Longinus to leave without losing face. Something told her that the lizards used for racing in Azyr bore little resemblance to the shy, pale creatures found in Damsport.

"You three sit in the back row," Reheeme told Rory, Rafe, and Adelma.

The guards had already taken position, flanking the entrance to their box. Reheeme and Jabir took their seats in the front row, and Longinus sat next to Jabir. Cruikshank sat last, next to Longinus. Rory saw her whispering something into his ear, and she hoped he would be alright. Maybe he could keep looking at his feet so as to not see the racing.

A servant materialised—a young girl with simple copper studs at her eyebrows—and Jabir ordered food and drink, but he spoke in Airnian, probably so his guests would understand.

"Would you like to see the lizard almanac before you bet, sir?" the girl enquired.

Jabir shook his head. "Deaths before the midpoint on all races. Please put it on my account." He spoke quickly and with evident disgust.

Rory frowned, wondering why there would be deaths in the races. Did the lizards attack each other?

Across from the arena were the seats for Maksur. They had no boxes, no awnings, and no shadowy corridors that Rory could see. Instead, the area was a simple set of large stone steps on which people sat. There were ragged cushions, and Rory guessed that without them, the stone would be hot enough to fry an egg on. The Maksur side was raucous and loud compared to the hushed whispering on her side of the arena.

"You can find binoculars and something to help with the smell under your seat." Reheeme reached below her chair.

Rory followed suit, frowning when she brought up a set of binoculars and an orange studded with cloves.

Cruikshank looked unimpressed as she retrieved her orange. "Is that really all there is to combat the smell?" she asked incredulously. "This orange and that horrible incense back there? Surely you could create something to neutralise the smell and spread it through vents or something of the sort."

"The races are a tradition that go back hundreds of years," Reheeme replied. "Incense and oranges were used back then, so we have preserved that tradition."

Rory shook her head. Bloody ridiculous.

They waited in tense, uneasy silence. The drinks Jabir had ordered arrived, a bright-green liqueur that tasted of mint and aniseed and cooled the throat as it went down.

The stone of the arena seemed to be radiating heat, and Rory was soon sweating despite the cooling drink. The heat made the smell even worse so that Rory could hardly breathe.

The noise seemed to grow louder, and Rory shifted listlessly in her seat. Between the noise, the smell, and the heat, she was starting to feel hemmed in. She ran her forearm across her forehead, wiping some of the sweat, hoping the racing would begin soon.

***

Rory adjusted her binoculars and took another sip of the emerald-green liquid. They'd been waiting in the box for what felt like an age, making strained small talk while Longinus breathed noticeably through his mouth.

Finally, something happened. The gate at the end of the arena slowly lifted open. It led into darkness, the shadows too thick for Rory to see through. The binoculars were remarkably effective, to the point where Rory could make out the coarseness of the sand, but the shadows provided a blunt end to what she could see.

Excited chatter rippled through the crowd, the sense of anticipation growing. Rory peered into the shadows, waiting for the first appearance of the lizards.

A low, rhythmic drumming began, reminding Rory of the mines down in the Lower. Beranthium was the main source of Azyrian wealth, yet how few of the people present would be thinking of the people in the Lower who did the backbreaking work that enabled their wealth?

The rhythm of the drums increased, whipping up into a frenzy, until it came to an abrupt stop. A hush settled on the crowd as if they held their breath, waiting. Rory held her breath, too, staring at the open gate.

"Over there," Rafe whispered, touching her elbow and making her jump.

She turned her binoculars to the other end of the arena, where part of the wooden palisade had lifted to reveal the bars of a cage. Behind the bars was a man. Rory wasn't sure where he was from, but his skin was paler than hers and golden, although not white enough to be a milk skin. His shoulders and arms were sunburnt as well as his face, an angry red that spoke of exposure to the harsh Azyrian sun. His chest was bare, the sunburn at his shoulders stopping in a straight line as though he were wearing a skin-coloured tunic.

The holes at his eyebrows marked him as a slave, and his eyes were wide with fear. Through her binoculars, Rory could even make out that he was sweating profusely.

And then Rory heard hissing and an odd clicking, scrambling sound. The man heard it too, and he started, eyes widening in terror, mouth speaking a silent prayer. Rory hoped she was wrong in her guess of what she was about to witness.

A loud trumpeting sound startled her.

The bars of the slave's cage fell open with a crash, sending out fine sprays of sand. At the same time, the rest of the wooden palisade lifted.

The man didn't wait but broke into a run. He glanced back over his shoulder as he ran.

Out of the gloom, a lizard larger than anything Rory had ever seen appeared. The man let out a small cry as he caught sight of it over his shoulder. The crowd cheered in response.

The lizard was huge—nearly three yards long—and whip thin, with gleaming black claws as sharp as talons. Its skin looked like it was made of beads the colour of sand, and it had spots all over its body, like a leopard. A crest of pale spikes ran all along its spine. Its massive head was flat at the top, and it sent a forked tongue slithering out, tasting the air.

It moved a few steps with alarming speed, rushing out of its cage, then froze in place, hissing and sending its tongue out again.

The slave raced on towards the gate, unable to stop looking over his shoulder at the monster behind him. He was about a third of the way along the arena, the deep sand slowing him down. He left clear footsteps behind him, and a reddish tinge appeared where he had run and displaced the sand beneath his feet. It looked as though he was already leaving a trail of blood.

"Come on, come on," Rory muttered through gritted teeth.

"What happens if he reaches the gate first?" Rafe asked.

"Then he wins his freedom," Reheeme replied.

Still, the lizard hesitated, moving its head right and left, its tongue darting in and out. The crowd was shouting, pointing fingers down at the arena, some standing up in their excitement.

The lizard ignored them.

Then its long, narrow neck suddenly inflated, expanding outwards to twice its width, revealing deep stripes of red-beaded skin. The beast launched itself forward, moving at impossible speed.

The slave cried out, but the sand prevented him from running any faster, his feet sinking a couple of inches deep with each step. His movements were already growing clumsy. He was tiring.

He looked back over his shoulder. The lizard was narrowing the distance faster and faster, moving like the wind over the sand.

"Don't look back, you fool," Rory shouted. "It will just slow you down."

The man looked back again. The lizard was just yards behind him. The crowd hooted.

The lizard reached the man and gouged a large tear in his back with one of its talons.

The man stumbled but looked like he might catch his balance for a moment. The creature crashed into him. The crowd roared.

The lizard's mouth was full of razor-sharp teeth, and they tore the man open. Rory dropped her binoculars, sickened.

The crowd was loud but not quite loud enough to drown out the screaming of the man being ripped apart.

Longinus threw up, and Rory noticed dispassionately that his vomit was green—the colour of the liquid they had all been drinking. She shuddered and looked away.

The servant from earlier reappeared, informing Jabir in a pleasant tone that his winnings would be added to his account. Rory looked up and noticed that the dying slave was only a few feet shy of the midpoint—Jabir had bet well. Jabir grimaced and gave the faintest nod.

"Pull yourself together," Reheeme said to Longinus. "People are looking. We can't afford a scene now, or people will be paying attention to what we do."

Rory saw that Longinus was in danger of falling forward. Cruikshank held him back.

"Unless you're as big a fool as that lizard was fast, Reheeme," Adelma said, "it should be obvious to you that Longinus ain't well, and therefore, he ain't able to pull himself together."

"I will take him back inside, to the shade," Jabir said, rising.

Longinus nodded weakly but didn't say anything. He pressed a white handkerchief to his mouth.

"It will do me good also," Jabir added. "I find the sight of these races sickening."

"I'll come too," Rory said at once. Longinus's bouts of sickness at the sight of blood didn't last, but all the same, she didn't like the thought of him weak and alone in that shadowy, incense-choked passage.

"We can all come," Cruikshank said. She too was a little pale.

"It's best that you all stay here," Jabir said in a low voice. "It is expected that as our guests, you will see at least a few races before we retire. If you all leave after the first race, it will draw attention, and people will gossip. There will already be enough talk about all of you. I'd rather not add to it."

Rory nodded, grudgingly admitting that it made sense.

"We won't be long." Jabir held out his hand and helped Longinus to his feet while Reheeme looked on with obvious impatience.

As Jabir ushered Longinus back to the shade, Rory found herself grateful for his kindness—unlike his nasty harridan of a wife. Rory smiled wryly to herself. *Harridan* was very much a Longinus word, and it was the first time she had used it, even in thought. She made a mental note to tell him about that later to cheer him up.

Down in the arena, a group of men had appeared. Five of them held long metal poles with large loops at the end. Ten more brandished steam guns. The creature hissed at them, backing away slowly. One of the men tried to slip the loop around its neck, and the creature hissed, lunging at him with its claws. Three of the steam guns blasted it, and it shrieked in pain, scuttling back.

Two men managed to slip their loops around its neck, and the lizard hissed, shaking its head, trying to wrench free.

"I thought the steam was hot enough to melt flesh," Rafe said.

"It is," Reheeme replied. "The lizards' skin is so tough that they don't even feel regular steam."

The lizard continued to move backwards, the men shepherding it towards the open gate at the other end of the arena. More men circled it, and gradually, using the steam guns, they guided the lizard back into the shadows. The men followed the lizard inside, the gate closed, and all that was left on the sand was the disembowelled slave, his entrails as livid and red as the slashes on the monster's neck.

His blood had poured out, and the sand soaked it all up greedily so that the stain spread like red wine on a linen tunic.

Finally, the body was dragged away, while men with rakes settled the sand into place, blotting out the stain left by the corpse.

"This is barbaric," Cruikshank said, her lips pressed into a grim line.

Reheeme shrugged. "It's tradition. The races used to be for criminals sentenced to death so they had one final chance to redeem themselves. Now it's a way for slaves to try to win back their freedom."

"How can you stand to watch that kind of thing?" Rory asked, revolted.

Reheeme looked at her flatly. "I watched my parents get butchered in the Prelate's personal fighting pit when I was seven. This is nothing."

CHAPTER
23

Once he was out of the sight of the racecourse and all the horror he had witnessed there, Longinus felt a little better. The shadows back in the passageway were a relief after the heat outside, although the incense made him feel claustrophobic. He wished he could step out of the racecourse altogether and breathe fresh air—even though the air in Azyr was anything but fresh. It was too hot, too filled with dust.

Jabir ushered him to one of the alcoves hewn directly into the rock wall. A twin set of simple stone benches were carved from the stone with a wooden table between them. Longinus sat down gratefully. From deep within the shadows, he could see everyone walking past, blasted on and off with light as they passed the entrances to the boxes.

He took a deep breath, and he could taste the incense, a nice change from the foul taste in his mouth. Jabir gestured at someone, and moments later, two drinks were brought over.

Longinus drank carefully, unable to meet the man's eye. The humiliation of having his deepest, darkest, most embarrassing secret aired so publicly ate away at him. Would they laugh at him? Maybe not to his face but probably behind his back. They would whisper and sneer.

It was all he could do not to bury his head in his hands. Only the desire to maintain a scrap of dignity held him back.

Lady Martha might hear of this too. Reheeme seemed utterly devoid of compassion or kindness, and she might think nothing of including his weakness in future communications with Lady Martha.

Longinus groaned and drank again.

"Are you alright?" Jabir asked, his brow creased with concern.

Longinus nodded, wishing the man would go away. The last thing he needed was a witness. He felt ridiculous and insignificant enough as it was without having to bear the weight of another's pity.

People strode past and milled around, greeting each other and carrying out conversation in gentle tones. Nobody looked at Longinus much, and he guessed the smoke and the shadows were dark enough to make his skin tone less obviously foreign. If only they could make him disappear entirely.

"I'm sorry you were unwell," Jabir said in a soft voice.

Longinus nodded but didn't reply, staring at his drink. Somewhere beyond the stone walls, the drumming started again, followed by the loud trumpeting that signalled the start of a new race. Longinus shuddered at the thought of what was going on out there.

"I've felt sick myself," Jabir continued, "countless times. Watching those awful races... it's expected for someone with my studs to show his face regularly, so I do, but I..." He shuddered. "I hate it. The races are archaic. A leftover from a time when, it pains me to say, we were ruled by savages."

On that Longinus could agree. Words like *savages* and *archaic* were understatements to describe the Azyrian races. "It's barbaric." He drank again, not wanting to say more on the subject in case it triggered another bout of nausea.

He and Jabir sat in silence. Longinus let the drone of the muted conversation wash over him.

"Can I ask...?" Jabir said cautiously. "I'm not trying to pry, but... is this the first time you've been ill on seeing death?"

Longinus didn't reply, his stomach sinking even further. He had assumed everyone had guessed, and it would be even worse to witness Jabir piecing things together. Once he realised that Longinus, an assassin, was afraid of blood, there would be smirking, maybe even a stifled laugh.

"Only," Jabir continued, "I was under the impression that you were an assassin, and so... it must be... I had assumed you'd be accustomed to that sort of thing."

Longinus pressed his lips into a thin line. "I'm a poisoner," he said, each word falling from his lips like hot stones. The humiliation of the moment burnt as hot as any flame. "I never draw blood."

"I see," Jabir replied.

They lapsed into silence, for which Longinus was grateful. He drank some more. At least the drink was washing away the foul taste in his mouth. It tasted sweet, like peaches.

Beyond the walls were muffled shouting and cries of pain, although they weren't as gut wrenching as the ones from the last race. A sharp hiss answered the cries.

"It must be quite an impediment in your line of work," Jabir said.

Longinus looked away, hating Jabir in that moment for prodding at something so deeply painful. Then a small part of him rebelled. He was tired of being rendered helpless by the sight of blood. Tired of carrying that shame around with him like a heavy stone around his neck.

Longinus knew there was little he could do to combat his affliction. The reaction to the sight of blood was so visceral, so immediate, that he didn't even have time to try to steel his mind against it.

But maybe I can use it to my advantage.

He was alone with Jabir, in a position of weakness. People were less likely to be guarded when dealing with someone they perceived as weak, and so far, Jabir had yet to offer that key piece of information: how he had gotten the letter from Kadelta.

Longinus decided to turn his unfortunate circumstance into an advantage.

"It is a huge impediment, and it's why I specialised in poison. You must think me a fool," he added without having to try very hard to add misery to his tone.

"Of course not," Jabir protested. "I think it is very courageous of you to come to the races, given your condition."

"Thank you. It's nowhere near as brave as what you do," Longinus replied, hinting at Jabir's role in the rebellion.

Jabir gave a small, modest smile. "To me it's not even a choice. I couldn't conceive of not doing what I do."

"And that should be commended."

Jabir gave him a wider smile.

"I do admire people of action," Longinus continued, sipping his drink. It was so wonderfully cooling on the throat, removing more of that awful smoke. And he found that in focusing on flattering Jabir in the right way, he was dulling the sharp pain of his recent humiliation. "I admire people who take things into their own hands." He nodded to himself, looking down at his drink. "Not many people do that."

"No," Jabir echoed softly. "Not many people do." He took a deep draught of his drink, seeming lost in thought.

Longinus looked up at him. "And to think you even went deep into the palace, all the way to Kadelta, to get that letter from him."

Jabir seemed caught off balance and actually stammered the first couple of words. "It-it w-was actually a machinist who works with him who got the letter to me."

"I see," Longinus replied.

He wondered if Jabir was lying or hiding something that would have caused the stammer. Jabir turned away, raising a hand to signal a waitress.

"I imagine Reheeme and the others will join us after another two or three races," Jabir said, obviously looking to change the subject.

"The sooner the better," Longinus replied with a polite smile.

The waitress brought more drinks and they drank in silence for a while.

Longinus decided not to press Jabir any further for now, so as not to seem suspicious. But he made a mental note to share Jabir's stammer with Rory and see what she thought. There might be something in it, or there might not. Either way, it was useful to know that Jabir had contact with one of Kadelta's machinists.

CHAPTER

24

They had watched five races, and Cruikshank was growing
more and more sickened as one type of lizard after another
killed slaves running for their freedom.

None of them made it.

One lizard had a frilled collar around its neck, its skin the
colour of fire, and it spat a viscous black liquid at a woman
running away from him. The woman screamed and fell,
clawing at the arm that was covered with the poison.

Another race involved a horde of bright-green scorpions,
each the size of a large rat, boiling out of the door, skittering
along the sand and up the walls. The men with the steam
guns kept them from spilling out of the arena, forcing them
to continue after their quarry.

Cruikshank had noticed that during several races that the
lizards and scorpions didn't always want to run after the
fleeing slaves. Some of them had to be forced with blasts of
alchemically treated steam. It seemed all the more cruel to
force these animals to kill when they had no desire to do so,

ensuring that the slaves vying for freedom were bitten, clawed at, or simply torn apart for the crowd's amusement.

And the sand grew more and more red, glutted with blood.

Cruikshank never turned away, feeling like it would be cowardly to look away from the men and women making their final, desperate dash for freedom. She had gagged on more than one occasion, though.

A commotion at the entrance of their box caught her attention, and she turned away gratefully from the arena. A man entered, wearing a headdress as elaborate as the woman from the entrance, slaves framing him as they helped support the elaborate fan structure. The headdress was of rich green silk, and it dripped with rubies.

The slaves looked distinctly uncomfortable as they bore the headdress's weight. The man himself seemed oblivious to their presence, bearing a distant, haughty expression as though he was above everyone around him.

"Riamir," Reheeme said, standing and giving him a warm smile.

She bowed low, making elaborate greetings, before introducing Cruikshank in Airnian.

"Ah, yes," Riamir said. "I'd heard you had Damsians with you."

"This is Councilman Riamir," Reheeme said to Cruikshank.

Cruikshank bowed low.

"Are they here to help us with our cause?" Riamir murmured, leaning and forcing the slaves around him to lean with him.

Behind her, Cruikshank heard a sharp intake of breath. She was equally shocked to find that this was a member of the rebellion. It was one thing to keep slaves for appearances' sake, but to have them carry the Councilman's ridiculous headdress around was beyond the pale. It was all she could do to keep her expression neutral.

"They are indeed here to help us," Reheeme replied in a low voice. "Bringing support from the Marchioness of Damsport and the promise of trade deals once *it* is done."

The Councilman's eyes gleamed. "Trade deals?" He looked at Cruikshank like she was a golden goose.

"Conditioned on the fair representation of Maksur and Azyr the Lower in the Council," Cruikshank said at once, keeping her voice as low as she could. "And also on slavery being abolished as well as Maksur being given full access to water."

Riamir gave a dismissive wave of his hand. "Yes, yes. Those Maksurians, always harping on about their water. But the Marchioness has given her assurance of trade deals?"

Cruikshank nodded.

"Excellent, excellent." Riamir smiled. He stepped back. "I wish you an enjoyable and productive stay in our fair city," he added in a normal voice. He nodded at Cruikshank, then at Reheeme before slowly turning around.

It was quite a feat for him to turn with all his slaves around him, and yet they all managed it without the headdress being knocked off.

As soon as he was out of sight, Reheeme abruptly wiped the smile from her face. "He was the first to turn on my parents," she murmured through gritted teeth. "The first." She swept back to her seat, sitting ramrod straight, her face colder than stone.

Cruikshank glanced over at Rory, Adelma, and Rafe. All three looked as angered by the exchange as she felt. One thing was abundantly clear: if Riamir was anything to go by, the Sons and Daughters of the Elephant had no real interest in bettering the lives of the rest of the city. This was purely about profit.

Cruikshank sat back down.

They had to endure two more races before a short drum rhythm announced an interval.

"Let us go check on Longinus," Reheeme said with the kind of bland, pleasant tone she might have used at the interval of a play. "I have friends I would like to call on."

Cruikshank stood up, feeling weak with relief. She didn't think she could bear to witness another slaughter. She wondered again at what Reheeme had said about watching her parents die in this manner when she was a child. She didn't like to make excuses for the woman, but that kind of trauma would explain some of her current attitudes.

Watching her with the Councilman had been interesting, and Cruikshank expected to get a better sense of her still once she saw her interacting with the Risen. She still wanted

166

a better understanding of who exactly she was dealing with. She didn't feel like she fully grasped what everyone's agenda was, and that troubled her—especially given that Longinus had discovered that someone watched them through peepholes.

"Are you alright, lovey?" Cruikshank asked Rory as they filed out of the box. The girl nodded.

They stepped back in the incense-choked passage, and Cruikshank felt relieved to be out of the stink of blood cooking in the heat. They headed over to Longinus and Jabir who stood up. Cruikshank was pleased to see that Longinus no longer looked sick, although he still looked weary.

"How are you all?" Jabir asked, his brow creased with concern. "It's always a trial to watch the races, isn't it?"

Cruikshank nodded. "Very much so."

"Well, it's done, now," Reheeme said impatiently. "This way."

***

Their route to where they would meet the Risen was long and convoluted. They went deep underground, past the cages where the lizards and other creatures were kept. Jabir smoothly bribed the creatures' handlers so they would forget that anyone had gone by. The way it happened was so smooth and easy that Cruikshank guessed this sort of thing happened often.

The lizards hissed and clicked in the darkness behind their bars as Cruikshank and the others walked past, and she found herself feeling sorry for them. They should be out in the desert beyond Azyr, not locked up in small, dark cages. They hadn't asked to be turned into ruthless executioners.

"Where are we going?" Cruikshank asked Reheeme after a time. "Where are we meeting them?"

"There is one place beneath the races where people from Maksur and Tarwa can mix without passing through the Watch's scrutiny," Reheeme replied. "A gambling den."

"Gambling is illegal in Azyr," Jabir explained, "save for betting on the races. Hence why it is expected that people with our studs place bets on each race. This is the only gambling den to be found in Azyr. It is illegal and doesn't officially exist, but the Seneschal knows of and tolerates it because he gets a significant share of the den's takings."

"And he doesn't monitor the den?" Cruikshank asked.

"If he does, nobody has managed to identify it," Reheeme said. "And believe me, there are many who check."

They eventually reached an innocuous-looking door.

Reheeme tapped a pattern on the wood and opened the door. Beyond was a sort of antechamber, like a waiting room with plenty of seats and just as many guards. They did not wear the recognisable scaled armour of the Watch, nor did they have the neat uniforms of the private guards Cruikshank had seen about the city. Instead, they looked like civilians but heavily armed.

Behind a desk, an Azyrian man dressed in simple robes but with gold studs smiled at them. His teeth were made of gold, glinting in the yellow light from the alchemical globes.

"Good evening," he said, gold winking from his mouth at every syllable.

"Good evening, Petrik," Reheeme replied, stepping forward.

Jabir followed with her, producing a purse that jangled with coins.

"You are bringing foreigners to my humble establishment?" Petrik asked.

Jabir smiled. "They want a taste of illicit excitement."

"Ah." Petrik took the purse and counted the coins carefully. Jabir looked pained at the insult, but Petrik didn't seem to care. He even went as far as to examine a couple of the coins, as if doubting their authenticity.

"There's an extra charge for foreigners," he said at last.

Jabir frowned. "What? Since when?"

"Since I just told you."

Jabir's mouth twisted. "Do you know who I am? Do you see my studs? How dare you try to rip me off as if I was nothing more than a common merchant!"

Petrik grinned. "Gambling is the great equaliser—on the card table, studs don't mean a thing." His smile faded. "And it's extra for foreigners."

The guards dotted about the room edged closer. Cruikshank looked about her, feeling the tension in the air thicken.

"Keep coming closer," Adelma growled to a man only a few steps away from her. "Come and help me check if I've sharpened my axes properly."

She rested both hands on the battle-axes at her sides. She was a good head taller than the man, and he looked at her axes, suddenly uncertain. She gave him a satisfied nod. "Wise."

Cruikshank found herself wishing that she had a weapon, but even with Adelma and Rafe here, they were completely outnumbered.

"Oh, Jabir, for crying out loud," Reheeme snapped. "Nobody cares about your studs. Let's just pay the man already and go." She produced her own purse and threw it contemptuously on the desk.

Petrik smiled, opening it. "I think I prefer doing business with your wife," he said to Jabir. "Please," he added to Reheeme, gesturing for everyone to go through.

There was a door across the room, and Reheeme led the way to it. She opened the door, revealing a thick leather-backed curtain, and pushed past it into the gloom beyond.

CHAPTER 25

Beyond the drape was a small chamber panelled with steel. There was another doorway ahead, also covered by a thick leather curtain. Reheeme pushed the leather curtain back and opened the door. Rory stepped out after her into a room that stretched out around them, completely dark other than spots of red light from alchemical globes hanging on top of each card table.

The light cast deep shadows on the players' faces, exaggerating noses and cheekbones and turning eye sockets into black pools. The ceiling was so low Adelma had to stoop. Rory reached up to touch the stone, feeling the roughness against her fingertips.

The tables were covered with red felt, the cards dealt by men and women with bare arms, no doubt to show the dealers weren't interfering with the cards. At some tables, the players had their sleeves rolled up, whilst at others, all had their sleeves down. Rory smiled.

"I bet them over there are all cheating," she whispered to Longinus, gesturing at a nearby table where everyone had their sleeves down. "My kind of table. I reckon I'd make a good cardsharp if I got to learn the trade. Nimble fingers and all that."

Longinus shook his head. "In the interest of all our safeties, please abort this type of thinking with immediate effect. I dread to think what would happen if you got caught stealing or cheating in this city."

"Don't worry yourself—I ain't gonna do nothing. But you know, once a thief, always a thief."

The dealers also had odd skullcaps with long ribbons that dangled down either side of their faces so that they looked almost like religious figures. Rory remembered her old partner in crime, Jake. He'd had a gambling problem, an addiction really, and she supposed that for some, gambling was a kind of religion—the kind that consumed you and all that you possessed.

As Reheeme led them through the dark room, Rory noticed something else: the red light meant that all eyebrow studs looked similar. The den owner had been right—gambling was a kind of equaliser. There was no telling rich from poor here—no shiny jewels or flashy displays of wealth.

Reheeme led them to a curtain about halfway down the room. A red globe hung above it, and two Azyrian men stood guard. They weren't Watchmen, and they wore no uniforms, but they were different from Petrik's muscle.

Reheeme showed them a token of some kind, too quick and too dark for Rory to see, and they nodded, parting the curtain.

Everyone filed through. Adelma grunted as she misjudged the height of the door and smacked her forehead against the frame. "Bloody short-arse Azyrians," she grumbled, ducking low and passing through.

Inside, an old Azyrian woman with a face more seamed than a coal mine waited. She sucked on a long-stemmed pipe as she watched them come in. Her lower lip protruded as if years of sucking on the pipe had deformed it.

Rory's eyebrows shot up as she recognised her. She had been playing the board game back in Maksur when Reheeme and Jabir's elephant had been forced to divert to get around her.

The room was small—so small that by the time everyone was inside, it felt cramped. The only furniture was a card table, and behind it was a dealer. The old woman had taken one of the seats at the table, with four seats remaining.

"Welcome," she said, rising. Her voice was like the scraping of a dry husk on a stone. "This is my grandson, Urzo." She gestured towards the dealer. "He is an integral part of the Risen, so we can speak freely in front of him."

"Thank you for agreeing to see us, Oma," Reheeme said.

After a bit of confusion during which everyone seemed to get in the way of everyone else, Reheeme, Cruikshank, Jabir, and Adelma took the remaining seats, Adelma muttering about the stupidity of building such low ceilings.

"And why should we build high ceilings when we are a small people?" Oma rasped.

"Ha," Adelma snorted. "Good point. Say, what's in that pipe? Mind if I have a taste?"

The woman looked surprised. "Most cultures would consider it rude to make demands before even having shared your name."

"Well, I ain't pretending to be a diplomat," Adelma replied.

"An understatement," Rafe added.

"Anyway, I'm Adelma, that's Rafe, that scrawny bit over there's Rory, Cruikshank's the sour one with the big tattoo, and Longinus is the toff at the back."

"It's a wonder you don't get sent out on more diplomatic missions," Rafe said, although Rory couldn't quite tell if he was genuinely amused or annoyed and hiding it behind his facade of sardonic amusement.

"You're telling me," Adelma replied. "I'd get things done a lot quicker than all them mincing fools what use all that complicated mumbo jumbo and never say anything of use. Like telling you straight up that we got a way to cut communication between the palace and the Dividing Wall."

"Be quiet," Reheeme snapped. "Oma, please ignore that. They are foreigners, Damsians, that my husband took upon himself to invite to Azyr, asking them to help me with the revolution."

Oma looked amused. "Help *you*? Well, if they're only here to help you, I fail to see the need for Urzo and me to be here." She made as if to stand.

174

"You know what I meant," Reheeme said crossly.

"Do I?" Oma said coldly.

"This is *our* revolution," Reheeme said in an exasperated tone. "You know that. We are in this together. I have brought the foreigners here, first, before bringing them to any of the Sons and Daughters. Surely that's a sign of the mutual trust and respect we share."

"Really?" Urzo said, all heat and anger where Oma had been cold. "Don't try to play us for fools, Reheeme. If you brought the Damsians in to help with the rebellion, why weren't we consulted first? You're only thinking of telling us about the Damsians now—how is that a sign of respect? Respect would have been notifying us of your plans *before* executing them. We may have simple studs, but we're far from stupid. We know you don't respect us. We know you don't take us seriously. And we know that the only reason you bother to talk to us is because you have no other way to get into the palace. Otherwise, you'd be perfectly content to only deal with your precious Sons and Daughters of the Elephant."

"I didn't notify you because I didn't know the Damsians were coming," Reheeme fired back. She glared at Jabir. "*He* arranged for them to come."

"I'm sorry," Oma said calmly, "but if you don't trust each other enough to communicate between yourselves, how is this supposed to convince us to trust the Sons and Daughters?"

"I acted the way I did," Jabir said, "because I didn't want more time to be wasted in endless stalemates and arguments. This way, the Damsians are here, and we can move forward."

Reheeme was still glowering at him. Urzo looked mistrustful and angry, while Oma was unreadable. Rory could feel the tension on the air.

The meeting was off to a bad start.

CHAPTER
26

Cruikshank pulled out a cigar. "I'm quite fond of tobacco myself, although I've yet to try Azyrian leaf. You might enjoy this cigar, one of the best in Damsport. Well, the best in Damsport, in my humble opinion."

She spoke slowly, as though relaxed, and she felt the tension ease somewhat as she handed Oma the cigar. Cruikshank had noticed that she had been amused rather than offended when Adelma had asked about her pipe. She hoped the abrupt change of conversation away from the revolution might set things on a better footing.

"I don't smoke cigars, but Urzo might like to try it," Oma rasped.

Cruikshank recognised the rough tones of someone who had smoked all her life, and she briefly wondered if she would one day rasp like Oma.

She handed the cigar to Urzo. "It's a very fragrant tobacco and very smooth."

Urzo took the cigar, nodding curtly. He was in his early twenties, but he looked serious beyond his years. Cruikshank guessed he had no interest in the cigar but was humouring Oma, who had seen her attempt to defuse the situation and gone with it. She was surprised that Jabir, who had in the past been quick to smooth tensions arising from his wife's prickly demeanour, wasn't trying more actively to move things forward and defuse the tension. Other than justifying his actions, he had been completely silent.

"I realise that our presence is a bone of contention," Cruikshank said, "but whatever the relationship between all of you, we genuinely want to help the rebellion. We also want to rescue one of our own who is being kept as a slave in the palace. He's an inventor called Kadelta, and he has been working on making a submersible ship." Cruikshank decided there was little point in holding anything back. The Risen probably already knew of Kadelta, and she didn't see the point in potentially antagonising them by hiding information from them.

"We came to Azyr to liberate him," she continued, "but also to ensure that the Seneschal doesn't get the finished submersible, as that could allow him to engage in international slave smuggling with terrible ease. We understand that you could smuggle us into the palace so we could get to him. In exchange, we bring you a couple of things. The first, as Adelma mentioned, is that we can cut communications to enable the successful attack of the Dividing Wall, allowing your rebel force to reach the palace. The second is that the Marchioness of Damsport is not only prepared to publicly recognise the new government you establish after the coup, but she will also condition any future trade deals on Maksur being granted full water access and on slavery being abolished." Cruikshank leaned forward. "We are all serious in our desire to help end the awful practice of slavery in Azyr."

"And the oppression of the Lower Azyrians," Rafe added. "The trade deals will also be conditioned on both Maksur and Azyr the Lower being adequately represented in the new Council."

Oma looked at him with interest. "Why do you care about the Lower Azyrians?"

Rafe frowned. "Because I have morals and principles. And the way those people live down there in the shacks, working in the mines by hand... it's like going back to the dark ages."

"I grew up in the poorest area in Damsport," Rory said. "And it were nothing like this. I grew up like a princess next to them. I were free to roam as I pleased, free to pick pockets and run on the roofs, and just... I was free. And now I'm here. I had a chance to do well for myself. The Lower Azyrians, they're stuck down there, and ain't no chance of them ever moving up to the Higher, is there? Just because they were unlucky enough to be born down there don't mean it should dictate their whole life. That ain't right. So if you're gonna be looking to change all that, then we're happy to help."

"Nobody ever remembers the Lower," Urzo said slowly. "Nobody ever thinks of them. They toil away down there

179

and die, and nobody thinks of them. Nobody but the Risen."

Oma had been sucking thoughtfully on her pipe, and she pulled it out with a wet suction noise. "You said you have a means of cutting communications between the palace and the Dividing Wall?" she asked Adelma.

"Cruikshank does," Adelma said.

"So you see," Reheeme said, "we could have communications disrupted while the Sons and Daughters attack the Wall from the inside to let the Risen through. Then once the palace gates are open, we can all storm in together."

"Wait, why even bother with the Wall?" Adelma asked. "Why don't you just force your way through the gambling den? There's a door at the other end, right? I'm guessing it leads to Maksur. Why not gather up your army and march through? Won't take much to overwhelm what's-his-name's guards."

Reheeme shook her head. "Do you remember that small chamber we passed through between Petrik's office and the den? That's an incinerator. It has a twin at the Maksur entrance. If anyone tries to force their way through, Petrik turns on the incinerators. He is able to keep operating precisely because he doesn't allow any movement through his den. The Maksurians go back out into Maksur, and the Tarwanese go back to Tarwa."

"Petrik isn't a man we can count on to help with the rebellion," Oma rasped then sucked on her pipe. "He's too pragmatic to have any vision or morals."

"Hmm, I see," Adelma said. "And tell me, how exactly are you going to smuggle us into the palace?"

Urzo smiled. "I'll be the one doing the smuggling."

"A fellow smuggler?" Adelma asked.

"Not quite. I work the sewers."

"Ahhh. Very good. And I can't imagine them palace folk like to pay too close attention to the sewers," Adelma said with a wink.

"They don't," Urzo confirmed. "The palace is vast, and a lot of it is now abandoned because the Prelate is running out of money to maintain it all. Plenty of places where we can come out of the sewers unobserved."

"And where in the palace will you come out?" Jabir asked.

"That's for us to know until the day comes," Oma said sharply.

Reheeme raised an eyebrow. "It wouldn't do for you to trust us, would it?"

"Only as much as you trust us." Oma clamped her pipe back between her teeth and nodded thoughtfully. "Very well," she said at last. "We will smuggle the Damsians into the palace in exchange for complete details of how to interrupt communications, including any tools or equipment we might need to do it, and written assurances confirming Damsport's support and the conditions on future trade deals." She gave Reheeme and Jabir a look. "If the fat merchants of Tarwa sense they will miss out on even fatter profits, I'm sure they'll suddenly find themselves willing to give us full access to water."

"It would be better if the Sons and Daughters took care of the disruption in communications," Reheeme said, frowning. "They have a greater force this side of the Wall."

Oma shook her head. "We also need to disable communication between the Wall and the Great Gate so we can tear that from the inside and allow the Lower to rise up."

"I don't think the Lower will make any kind of significant contribution to the rebellion," Reheeme said. "They have the numbers, sure, but they aren't armed, and they're malnourished and weak. It's far more important for us to disable communication between the Wall and the palace."

"The arming of the Lower is *our* concern," Urzo said curtly. "But if you want a great force backing the Sons and Daughters when they mount their attack on the palace, the Lower will be a part of that force, and therefore, we need to disrupt communication between the Wall and the Great Gate."

Cruikshank decided then that she liked Urzo. She guessed what he wasn't saying. The Lower might be far, far removed from formidable soldiers, but if there was a citywide uprising, they deserved to be there among the rebels, to rise up with the rest and shout out their rage and their desire for change. They deserved a chance to fight for their freedom.

"Are the two communication systems the same?" Cruikshank asked.

"I believe so," Oma rasped.

"I'll need to check the plans to see if the communication pipes go over any kind of rise in Maksur. If they do, then I should be able to give both factions the means to disrupt all communications."

"Hold on," Longinus said. "There's an important point missing. We are negotiating with Cruikshank's method of interrupting communications, but before we do any kind of a deal, we also need some guarantees."

"We'll be smuggling you into the palace," Urzo pointed out.

"Yes, but what happens after that? How are we to find Kadelta? Are we simply to help you open the gates, wait for the coup, and hope that those in power will release Kadelta and his machine? Surely, you can see why we might not be comfortable with that."

Cruikshank nodded. "The submersible would be a huge advantage to anybody controlling it."

"Which is why," Longinus said, "we should be given Kadelta's location *before* any of this takes place so that once the gates are open, we can go find him ourselves. We are here to help the rebellion, but we are also here to free a fellow Damsian and retake his submersible."

Reheeme shook her head. "I don't know where he is kept."

"Neither do we," Oma said.

"Jabir does," Longinus said, earning himself a shocked look from Reheeme.

She turned to face her husband. "Is this true?"

Jabir gave an apologetic smile. "Not quite. I think there was a misunderstanding with Longinus earlier, probably given his… condition." He gave a slightly patronising smile dimly disguised as concern.

Cruikshank found herself wondering about the man's sincerity.

"It was pure happenstance that I came across Kadelta's letter," Jabir continued. "I was in the palace, and by complete coincidence, I bumped into a machinist we had hired a year or so ago."

Reheeme frowned.

"When we had to repair our water pump," Jabir said a little awkwardly.

Urzo's face set in grim lines. Maksur only just managed to get enough water from Tarwa to survive, while the Tarwanese had the luxury of running water in their homes. Cruikshank could very much sympathise with how the Maksurians had to feel about this shocking inequality.

"Anyway," Jabir continued quickly. "Since he knew me, I guess he thought he would take a chance, and he gave me Kadelta's letter, begging me to send it to Damsport. Which I did, and I added a letter to the Marchioness, sensing an opportunity to help us move the rebellion forward. So you see, I don't actually know how to get to Kadelta."

"But surely," Longinus said, "you should be able to get in contact with this machinist. If he is free to come and go in the palace, there must be others who know where he works. He must have family who can relay a message to him. I can't imagine such a small problem getting in the way."

Jabir looked uncomfortable, and Cruikshank wondered if it was because he was becoming more directly involved. He had probably kept out of it all until now, planning in the abstract. Then again, he had written to the Old Girl.

Cruikshank frowned, unsure what to make of his reaction.

"Yes, you're right," Jabir said slowly. "I could try to find his family."

"So we are agreed, then?" Cruikshank asked. "Once we have been given Kadelta's location in the palace, I will provide the Risen and the Sons and Daughters with the means to interrupt communications between the Wall and the palace and between the Great Gate and the Wall. We will then be smuggled into the palace, and we will open the small Eastern Gate. Between the Risen and the Sons and Daughters, you should then have enough to attack the palace. Meanwhile, the five of us will seek out Kadelta and get him out."

Oma nodded slowly. "That seems fair to me."

Reheeme matched her nod. "Yes, I agree."

"Then we're all agreed," Cruikshank said. "Now, onwards."

She ignored the sense of unease and trepidation, which pervaded the room as though coming to an agreement were a disturbingly foreign thing.

CHAPTER
27

Rory awoke at the first knock that signalled Longinus was coming to get her for her night shift. She padded to the door and opened it without bothering to shake an alchemical globe to life. If someone was watching, a globe would only make it easier for them to see what was going on.

Longinus slipped in. "Do you think we're being watched?" he murmured.

"I doubt it," Rory whispered back. "I been asleep all this time, and I can't see why anyone would want to waste their time watching me sleep."

Just in case, she led Longinus to the window, throwing back the shutters. She inhaled the night air. Even the night smelled different in Azyr—like spices and dust. From her window, she couldn't see much beyond the wall of the next house, but the cooler night breeze was refreshing.

"If anyone's watching, they can get an eyeful of our backs," she murmured. "And nobody will be close enough to overhear us." She glanced over at Longinus. "You alright?" That was the closest she'd get to referring to the incident at the races.

He nodded. "Fine now. Actually, I wanted to run something past you." He told her about his conversation with Jabir at the races. "I might be making too much of it, but when I first asked him about the letter, I got the feeling that I caught him off guard, and he even stammered on his answer. Of course, by the time we were with the Risen, he seemed fine, but I couldn't help but think he was hiding something back at the races, or maybe he hadn't given me all the information. It doesn't make sense for him to be startled by my question. He must have expected that we'd ask where Kadelta was."

"Hmm," Rory said, pensive. "It's tough because them Azyrians are so odd. Could be something in there about their culture. You know, like, he might be shocked that someone without studs questioned him. Then again, could be something else."

"I think it would be best to keep this in mind in our dealings with him and Reheeme. I like Jabir far more than I like her, but I don't think we should trust him fully yet."

"I agree. I got a better sense of the Risen, though."

"Me too. They're more upfront. More transparent. They aren't surrounded by slaves while claiming they seek to end slavery in Azyr, for example."

"Exactly that," Rory said. "They make sense."

Longinus sighed. "Well, it was never going to be straightforward. We're making progress, though."

He wished her a good night and headed off to his room.

Left alone, Rory went out into the communal sitting room. She flung the window open, enjoying the night air again. She stared at the wall across the street and at the window there. She noticed with a smile that there was a simple lock at the window, just the kind with helpful tumblers that responded oh so readily to her lockpicks.

The thought of breaking into the house suddenly made her crave the outdoors, the freedom of the roofs, and without pausing to think, she got out her grappling hook and silk line.

It was child's play to get her hook into position so she could climb up to Jabir and Reheeme's roof. There was one more story overhead, and Rory paused, looking up at it. It most likely housed the servants and slaves, but the windows were dark. She doubted anyone would be working at that hour.

Grinning, she put on her leather gloves then swung herself out onto the windowsill. She began to climb, feeling the old familiar thrill as she hoisted herself up. She was passing the window above hers when she was startled badly enough to slip, barely managing to keep her footing.

Someone was watching her. The boy poked his head right out of the window, and Rory recognised him.

"Terrell," she said, relieved. "You scared me half to death."

She climbed up onto his windowsill, keeping a careful hold of her silk line. Beyond was a tiny room with just enough space for the bed, which was pushed up against the wall. It was cramped and hot, and Rory could feel the contrast with the cooler night air.

"How you doing?" she asked, examining the boy's face.

One eye was painfully swollen, as was his mouth, and the lump on his forehead had grown. More angry marks could be seen on his bare arms.

But he did seem to have been well tended to. There was no sign of dried blood anywhere, and the lumps and bruises gleamed as if some kind of cream or ointment had recently been applied.

"Thank you," the boy said shyly. "For before. If you hadn't come along, I don't think the man would have stopped."

"Jabir would have done something even if I hadn't."

The boy shrugged and looked over her silk line with his one good eye. "What's that?"

"I'm climbing up to the roof," Rory said.

"I wish I could do something like that," he said with obvious envy. "Just because I wanted to."

Rory wasn't sure what she could say in reply without sounding trite. She couldn't imagine what it would be like not to be free to do as she pleased.

"Things will change," she whispered.

The boy shrugged.

"No, I mean it," Rory said. "That's why we're here. Things *will* change."

She felt silent, not wanting to say any more. There was little chance Terrell could betray them, but she wouldn't take unnecessary risks. Instead, she took his hand and squeezed it. "Look after yourself. And keep an ear out. You'll hear about the changes real soon."

She slipped back out and climbed up to the roof with Terrell's eyes on her until she reached the top.

Rory took a deep breath, finally feeling like she could breathe properly. She could see across the Azyrian rooftops, a view both familiar and alien. The palace gleamed in the distance, its white stone turned blueish grey in the moonlight. Rory had pored over a map of Azyr, and she knew that after the palace, there was only desert, which legend had it no man or woman had ever yet crossed.

The air felt cleaner up here, too, with more room for the wind to dispel the dust and flower perfumes. Rory stretched her arms high overhead, enjoying the sensation of space. She briefly amused herself by leaning over the parapet wall, peering down at the shadowy streets below.

She was looking down above the house's entrance when she froze. Someone was at the door. She heard the person knock.

The door opened, a square of yellow light spilling out into the street. It illuminated a man dressed in dark, sober clothing—just the kind of clothing you might wear to make sure you weren't spotted out at night. The man said a few words, too quiet for Rory to hear.

She sprung to action, rushing back to her side of the house. In a moment, she had swung herself over the parapet wall and was abseiling back down. She swung into the communal sitting room, landing on silent feet. The grappling hook she left behind, not wanting to waste precious seconds taking it down and miss overhearing something.

In a few quick steps, she was at the door to the sitting room, which opened out onto a balustrade over the internal courtyard. She listened for a heartbeat or two, checking that there was nobody outside. Then she took off her boots and slipped out the door.

Rory heard footsteps ahead, coming from lower down in the courtyard. She padded over to the balustrade.

Down in the courtyard, the mysterious arrival was following a servant towards the stairs. The servant held an alchemical globe that swayed at the end of a curved handle, the light lurching with each of his steps. It bounced off the plants that lined the courtyard, briefly illuminating them in flashes of green before leaving them to the shadows once more. The man behind him kept back a couple of steps, so his face remained in shadow.

Rory watched their progress, careful to remain in the dark. The two men briefly disappeared once they reached the stairs, reappearing at the upper floor, directly across from the internal courtyard. She took two steps backwards, her hand finding the door handle, ready to duck away at the first sign that they were headed towards her.

The men came out of the stairwell and headed down the cloister. The servant turned to the man and whispered something, slipping through a door. He'd probably told the man to wait until he had permission to enter from either Jabir or Reheeme.

She wished she knew if the door led to Jabir or Reheeme's quarters.

After a time, the servant reappeared and gestured for the man to step inside. The door closed behind them both, leaving Rory alone in the dark.

CHAPTER 28

Jabir was beside himself. His servant had roused him from sleep, and on hearing who had come to see him in the middle of the night, Jabir had almost fallen out of bed. He'd snapped at his servant, telling him to make the man as comfortable as possible, while he rushed to make himself presentable.

Jabir slept with his studs in, of course. Some people from the preslavery days had kept up the practice of removing them at night, but the thought of looking like a slave, even just in his sleep, was too much for him. He splashed some water on his face to wash away the last remaining sleep cobwebs and threw on a robe, fumbling with the sash.

Why, oh why, was the Seneschal's personal secretary waiting to see him in his personal quarters?

When at last he was ready, he took a deep breath. The only people who panicked were fools, incompetents, or those who were guilty, and he was none of those things. The Seneschal obviously had a message for him of such great importance that it couldn't wait till the morning. Jabir smiled at the thought.

He wasn't a Councilman yet, but he would be once the rebellion had fallen to the Seneschal and the Damsians were locked up in the palace. Tonight was no doubt a taste of life as a man in the Seneschal's trust. This was what happened to men who took matters into their own hands.

Jabir had initially believed in Reheeme's rebellion—it was, in fact, one of the key points that had pushed him to marry her. He had hoped to secure for himself the opportunity to partly rule Azyr when the Seneschal was overthrown, while at the same time gaining a beautiful and like-minded companion. Instead, Reheeme's rebellion slowly ran to the ground in endless arguments, and on their wedding night, she talked of nothing other than the Seneschal and made it clear that this was a marriage of convenience, nothing more.

At first, Jabir thought he would be able to help spark the rebellion and even change Reheeme's mind. He'd since let go of that foolish thinking and instead found a way to turn the rebellion's stalemate into an opportunity. Once the rebellion was crushed and the Damsians were in the Seneschal's keeping, Jabir would be rewarded with riches beyond his imaginings, a place on the Council, and a set of studs that only Council members could wear.

Jabir had also negotiated for Reheeme to be stripped of her position as Head Alchemist and forced to wear plain studs rather than being sentenced to death for treason. He would have his wife where she should be: by his side and obeying *his* orders.

And maybe once she was rid of her obsession with the Seneschal and the rebellion, things would be different.

It was all going well too. Arranging for Terrell to be beaten had come off perfectly, and after his considerate treatment of Longinus at the races, he felt quite sure he had regained the Damsians' trust and undone the damage that was caused by the incident at the docks. They would be well disposed towards him and wouldn't oppose him when it came to taking them to the palace, he felt quite sure. They would follow like docile lambs going to the slaughter.

Jabir stepped out of his room to greet the Seneschal's private secretary. "Carrit," he said, bowing formally. Jabir's studs were significantly superior to Carrit's, but he bowed anyway, acknowledging the man's connection and closeness to the Seneschal. If nothing else, it couldn't hurt to have the man on side.

"Jabir. The Seneschal has sent me on the most urgent of missions."

Jabir gestured for the man to sit, walking over to the sideboard. "Drink?"

To his anger, Carrit ignored the invitation, remaining standing. Jabir felt his face grow hot at the snub. He had offered generous courtesy, and Carrit was responding as if Jabir was a nobody.

"The Seneschal would like to see you," Carrit said curtly. "He's most displeased."

Jabir felt a cold jolt of fear. "Displeased?"

He cursed himself. He sounded weak, like a supplicant and not a powerful man in control. He knew why the

Seneschal was unhappy: they had initially planned for the Damsians to be taken to the palace first thing upon their arrival. Of course, things had worked out differently, with Reheeme directly opposing those plans. Jabir had known the Damsians would be suspicious after the incident at the docks, and he had thought it better not to risk sparking further mistrust by forcing the palace issue. Instead, he had focused on regaining the Damsians' trust—strategy and planning rather than thoughtless speed.

"I'm not at liberty to discuss why the Seneschal's disappointment," Carrit said coldly. "Are you ready to leave? I'm sure I don't need to remind you that the Seneschal doesn't like to be kept waiting."

Jabir willed his smile to look confident and patronising. "There is no need for that kind of reminder. I am at the Seneschal's disposal."

It was three in the morning. He prayed Reheeme was asleep.

The two men stepped out, Jabir giving instructions that nobody was to know that he was going out. Carrit took the lead the moment they were outside. They had barely reached the first corner beyond Jabir's house when they came across a whole platoon of the Seneschal's personal guards. They were dressed differently from the palace Watch, their uniforms sleek and black so they looked like shadows. They carried halberds, the blades gleaming cruelly in the moonlight.

Everyone set off on foot for what felt like the longest walk of Jabir's life. The Seneschal was not a forgiving man.

Jabir felt sure he had done nothing that needed forgiving, and yet the longer the walk continued, the less sure he became. The streets seemed to stretch longer, the palace somehow looking farther and farther away until suddenly it was on them, looming menacingly.

Jabir noted that he was being taken through one of the lesser-used gates. He knew that some people went to the palace and then vanished. Was that why they had brought him this way, or was it a simple precaution in the name of discretion?

Jabir began to realise the sheer magnitude of what he had done in getting into bed with the Seneschal. The man only had to decide that Jabir was no longer useful, and Jabir would cease to exist. He shuddered as he passed through the gate and into the palace.

***

Everything about the Seneschal's office whispered of his power, because it was so simple. The smooth pale walls, the understated trinkets that were in fact beyond the price of rubies. Only a certain calibre of person would know, for example, that the vase behind the desk wasn't just a regular vase but was, in fact, the finest porcelain, shipped from a distant country to the east.

The Seneschal's office made it clear that he didn't need to impress anyone. He was above requiring showy displays to establish his status.

There was a painting in the Seneschal's office that always made Jabir feel uncomfortable. It hung to the left of the door, a stunningly rendered landscape of Azyr, both Lower and Higher, during the golden hours of late afternoon. The colours were exquisite, the painting both striking and subtle.

A vastly inferior copy sat in Reheeme's office. She had commissioned it, scouring Azyr for a painter who had seen the original at her parents' house and could reproduce it from memory. She had done her best to give him directions, the painting being intimately familiar to her, but for all her efforts, the new one was dull, lifeless, a poor imitation of the vibrant original.

The Seneschal was seated in a chair, fingers steepled, elbows resting on the armrests. He wore flowing black robes with gleaming black studs at his eyebrows. He was a tall man, unusually tall for an Azyrian, and as thin as a rake. His head was shaved, the skin stretched tightly over his skull, showing prominent cheekbones.

He watched Jabir entering the room with heavily lidded eyes, and there was something reptilian about his stare that reminded Jabir of the lizards kept both at the racetrack and in the Prelate's private fighting pit.

"Please take a seat." The Seneschal's voice was no louder than a whisper of silk so that Jabir almost had to strain to hear him.

Jabir moved to the offered chair, his heart pounding. He was overly aware of his movements, suddenly finding his arms and legs awkward, not knowing what to do with his hands.

"If there is anything I can do to assist Your Grace—" Jabir began.

"Is there something you can do?" the Seneschal asked, his voice soft and quiet but with an edge that could have cut diamonds.

Jabir paused, unsure what to make of this. "Well, if it is within my humble powers, I will certainly strive to—"

"Ah, you strive, you strive, Jabir. And what does your striving get me? Are the Damsians in my care?" The Seneschal looked around as though one of them might be hiding behind the furniture in his office.

Jabir swallowed. It felt as though a hard lump had taken residence in his throat, closing most of it off. How could he have been arrogant enough to think that the Seneschal would tolerate a day's delay? He should have risked Reheeme's suspicion and anger and the Damsians' suspicion. He should have risked everything rather than anger the most powerful man in Azyr.

"Th-they will be here tomorrow," Jabir stammered.

The Seneschal lowered his eyelids and looked at Jabir through his eyelashes. Jabir could feel sweat trickling from his armpits.

"Walk with me," the Seneschal said suddenly, standing up.

He led the way out of his office. The Seneschal didn't have his rooms up in the higher levels of the palace as one would expect of a man of his status. Instead, his office was down in the foundations, and it was windowless. Jabir had heard whispers that this was so that the Seneschal could be close to the torture chambers he liked to amuse himself with.

Jabir grew colder as they walked down empty corridors. When the Seneschal turned into a long, narrow corridor lined with heavy wooden doors studded with metal, Jabir nearly fainted.

The floor was simple flagstone, and their footsteps echoed loudly. Weak alchemical globes cast a sickly yellow light, and the air was hot and stuffy.

The Seneschal stopped at the first door, opening a small square shutter that allowed him to peer inside the cell. Jabir felt sick as he heard a man wailing with pain. There were words within the wailing, gibberish, beyond even the rantings of a madman. The Seneschal nodded to himself, as though satisfied, and closed the shutter with a smart snap.

Jabir realised then that the air was full of muffled sounds of pain—sobs and cries and pleas.

The Seneschal turned to Jabir. "I am a patient man, but I do not appreciate incompetence. Out of respect for the level of your studs, I went with your suggestion that you bring the Damsians to the palace. It was also a wise move, ensuring that no rumour of the arrest could circulate and somehow get back to Damsport. We agreed that you would bring them today, and because I took you for a man of ability and of some power, I trusted that you would deliver on your promises. I see that I was wrong. This is the Damsians' second night in the city, and they are still in your house. I hope, Jabir, that you haven't reversed your cloak and chosen to side once more with the rebels?"

Jabir immediately protested that he hadn't, tripping over his words in his hurry to get them out.

The Seneschal looked at him impassively. "You will receive an official summons from the palace for tomorrow. I cannot afford to risk a public arrest where a witness might manage to get word back to Damsport. I want the Damsians all in the palace tomorrow morning so I can simply collect them without any fuss or problems. Do I make myself clear?"

Jabir nodded shakily, blinking as beads of sweat rolled into his eyes.

The Seneschal gave the faintest ghost of a smile. "Good. You may see yourself out."

He turned and walked away, back to his office. Jabir sagged, leaning an arm against the nearest door. He was breathing heavily as though he had just run a great distance.

Only when he could once again make out the muffled wailing beyond the door did he jerk himself upright, snatching his hand away as though the door had burned him. He hurried out, walking as fast as his dignity would allow, fleeing the long corridor with its many wailing doors.

Rory had waited in the dark while the messenger went in to talk to either Jabir or Reheeme, then she'd watched as a hooded figure came out after the messenger. It was too dark for her to make out anything, and she was still none the wiser as to whether the second person was Jabir or Reheeme.

She'd considered following them, but Cruickshank's steam-powered spider was still packed up. The streets of Tarwa were narrow enough here for her to follow via the roofs, but that might not remain the case. And the city was too foreign for her to go out alone in the middle of the night without notifying anyone. That would be just stupid.

So she was waiting, hoping that whoever had gone out with the messenger would be revealed on returning, when Adelma came up behind her, startling her half to death.

"What you doing out here?" Adelma whispered, frowning. "I were almost about to rouse all the others, thinking something had happened to you."

Rory explained.

"Interesting," Adelma whispered. "What's gonna be even more interesting is whether we find out about the messenger first thing tomorrow morning or whether they'll hide it from us."

"Exactly," Rory whispered back.

"Uh-huh. So I'll wait and see who comes back."

She settled herself, sitting next to Rory.

"I'll wait too," Rory said. "I want to see for myself."

"Good idea. That way you can keep me company. Keeping watch can be dreadfully dull if there ain't a sea to focus on."

They sat in silence for a while.

"Say," Adelma whispered, "what's the deal with you and Rafe?"

Rory almost choked on her own saliva. There was bluntness, and then there was Adelma.

"You and Rafe?" Adelma whispered again. "I seen you two in your cosy little sessions at the prow of the *Slippery Eel*—don't think I don't know everything what goes on in my ship. And mind, you should also know that if you two decide to bump uglies on the *Slippery Eel*, I *will* know about it."

"Oh, stone the gulls," Rory groaned. She had never been more uncomfortable in her life. "Rafe and me, we're friends, alright? That's it. There were a bit of confusion in the beginning and all, but that's past now. Anyway, you and me are watching for something important, right, so now's not the time to talk about that."

"Think that excuse's gonna work on me?" Adelma snorted. "We can talk and watch, my girl. Women are supposed to be able to do more than one thing at a time. Ain't you got the message? And anyway, your boy Rafe went to the prow of my ship every night since the first time he clapped eyes on you sitting there. That don't look like someone who's just your friend."

Rory was too surprised to come up with an answer. Rafe had been coming to the prow looking for her?

"I also heard he wants to train you in some new fighting style," Adelma added.

"So what?" Rory said stiffly, "Longinus is training me, and it don't mean nothing. Or you gonna try to tell me there's something going on with him too?" Rory repressed a shudder. That felt as wrong as having something going on with her brother, if she had one.

"It don't mean nothing with Longinus because you're about as much his type as skinny little runts are mine."

Rory turned to Adelma. "I ain't a runt."

Adelma cuffed her on the head. Rory gasped in surprise but knew better than to make a sound of protest. "The hell?" she whispered, rubbing her head.

"See? You don't hit me back," Adelma whispered, grinning.

Rory glared at her. Adelma was several times larger than her, a walking slab of muscle.

"I ain't suicidal," she muttered. If there was one thing Rory had in spades, it was an instinct for survival, and brawling with Adelma went right against that instinct.

"The others would." Adelma's grin widened. "That makes you the runt of our group." She slung an arm around Rory's neck, pulling her in closer. "Now, ain't a problem being a runt, especially if you find someone interested in runts. And methinks Rafe likes to go for the nonobvious choice. That would be you," she added for clarification.

Adelma paused, eyes flicking over Rory's shoulder.

Rory froze. "Someone?" she murmured.

"Yep," Adelma murmured back. "Trying to keep from being seen but definitely listening to us." She squeezed Rory's shoulder hard enough to break bones. "Misdirection." Her voice rose to a loud whisper that was sure to carry halfway across the internal courtyard. "Now, I'm about to drop some pearls of wisdom, so make sure you pay attention and pick them up."

Rory felt her face burn at the realisation of what Adelma was going to use as misdirection. She also realised that trying to change Adelma's course was as likely to be successful as expecting a curtain to prevent an elephant from stepping forward. She just prayed that Rafe wouldn't be anywhere within earshot, which he hopefully wouldn't be since his shift had been earlier that evening.

"The greatest stupidity of youth," Adelma said, "is making things far more complicated than they need to be. Take you and Rafe, for example. The way I look at it, you're in one of four situations. One, you don't like him, and he don't like you. Well, then, ain't nothing to be done and nothing to worry about. So stop sulking about it. Two, you like him, but he don't like you. Why, nothing you can do about that either. Ain't no changing the way someone feels about you. So chalk it up to experience, and move on. Three, he likes you, but you don't like him. Again, nothing you can do about the way he feels about you. Take it as a compliment and move on. Or finally, four, you like each other."

Adelma smiled at Rory. "Still listening," she murmured so low that Rory barely heard. "In which case," she said in her loud whisper once more, "just get on with it. Although realise that if it's in my ship, I will know and make excellent use of the opportunity to take the piss out of you both."

If it weren't for the fact that she wanted to see who came back from the mysterious nighttime errand, Rory would have been happy to disappear into the ground.

"Rafe and I are just friends," she said through gritted teeth, barely bothering to whisper.

Adelma snorted again. "I told you about that already. Burn my body, girl, but you're useless. It's a wonder you've ever managed to find yourself a man."

Rory's face seemed to spontaneously combust, it was so hot. No stone of Azyr had ever reached such a temperature, and nobody had ever felt this awkward before, she was certain.

Adelma seemed to notice her discomfort, and she gave an incredulous snort.

"Gone," she murmured. "Back inside." Again, she let her voice rise. "My girl, have I got knowledge to share with you. But first, my throat is dry with all them pearls of wisdom I've had to produce, so let's get it lubricated first."

She stood up, her knees crunching like old gears, and gestured for Rory to follow suit. They returned to their communal sitting room, closing the door. Rory immediately dragged Adelma to the window in case anyone was watching.

"What about watching to see who comes back?" she murmured.

"Can't happen now," Adelma replied in the same tone. "If we keep watch, we'll look suspicious. Also, I'd wager that whoever was listening to us will send out a warning that we're there, which means whoever went out won't come back in until we're gone. The longer we stay out, the more it will look like we know something's up. Anyway, we'll still learn something when we find out whether Jabir or Reheeme mentions anything about this tomorrow. Just knowing that they're hiding something from us is already good information."

She clapped Rory on the back. "Now, I don't care if you don't want to hear what I got to tell you. Go pour me a drink, and I'll explain all you need to know about men."

CHAPTER 30

Dawn found Cruikshank up and working on the drill she was creating to help disconnect communications between the various walls and gates of Azyr. She was enjoying the challenge. The drill she was making was complex, but the way it was going to be used was just a matter of physics. The simplicity and elegance of the solution pleased Cruikshank greatly, and she found herself humming as she worked. That this would also help bring down a ruler who believed in slavery and oppressed his people made it even better.

Cruikshank had successfully transformed her bedroom into a small, exotic version of her workshop, and it gave her a sense of comfort and familiarity, like being home. Now that she had stopped using her furnace, sketches and formulae scrawled on sheets of paper littered the bed, many of them crumpled. She had pulled most of her tools out, laying them all out on the floor so that she had to weave her way between them to get to the door. The only part of her bedroom that was neat was the area she had transformed into her workbench.

She'd worked throughout most of the night, as was her habit. She was most definitely a night owl and didn't need much sleep. As a result, she now had two working prototypes of the drill that would disrupt communications.

Cruikshank absentmindedly scratched at the new tattoo of the partially completed cog on her abdomen. She would enjoy telling Liv about what this tattoo represented.

A knock had her looking up.

"Come in."

Rafe opened the door. "I saw the light under your door. You're already working?"

Cruikshank grinned. "A machinist's work is never done."

"Mind if I come take a look?"

"Of course, if you can pick your way past my tools without stepping on anything."

Rafe danced across the floor easily, his Varanguard training evident in every step. He reached Cruikshank, and looked at the piece she was working on. "How will it work?"

"It's very simple really. From what Reheeme mentioned, they are able to detect any leaks and alchemical interference with the solution inside the communication tubes. So what we're going to do is insert a large bubble of air in the pipes at a point where they will be curving upwards to follow the curve of a hill. The air bubble will rise and settle at the summit of the hill, or rise, and stay there. Reheeme confirmed that the alchemical signal cannot travel through

Celine Jeanjean

air. The solution is also unaffected by air. So the bubble will very simply block any signal from passing. Simple, isn't it?"

Cruikshank smiled, once again enjoying the smoothness of the reasoning. It gave her the same satisfaction as tracing the slippery-smooth contours of a pebble with her fingers.

Rafe regarded at the drill with interest. "Very efficient. How will the machine work, then?"

Cruikshank was surprised. She hadn't realised the lad had an interest in machinery. "You really want to know?" she asked.

Rafe nodded. "Before I became a Varanguard, I always thought I'd be a machinist."

"Well, grease my gears. I had no idea. Lovey, you are in for a treat. It's quite simple really. This bit here is a hand-operated drill. As it drills into the pipe, this part here expands to fill in the hole and prevent any leaks. And we can insert air into the pipe like so."

Cruikshank showed him everything, including the dials that would control how much air was pushed into the pipe.

Rafe watched with curiosity. "And to seal the hole?"

Cruikshank smiled, and she felt her first craving of the day for a cigar. She pulled one out, realising that she had probably hadn't brought enough for the whole trip.

"A resin can be pushed into the gap as the drill is removed like this. The whole setup is very simple, but the best things often are," she said, lighting her cigar. She exhaled blue smoke. "The flashier and more complex a piece, the more you have to wonder if the machinist in question is trying to prove something, and the easier it is for something to go wrong."

Rafe nodded. "It's elegant. Even Longinus would think so."

Cruikshank gave an affectionate snort. "Longinus would want me to make the metal parts shiny and polished. But this will do the job. It's pretty much done. I just need to calculate where on the pipes to do the insertions and finesse the calibration for the amount of air to be inserted."

She paused and looked the lad over through the haze of smoke. "I'm hoping you and Rory have patched up your disagreement, by the way. I never like having team members not getting along. It can make things more difficult."

Rafe shrugged, looking away. He picked up a pair of pliers and fiddled with them. "I don't really know. I guess so, but then, the other day I tried to suggest she use another weapon than a sword, and she told me to leave."

Cruikshank nodded. "I don't know much about Rory's past from before I met her. She won't talk about it. But I do know that her dream of being a swordswoman goes way back. I think she had a friend, a very close friend, who died. I imagine that her fixation on fighting with a sword comes from that in some way."

Cruikshank took a drag on her cigar. She wasn't sure if it was a good idea talking to Rafe about Rory's past. But she had a hunch, and she went with it. "You know, Rory might seem straightforward at first glance, but she's quite a complex girl. I think anyone who might be... interested in her, would need a lot of patience. Would need to put in the time and really get her trust."

Cruikshank almost added that not taking the time could result in getting bracelets flung at one's face, the way Rory had thrown the bracelet Rafe had bought her, but she thought that might be a bit much.

"Time," Rafe muttered to himself still fiddling with the pliers. He seemed to realise that he'd spoken out loud, and he looked up abruptly.

Cruikshank decided not to increase his embarrassment, and she changed the subject. "I think I'm going to go see Reheeme and find out if she's awake. I want to go look at the site of the pipes myself and also see if I can get a look at the reader and transmitter at the Dividing Wall. The plans Reheeme gave me say nothing about the width of the pipes, and I need to know how to calibrate the air-bubble insertion. I also want to check that there'd be no way to detect the extra space the air bubble would take. Reheeme said they wouldn't be able to detect it alchemically, but I need to know what I'm working with. Probably best if I do all that before the streets get too busy."

Rafe nodded. "I'll leave you to it."

CHAPTER
31

Reheeme was pleased to hear of Cruikshank's progress, and she quickly drew up paperwork to arrange a visit to the Dividing Wall. She was adamant that Cruikshank have an escort, so the machinist suggested Adelma. But Reheeme insisted on sending her own guard as well.

Cruikshank was less than pleased at first, but now that they were walking through the Azyrian streets, she was grateful for his presence. People looked at her and Adelma with frowns and suspicion until they saw their escort, and then their faces cleared.

Cruikshank wanted to go look at the two areas she had earmarked as the disruption sites, to ensure that the slope of the ground was sufficient. They reached an area of Tarwa with more bustle than what they had seen so far and less luxury too. Shops were opening, and delicious smells began wafting out as eateries got their food ready for the day. Slaves darted in and came out with steaming parcels that they hurried to bring back to their masters.

The streets were a little wider here and the buildings looked newer, too. They weren't quite as beautifully decorated as the area around Reheeme and Jabir's house. They were all in bright colours but without the stunning displays of mosaics and carvings.

Adelma walked alongside Cruikshank, large and almost incongruous in the crowd. Azyrians were a lot more delicate than Damsians—they were lithe and dark, and next to them, Cruikshank and Adelma looked pale and clunky, like old pieces of machinery. Adelma didn't seem to notice, or if she did, she didn't care.

Cruikshank had covered up her tattoo with a loose white shirt lashed to her waist with a wide leather girdle, which she wore over black cotton leggings. Her tattoo was too recognisable, and she didn't want to draw any attention to the fact that she was a machinist. Despite her long sleeves, she was comfortable, enjoying the feel of the lightweight fabric against her skin. Adelma, on the other hand, had refused to go without her fighting leathers, and the smuggler was already sweating profusely. Cruikshank resisted the urge to tell her she should have changed before they left, knowing it wouldn't achieve anything. Instead, her eyes fell onto Adelma's right hand, which stayed worryingly close to one of her battle-axes.

"Don't forget," Cruikshank told her in a low voice, "we're just foreigners, here to see the sights of the city. Try to look less intimidating."

Adelma grunted. "Intimidating is my natural state of being. Not sure now to be anything else."

"Well, try. Like, for example, you could remove your hand from your axe."

Adelma grunted and let her hand fall to her side. There was still a tension to her, but it was an improvement.

Cruikshank had brought two pairs of dark-tinted goggles to give them some relief from the blinding sun. They were simple things. Stiff leather on the sides acted like blinkers of sorts, keeping the sun out, while the lenses were smoked glass. Adelma's glasses suited her. With the shaved sides of her head and her long plait, the goggles gave her, if that was possible, an even more formidable air than usual.

"Look at that building over there," Cruikshank said, not having to exaggerate her admiration much. It was stunning, reminiscent of the older area of Tarwa where Reheeme and Jabir lived. The whole thing was covered in the tiniest tiles in white and various shades of blue, the mosaic depicting graceful vines curling up the walls all the way to the roof.

"Very nice," Adelma replied.

"It's beautiful," Cruikshank said. "A real work of art."

Adelma shrugged. "Ain't a ship."

Cruikshank repressed a laugh. "Is that really all you can say?"

"Well, it ain't, is it? I didn't become a smuggler 'cause I wanted to see the world or any of that nonsense. I like ships, I like smuggling, and I like money. The rest of it just don't matter to me, and if foreigners want to waste their time putting tiny bloody tiles all over their walls, well, that's their business. I ain't gonna get into a tizzy over it."

Cruikshank quirked an eyebrow. "I suppose that's as good a life philosophy as any other."

"Served me well over the years," Adelma replied with a shrug.

"All the same—we're supposed to be taking in the wonders of Azyr while Longinus carries out his alchemical business, so try to look like you're enjoying yourself."

Adelma grunted.

"This is the new money part of Tarwa," the guard said behind them. Cruikshank turned, surprised.

He looked contemptuous as he gestured toward the buildings around him. "That house you pointed out is only ten years old."

"I see," Cruikshank replied. It seemed that even the guards of the wealthy felt the need to be snobs in Azyr.

They walked down a wider road, taking in the full heat of the sun. Cruikshank began to sweat, feeling it run down her sides under her linen shirt. She found herself envying Adelma's bare arms despite how uncomfortable her fighting leathers must have been.

They turned into an even wider road.

"This is it," the guard said.

Cruikshank hadn't wanted to draw attention by bringing the plans with her to map out the route to the disruption sites, so instead, she'd had to rely on the guard's directions. She looked ahead and nodded with satisfaction. Farther on was quite a noticeable rise in the ground—perfect for her purpose.

Not only that, but a strip of cobblestones ran all along the street, darker than the rest where the sun hadn't yet had the chance to bleach them to the colour of old bones. Cruikshank guessed the pipes were beneath.

They walked to the top of the rise. Shaded cloisters lined either side of the street, just right for a nighttime approach. The shadows there would be thick enough to hide the rebels. The shops sold things made of wood, leather, and silver.

Cruikshank nodded to herself. Again, this suited their purpose well. The shop owners would be unlikely to be getting up at the crack of dawn like those who had to prepare food each day.

She tapped the cobblestones with her boot. She'd have to make sure whoever disrupted the communications also had the right tools to pull out the cobbles without making too much noise. But overall, so long as there was no way to detect an air bubble in the pipes, this would be perfect as one of the disruption sites.

"Alright," she said. "Let's go to the Dividing Wall and then to the next disruption site."

**

The Wall was huge, splitting the Higher city into the areas of Maksur and Tarwa. Reheeme had written up documents that would allow them access to the Dividing Wall itself under the pretence that they wanted to visit one of the landmarks of Azyr.

Cruikshank and Adelma aimed for the part of the Wall where the plans showed it intersecting with the communication pipes, since the mechanism that read the alchemical signal was sure to be housed there. The Watch who manned it had silver-coloured scaled armour over a blood-red uniform.

"When we get there," Cruikshank murmured to Adelma, "can you create a diversion?"

Adelma grinned. "Can I just. You seen me? I'm practically a walking diversion."

As they got close to the Wall, Cruikshank could see a stream of foot traffic coming through to their side of town. They were dressed more soberly than the inhabitants of Tarwa and in cheaper fabrics. They walked briskly, no doubt hurrying to their places of work. Cruikshank guessed that a lot of the workers in Tarwa lived in the poorer area of Maksur and came in each day to tend to the wealthy.

Cruikshank and Adelma reached the Dividing Wall, just to left of the arched gate that let all the workers through. Reheeme's guard stepped forward, producing the paperwork and thrusting it at the woman of the Watch standing by the gate. Her scaled armour gleamed so brightly in the sun that she was almost painful to look at. Her helmet marked her out as a captain.

"My mistress has arranged for the foreigners to visit the wall," the guard said.

The Watch captain took the papers, giving him a cold, unreadable look. She glanced over Cruikshank and Adelma, and Cruikshank did her best to look like someone just sightseeing. Adelma of course, looked like Adelma, but there was nothing to be done about that, and Cruikshank found her presence reassuring.

The captain looked over the papers slowly, peering at the signature.

"I hope you're not questioning my mistress's integrity," the guard snapped, growing angry at the perceived insult.

The Watchwoman ignored him, still looking the papers over. Cruikshank looked up to where she thought the communications room might be—a small windowless structure up on the wall, just to the left of the gate. She wondered if someone was signalling the palace, informing them of two foreigners wanting to see the Wall, but she doubted it. If the communications system was overrun with such pointless information, it would lose its effectiveness in the case of an emergency, which was, after all, its chief purpose.

After what felt like an age, the Watch captain returned the papers with a curt nod. "You can go to the top," she said to Cruikshank and Adelma. "But not more than a few meters either side. I won't have you running around up there. We have work to do, and we don't have time to look after foreigners."

"Of course," Cruikshank said. "I'm ever so excited at the thought of seeing the great Dividing Wall and the view from the top. I've heard so much about it."

"Yes," Adelma echoed. "Very excited." She sounded about as excited as a tombstone, but the Watchwoman didn't seem to pick up on it.

They began walking up the steep steps that led up to the top of the Wall. Reheeme's guard tried to follow but the captain gestured for him to stop. "Not you. The papers are for the foreigners only."

"But I'm under strict orders to escort them," the guard protested.

The captain shook her head.

"We'll be fine," Cruikshank told him. "You'll be able to see us from down there."

They climbed up the stairs slowly, the Watchwoman leading the way. Cruikshank looked as unobtrusively as she could towards the communications room. The door was half-open, and when they reached the top, Cruikshank saw machinery inside, something that looked like it could be the reader for the alchemical signals.

"Alright, go for the diversion," Cruikshank murmured to Adelma, who gave the tiniest of nods in reply.

"Now you can see the view on either side," the Watchwoman said, clearly annoyed at having the two foreign women there. "That's city Watch standing guard, and that's about all there is to it. I really don't know why your host arranged for you to come to see this."

Adelma narrowed her eyes at one of the Watchmen. Cruikshank slipped discreetly back so as to be behind her, partly hidden from sight.

"You. I know you," Adelma said, pointing her finger at the Watchman. He was smaller in stature than the rest, and Cruikshank could tell from his youth and the way he carried himself that he was probably a recent recruit. She felt a pang of guilt that he was about to be the recipient of Adelma's diversion. The Watchman looked understandably confused at having been singled out by Adelma.

"Don't try to pretend you don't recognise me," Adelma said, sounding furious. "You should be ashamed of yourself. You never wrote. You never came to see me when you made all them pretty promises." She loomed over the Watchman, but she was smart enough not to make any kind of contact.

"What's going on?" the captain asked.

Cruikshank took one step back and then another. Nobody was paying attention to her.

"What's going on?" Adelma said. "I'll tell you what's going on!"

Cruikshank slipped into the communications room. It was hot inside, the air trapped in the windowless room. A number of concentrated alchemical globes hung overhead, diffusing a hard white light into the small space. The light would be clear as day even in the dead of night.

In the centre, a twin set of tubes rose up through the floor, linking into a complex set of dials. Cruikshank saw the receptor at the top of one tube that would read the alchemical signals. Atop the other tube was the transmitter. A tiny container poked out of it, filled with the same solution as in the tubes. No doubt, the appropriate alchemical solution could be placed in the container, and it would travel throughout the length of the tube in seconds, reaching the palace.

Interestingly, there was a large tank overhead with two thin pipes connected to each tube—a surplus of the conducting solution that could be fed into the tubes to handle any minor leaks, most likely.

Another reader was attached to the tank—some kind of warning system should the reserve solution fall beneath a certain level. That would allow them to quickly identify any leaks, whether accidental or planned, while ensuring communications weren't immediately stopped by topping up the communications liquid. It would give more than enough time for the palace and the Dividing Wall to signal each other that there was a problem. It might even give them time to investigate the potential leak before communication broke down. It was a very clever system.

Cruikshank craned her neck to get a good look at the figures on the reader. Adelma's voice drifted to her, still haranguing the Watchman about their made-up tryst. Cruikshank had to give it to Adelma—she was effective at creating a distraction.

Looking at the setup, she felt pretty confident that the air bubble wouldn't be picked up, which was good. She got a good look at the reader, too, memorising the figures she could see there and the point at which the alarm would be sounded. She needed to know just how much room they'd have to play with when installing her air drill—there could possibly be minor leaks before the air was forced in and the seal was made. It was always best to provide wiggle room for things going wrong.

"What are you doing here?"

Cruikshank started. She turned and gave the Watch captain a smile. "Grind my... uh, biceps," she said, only just managing to swallow down her usual expression. "You startled me half to death. This is fascinating. What is it?"

"Get out," the Watchwoman said. "You're not supposed to be in here." She marched over and dragged Cruikshank out by the arm.

Cruikshank let herself be led without resisting. "Oh sorry. I didn't realise this was out of bounds."

The Watchwoman shoved Cruikshank forward into the sunlight. It was barely brighter outside than it had been in the communications room. "Both of you, off my Wall," she snapped.

"Don't think this is over," Adelma warned the poor Watchman she had been yelling at.

He had gained confidence, being backed by his peers and supervisor, and he sneered at her. "Off the Wall, you crazy foreigner."

"Come on, Adelma," Cruikshank said. "I think we're getting in everyone's way."

They climbed back down the stairs.

"That was some distraction," Cruikshank murmured.

"Get what you wanted?" Adelma asked.

"Yep."

CHAPTER
32

Jabir hurried over to his wife's quarters, the summons from the palace fresh in his hand. It had been a nightmare getting back to his house, his trusted servant fortunately having intercepted him to warn that Rory and Adelma sat within sight of the internal courtyard. Gossiping about boys, of all things! Jabir was practically twitching with nervous energy and anger.

By the time the two women had left, it was too late to risk reentering the house without Reheeme noticing—she was an extremely early riser. So he'd had to pretend to have been out on early-morning errands, going to see those traders who began their days at the crack of dawn.

Now it was late, and he had yet to speak to his wife about the palace summons or make suitable plans for the day. Why had Adelma and Rory felt the need to sit outside of their suite to have their inane conversation? For the hundredth time, he cursed them and their studs before remembering that they had no studs.

Jabir stopped and took a deep breath. Panic was for amateurs and fools, and he was neither. Today was too important to risk messing anything up. He took another deep breath. Nothing was ruined. He just had to remain calm and take the Damsians into the palace. That was all.

He announced himself to Reheeme's personal servants and was let into her rooms. He found her in her office and, for a heartbeat, felt his nerves return to him as he saw, behind her desk, the poor imitation of the painting in the Seneschal's office.

"Yes?" Reheeme asked coldly.

"And a good morning to you too." Jabir took a seat. "Dear," he added just to spite her. "We have all been summoned to the palace." He placed the summons on her desk. "It seems the Prelate has heard of the Damsians' presence in Azyr, and he wants to meet all of them."

Reheeme frowned as she read the summons. "Well, he can't."

Jabir's stomach lurched. "What?"

"I said he can't meet them all. Cruikshank and Adelma have already left. Cruikshank wanted to inspect the communication pipes before the day got too busy, and Adelma went with her as her escort. I sent a guard with them as well, of course."

Jabir felt his throat tighten with panic. "Call them back," he snapped. "The summons is for all the Damsians."

"I see that," Reheeme replied with infuriating calm. "But I can't call them back. I have no idea where they are. And since the summons is for this morning, we can't afford to lose time. Better that we show up on time with two missing than hours late with all five of them."

Jabir began to sweat again. He should have been there. If it hadn't been for Adelma and Rory, he would have slipped back in early enough to ensure that Cruikshank pushed back her plans to inspect the pipes and instead came to the palace. What would the Seneschal do to him if two Damsians were missing when they went to the palace?

"I think I will go pay my respects to my parents' resting place while we're there," Reheeme added.

Her parents had been fed to the Prelate's private lizards in his private fighting pit. There hadn't been enough left of them to bury, and Reheeme had developed the macabre habit of going to see the fighting pit when it was empty.

"I will leave you to come back from the palace with the Damsians, and I will follow later," Reheeme said.

Jabir nodded distractedly, barely listening.

"Well?" Reheeme asked impatiently. "Was there anything else?"

Jabir shook his head. An impossible situation—he was in an impossible situation. He closed his eyes, picturing that long corridor of cells and the muffled sobbing that came through the doors.

CHAPTER
33

Longinus watched as the palace drew nearer. It was enormous and dazzlingly white. Around it was a ring of high, smooth wall, the tops of which bristled with spears and guards. The wall was so smooth, in fact, that it gleamed as if radiating its own light. Luckily, Longinus had, as usual, made appropriate sartorial preparations. He wore dark purple-tinted optics that absorbed most of the sun's harshness. He quite liked himself with the tinted optics on.

It made him look debonair.

The mechanical elephant bearing them headed for a large gate in the middle of the wall. As they drew up to the gate, Longinus quirked an eyebrow in surprise. The wall was marble—an unbelievable waste of a precious material, to say nothing of how appalling it was to juxtapose spears with such a precious and elegant material.

"Stone the gulls," Rory muttered next to him. "That must have cost a bloody fortune."

"It did," Reheeme replied grimly. "Not just in gold but in the lives it took to build it too."

Longinus glanced at her, surprised. It was the first time the prickly woman had made a reference to the people her revolution was supposed to help. Rory had told him about the late-night messenger and the mysterious outing. So far, neither Jabir nor Reheeme had mentioned anything, and Longinus couldn't decide which of the two it might have been. That was concerning. Clearly, one or both of them had a hidden agenda.

The gate looked like a small palace in itself, towering far higher than the walls and flanked by two small towers. It was large enough for three mechanical elephants to walk through abreast, and it arched high overhead, terminating in a point. The gate was of white marble, as were the walls, but its surface was covered with fine engravings depicting scenes of war and hunting.

"Such lack of taste," he whispered, disgusted. He pushed down his purple optics to glare at the marble over them. "War and hunting engraved in such fine marble. What next—bloody executions and beheadings printed on silks?" He sniffed and pushed his optics back up. Money obviously didn't buy class.

Two huge engravings on either side of the arch showed a very impressive specimen of male Azyrian, wearing only a simple wraparound skirt, displaying a perfectly muscled chest, and raising his hands to the heavens. Longinus guessed that was the Prelate. Yet another ridiculous display.

How could a man be taken seriously if the first impression he gave his guests was of himself stripped to the waist?

Then the elephant plodded through the gate. It was so deep that the whole mechanised animal was swallowed up in its shadows, while overhead were murder holes and the tips of what must have been an iron gate. The palace might have been all white marble and fine engravings, but there was no mistaking the wall's purpose. More Watchmen manned it, but their scaled armour and uniform were white, in stark contrast to their black skin. They seemed to blend in with the marble like a living part of the palace.

The air seemed hotter within the palace walls, too, probably because the sun and heat were reflected off every surface, blasting at them from every direction. At this rate, Longinus was in danger of arriving at the palace sweating.

I really must find some alchemical treatment to prevent that in the future.

As they got closer, the intricacies of the palace walls became visible: every single surface was engraved in fine, complex patterns so that it all looked as delicate as lace.

Finally, an appropriate use of marble.

They reached the entrance, climbed down from the elephant, and were quickly admitted inside once Reheeme and Jabir had made themselves known.

Whereas outside had been harsh and bright, inside was wonderfully cool and dark—so dark, in fact, that with his sun-soaked vision, Longinus could barely see a thing with his optics on. He allowed himself a brief moment of foolishness, wishing he could keep them on. Taking them off would diminish the effect of his outfit, and he wanted to make a strong first impression on the Prelate, but he wasn't about to walk around the palace half blind. With a sigh, he removed the optics.

Reheeme led the way up a sweeping staircase. As they climbed, a young woman walked down past them, nodding once briefly at Reheeme. She had simple studs at her eyebrows, and Longinus grimaced at the sight of an ugly bruised lump in the middle of her forehead. Reheeme and Jabir didn't express any surprise or concern, so Longinus thought it best to keep silent.

The staircase opened up into a long succession of passages that stretched into the distance to a large, heavily guarded entrance.

"The preaudience chambers," Reheeme said in a low voice. "Four of them." Every surface was of stone without anything soft to absorb the sound, and her voice bounced off the marble.

They walked through the parade of preaudience chambers, each one bisected by a straight path of encrusted gems. Yellow jasper for the first chamber, then red carnelian, and then green garnet. The stones had been shaped into points that had obviously been worn down over the years, although Longinus could still feel them poking through the soft leather soles of his boots.

"When the palace was first built," Jabir explained in a hushed voice, "subjects came to the audience chamber barefoot. And the stones were sharp. Arriving with bleeding feet was considered a sign of respect for the Prelate." He glanced at the silent guards. "But now our benevolent Prelate, as many before him, has declared that we may approach with shoes on."

"How generous," Rafe said, his tone ambiguous enough that it could have been mistaken as genuine.

They continued walking in silence, their footsteps echoing loudly against the marble. When they reached the fourth room, Rory gasped. The path cutting across the space was made of sapphires. There was no mistaking the stones. They were polished to a brilliant blue, smooth and unbroken, and some were as large as eggs. Even Longinus had to admit that he was shocked.

They were walking atop a fortune.

And then they reached the throne room.

CHAPTER
34

Two ceremonial Watchmen clad in white-scaled armour stood on either side of the doorway to the throne room, blocking the way with their extended halberds. A small man in fine but civilian clothing stood waiting. Reheeme and Jabir each handed him a card.

"We bring guests to His Radiance, Chamberlain," Reheeme said reverently.

Longinus raised an eyebrow. *The she-devil, the harridan, is capable of respect. Who knew?*

"Foreigners, from Damsport," Reheeme added.

She could have mentioned that there's a gentleman alchemist among the foreigners.

The Chamberlain scanned the cards and looked over at Longinus, Rory, and Rafe with just a hint of superiority. Longinus wished he still had his optics on. There was nothing quite like glancing over the top of optics to imply condescension. The Chamberlain nodded and made a gesture for them to wait.

Longinus had a good view of the room beyond, only partially blocked by the halberds. It was brilliant-white marble. There were windows, unlike the previous chambers, with the sunlight pouring through so that the path leading up to the throne glittered hard: it was made of diamonds. The throne sprawled atop a small set of steps, and it carried the fattest man Longinus had ever seen.

The Prelate seemed to have been molded out of a block of fat, spreading without shape across the huge throne as if he had been made of wax and the sun had reduced him to a quivering mass. He was dressed, from his bulging neck to his ankles, in loose white silk robes and out of the puddle of clothing his head, hands, and feet stuck out, his black skin a sharp contrast to the bright white. His head was perfectly bald and shining, beads of sweat shimmering at his forehead and upper lip.

Longinus struggled to keep the disgust from his face. The carvings at the entrance of the palace seemed like a joke. Surely all of Azyr had to be laughing at the enormously fat man who liked to represent himself as a man at the peak of his strength.

Diamonds glittered at the Prelate's eyebrows and fingers, the first time Longinus had seen diamond studs in Azyr. No doubt, diamonds were specifically reserved for the Prelate. He held a long leather leash that was tethered to a beautiful leopard, its collar encrusted with yet more diamonds. It lay on the floor at the Prelate's feet, and it yawned lazily, showing a pink tongue. A gaggle of courtiers stood on either side of the Prelate, each one more finely dressed than the last. They all had the heavy, complicated headdresses

Longinus had seen before at the races, each one requiring a number of slaves to hold them up. Bells, flowers, and jewels cascaded down from the headdresses so that the courtiers looked like tropical birds.

An Azyrian man sat on his knees at the base of the throne, his loose robes bunched up around his legs.

"I thank His Radiance the Prelate for such generosity," the man stuttered. "I thank—"

The Prelate looked both annoyed and bored, and he flapped his free hand at the man, interrupting him. A young slave stood at the Prelate's side, holding a chiselled crystal bowl full of sweets, and she pushed a sticky-looking confection into his mouth. He didn't even seem to notice.

"Your Radiance," the supplicant murmured. He placed both hands on the ground and bowed forward as if to touch his forehead to the marble. To Longinus's shock, the man whacked his forehead loudly enough to make a dull knocking sound. Longinus muffled a gasp. The man got to his feet, a little unsteady.

Longinus remembered the woman they had seen earlier with the ugly bruised lump on her forehead. "This is customary?" he whispered to Jabir, appalled.

Jabir didn't look at him, but he gave a small nod.

The supplicant walked out of the throne room, an angry lump already visible on his forehead. The two Watchmen let him pass, and the Chamberlain announced Reheeme, Jabir, and the Damsians. Reheeme led the way in, and Longinus followed, Rafe and Rory behind him since they played the part of his retinue.

Up on his throne, the Prelate thrust his head forward, staring myopically at them. "Damsport? Damsport, is it?" he called in a surprisingly high, nasal voice.

Longinus suppressed the urge to laugh. *Gods alive, the man is ridiculous!* With his extended neck and his enormous body, the Prelate looked like some kind of mutant turtle blinking at them.

"Yes, Your Radiance," Reheeme answered, gracefully getting down on her knees.

Longinus watched her, horrified. Surely she wasn't going to bang her head against the floor? Would they expect him to do the same?

But Reheeme only touched her forehead to the marble. Longinus followed suit, lowering himself to his knees. The marble was cold and smooth against his forehead.

That done, everyone sat back on their ankles, Rafe and Rory settling into place on either side of Longinus, just behind him.

The Prelate continued to blink at them, his expression strange and slightly malevolent. "Damsians, huh? Damsians…"

"I am here to represent Damsport in matters of alchemy, Your Radiance," Longinus said smoothly. "Reheeme and I are working to increase both Azyr and Damsport's—"

"You are spies!" the Prelate exclaimed, pointing a sausage-like finger at them.

Longinus froze. He shot a quick glance at Rory and Rafe, who seemed as shocked as he was.

"Of course not, Your Radiance," Reheeme replied evenly. "They are friends of Azyr's. Allies."

"Allies?" the Prelate squeaked. "*Allies?*"

"Yes, Your Radiance," Longinus replied. "Allies."

"No, you are spies. I have no need for allies. I want spies!" The Prelate sprayed spittle as he spoke, his face like a petulant child's.

Longinus looked bemused. "Your... Your Radiance?"

"Why aren't you spies? Hmm? Hmmm? Azyr is the greatest city in the world, so why aren't you here..." The slave girl pushed a sweet in his mouth. "Why aren't you here to spy on me?" He spoke with his mouth full, chewing the sticky confection.

Longinus threw a panicked look at Reheeme, who seemed equally at a loss.

"Seneschal! Seneschal," the Prelate called, his voice rising in pitch. He was agitated, squirming about his throne. Beads of perspiration flew off his forehead, and another young slave stepped up to dab his brow with a pristine white-linen cloth.

"Your Radiance," said a voice soft and smooth as silk.

Longinus glanced over his shoulder. Behind Rafe and Rory, an Azyrian man he hadn't noticed before had stepped forward. He was tall for an Azyrian and thin as a rake. His skin stretched taut over his shaved skull, making deep pools of his eyes and sharp angles of his cheekbones. The man was dressed in flowing black robes and had gleaming black studs at his eyebrows. His dark skin was so perfectly smooth and unlined that he seemed ageless. His eyes were heavily lidded in a way that reminded Longinus of a reptile.

He stepped forward, moving with disconcerting smoothness. "Your Radiance," the Seneschal repeated, taking a small bow.

"Why aren't these people here to spy on me?" the Prelate asked. "I want to arrest them. Find reasons to arrest them— I want to sentence someone to death today. And Damsians too! How can they be entering *my* city and not spy on me? Your standards are slipping, Seneschal! Damsport is like a boil on the ear of an elephant next to the magnificence of Azyr. The Damsians should be awed, cowed—*they should be spying!*" The Prelate's voice had gone painfully shrill.

The slave girl at his side dabbed at his chin with her cloth, removing the spittle, while the other slave pushed a new sweet into his mouth.

"Your Radiance is, of course, absolutely right," the Seneschal said softly, his face remaining perfectly bland. His eyes, however, were cold and calculating, and something about the man made Longinus's skin crawl.

Everyone had gone quite still, as if in fear of speaking up when the Prelate was angry. Longinus repressed the urge to release the safety catch of his poison spitter. He looked slowly from the Prelate to the Seneschal, frantically groping for some way to defuse the situation. Rafe caught his eye. The lad was coiled like a spring, hands resting on his thighs so he would easily be able to draw his knives.

"The Marchioness of Damsport has nothing but the highest respect and admiration for Your Radiance," Longinus said. "She has also heard just how efficient and ruthless you are when it comes to eradicating spies. She knows better than to try to pit herself against such a superior adversary. For her to try to send spies to Azyr would be an exercise in futility."

The Prelate looked surprised, then mollified. "Huh," he said, leaning back. "So she should. Trying to pit herself against me, indeed. Did you hear that, Seneschal?"

"I did, Your Radiance."

The Prelate watched Longinus balefully, his small porcine eyes gleaming. Then, to Longinus's shock, he burst into laughter. Around him, the Azyrian courtiers joined in, polite, strained laughter filling the room.

"Futility, haha, yes! Futility! Did you hear that, Seneschal?" the Prelate said. "Futility!" The word rang out loudly against the marble.

"I did, Your Radiance."

The Prelate giggled on, his laughter tinged with hysteria. He slowed then stopped with a hiccup. It was unnerving, like the behaviour of a monstrous child.

"Still, why can't you be spies? I wanted to arrest some spies," he whined. The Prelate stopped and considered Rory, Rafe, and Longinus. "Seneschal, give them the run of the palace. You." He turned to Reheeme. "Show them around. I want them to see how magnificent it is."

"Your will, Radiance," Reheeme said, touching her forehead lightly to the ground.

Longinus frowned. He wouldn't for a moment believe that this madman was prepared to give them the perfect opportunity for reconnaissance just like that.

"You can all report back to that sour old cow in Damsport," the Prelate said. "Tell her of Azyr's true magnificence. Tell her of the palace."

"Of course, Your Radiance," Longinus said. "I am a writer of great talent, and I shall compose essays and poems to the magnificence of Azyr and its palace."

"Good, good." The Prelate rubbed his hands, his flesh quivering like jelly in a dish.

Reheeme and Jabir touched their foreheads to the ground once again, and Longinus did the same.

"And, Seneschal, when they're done reporting on Azyr's magnificence," the Prelate said, "have them killed for spying."

Longinus's stomach dropped into his boots. The others also seemed to have frozen into place.

"I have a new lizard I want to try out," the Prelate continued blithely. "It will be ready in three days, which should be enough time for them to make a report and then be arrested for spying."

The Seneschal bowed. The Prelate frowned at Longinus and the others. They were all still frozen in disbelief.

"Well? Well? Dismissed. Dismissed!" the Prelate snapped, waving a hand at them. "Run along, and go report to the old cow in Damsport."

They all once again touched their foreheads to the marble ground and quickly walked out of the throne room. Longinus felt dizzy. He hoped Cruikshank and Adelma were making better progress.

CHAPTER 35

After they left the Wall, Cruikshank and Adelma went to see the potential site for disrupting communications between the Dividing Wall and the Great Gate that led down to Azyr the Lower. Cruikshank found it suitable for her purpose.

By that time, they had been walking for a while, and the sun was out in full force. Cruikshank was growing thirsty and was keen to get some shade.

"Alright," Adelma said. "I been following you all this time, but we're gonna do it my way for a bit."

"And what way is that?" Cruikshank asked.

"We go to where the sailors and smugglers go, see what gossip we can gather about the place. Could be there's something useful."

"That works for me, so long as I can sit somewhere in the shade with a drink."

Adelma grinned. "Finally, you and I are on the same page." She turned to their escort. "Take us to Sookadeen."

Cruikshank vaguely recognised the name. It was an area in Maksur not far from the Great Gate.

The guard looked startled. "Sookadeen? That's not... it isn't an area remotely appropriate, given your Azyrian connections. I can take you somewhere more—"

"Couldn't give a rusty anchor about what you think is appropriate," Adelma replied. "Take us there."

"If you're after refreshment, I can certainly recommend more—"

"Appropriate places?" Adelma asked. "Listen, it's pretty simple. Either you take us there, or you give us directions so we can get there ourselves, and you can go back to Reheeme on your own."

The guard looked decidedly unhappy.

Adelma smirked. "Correct me if I'm wrong, but since we're guests of Reheeme and Jabir, that means we got a close enough connection to them to exceed your studs. So you need to do as we say."

The guard looked surprised. Cruikshank mirrored his expression.

"What?" Adelma said. "You think I weren't paying attention all them times we had to fanny about when we crossed paths with people in Tarwa? Well, I was. So do as you're told."

The guard nodded stiffly. "Very well." He turned to the rest of the guards in their escort. "Stay close."

Adelma rolled her eyes and turned back to Cruikshank. "Don't see why he thinks we need them to stick close if I'm around."

Cruikshank smiled, surprised to find she was enjoying herself. "He obviously feels like he needs protection," she said with a wink to the guard. "Don't worry. We'll protect you."

The guard didn't seem to take the joke well.

"Oh, lighten up, lovey," she said. "We're teasing you."

It didn't take them long to reach Sookadeen. There were far more foreigners in that part of Azyr than anywhere they'd been so far. As they walked through the streets, Cruikshank saw some milkskins from the north—men and women with the slanted eyes and golden skin from beyond the Jade Seas and even a couple of Damsians. Cruikshank and Adelma smiled and exchanged quick greetings with the other Damsians, enjoying the reminder of home.

Sookadeen was still as dry, cracked, and poor as the other parts of Maksur they had seen, but there was something reassuringly familiar about the sight of drunks and foreigners. It felt almost like Damsport, although it was missing quite a few pickpockets and cutthroats to really feel like home.

"I ain't never been here before," Adelma said, "but I heard it's where all the sailors come while they wait to head back out to sea. Will be a good place to get some gossip and information. I like to know the lay of the land before I go charging in."

"Funny," Cruikshank said, "you strike me as the kind of person to charge first and get information later."

Adelma grinned. "I know. Takes a lot of work to build that kind of reputation, but you'd be amazed at how useful it can be. 'Course, there are many times I do just charge and think later—awful fun." She winked. "Ah, that place there will do for us. You wait out here," she added to the guards.

They had come to a stop outside a shabby-looking drinking hole.

"I'm not sure that's necessary," said Cruikshank. "It's pretty hot out here."

"I also shouldn't leave you alone," the guard added.

"Nope, you ain't coming in. Go drink somewhere else if you need to get out of the sun, and be here when we get back. Now come on," Adelma added to Cruikshank.

Cruikshank gave the guard an apologetic look, but in truth, she wasn't sorry to be rid of him for a bit. She wasn't entirely sure he was only keeping close for their protection, and she wondered if he would be reporting back to Reheeme. The question was why Reheeme might want to keep tabs on them.

Inside was dark and smoky, so much so that it was hard to see. And it wasn't the smoke of incense like at the races but good old-fashioned pipe and cigar smoke. Cruikshank realised that she was craving a cigar, and she pulled one out.

The place was foul, which didn't bother her too much. Foul places were common as rats in Damsport, and while she didn't particularly favour them, she was very much used to them.

Great swathes of fabric hung from the ceiling in the Azyrian way, although it was hard to identify the fabric's colour, filthy as it was from the thousands of dirty hands that had touched it. The fabric hung limp and ragged, torn in many places, seeming suspended in the heavy smoke. The walls were streaked with greasy black marks, and the floor was sticky underfoot. All around them, people spoke in low voices, a constant hum that filled the large room.

Adelma led the way, weaving with the confidence of one at home in this kind of establishment. She selected a table against a wall, so they had as uninterrupted a view of the room as the drapes would allow. The table was low in the Azyrian fashion, the wood so scraped and scuffed it looked as if someone had attacked it with a blunt metal tool. The floor cushions were torn, their pale, yellowing stuffing sticking out in thick tufts.

Adelma sat down, cursing Azyrians and their low tables. Cruikshank followed suit. She did her best to ignore the smells of sweat, stale alcohol, and urine that wafted up from her cushion as she sat on it. A waitress came to their table, a cantankerous-looking old Azyrian woman with missing teeth.

"Two of the strongest drinks you have in this shithole," Adelma said.

"Seriously?" Cruikshank lit her cigar. "We need to be clearheaded—this isn't the time to be getting drunk." She exhaled with a satisfied sigh.

Adelma gave the cigar a pointed look.

"What?" Cruikshank asked.

"It's alright for you to crave cigars but not for me to crave a drink?"

"Smoking doesn't affect me."

"'Course it don't. That's why you become even more of a grumpy, sour pain in the arse than usual if you don't get to smoke for a bit."

"I don't become grumpy when I can't smoke," she said defensively and, she realised, insincerely. "Anyway, that's different."

Adelma snorted. "You keep telling yourself that. Reality, though, is that you're addicted to cigars, and I'm addicted to alcohol. Difference is that I'm aware of it and comfortable with it."

Cruikshank gave her a cold look. "Please don't use cheap, two-bit philosophy to try to justify your drinking." Adelma's little speech was far too reminiscent of things her father used to say, and she could feel her hackles rising.

Adelma laughed. "I ain't justifying nothing. I don't care what you think. You, however, you got a chip on your shoulder. My drinking ain't had any negative impact on the mission, has it? And it won't have, 'cause I got it under control. So you should leave it alone." She paused. "Your mother drink?" She narrowed her eyes, scanning Cruikshank's face. "Ah, your father."

Cruikshank's mouth narrowed to a thin line.

"You know, people are just people, even if they are parents," Adelma said.

Cruikshank crossed her arms. If this was Adelma's attempt at justifying being a drunk while raising Tommy, Cruikshank wasn't going to have any of it.

The waitress returned, plonking down two goblets of something so strong that Cruikshank felt pretty sure she could get drunk on the fumes.

"Excuse me," she called just as the waitress was leaving.

The woman turned back, scowling.

"Do you have something like an ale or a beer? Or even some wine?"

The waitress gave her a look as if Cruikshank had just demanded her firstborn, and she skulked off without replying.

"Friendly," Cruikshank said.

Adelma took a sip from her drink, and she gave a small cough as she swallowed. "That's strong," she wheezed.

Cruikshank gave her a dark look. "Tommy deserves better."

Adelma put her drink down. "I ain't never drunk with Tommy. When I'm with him, I'm sober and I'm as good a mother as I can be. And you ain't got the right to judge me. You're lucky you're not a mother, you know. People seem to think they're entitled to tell you the way you should behave when you're a mother. Nobody cared a whit what I did before Tommy. Then he comes along, and all of a sudden, everything I do is fair game for everyone to judge. I make short work of that, let me tell you."

Cruikshank took a drag on her cigar, not quite sure how she wanted to respond. She was all too aware of how judgmental people could be with mothers. It was something she hated, and she felt deeply uneasy at the fact that she had just taken part in that kind of judgement. She took a deep drag on her cigar.

"I never wanted to be a mother," Cruikshank said at last.

Adelma shrugged. "Me neither, but Radish wanted it so bad…" She waved a hand in the air, and for a moment a deep, weary sadness sank into her features. Then she smiled—a completely genuine, light-her-whole-face smile. "And now my Tommy's the love of my life."

Cruikshank watched her through the haze, adding to it as she blew a plume of smoke. It was so easy to reduce Adelma to her brutish exterior, and Cruikshank was surprised to find the woman had a good head on her.

"For what it's worth," Cruikshank said, "I'm really, truly sorry for the way things turned out with Radish."

"Thanks." Adelma downed the contents of her glass. At that moment, the waitress returned with something vaguely resembling ale. Cruikshank took a hesitant sip. The drink was tepid and had more in common with cat's piss than actual ale, but it would do.

"Radish gave up the life for Tommy, you know," Adelma said, fingering her empty goblet between her fingers. "Wanted Tommy to be given the best possible start."

"Do you ever consider giving up the life?" Cruikshank asked.

"'Course I do. All the time. But see, thing is, I do that, and I know what will happen. I'll get into fights. I'll get drunk all the time. And worse, I'll resent Tommy. Smuggling… I don't know. It keeps me level. The sea, the excitement, the people… I figure best way to look after

Tommy and give him an example in life is to be true to who I am, and I'm a smuggler to my core, so…" She shrugged. "Anyway," she said, her voice hardening, "I ain't a walking set of ovaries, and just 'cause I got Tommy don't mean I should start being some idiot's fairy-tale idea of a mother. Swanning about like a milksop, dispensing insipid thoughts of love for the world…" Adelma shook her head. "That ain't for me. And if you ask me, that's no good an example to give my boy. Can't expect him to live his life and not someone else's if I can't even do that, can I?"

Cruikshank took another sip of the cat's piss posing as ale. "I don't think I agree with even a quarter of what you said, yet somehow, overall, I agree with you."

Adelma was endlessly frustrating—a drunk, a walking disaster, but Cruikshank found herself feeling genuine respect for the woman.

"Ha!" Adelma said, laughing. "'Course you do, because I talk a lot of sense. Longinus had the right of it when he said modesty's for amateurs. That one's got his head screwed on. Now, enough of all this chitchat. I'll show you what I do best."

She downed the rest of her drink, gave a quick cough, and stood up.

***

Cruikshank stayed at their table, as Adelma had suggested, while the large smuggler went to work the room, drifting from one group to another, buying drinks, clapping shoulders, and letting out raucous laughter.

After observing her for a bit, Cruikshank pulled out the notebook and pen that she always carried with her. She wanted to do some calculations to estimate the amount of air they should insert into the pipes and, from what she had seen of the dials, how much of a leak they could get away with before triggering the alarm. It didn't take long for the numbers to come to heel beneath her pen.

She was almost done when a hand shot out from behind her and snatched her notebook away.

"What the…?"

Adelma had returned, her face and body tenser than a coiled spring.

"What happened?" Cruikshank asked.

"Put that away immediately," Adelma murmured. "We got to leave. *Now.*"

Cruikshank took her notebook back, closing it so the figures would be hidden from sight. She had no idea what Adelma had found out, but she knew better than to question her now.

They were headed for the door when a man came across their path. Cruikshank couldn't tell exactly where he was from—his skin was somewhere between a Damsian's and an Azyrian's, and he had very harsh angular features. His head was shaved, his hands heavily tattooed.

"What?" Adelma snapped.

"Just wondering who this is you just picked up," the man said.

"That's my cousin," Adelma replied. "I told you, if I hear anything about a Damsian machinist, I'll send word. And like I told you, I want to get back to my ship."

The man didn't seem to listen and kept staring at Cruikshank. "What about her?" His eyes narrowed. "If you're going to try to cheat me out of my reward for finding the machinist…"

Cruikshank kept very, very still.

Adelma burst out laughing. "That's my cousin. She's a bit simple, so I keep her with me—people don't always treat the simple ones kind. She don't speak much, and she thinks even less. If she's a machinist, then I'm the Marchioness of Damsport."

Cruickshank took on what she hoped was simpleminded expression. The man kept looking at her.

"She got hit in the head when she were a baby," Adelma added.

"She was writing something in her notebook before," the man said.

Cruikshank sensed Adelma's hands moving carefully to her axes. She managed to collect saliva in her mouth, and she shook her head, letting it dribble slowly onto her chin, pretending she wasn't aware of it. The man's lip curled back in disgust.

"Leave her be," Adelma grunted. "She likes to write her name and do some drawings in that thing. It keeps her happy and out of my hair."

The man hesitated then grunted. "Well, let me know if you see that machinist," he said, turning away.

It was all Cruikshank could do not to sag with relief.

"Will do," Adelma said curtly. She grabbed Cruikshank roughly by the arm and marched her out the door.

"What was that about?" Cruikshank asked as soon as they were outside, but Adelma kept moving, dragging Cruikshank behind her at a fast pace. Her face was like thunder.

"Hey!" Cruikshank said. "Adelma, what's going? What about the guard?"

"Forget the guard," Adelma replied, looking quickly around her and bustling Cruikshank down a side street. "We got to lose him. We've been set up."

"Set up? What setup? By who?"

"There's rumours that the Seneschal is after a Damsian machinist staying in Azyr. Rumour says there could be a pretty profit to be made for whoever brings him that machinist because he needs help with a machine he's having built."

Cruikshank went cold.

"We wasn't brought here for the rebellion," Adelma continued. "That's why Reheeme didn't know we were coming. That's why none of the rebels knew about us before we got here."

"Greased gears," Cruikshank muttered. "If you're right, that means Jabir is working with the Seneschal. And Rory and Longinus and Rafe are in the palace with them both."

Adelma nodded darkly.

251

CHAPTER
36

Jabir was sweating profusely by the time they left the throne room. He fancied he could still feel the Seneschal's gaze on him, like hot coals boring into his back.

He heard footsteps behind them, and he knew without looking that it was the Seneschal. His gut twisted with panic. His one hope was that the Seneschal would still need him to get Cruikshank and Adelma. And when Jabir got his hands on the two women, he would make them regret messing up his plans.

"My apologies for what happened just now," the Seneschal said as he reached their little group.

His voice was soft and so low it didn't echo against the marble. It gave the odd impression that he was a part of the palace while everyone else was intruding.

"As wise and benevolent as our leader is, he can sometimes be... volatile. His Radiance didn't really mean what he said. You are honoured guests of Azyr, and His Radiance wishes for you to continue enjoying your stay in our wonderful city. Please have no concern about your safety, and give no more thought to all this nonsense about spying. You are still free to visit the palace if you wish, but you aren't expected to do any kind of report, and of course, none of it will be construed as anything other than a visit to one of the world's greatest palaces. For now," the Seneschal continued pleasantly, "I need to have a word with Jabir, if you don't mind."

Jabir's bowels turned to water.

"Of course," Reheeme said. Her face betrayed nothing, but Jabir knew she would be burning to know what that was about. And suspicious. Not that it would matter if he couldn't survive his interview with the Seneschal.

Jabir followed the Seneschal, not looking back. He felt as though his entire world were unravelling beneath his feet so that soon he would be falling, falling down into the abyss. He had to find a way out, and quickly.

As he followed the Seneschal, his mouth grew dryer, which made it tricky to answer the Seneschal's polite chitchat. By the time they reached the Seneschal's office, Jabir was so tightly wound that his shoulders and neck felt like they had fused into one painfully tense mass.

The Seneschal took a seat, gesturing for Jabir to take the chair opposite him. Slaves brought tea-making implements, and the Seneschal prepared the tea himself, his long, spindly fingers moving dexterously.

Jabir found himself wishing he had left Reheeme alone to conduct her rebellion. It would have failed, quietly fizzling out. He might not have gained a place on the Council, but he would be alive and well. Instead, he had overreached himself, grasping for a position and money and power, and he was on a knife's edge, about to lose everything. He had to pull himself together. He had to be calm and assertive, show the Seneschal he was someone to be respected, not a fool who had just failed on a momentous scale.

Jabir realised the Seneschal was watching from beneath hooded lids, and a jolt of fear stabbed through him.

"Your Grace," he began, but the Seneschal stopped him with a raised hand.

"I am preparing the tea," he said softly, his tone reproachful.

Jabir closed his mouth abruptly, waiting as the Seneschal continued his careful ministrations. Finally, the Seneschal handed him a cup of dark, smoky liquid.

"I was under the impression all five Damsians would come to the palace today," the Seneschal murmured, stirring honey into his tea. His voice was almost drowned out by the pounding of Jabir's heart.

"Yes, I tried to bring them all." Jabir cursed himself for sounding so weak, as if he was making excuses. "They were all supposed to come," he tried again. That was barely better. "But Cruikshank and Adelma decided to leave before I was back from last night's excursion."

The Seneschal frowned. "Are you trying to imply this is my fault?"

"No, no, not at all," Jabir rushed to reply.

The Seneschal sipped his tea. "This is all so disappointing." His voice remained soft and low, yet the level of threat he was able to inject was incredible.

Jabir's blood felt like ice in his veins. "I'm so very sorry," he babbled, his voice sounding shrill to his ears. "They will all be at my house later today. Perhaps you could—"

The Seneschal shook his head slowly, tutting. "My dear Jabir, surely you're not suggesting that I do your work for you?" His voice grew unctuous, almost oily. "After those initial discussions we had, I thought I could rely on you. You seemed capable, reliable. I have, by the way, made preparations for my end of the deal. The funds have been made ready, as is the paperwork to bestow your title and place on the Council. The studs have been made. And now you have only brought me half what we agreed to, and you are expecting me to do the rest for you?"

Jabir licked his lips. "The three Damsians in the palace could be arrested now and—"

"What value exactly would those three Damsians have to me?" the Seneschal asked, a diamond-hard edge creeping into his voice. "The only value of those Damsians is to ensure that they don't take word of Cruikshank's capture back to their filthy city. If I take them and not the Head Machinist, what exactly am I getting out of it?"

The Seneschal put down his tea and crossed his long fingers, bringing them against his chin as he regarded Jabir.

Jabir swallowed, his mind groping blindly for something, anything. "We could send a message," he began, but the Seneschal shook his head.

"Too much potential for error."

A knock interrupted them. A slave appeared. "A message from His Radiance," he said in a low voice, never taking his eyes from the floor.

The Seneschal silently extended his hand, and the slave hurried over, handing him the note. The Seneschal dismissed him with a wave, scanning the message. Tension appeared between his eyes, the skin pinching in displeasure or frustration, Jabir couldn't tell which.

The Seneschal tucked the note away in a pocket and took his tea once more. "I shall choose to trust you one last time. My personal guards will come to take the Damsians from your house. It irks me to have to do someone else's job, and even more so to make the arrest in the open with the risk of word getting out. But the stakes are too high. I need the Damsians, and I need that machinist. The submersible can't be finished without her input. So I will fetch the Damsians with my own guards. But," he added, his voice dropping several degrees and decibels so that it was barely audible, though the very sound of it made Jabir shiver. "If so much as one of the Damsians is missing, you will be fed to the Prelate's new lizard. It goes without saying that all offers of a title and wealth are retracted. I think you keeping your life is reward enough, given your level of incompetence."

Jabir nodded shakily. He heard a clinking and realised that his hands were shaking so badly that his cup was knocking against his saucer. He placed it hastily back on the table.

"Really, Jabir," the Seneschal said, his voice returning to its normal level. "There is no need to shake like that. I have full confidence in your ability to ensure all five Damsians remain in your house as you have said they will. I have no doubt you have already set up measures to make sure they do exactly as you say."

Jabir nodded again, not trusting himself to speak.

***

The moment Jabir reached the ground level and felt the sunlight on his face, he was overwhelmed by both relief and blind panic. He breathed deeply as he hurried along, doing his best to calm the rising sense of hopelessness. Gathering all five Damsians in his house within the next few hours should have been child's play, but with the damned foreigners and his wife, it was like herding cats. He needed to ensure that they did nothing other than wait in his house until the Seneschal's guards arrived.

He was hurrying along, and as he turned a corner, he almost crashed into Rory.

"Rory," he said, heart pounding. "What are you doing here?"

"We split up so we could cover more ground."

"I see, I see," Jabir replied.

"So what was that about?"

"What?"

"The Prelate saying we were to get arrested in three days. And then the Seneschal saying he didn't mean it. You reckon that's true?"

Jabir swallowed down a sigh of relief. All was still well—she still trusted him enough to talk to him.

"And why were you talking with the Seneschal?" she asked.

Jabir had a flash of inspiration then, an idea of pure genius, and he took Rory's elbow, ushering her forward. He put a finger to his lips, glancing around him. "We are betrayed," he murmured.

"Who? What betrayal?" Rory asked, face intent.

"I'm so glad you found me. I wasn't sure how to get a warning to you and the others—it's Reheeme," he added, his features twisting into a mask of anguish.

Rory frowned. "Reheeme?"

Jabir winced internally at her expression. Was it too farfetched? Still, too late to go back. "I got a message late last night, a warning. I met with Oma in secret. She was the one who told me that Reheeme has been in secret communication with the Seneschal. I'd noticed something odd of late. I-I thought she was having an affair, but it turns out she was going to the palace. She was seen a couple of times."

Rory looked at a loss. "Why would she do that? I thought she were obsessed with her revolution, her parents' legacy…"

Jabir shrugged miserably. "She has apparently sold out the revolution to the Seneschal in exchange for a place on the Council and a lot of money. I'm sure she doesn't care about the money, but a place on the Council would give her a lot of power. She might be aiming for her own advancement rather than that of the city. I don't know… I don't know…" Jabir gave a deep sigh.

Rory didn't seem taken in by the emotional display, and he reined it in a little.

"I also don't know what she has said of our involvement yet," he continued. "The Seneschal wanted to talk to me about a matter of taxes, but there was something odd in his questions, in the way he spoke to me. The fact that we haven't yet been arrested is a good sign, but I don't think we have much time."

Rory looked panicked. "Longinus and Rafe are still with Reheeme. We have to warn them."

"Yes, and as soon as possible." Jabir was careful to keep his face looking worried, but inside, he was triumphant. It had worked. Reheeme had mentioned earlier that morning that she wanted to go to the Prelate's fighting pit to pay her respects to the place her parents had died. The situation was perfect: she would leave the Damsians alone with Jabir to go back home and wait for the Seneschal's guards.

Jabir felt almost giddy. It would still work out. "We need to move quickly," he said. "We need to get warning to the others and get Cruikshank and Adelma back to the safety of my house as soon as possible."

"Is that wise?" Rory asked. "Reheeme will know to find us in the house."

"If we don't go back to the house, it will look suspicious. We should all regroup there long enough to figure out our next step."

And long enough for the Seneschal to send his men.

CHAPTER
37

Jabir and Rory found Reheeme giving Longinus a detailed tour of the palace's laboratory while Rafe looked on. Rory didn't want to risk tipping Reheeme off, so she had to bear the agonising wait while Reheeme finished. She knew the three had already had a reconnaissance of the Eastern Trade Gate, the one the rebels would be opening to allow the main force to sweep in.

Reheeme had also earlier taken them near the areas where Kadelta might be held. At least now they had a rough idea of the palace layout. However, having seen the number of Watchmen about, Rory felt quite sure they could only successfully get Kadelta out if the rebellion was raging, keeping most of the Watch focused elsewhere.

The laboratory tour was just for show, in keeping with their official cover of an alchemical exchange. After what felt like an age, the tour finished, and the party headed out of the palace.

"Did you see all you needed?" Jabir asked Reheeme.

She gave him a curt nod and turned to the Damsians. "I have another engagement, so I will let you get back to the house without me."

Rory resisted the urge to glance over at Jabir, not wanting to give anything away. Few things would be as pressing or important as what was going on at the moment. What engagement could Reheeme possibly have, if not to go see the Seneschal?

"We'll head back to the house and meet you there. Take the elephant to come back, then," Jabir said gallantly to Reheeme. "We can go back by foot. We have enough of an escort."

Something shifted in Reheeme's expression—she mellowed into a smile. "Thank you," she said, placing a hand on his arm.

Rory was a little thrown by the display of warmth. A final moment of guilt or some impressive acting?

"Oh, it's nothing," Jabir said. "It will give the Damsians a chance to see the lay of the land from a different viewpoint."

"Yes, of course," Reheeme replied. "You're right. Well, safe journey back."

"Shall we?" Jabir asked, gesturing for them all to step forward.

They set off, flanked by a heavy complement of guards.

"Have you had a chance to warn them?" Jabir asked Rory in a low voice.

They were crossing the vast white expanse before the palace. Rory shook her head, squinting against the heat and the sun.

"What?" Rafe murmured, never taking his eyes off the guards.

"Reheeme betrayed us to the Seneschal," Rory whispered, not daring say more until they were out of the palace.

They walked in silence, and somehow, the space between the outer palace wall and the palace itself seemed even bigger and hotter than before. It took eons to reach the outer wall, and Rory was wiping her forehead by the time they got there.

Once they were out of the palace, Longinus turned to Rory.

"Tell us everything."

Rory eyed Jabir's household guards who were escorting them back.

"You can trust them," Jabir said.

"How d'you know they don't work for her?" Rory murmured.

"Because I'm the one who pays them."

Rory nodded. That, at least, made sense. She quickly explained everything to Longinus and Rafe. "We need to find Cruikshank and Adelma and get them back to the house."

"That's not a good idea," Jabir said. "Let me send some people to go look for them. I don't want to jeopardise your safety at this point. It would be better if you stayed in the house. Cruikshank and Adelma will be coming back there anyway, and if they come back while you're looking for them, you'll waste time."

"No," Rory replied stubbornly. "We're going after Cruikshank and Adelma, and that's all there is to it."

"I agree," Rafe said. "And waiting in that house, we'd be sitting ducks."

"Even I concur," Longinus said. "And much as she has all the grace of a lumberjack when she fights, Adelma is ruthless in her efficiency, and I would feel better for having her by our side."

"Alright," Jabir said, raising his hands in a placating gesture. "How about this. Let's go to the house and see if Cruikshank and Adelma are already back. There is no point going after them without checking first. And then we can head out with more guards. I'm not taking any chances."

"Fine," Rafe said.

Rory nodded.

They walked on in silence. Rory took the time to mull over the last few hours. Reheeme's warmth earlier still felt weird, and something else was bothering her. If Reheeme had always planned to betray the rebellion, why had she insisted the Damsians meet Oma? That didn't make sense.

All this was just based on Jabir's word. Rory sidled a glance at him. She had always thought more of him than of Reheeme, especially after the incident with Terrell, but was she willing to trust him that much?

She gave Longinus and then Rafe a look, hoping to communicate that something wasn't right. She didn't want to say anything with Jabir listening. Maybe stopping by the house wasn't such a bad idea after all. She could pull both of them aside and tell them what was troubling her.

Rafe seemed to understand what she was about, giving her a tiny nod before walking up to Jabir, taking his arm and drawing him into a low conversation. They spoke too softly for Rory to hear, but Jabir looked serious, listening attentively. He glanced back over his shoulder at Rory and Longinus but quickly went back to his conversation with Rafe.

Rory felt a surge of gratitude for Rafe's understanding. It was both comforting and unsettling how fast he seemed to have learned to understand her.

Rory murmured her misgivings to Longinus, never looking at him, so that they just looked like they were walking side by side. The general noises of the street easily drowned out her voice for anyone not standing right next to her, so Jabir and the guards wouldn't hear a thing.

Longinus listened to her thoughtfully, nodding slowly. "For all her enormous failings," he whispered, "Reheeme isn't stupid. She has made mistakes—of that there is no doubt—but why would she have taken us to see Oma to try to resolve the stalemate? It would have been in her best interests to keep us away."

"Exactly."

"Right. I say get Cruikshank and Adelma, and we find a way to disappear. Then we reassess. But we need to get away from both Reheeme and Jabir until we can figure out who we can trust."

Rory nodded. "I agree."

Part of her wanted nothing more than to creep out of Azyr and head back to the safety of Damsport. But the thought of leaving with so many Azyrians enslaved and so many Maksurians without proper access to water left a bad taste in her mouth. Which was odd. She was a thief after all, and creeping away like a thief in the night was what she did.

Rory sighed. She missed Cruikshank. The machinist would know what to do. Once they were all together again, things would make more sense.

***

They reached the house without incident. The moment the door opened, Rory rushed in to see if Cruikshank and Adelma had returned. But the servant at the door informed her that they hadn't been seen since heading off that morning.

"Fine," Rafe said, following behind Rory at a less frantic pace. "I'll go upstairs and fetch my helmet, and then I'll be ready to go after them."

"I'll come up with you," Rory said, "I want to get my lucky dagger."

It wasn't a completely made-up excuse—she did have a dagger that she'd stolen when she was a little kid, and she had left in her room, not wanting to risk an Azyrian pickpocket lifting it from her. But she also wanted to go upstairs alone with Rafe so she could explain her misgivings.

She gave Longinus a quick glance and knew that he'd guessed her meaning.

"Well, *I* am ready," Longinus said. "A good assassin is ready for all eventualities. I shall wait down here."

He adjusted his ornate gloves, which Rory knew to be an ingenious tool for spraying his deadly skin poison. She also realised that he was offering to act as a lookout, in case anyone else came into the house behind them.

"I need to get something from my office," Jabir said.

Rory nodded, wondering if this was real or some way to get a message out.

"We need to hurry," she whispered to Rafe as they climbed up the steps.

She heard Jabir order some refreshment for Longinus.

As soon as she and Rafe entered their suite, Rory quickly brought him up to date on the misgivings she'd shared with Longinus about Reheeme's betrayal.

Rafe nodded slowly. "I've been thinking along the same lines. It was one reason why I wasn't comfortable with the idea of staying in this house. The thing that bugs me is that I can't understand the motivation for Reheeme betraying this revolution any more that I can understand the motivation for Jabir lying about it."

"If Jabir's lying about it, maybe it's to cover up the fact that *he's* the one who plans to do the betrayal."

"Possibly, but then we're right back to the reason for us being here. If he was going to betray the rebellion, why bother to contact the Marchioness or even pass on Kadelta's message?"

Rory froze, an idea forming in her mind—something about Kadelta and his machine—but it vanished like mist in the morning when she heard Cruikshank's voice.

"They're back!" Rory exclaimed, turning and rushing out the door.

She crashed into Terrell, almost knocking him off his feet. She caught him, steadying him. "You alright?"

The boy put a finger to his lips, gesturing for them to be silent. "Come with me," he whispered. "You can't go down there. Come quick."

"What? Why?"

"Because the Watch is coming," Terrell replied, a panicked edge creeping into his voice. "Quick, quick!"

He tugged on Rory's arms, pulling her away from the corridor that led back to the internal courtyard.

"The Watch?" Rafe asked.

"I saw the master put out a signal," the boy whispered. "And just now, I overheard the master's personal secretary say the foreigners would soon be taken away. The Seneschal's personal guards are coming for you. You have to hide!"

Rory felt a chill on hearing the Seneschal mentioned. She heard Longinus talking to Cruikshank and Adelma, telling them that Rory and Rafe were just upstairs.

"We have to warn them," Rory said, heading down the corridor.

"No time!" the boy wailed. "Come, come quick, or I won't have time to hide you."

There was a loud pounding downstairs on the door. Someone opened it.

"The boy is right. We have to hide," Rafe said, grabbing hold of her other arm.

Footsteps rushed in downstairs. Rory stood frozen to the spot, unable to move at the thought of leaving the others behind.

"If we get taken, we can't do anything," Rafe said urgently. "We have to *go*!"

He dragged her away, following Terrell, while downstairs, Adelma roared in anger.

CHAPTER
38

Longinus had been pacing for what felt like an eternity, even though it had only been ten minutes or so. He had checked his poison spitter twice, made sure his sword came smoothly out of the scabbard and, of course, ensured that his clothing was nice and straight and as it should be.

The latter might have seemed superfluous, but Longinus firmly believed in the importance of being well turned out when facing difficult situations. It allowed one to be calm, to feel prepared, and if nothing else, it gave an impression of confidence, which was always beneficial.

When the door opened to reveal Cruikshank and Adelma, Longinus let out a relieved cry, hurrying over to them.

"Thank the gods you're back," he said just as Cruikshank began to speak.

He shook his head. "No time. We are betrayed."

"I know," Cruickshank replied. She looked around. "Where are Jabir and Reheeme?"

"Reheeme is back at the palace, and Jabir is in his office."

Cruikshank took him by the arm. Longinus noticed that Adelma was tense, looking around her with both her battle-axes ready, as though she expected an attack.

"The Seneschal is after me," Cruikshank told Longinus in a low voice, also looking around. "They need me to complete the submersible. That's why Jabir had us brought here without Reheeme knowing. Nothing to do with the rebellion."

Longinus was thunderstruck.

"Where are Rory and Rafe?" Cruikshank asked.

"Upstairs."

"Good. Let's go get them—we're leaving."

Someone pounded at the door. Longinus froze.

The entrance door crashed open, heavy boots ringing against the floor. Guards poured in through the doorway like water out of a jug. Adelma bellowed in anger, drawing her axes. Longinus released the safety catch on his poison spitter.

"Stay clear of me," he warned Cruikshank and Adelma.

"Buy me some time," Cruikshank said.

Longinus was aware of her darting off behind him.

He swung his arm wide, sending a spray of poison at the charging guards. He aimed high, for their faces. The first line staggered as instant paralysis began on contact with the poison. They collapsed.

There was a brief moment of confusion as the guards behind them stumbled over the bodies. Longinus sent a second spray of his deadly poison, but the guards were well trained, and they protected themselves with their armoured forearms, the poison running harmlessly off the metal.

Guards reached him and Adelma. Longinus was forced to step back and draw his sword to deflect a spear. It was an easy move. He parried, leaning into the movement so that he swung around against the body of the spear, pulling up right in the man's face. He touched his spitter to the man's cheek, sending him down. Behind him, Adelma hacked and grunted, and Longinus did his best to convince himself she was chopping wood. An awful metallic tang filled the air.

Longinus engaged a second opponent, drawing him in so he could administer his signature move that would send the man's sword clattering away. Something hissed past his face. Before he could wonder what it was, there was a second hiss, and something sharp pricked his neck. He staggered back away from his opponent, who didn't press the advantage. He heard Adelma make incoherent, angry noises, but they sounded distorted as though deep underwater. Then a heavy thud, and she fell silent.

Longinus had the presence of mind to push the safety catch back on his spitter, dropping his sword. Icy numbness washed over him. His mind seemed to detach from his body, calmly analysing the effects to determine if he was dealing with poison or a narcotic. He turned away from the guards, his thoughts slowing. He had enough time to decide it was a narcotic and to see Cruikshank once again in the internal courtyard before he felt his legs give way beneath him.

He fell slowly, slower than a leaf on the wind, and the floor rushed up at the same time, meeting him at great speed. Cruikshank shouted something, but it was drowned out by the low roar that had taken up in his ears. Longinus's last thought as the world went dark was to hope that Rory would be able to get away.

The space Rory and Rafe were hiding in was so narrow it would have made a coffin look roomy. They were in a cache beneath the floorboards, lying sideways, face-to-face, the space barely wide enough for both of them in that position. The wood at Rory's back seemed to press into her, and her legs were placed at an awkward angle, tangled up with Rafe's, so that a cramp was already creeping up her left calf.

From somewhere in the house, she could hear voices and heavy footsteps. Rafe's breathing was loud in her ear, almost as loud as her own. She kept catching herself trying to hold her breath for fear that someone might hear them through the floorboards.

Rory could feel Rafe's heartbeat too—her arms were wedged awkwardly between them, and his heart beat against her right forearm. She had never been so close to him, and she could smell his skin—sandalwood, soap, and leather mixing with the old, musty smell of their hideout.

Light filtered through the gaps between the floorboards, striping Rafe's face. Waterfalls of tiny particles of dust drifted through the slits of light, never seeming to land anywhere.

A male voice shouted that they had to be in there somewhere. Rory exchanged a look with Rafe. Footsteps drew nearer.

Rory held her breath as she heard the loud creak of the floorboards above them.

Someone was in the room.

Boots rang out heavily against the wood. A scrape as the person stopped, turned around, and went back in the original direction. The boots were directly above Rory and Rafe now.

A heavy sprinkling of dust fell onto Rory's face. She clamped her fingers over her nose to stifle a sneeze.

Rafe gave her a worried look, and Rory gazed back at him, unable to tell him that the sneeze had passed. She didn't even dare move her arms to gesture that she was alright.

The boots continued past them.

Rory heard the sound of a cupboard being opened. Hands rummaged inside the contents. Something metallic fell on the ground.

To Rory's horror, it had some kind of lid that went rolling slowly across the floor. It turned just as it reached the space above her face, spinning on itself faster and faster until it fell into place with a dramatic, cymbal-like rattle.

The lid straddled the gap between floorboards exactly over Rory's face. The stripe of light over her eye disappeared, replaced by shadow.

The man grunted, and Rory heard his boots heading over to the lid. She held her breath, her heartbeat so loud and fast it seemed impossible that he wouldn't hear.

The boots stopped just behind Rory's head. Had he seen?

Fingers reach down at the edge of the lid. The fingers paused.

Rory felt sick.

The pad of one of his fingers was touching the gap between the floorboards. The fingertip was pale compared to the rest of the man's dark skin. His finger was so close to her face she could see that the nail was dirty and needed trimming.

Time seemed to grind to a halt while Rory's heart beat madly on. He had seen them—it was impossible that he hadn't seen them. She could picture his fingers digging at the floorboard edges and ripping it up, the light flooding in the cache, while she and Rafe blinked, trapped.

And then the fingers curled around the edge of the lid, lifting it up. The boots rang out, heading back towards the cupboard.

Rory felt dizzy with relief.

The man continued to rummage about the room, moving back and forth but without stopping above them again. Furniture scraped along the floor, and more items were scattered about.

Finally, his footsteps retreated towards the door. "Not here," the man shouted.

"I don't care if you have to rip this place apart," Jabir's voice came back, shrill to the point of hysteria. "They are in here somewhere. Find them. *Now!*"

The man grunted, and the door slammed. Rory heard his footsteps retreat.

Rory exchanged a look with Rafe, who looked as relieved as she felt. Almost immediately, the cramp in her leg decided to remind her of its presence. Her entire left leg seized up, the cramp travelling all the way up to her bum cheek. She winced against the pain.

When she hadn't heard anything for a few minutes, she tried to shift her leg. It made a faint scraping sound, and she froze. Rafe shook his head, his eyes anxious. Rory nodded and stopped moving. She didn't think anyone was still in the room, but the discomfort wasn't worth the risk. She ground her teeth against the twisting pain in her leg.

Rafe squeezed her hand awkwardly, only managing to grasp it between the tips of his fingers. His eyes were a question: was she alright? She gave a quick nod, lying. No point in worrying him any further.

Time trickled past. Still, they heard nothing but distant voices in the house. The pain in Rory's leg was growing unbearable, and it was all she could do not to cry out as the muscles twisted, the cramp crushing them in a viselike grip. Rory looked at Rafe then down at her leg. He nodded. She tried to shift it again, while he tried to move to give her more space. But the wood behind her pressed harder, and no matter which way she tried, she couldn't change position. She couldn't even brace herself on her arms, not with Rafe there and the floorboards so close to her.

Sweat was beading on her forehead, and she closed her eyes, wondering how much longer she would have to bear it.

"D'you think he'll interrogate the boy?" Rafe murmured in her ear so low she barely heard. His breath tickled her cheek.

"I don't know," Rory murmured back.

It hadn't occurred to her until they were already in the cache that by accepting Terrell's help, they had potentially signed his death warrant. He was too young and far too frail to be able to withstand any kind of interrogation, and if Jabir found out he had helped them, the boy would certainly be killed.

Rory clung to the hope that Jabir would consider him too young, too unimportant to bother with. That was the greatest gift of being small and insignificant-looking—it was so easy to be overlooked.

That Jabir was a traitor was a given, but Rory wondered if Reheeme was involved too. She didn't think so—not given the woman's behaviour. If she was involved, she'd have tried to stop Cruikshank and Adelma from going to the Dividing Wall, instead making sure all the Damsians stayed together.

It was no coincidence that they had been attacked when they had all been in the house. An attack with one or two of them missing ran the risk of word getting back to

Damsport, and that would mean consequences. There was no doubt that, had Cruikshank and Adelma been at the palace, they would all have been arrested there and then.

Darkness gradually fell, the light that seeped through the floorboards growing fainter and fainter. It had been hours since Rory and Rafe had heard any sounds, but neither of them dared to move. If anyone was left in the house, it would only take a little noise to give the two of them away.

All was silent save for Rafe's breathing and his regular heartbeat. Rory was surprised to realise that she didn't feel scared or awkward being so close to him. In fact, his closeness felt weirdly natural, which was a relief. The last thing she needed was a case of the awful awkwardness she had felt around him before.

It wasn't until it was pitch-black that Rory heard footsteps again. The night was so complete that she couldn't even see Rafe's outline. She tensed immediately, feeling Rafe's body do the same.

"It's me, it's me," Terrell whispered. "They've left."

Nothing had ever sounded so sweet as the floorboards being pried up.

CHAPTER

40

Cruickshank came to, her mouth as dry as sandpaper. Her head was pounding almost to the point of feeling swollen, as if she had a bad hangover. Her eyes were still closed, but beneath her, the ground seemed to rock and lurch, making her feel nauseous. She wondered whether she was on a ship.

She opened her eyes—or at least, she tried to, but they were gummed together. Slowly, her right eyelid peeled open, her upper and lower lids separating slowly and painfully. She felt something crusty in her lashes and raised a hand to rub her eyes. Her fingers flailed clumsily at her forehead, struggling to find her lids. Then her left eye opened.

Her vision was blurry, and all she could see was a dark-orange, almost rusty colour. And then a face, too fuzzy to make out, appeared before her.

"You're awake," the voice said.

Cruickshank blinked, her mind working so slowly it was like thinking through molasses. It took eons for her eyes to focus enough to identify the person before her.

Kadelta.

Or rather, what looked like the ghost of the man who had once been Kadelta. He was gaunt, his cheeks hollow, his cheekbones standing out painfully. His eyes were sunken deep within dark-purple rings that stood out starkly against his pallid skin. Despite having the brown skin of a Damsian, he had grown so pale it was obvious he hadn't seen the sun for months.

"Here, I'll get you water," he said, disappearing from sight. Cruickshank blinked again. Everything felt slow, as if she were moving through water. She tried to push herself up, but the ground lurched beneath her, and she fell clumsily back down, nauseous and dizzy. It was all she could do not to be sick.

"Here." Kadelta handed her a cup of water.

When she tried to close her fingers around it, her grip was too weak, and if Kadelta hadn't been holding the goblet, she would have dropped it. He brought it up to her mouth and tilted it so she could drink.

The water felt heavenly, running down her throat and soothing the raw sandpaper feel. It seemed to help with the nausea and fuzziness too, and by the time she had finished the water, she felt a little better.

Cruikshank looked around her. She wasn't on a ship at all but in some kind of underground workshop. A screen obstructed her view, but she could see past it to a furnace and, close to that, a workbench with the kinds of tools used by a machinist. Voices hummed in the distance, and the familiar sound of metal grinding against metal rang out.

Beneath Cruikshank was a lumpy mattress placed straight on the floor, which was made of dark rust-orange brick, as were the walls and ceiling—a far cry from the dazzling white marble of the palace.

Kadelta returned with more water, and she drank gratefully.

"It will pass in a bit," Kadelta said. "The effects only last a few hours after you wake up."

Cruikshank remembered then the sharp prick at her neck that had preceded the darkness. She winced at the memory—Adelma fighting valiantly and collapsing as a little dart sank into her neck and Longinus following just moments later. She wondered whether Rory and Rafe had managed to escape, and she feared the fate reserved for Longinus and Adelma.

Cruikshank closed her eyes. Worrying about them would achieve nothing. What she needed was to keep her head screwed on until she could find a way to get out of the workshop.

"I'm so sorry," Kadelta whispered. "I'm so sorry. They've held me for months. I stalled, and I stalled. I worked as slowly as I could. But when I got to the point where I genuinely couldn't continue without your vibration-activated valve… I tried to replicate it, but I couldn't get it to work, and neither could any of the other machinists. I never thought that when I told them about it, about you… I wanted to buy more time and maybe to get word out about my situation. I never thought they would bring you here too. I'm sorry. I'm so sorry—"

His voice was thick with emotion, his eyes huge and haunted, and Cruikshank quietened him with a hand on his arm. "It's alright, lovey. It's alright. It's not your fault."

She noticed then that he had holes in his eyebrows, like an Azyrian slave. "They even gave you holes at your eyebrows."

"They made me a slave when they took me. That way, I legally belong to the Prelate, and anything I create is also legally his property."

"I'm surprise they care about the legality of anything," Cruikshank growled. "And I guess I can expect a similar fate in the not-too-distant future."

Kadelta winced and looked down, shame written all over his face. "I'm so sorry."

Cruikshank pushed herself up from the lumpy mattress. Kadelta helped her until she stood on uneasy legs. Whatever they had stung her with, it was damned effective. She had no idea how long she had been out, but her body ached all over as though she hadn't moved for a long time.

She took a deep breath, drawing strength from the familiar smell of soot and hot metal. If she closed her eyes, she could almost pretend she was back in her own workshop.

Almost.

At least she was in a workshop, which was familiar territory. Cruikshank staggered forward like a drunk, stumbling past the partition.

The workshop was enormous. The ceiling was arched and low, each arch supported by pillars. Cruikshank guessed she and Kadelta were somewhere in the foundations of the palace, given the low ceiling and the lack of windows. Alchemical globes cast a yellow light on the space while more powerful globes shone white, illuminating the workbenches.

And of course, in the middle of it all, hanging over a large pool of water, was the submersible. It was suspended from the ceiling by thick cables and buttressed by a wooden cradle. Ladders and platforms had been erected all around it, and a large handful of machinists worked on it, crawling over it like insects. Cruikshank noticed they were all Azyrians, and she wondered whether they were free workers or slaves.

"I give the orders, and they carry them out," Kadelta said. "If I had been working on my own, it would have taken much longer. As it is, it's virtually finished."

"Does the water lead anywhere?"

Kadelta nodded. "There's a tunnel to the underground river. That's how the submersible will be moved to the sea." As he spoke, his left hand found the little finger of his right hand, which was crooked, and rubbed it. He had limped when walking out from behind the partition, which Cruikshank didn't remember from before. She didn't ask what had caused the limp or the crooked finger, dreading the answer.

"Any chance of a person getting out that way?" she whispered as low as she could.

Kadelta shook his head. "There are bars on the tunnel entrance. They can be lifted up, but only from the Seneschal's office."

Cruikshank pressed her lips into a line. Even if she could get the bars open, the workshop was under guard, and they weren't likely to let her construct a breathing apparatus. No, there would be no escaping that way.

Looking around the workshop, she saw only one way out—the door that was heavily guarded. Overhead was a large hole through which the exhaust for the furnace and other tubes disappeared, but they filled the hole completely and were likely to be boiling hot.

Cruikshank's eyes ran to the furnace. Furnaces could be made to overheat and explode.

The door opened, interrupting her thoughts.

"The Seneschal," Kadelta whispered.

The Seneschal's skin had the smooth, velvety look of a wealthy Azyrian, but it was the only soft thing about him. His eyes were black pools in the yellow light, the studs at his eyebrows gleaming menacingly, and his smile was more a showing of the teeth while his eyes remained cold and reptilian.

"Well, Kadelta," the Seneschal said. "It seems to me you have everything you need now. Cruikshank will make your valve, and you will finish my submersible, yes?"

Kadelta gave a jerky nod of his head. The Seneschal looked pained.

"I'm sorry," he said, his voice like caramel. "I didn't quite hear you." He tilted his head so that his ear was pointing at Kadelta.

"Yes, sir," Kadelta said in a shaky voice.

The Seneschal smiled again, all white teeth and cold eyes. "Glad to hear it."

He glanced behind him, and Cruikshank saw that a small Azyrian man had followed him in. He had on simple clothing, and his studs were common semiprecious stones. Some palace official, Cruikshank guessed, but not one very high up the ladder.

"Just one more detail to attend to," the Seneschal said.

Cruikshank saw that the little man carried a needle, and she braced herself as two guards grabbed her arms. She certainly wouldn't give any of them the satisfaction of protesting or squirming. She looked at the Seneschal defiantly. If he thought he would break her, he had another thing coming.

"Ah," the Seneschal said. "I do admire spirit. So brave. So... stupid."

The little man stepped up to Cruikshank. He had a tic in his left eyelid that caused it to blink continuously. "Hold still," he said, pinching the skin at Cruikshank's right eyebrow.

CHAPTER
41

Rory felt like a piece of origami as she gingerly stretched out, pulling herself out of the cache. She winced at the sharp pricking under her skin as blood flowed back into her limbs. Rafe followed after her, groaning with relief as he massaged blood back into his arms and legs.

He turned to Terrell. "Thank you for saving us," he whispered, gripping the lad's shoulder. "Really. Thank you. We won't ever forget it." His face was more serious and earnest than Rory had ever seen it. Terrell gave a small smile and shrugged as if it was nothing.

The house was perfectly silent, the darkness around them complete save for the small circle of light from Terrell's alchemical globe.

"Jabir has gone?" Rory asked in a whisper.

Terrell nodded.

"And Reheeme?" Rafe asked.

"She's back," a familiar voice said beyond the light.

Rafe tensed and immediately drew out his knives. Rory drew her sword more slowly, her numb fingers clumsy. Reheeme stepped into the light, raising both hands to show she was unarmed. She looked like a different person from the prickly, arrogant woman Rory had grown to dislike so thoroughly. She still had the flamboyant clothing and the brightly dyed hair teased out into a flamelike halo around her head, but her face could almost have been another person's. Her eyes were dull, her expression that of someone who'd resigned herself to massive loss. Her shoulders slumped, and she no longer looked like she imperiously commanded the room.

"I'm not here to harm you," Reheeme said, sounding exhausted. "I had nothing to do with your friends' arrest. In fact, I had nothing to do with any of it. I had no idea, *no* idea about Jabir…" Her voice drifted off. She seemed to sag beneath the weight of it all. "All the Sons and Daughters have withdrawn their support. All of them. The Seneschal promised to lower taxes, and he threatened to seize all assets of anyone who continued to have anything to do with the rebellion after that. He didn't even threaten their lives. He lowered the taxes, and that was enough for most of them. The rest left to save their assets." Her voice was heavy with defeat and bitterness.

"Right," Rory said, growing angry. "Well, if you're expecting us to feel sorry for you because a bunch of toffs turned their coats at the first sign of trouble, you're wasting your time. Our friends got taken to the palace because *your husband* betrayed us to the Seneschal. So we got better things

287

to do than stand around listening to you moan about your precious Sons and Daughters of the Elephant. And for the record, the rebellion was never about them. It's about the Maksurians and the Lower Azyrians and all the slaves kept in Tarwa. And *they're* all still here."

"They'll never trust me," Reheeme said miserably. "How can I lead them?"

"So what if you can't lead them? They already got a leader. This ain't about you. It's about helping them get free from oppression. When will you get it, woman? This revolution ain't about your parents or you or Jabir. 'Course they don't trust you—you don't even acknowledge that this is about them!"

Reheeme looked ashen. "Oh god," she said in a low voice. "Oh god, I've been such a fool." She sank into a chair. "There was a painting my parents treasured, a painting of both halves of the city. My mother used to tell me that one day she'd have it repainted when all of Azyr's walls had been torn down."

"She probably knew that what she and your father were working towards wasn't about them—and that it was far, far bigger than that," Rafe said. "Maybe their focus was on the people of Azyr."

Reheeme nodded slowly. "I was so focused on the people who betrayed my parents," she whispered. "I forgot about the people who didn't."

"Well, now you see the light," Rory said impatiently. "But we ain't got time for this. Rafe, we need to get to the palace."

"Yes, and for that we need to see Oma again," Rafe replied.

"I can help you with that," Reheeme said.

"We don't want your help," Rory snapped. "Look where it got us."

Reheeme stood up. "You need my help to get word to Oma. And I am not going to stand by passively while the rest of Azyr rises up. One way or another, the rebellion *will* happen, and I *will* be a part of it." She added in a softer tone, "I do also want to right the wrong that was done to your friends."

"Could you please give us a moment?" Rafe pulled Rory aside. "Listen," he whispered. "I know you don't want to hear this, but she's trying to make amends."

Rory jutted her jaw. She didn't want to listen, not when Longinus, Cruikshank, and Adelma were in danger at the palace. She wanted to hit someone. Several people. And she wanted to leave this god-awful city.

"Think about what we need," Rafe urged, grabbing her arm and squeezing hard enough to be painful. "We need to get to Oma and Urzo. We need to get into the palace. We *need* Reheeme's help. Swallow your anger down if you have to—push it aside—but don't be stupid enough to refuse help when we have so few resources."

Rory nodded grudgingly, knowing that he was right. The key was to get to the palace and then to Longinus and the others. The rest didn't matter.

She turned back to where Reheeme and Terrell stood. "Terrell," she called. "Do you trust her?"

Terrell's eyes widened, and he looked up at Reheeme.

"Don't worry about her," Rafe said. "She can't do nothing to you even if you say no. She lays a finger on you, and I'll beat her bloody."

"I don't beat children," Reheeme said through clenched teeth.

"No, but you keep slaves," Rory said coldly. "And you threatened Tommy with spears. Don't think I forgot about that." She knelt before Terrell so she was level with him. "You can whisper it in my ear if you want. Rafe and I value your opinion. Can we trust Reheeme?"

Terrell hesitated. Then he whispered "Yes. She's not nice, but she's not like Jabir. She gave all the house slaves their freedom."

Rory's eyebrows rose, and she realised that Terrell now had simple metal studs at his eyebrows.

"So?" Reheeme asked.

"You gave all the slaves their freedom?" Rory said, standing up.

"Of course. I've dismissed every single servant and guard from the house. I've given the slaves studs and sent them on their way with money. We are completely alone except for Terrell. I didn't want to risk anyone reporting back about you to Jabir. The house is under surveillance, as you'd expect."

"Surely releasing your slaves will alert them that something is going on," Rafe said.

"They already know something is going on," Reheeme scoffed. "They know I was heading the rebellion. They

290

know everything. The only reason I'm still here is they're hoping I'll lead them to you. They have to find you before you can report back to Damsport on what happened here. The Marchioness would be justified in interpreting this as outright aggression against Damsport and therefore in calling her allies in a war against Azyr. The Seneschal can't afford that, which means you must be found quickly."

Rory nodded. That all made sense.

"But the Seneschal also has an ace to play," Rafe said. "He holds Cruikshank, Adelma, and Longinus. He knows we won't skip town. He must expect that we will come for them, and he has Jabir—which means that he knows what our plans were until now." He looked meaningfully at Rory. "All the more reason for us to work together."

"Yes," she replied with a warning look at Reheeme. "For now, we work together."

"Good," Rafe said.

"I can get word out to Oma," Reheeme said, "but the real trouble will be getting you two to the races without anyone seeing you."

"That I can arrange," Rory said.

Rafe looked surprised.

"The spider," Rory explained. "Cruikshank brought it."

"A spider?" Reheeme asked.

"You'll see," Rory replied.

***

Rory thanked every god she could think of when she found Cruikshank's spider. The abdomen had been tipped out of its trunk, the legs scattered about as though it had been attacked and torn apart.

Moonlight streamed in through the window, highlighting the mess that was Cruikshank's workshop. Whoever had searched the room had pulled out all of her belongings, all her tools, scattering her sketches all over the floor. Rory and Rafe worked by moonlight, retrieving all eight legs of the spider.

Cruikshank had shown her how to assemble and disassemble the spider for travel, and Rory hoped she would remember all the delicate manipulations needed to attach the legs to the body.

"Will it work?" Reheeme asked, watching from the doorway.

"Let's hope so," Rory said.

Reheeme stood alone, Terrell having been sent to Oma. Reheeme had given him a proper servant's livery rather than his slave's tunic. The boy had also been given an inconspicuous message, something that wouldn't draw any attention or concern when the city Watch stopped him at the Wall.

It wasn't unusual for late-night messages to be sent, but given the recent arrests, it stood to reason that the Watch would have been instructed to look out for anything suspicious.

Rory was getting to work when the spider's abdomen caught her attention. A bit of paper stuck out of a tiny gap at the top of it, near the head. Rory grabbed hold of the paper by thumb and forefinger and tugged.

"What is it?" Rafe asked, coming to look over her shoulder.

Hastily scrawled on the paper was a note beneath a set of numbers and calculations as well as two addresses. Rory recognised Cruikshank's handwriting, and her chest tightened with emotion. She ran a finger over the writing, then she pushed the feeling away, steeling herself. Getting emotional wouldn't help Cruikshank.

"This is to ensure that we can operate the drills for the communications pipes," Rafe said, taking the note and peering at it. "The address will be the drilling sites, and this is so we can properly calibrate the air bubble to be inserted."

Rory frowned. "How d'you know all that?"

"Cruikshank explained the drill to me. And I've always liked machines. They're logical. We'll need to give this to the Risen along with the drills if they're to smuggle us into the palace." He pocketed the note. "I'll go look for the drills while you keep on with the spider."

It took Rafe a while to find both drills. That done, he helped Rory reassemble the spider. It took them a good couple of hours before the spider was finished.

Rory climbed on, testing the controls to check that the legs worked alright.

"We're good to go," she said to Rafe.

***

As soon as she found herself on the spider, running across the rooftops, Rory immediately felt better. It felt like home, riding the spider, even though the rooftops stretching around her looked foreign. In the distance, grey-pink dawn was creeping across the horizon, and the air was cool. The spider moved rhythmically beneath her in a way that was familiar and comforting.

Rory wished she could go fast enough for the wind to stream through her hair. She wanted to rush the spider at full speed towards the palace, straight to Longinus, Cruikshank, and Adelma.

But of course, that wasn't possible. They were going to the racecourse, not the palace, and Reheeme was walking in the street below while Rory and Rafe followed along the rooftops on Cruikshank's spider.

Rafe leaned to the left so he could see over the edge of the roof to where Reheeme was walking. As he did, he grabbed hold of Rory's waist to steady himself. "Turn right," he whispered.

Rory followed the direction.

Down below, Reheeme walked alone. She had slipped out of the house into empty streets that seemed quiet and asleep. But from the rooftop, Rory and Rafe had seen two shadows detach themselves from the rest and follow Reheeme.

"They're still following," Rafe murmured.

Rory nodded. They had discussed how best to deal with anyone tailing Reheeme.

After a couple more turns, they reached a long, straight road that was wider than the rest. Rory stayed as close as she dared to the roof edges—close enough for Rafe to lean over and catch a glimpse of the street below but not so close that she would be easily visible to Reheeme's tails.

"Here goes," she whispered.

She pushed the spider forward, its legs clicking in a blur of speed against the rooftops. The increase in speed was abrupt, and Rafe was jerked back, snaking an arm around her waist to steady himself. For the briefest of moments, Rory enjoyed herself, racing across rooftops with Rafe's arm around her. It only lasted for a heartbeat or two before her grim determination returned.

The spider jumped gap after gap between roofs, barely needing any steam to close the narrow spaces. The roofs were stone, so the spider's legs made only the faintest noise.

At the end of the street, Rory stopped. She and Rafe undid their harnesses and slid off. Rory found a suitable spot and secured her grappling hook, the silk line trailing down into the dark of the alley below.

"Be careful," Rory whispered.

Rafe winked at her. "Don't worry about me. Love interests always survive, don't they?"

Rory was so taken aback that she fumbled her reply, making an indistinct noise. What about their agreement that there was nothing going on? But then, Adelma had said he'd been looking for her at the ship's prow.

Rafe vaulted gracefully over the edge of the roof, lowering himself down. Rory pushed the whirling confusion out of her mind. There was absolutely no time for this— although she was surprised to realise that his silly comment had cheered her up a touch, giving her a little release from the awful tension in her stomach.

She watched the shadows down below, but Rafe had settled in place, and the darkness was impenetrable. He was down in a narrow side lane just off the street Reheeme was walking on. Rory heard footsteps, and she moved to another edge of the roof to see Reheeme approach.

Behind her, the two shadows still followed. As agreed, Reheeme wasn't looking back or checking how close her followers were, to give the impression that she didn't realise she was being tailed. She carried a knife as a precaution, and Rory could see from the way she held her right hand against her chest that she had it out and ready to use.

Rory wondered if Reheeme had it in her to kill.

Reheeme passed the lane where Rafe was hidden. A few heartbeats later, the two shadows passed Rafe.

Rory saw the shadows move, a sharp dart outwards like a snake striking. She heard a muffled cry then the wet tearing sound of blade meeting flesh.

"Clear," Rafe called in a low voice.

Footsteps again. Reheeme returned. "Who was it?" she whispered.

Rafe dragged one of the bodies out into the street, where the watery predawn light caught the man's face. Reheeme bent over him then straightened. "Someone who works for the palace. Nobody I know." She spoke completely dispassionately, without a hint of the emotion most people felt on seeing death.

Rory decided then that Reheeme would be able to kill someone. That made her respect the alchemist a little more, despite all her shortcomings.

"If we see anyone else, we'll take them out the same way," Rafe said to Reheeme.

Reheeme nodded. "We haven't got that far to go now."

Moments later, Rafe was hauling himself onto the rooftop. He removed the grappling hook and coiled the line up.

"Efficiently done," Rory said as he handed her the hook and line.

He gave a shrug. "All in a day's work." His voice didn't have its usual sardonic ring. Death was obviously not something he took lightly, and he would be just as aware as Rory of how much rode on whether they succeeded or failed.

As Rory pushed the spider forward once more, her mouth set in a grim line. They would get Longinus, Cruikshank, and Adelma out of that palace if it was the last thing they did.

CHAPTER

42

Longinus awoke to find himself in a cell. His mouth felt furry and tasted of something awful—a not-unexpected side effect of having been forced to consume a narcotic. He still felt the detached calm that had begun as soon as the dart hit his neck, and he ran through a slow inspection of his body, checking for pains or anything else that might suggest an injury or poison.

His thoughts weren't their usual sharp selves—no doubt the aftereffect of the narcotic. If not for the fact that he regularly consumed a concoction of his own making to diminish the effects of poisons and narcotics, he would have been in a far worse state.

Longinus moved his head slowly, blinking as his vision focused. There were metal bars straight ahead of him, running from floor to ceiling, while the other walls were of rough stone, the same pale colour as at the racetrack.

Adelma was also in the cell, sitting with her back against the wall to the left, her knees bent. She had tilted her head back until it rested against the wall, and her eyes were closed. Longinus guessed that she had already woken in order to move into that position.

The walls looked old and were heavily marked. A number of people had carved their names, one just next to Adelma's head. Rings were screwed into the back wall, chains and manacles dangling from them.

Somewhere in the distance, Longinus heard the squeaking and clanging of bars being opened and slammed shut. The place smelled of animal dung, sweat, and oiled leather, and the air tasted old and stuffy.

He hoped that Rory and Rafe had somehow managed to get away. He took comfort in the fact that they had been on the upper floor. If Rory had made it up to the roof, she might have been able to jump to another roof and hide there. He was less certain about Rafe, but the lad was a Varanguard and capable. Longinus was careful to keep his thoughts away from examining the possibility of Rory being trapped in a cell similar to this one. That would achieve nothing, and it wasn't a possibility he felt capable of facing.

Instead, he focused on the one thing he could do: try to find a way out of this rather regrettable situation.

"Adelma, are you alright?" Longinus croaked. The words scraped painfully against his throat, and he wished for a drink of water.

Adelma nodded, lowering her head and opening her eyes. "You?"

"I think so." Longinus pushed himself up and winced as pain lanced through his body. He ached all over, and his hips and back were particularly tender as if he had been thrown around like a rag doll. He carefully felt his legs, arms, and ribs for any signs of broken bones, but it seemed all he had where heavy bruises. And that was bad enough.

Barbarians. Clearly, these people knew nothing of the procedure when drugging a gentleman. It certainly did not involve manhandling him like a sack of potatoes.

"I was probably too heavy for them to throw me around much," Adelma said, giving him a faint grin.

Longinus nodded. Occasionally—very rarely—but occasionally, there were disadvantages to being a man of lithe and elegant form. This seemed to be one of those rare occasions.

"Where do you think we are?" he asked.

Adelma shrugged. "Dunno. Nowhere good."

"You're in the cells beneath the Prelate's arena," a deep voice answered.

Longinus started, looking out beyond the bars. Across a narrow walkway was another row of identical cells. In the one opposite them, a man sat close to the bars, his back leaning against the wall. His arm rested on the horizontal bar level with his shoulder, his hand dangling languidly out as though he were enjoying a pleasant evening rather than sitting in the Prelate's prison.

The prisoner had the heavily scarred and even more heavily muscled look of a fighter—or, in less generous terms, a brute. Part of his right ear was missing, as was his front tooth, and a nasty scar slashed across his mouth, twisting and puckering the skin. An ugly patchwork of scars covered his left eye, and his hair was scraped short. He wasn't Azyrian, but Longinus couldn't place his features or his accent. He certainly wasn't from near Damsport.

"You mean we'll be put out to fight?" Adelma asked.

The prisoner shrugged. "Depends on your worth. If you're worth something, you'll be sent to fight. If you're worth nothing, you'll be sent to die with the lizards. Either way, it will be entertaining for them upstairs. And either way, it'll end in death for you."

"When?" Longinus asked.

The man shrugged.

"You fought before?" Adelma asked.

"I have," the prisoner replied, a note of pride creeping into his voice. "I've done several fights, and I survived them all. In fact, I'm the longest surviving pit fighter." He grinned. "I'm one of the Prelate's favourites."

Longinus nodded. He moved a little to get a better view of what was outside his cell. The passageway they were in was lined with rows of cells, and he saw a solid-looking door at one end but no guards, which gave him hope.

Alchemical globes of abysmal quality lit the passageway, casting a sickly yellow light that didn't so much illuminate the passageway as create shadows.

"Has anybody escaped from the cells?" Longinus asked in a low voice.

The prisoner raised both eyebrows then brayed with laughter.

"I fail to see what's so funny," Longinus sniffed, glaring at the man.

"Shut it," someone shouted farther down. "Trying to sleep here."

Longinus stood up and went to sit next to Adelma. They stayed in silence for a time, and after a while, the prisoner across from them moved deeper into his cell to lie down.

Once he felt quite sure they were unobserved, Longinus decided to show Adelma what would undoubtedly be their trump card. His gloves were gone, of course, as was his poison spitter, but he had other, secret resources.

"There's something you need to know," he whispered. Adelma raised both eyebrows, waiting for him to go on. "I keep small weights in the hems of my clothes."

"You what?" Adelma replied loudly.

"Shhh," Longinus hissed, gesturing for her to be quiet. He glanced over at the prisoner opposite them, but he didn't seem to be paying attention.

"I have small weights in the hems of my clothing so that the fabric will always drape properly even if it gets windy or I make an abrupt movement."

Adelma looked bemused. "The hell are you on about?" she said, thankfully this time keeping her voice low.

"You know," Longinus replied patiently. "Say there was a gust of wind. It would move my tunic like so." He showed her, flicking and crumpling the bottom of his tunic. "I would look all in disarray. With these weights, if there is a gust of wind or I make a sudden movement, the drape of the tunic remains." He placed the fabric back as it should be. "See?"

Adelma's face was perfectly blank. "I still have no idea what you're on about."

Longinus clucked his tongue. "Never mind," he whispered. "It's dark. You probably can't see very well…"

"Sure, that's what it is…" Adelma whispered back, the sarcasm in her voice as subtle as lime green matched with orange.

"Anyway, that's not important," Longinus whispered impatiently. "The point is that I am a professional assassin to my very core. Which means that I take every opportunity to arm myself, and I arm myself in the most ingenious and elegant of ways." He grabbed the hem of his tunic, feeling between his thumb and forefinger for the weights. "Each of the weights is, in fact, a small poison capsule. They are quick and effective, with a relatively fragile shell, but they need to be swallowed to work. They can be crushed and shoved into someone's mouth, for example. Crude, I grant you, but they will kill in a matter of seconds. Then I also have this piping there." He pointed to the piping on his sleeves. "It is, in fact, filled with a narcotic in powder form. It needs to be inhaled or swallowed to work."

"Ain't it dangerous, carrying all them poisons on you?" Adelma whispered.

"I have been careful to ensure that none of them can accidentally cause me harm. They all need to be ingested or properly altered before being effective. The narcotic, in fact, needs to be activated using… using…"

"Using?" Adelma frowned.

"Well, you have to understand that I needed to come up with something common enough that it could be found anywhere but not so common as, say, water, because the possibility of being drenched in water is very real. And I can't risk the narcotic being activated at the wrong time. So… I know this is crude beyond measure, but in times of great need, great sacrifices need to be made."

"Blood?" Adelma asked.

"Heavens no, woman. Are you mad? No. It's… ammonia. It can be found in alchemical lamps, or… or… micturition."

"Right. Handy, that."

Longinus was relieved she hadn't taken that as an opportunity to make stupid comments.

"What's micturition?" Adelma asked. "Some other kind of powder you got or something?"

Longinus sighed inwardly. *Of course she hasn't understood. It would have been too much to hope that I would be spared the indignity of having to explain.*

"Urine," he said, wrinkling his nose in disgust.

Adelma coughed and snorted and generally failed to keep her laughter completely silent. Longinus glared at her.

"It is a highly elegant solution," he snapped, only just managing to keep his voice low. "As I said, in times of great need—"

Adelma slung an arm around him, pulling him in. "I feel so much closer to you now that I know you're into getting pissed on." She was laughing so hard she barely managed to get the words out.

"Unhand me, woman." Longinus disentangled himself while Adelma continued laughing silently, holding her belly with both hands.

"Oh, no more, no more, I don't think I've ever laughed this hard," she wheezed.

Longinus gritted his teeth, rolling his eyes to the heavens. As if their current troubles weren't trying enough. "Glad to see you find our predicament so entertaining," he said icily. "Might I remind you that we are facing the very real possibility of death?"

"Exactly. Gotta laugh about something, 'cause crying ain't an option." She finally calmed down. "All jokes aside," she whispered, "that is excellent news."

Longinus nodded, pleased that she was finally behaving like a rational being. "When they come to give us food," he whispered back, "I can poison the jailer, grab his keys, and let us out."

"Save your poison. If he gets close, I can knock his lights out easy enough."

"You sure that's wise?" Longinus asked with a frown. "What if someone hears you attack the jailer?"

"We got to chance it," Adelma said. "We got nothing going for us but the element of surprise. Until we get some weapons, we save up your poison 'cause it's the only card we got. Let me see about that jailer. I'll get the better of him."

She cracked her knuckles.

***

It didn't take long before a jailer arrived. In the distance, Longinus could hear footsteps and voices, and he smelled something that could possibly be food. His stomach made the kind of noise he had come to associate with Rory. He nodded at Adelma, readying himself.

Now was the time.

Of course, they had no idea what they would come up against once they disarmed the jailer, but they would have to improvise. Adelma's idea of saving the poisons was good.

It took a few minutes for Longinus to realise something was wrong. He could hear voices, footsteps, bowls scraping against the floor—he even overheard a prisoner complain about the food. The thing that was missing as glaringly as his neighbour's front tooth was the sound of slamming bars.

"They're not opening the cell doors," Longinus murmured. "The jailer doesn't even sound like he has keys." And indeed, there was no telltale jangle of keys to match the jailer's footsteps.

Adelma shook her head, looking grim. "We'll wait. There'll be another opportunity."

By the time the jailer reached them, Longinus could tell he had no keys on him. His belt was empty and his clothing limited only to a grimy pair of trousers with no pockets, leaving his chest and taut, round stomach bare. Longinus swallowed his disappointment.

The jailer set down two bowls just outside the bars. They were small enough to fit through the bars and filled with something that made the street food in the poorest area of Damsport seem appetising.

"At last," Longinus said. "You do realise, good sir, that the service in this establishment is atrocious?"

The Azyrian simply grunted and walked away.

"I should be eager to speak to your supervisor," Longinus called after him. "I would like to lodge of complaint about the quality of the slop you have the gall to call dinner. Or breakfast. Or whatever meal this is supposed to be."

"Quiet!" a deep voice shouted, too far away for Longinus to see.

The lights outside his and Adelma's cell went out.

"Well, that's better," Longinus said to her. "Now at least I don't have to see it as well as taste it."

CHAPTER

43

The main doors to the race building were closed. Reheeme knocked against a smaller door cut within the main doors, and she said a few low words—a password, Rory guessed. She glanced back at the rooftop where she had left her spider. Cruikshank's spider, she corrected herself. She didn't like the thought of leaving it alone in a foreign city, but they had no choice.

Rory adjusted the hood of the cloak Reheeme had given her. Rafe had received a similar one, so they could both hide their faces. The fabric was thin and light, but the hood cast a deep shadow, and Rafe's face was completely hidden from sight.

The door opened, and Reheeme slipped in. Rafe followed, then Rory. Reheeme paid the man who had opened it, the coins gleaming dully in the early-morning light. They stepped quickly through the courtyard. It was odd to see the racetrack so quiet and empty. The air smelt of machine oil and dung, attesting to the two kinds of vehicle, alive and steam-powered, that had piled in earlier that evening.

Inside the building, the atmosphere was eerie. Reheeme held an alchemical globe, lighting their way, but it only made the darkness around them starker. To the left, Rory could see slivers of the arena below through the opening to the boxes. The sand was pale, almost grey in the morning light. It had been carefully raked, the blood hidden beneath a fresh layer.

Rory shivered at the thought of the countless men and women who had died down there. Even as they walked through the empty passage, past the dark nooks where people met and talked, there was a quality to the air, something that didn't feel quite empty.

It was a relief when they reached the stairs. Soon they found themselves in the underground passage that led to the gambling den. Rory fiddled with her hood again, careful to keep her head down so her face would be hidden.

They entered the antechamber before the gambling den. It was heavy with muscle for hire, far more than there had been the previous day.

Rory marvelled that her first visit to the races seemed so distant, yet only a day had passed. So much had changed.

"Well, well, well," Petrik said from behind his desk. "I didn't realise you had a gambling problem," he said to Reheeme, quirking an eyebrow.

Reheeme handed him an impressively sized purse. "I prefer no questions."

"Ah. And that's the real key, isn't it?"

The man's manner was different now that Jabir wasn't there, and Rory didn't like it. Petrik's gaze flicked up at Rory and Rafe as he handled the purse, weighing it in his hands. He stood up and came to the other side of his desk, leaning against it as he fondled the purse.

"Isn't the palace after a couple of foreigners?" he asked.

Reheeme produced a second purse the same size as the first. "There. Enough for you not to worry about who is coming or going."

Petrik's smile widened, not reaching his eyes. "Ah. Now, why didn't you offer me this right from the start?"

"Well, I've offered it to you now," Reheeme replied coldly.

She walked past him, gesturing for Rafe and Rory to follow. Rory kept a wary eye on Petrik as she stepped by him, still keeping her face in the shadows. As Rafe passed him, Petrik's arm shot out, catching his wrist. Rory stopped walking, hand flying to her dagger.

Rafe already had the tip of a small blade at Petrik's neck. His hood was still in place, his face hidden in its shadows.

"I say the word," Petrik said through gritted teeth, "and you will die at my feet."

"Probably," Rafe replied calmly. "But I'll be dying in a pool of your blood."

Petrik's face twisted into a semblance of a smile. "You make a convincing point."

"Seems to me," Rory said, "that we can kill each other, or you can take the very sizeable bribe you just received and leave us to lose our money in your den."

Petrik kept his eyes on Rafe, but he raised both hands, releasing Rafe's wrist. "I always found dealing with foreigners to be profitable."

"Glad to hear it," Rafe said, removing his knife from the man's neck.

"Please." Petrik gestured for them to step through the leather curtain.

Rory remembered that the next chamber they would be stepping into was an incinerator, and she shuddered as she followed Reheeme.

Reheeme turned the moment the door closed behind them. "We have to move quickly. He will be sending word to the palace of our presence here."

"Didn't we bribe him not to?" Rafe asked.

Reheeme shook her head. "Petrik will see that as a breach of balance. He has helped us so far by letting us meet in his gambling den. The balance tips in our favour. So now he will redress it by betraying us to the Seneschal. That is how he has survived so long: he is friends with everyone and no one. He keeps everyone on side yet isn't loyal to anyone. Come on. We have no time to lose."

CHAPTER 44

It was all Jabir could do to keep himself calm. He was being held in one of the Seneschal's cells. The space was bare save for a crude wooden table with shackles for wrists and ankles. Jabir had almost lost it when he'd realised there was a runnel around the edge of the table, as if it were a butcher's chopping block. The stench of blood in the air made it clear that the runnel had seen some use.

Beyond the walls, the moaning from the other cells was loud. "Shut up," Jabir called, covering his ears. "Shut up!" He squeezed his eyes shut.

He could feel himself growing hysterical. He had to keep a handle on his panic. Until the remaining two Damsians were found, he could still be of use to the Seneschal, and that could save his life. But if he completely lost it, he would achieve nothing.

Jabir couldn't understand how Rory and Rafe had gotten away. He'd had his place torn apart trying to find them, but it was as though they had vanished into thin air. He *really* couldn't understand it. It wasn't fair. Every time he was about to lay his hands on the Damsians, they split up and shifted and moved, flowing through his fingers like water.

When he heard a key turn in the door's lock, he scrambled toward it. Two of the Seneschal's personal guards appeared, grabbing him roughly. Jabir had never been so happy to be taken away by guards.

"Where am I going?" he asked.

They remained stonily silent as if he hadn't spoken.

After a while, it became clear that he was being dragged towards the Seneschal's office, and Jabir felt a gleam of hope.

The Seneschal remained silent as Jabir was dragged into his office. He sat on his chair like a Prelate throning over a room. His heavily hooded eyes watched Jabir over steepled fingers. The guards shoved Jabir forward so that he stumbled to his knees. His hat had been knocked off back at the house, and he had to push himself back up bareheaded like a supplicant.

"No, no," the Seneschal said, shaking his head slightly. "There's a reason my guards shoved you to the floor. Stay there."

Jabir's face was burning. He lowered himself slowly back to his knees. The Seneschal considered him, and what remained of Jabir's calm evaporated like morning mist.

"I don't know what happened, I simply don't know what happened," he babbled before catching himself and swallowing down the torrent of words that threatened to burst out of him. He knew well enough that excuses made no impact on the Seneschal.

The man regarded him quietly, not even blinking. Jabir felt sweat trickle down his sides. What was it about the Seneschal that was able to make him sweat at a moment's notice?

"I know their plans," Jabir said, suddenly struck by inspiration. "I know where the rebellion—"

"The rebellion is *nothing*." The Seneschal's voice cracked like a whip, and Jabir cringed. "I could have crushed them the minute you came to me if I'd chosen to. I let them continue because it suited my plans. And now that I have spoken, all the so-called rebels of Tarwa will be withdrawing their support, too cowardly to oppose me outright. The rebellion is *over*."

Jabir swallowed a hard, painful lump. The Seneschal was right, of course. He briefly wondered what Reheeme was doing right then, but he pushed the thought away. His wife no longer mattered. Survival was his only concern.

"The Damsians," he said. "I know them. The two that are missing, Rory and Rafe—they won't be running away and leaving their friends in the palace. They will try to continue with the plan to enter the palace unseen and rescue them. I know how they are going to be smuggled in. I know their plans."

Jabir explained about the sewers and the plan to open the old, boarded-up Eastern Trade Gate. He spoke so quickly that his words tripped clumsily over his tongue. The Seneschal didn't interrupt—a good sign. He interlaced his fingers, extending both index fingers and holding them against his mouth as he listened.

"We can lay a trap for them. Let them think they got away," Jabir continued. "Post Watchmen and -women around that part of the palace, and—"

He was interrupted by a loud knock at the door.

"Come," the Seneschal said.

One of his personal guards entered, boots ringing smartly against the polished wood floor. "We have received a message from Petrik's gambling den. The Damsians are there with Reheeme."

Jabir felt a jolt. Of course, they were going to meet Oma and Urzo to arrange the smuggling into the palace. He kicked himself for not having thought of that so he could have been the one to bring the idea to the Seneschal.

"Let me go get them," he said to the Seneschal breathlessly. "Let me take some of the Watch there and drag them back to the palace—"

"Like I had to have you dragged here?" the Seneschal asked. "Do you really think I would leave something so important to you *now*?" He turned to his guard. "Bring them to me."

The gambling den was unchanged despite it being late at night. The same low ceilings, the same spots of red lights beneath which shady figures hunched over cards, their eye sockets turned into black pools of shadows. Time seemed to stop here—day or night, dusk or dawn, it made no difference.

A woman draped languidly on her chair watched them walk past, her eyes following them without her moving her head.

Reheeme led them to the same private room as before. This time, it wasn't guarded, and the light in front of the curtain had been doused, so the curtain was barely visible in the shadows.

Rory wondered who had such a good relationship with Petrik that they were able to have this room whenever they wanted. It clearly wasn't Reheeme, and Rory doubted it was Jabir. Oma, then? But Petrik clearly wasn't a sympathiser to the cause.

Inside, Oma and Urzo were waiting for them, sitting at the same table as before. Rory realised with a pang how much larger the room felt without Cruickshank and Adelma to cramp the space. She spotted Terrell standing behind Oma and gave him a small smile. He smiled back then quickly turned serious once more. He stood with his feet slightly apart and his hands clasped behind his back. Despite his best effort to appear impassive, Rory could see pride written all over his features, and she felt a swelling in her chest for him. He deserved better than to be someone else's property, and now at least he had a chance to be part of something.

"We don't have much time," Reheeme said. "Petrik is probably getting word to the palace as we speak."

Oma nodded as though she expected nothing else. "I have sentries in the room and both sides of the wall. They will warn us if the Watch arrive. Urzo will take you out then."

"Terrell told you of Jabir's betrayal?" Rory asked.

"He did, and it will be remembered," Urzo replied darkly. "When our time comes."

Oma placed a hand on his arm. "Now isn't the time for revenge. What is our position?"

"We've lost all support from the Sons and Daughters," Reheeme said bitterly. "I'm so sorry."

Oma snorted as though this was hardly surprising.

"I spent years and years working on bringing them around," Reheeme said, her voice thickening with anger. "Gaining their trust, negotiating with them. I got their word, all of them. And they left at the first obstacle." Rory could feel the anguish beneath her anger, and she was surprised to find she felt sorry for her. For all that she was an unpleasant woman, Reheeme had been trying to do something good, even if she had displayed a rather surprising level of naivety in thinking the Sons and Daughters would stand by her if their positions and wealth were threatened by the Seneschal.

She hadn't realized that only the poor had nothing to lose.

"Longinus, Cruikshank, and Adelma were all taken," Rory said. "We think the Seneschal is focused on finding us to avoid us sending word back to Damsport. His actions would be justification for Damsport to call on its allies to attack Azyr."

Oma listened to all this, sucking on her pipe. "Wars are never good. They have uncertain outcomes. If we let that happen, there will be more deaths in the Lower than anywhere else."

Rafe nodded. "The best outcome for everyone is that we are able to get Longinus, Cruikshank, and Adelma out of the palace while you successfully manage to rise up against the Seneschal. We are still prepared to help, if you will still help smuggle us into the palace."

"We have the drills," Rory said. "The mechanisms Cruikshank created to disable communications."

Oma's eyes gleamed with interest.

"I can show you how they work," Rafe said.

Rory was still finding it hard to reconcile her idea of Rafe with his interest in and affinity with machines.

"Before we get into those details," Reheeme said, "we are facing a graver problem. Jabir knows our plans. Or at least, he knows the plans as they stood until now. That means they will be ready for us. Jabir knows we'll be targeting the Eastern Trade Gate, so they'll be waiting for us there. We can't open that gate from the inside anymore."

"All the other gates are much more heavily defended," Urzo said.

"Not as heavily as the Eastern Trade Gate will be now," Oma rasped. "Reheeme has a point."

"Which is perfect," Rafe said, eyes gleaming. "The more the Watch is focusing on the Eastern Trade Gate, the less they will be focusing elsewhere. Urzo, can we use the sewers to reach another part of the palace, one far from the Eastern Trade Gate?"

Urzo nodded. "The sewers connect the whole place."

"Great. So what other gate could we target? Where could we come out?"

"The Barraba Gate," Reheeme said. "It's on the other side of the palace, well away from where they expect us."

"We should make a distraction," Rory said. "I know Longinus would never admit to this, but sometimes his alchemical stuff goes wrong, and its explodes. If we can make something what would make noise and smoke, we can make Jabir and the Watch think we're coming out near the Eastern Trade Gate, get them to sound the alarm. All forces will go that way, and nobody will be paying attention to that other gate."

"Perfect," Rafe said, grinning.

Rory felt immeasurably better for having an actionable plan. Sure, there remained the problem of finding Longinus, Cruikshank, and Adelma before they were killed or hurt, and the challenge of getting them out of the palace—to say nothing of the importance of the rebellion managing to go ahead.

But all the same, there was a plan, and she could now see a way through the darkness.

The curtain at the entrance twitched. "The Watch," one of the sentries said. Rory leapt to her feet, heart pounding.

"Urzo," Oma said, "get everyone out of here."

"The Watch are already here, inside the den," the sentry said.

Rory swallowed.

"Our men must have been found out," the sentry said. "We never got word that the Watch had arrived."

"What are they doing?" Rafe asked calmly.

"They've fanned out across the den, and they're going to each table, one by one, looking at the players' faces."

"They know what we look like," Rory said. "Jabir will have told them."

"What about the exits?" Urzo asked.

"Both covered."

Rory edged to the curtain and snuck a peek. The room was indeed crawling with members of the Watch, who were checking each table. They moved in and out of the shadows like slow sharks. Back at the entrance, a thick cluster of Watchmen and -women stood menacingly, their silver armour glowing red from the light.

Rory's heart pounded. They were completely trapped. She saw a Watchman ask a card player to tilt his head to the light, and when the man refused, the Watchman yanked his head back by his hair, making the card player cry out in pain and surprise. The Watchman threw the man back into his chair and continued his inspection, moving to the next player.

The Watchmen and -women were slowly getting closer to the private room Rory and the others were in.

A touch at her shoulder almost had her jumping out of her skin. Rafe stood behind her, and he gestured with his chin at the curtain, asking to swap places with her.

Rory stepped back. "They're getting close, and I can't see no way out of this mess."

"First thing," Rafe whispered, still looking out, "is getting out of this private room."

"We can't go into the main room or they'll see us," Rory said.

"Hmm." Rafe finally pulled back from the curtain. "I think I have an idea." He turned to Urzo. "You've killed before?"

Urzo nodded once.

"Good," Rafe said. "Last thing we need is someone losing their nerve at the crucial point. There will be a lot of blood if all goes well. Here's what I propose."

Rafe explained his plan quickly. Rory nodded, growing excited. It might just work. Rafe spoke with the calmness of someone used to giving instructions in high-stress situations. At no point did he show nerves or even the slightest sign of worry. Rory had been quite close to panicking earlier, but now she found herself feeding off Rafe's calmness.

"Ready?" Rafe asked once he had finished explaining the plan to everyone. He looked at them all in turn.

Everyone nodded.

"Just remember to keep calm and breathe if anything has you worried. I'll be keeping an eye on it all."

Rory knew there was little Rafe would be able to do against all of the Watch outside, and she guessed he had said that to keep everyone feeling confident. She realised, with a wry smile, that it had worked. She could still feel trepidation at the thought of what they were going to do, but a part of her felt reassured by the thought of Rafe's calm presence.

They all got into position.

"Alright, here goes," Rory breathed.

CHAPTER

46

Cruickshank's eyebrows hurt like hell. After they'd been pierced, the Seneschal left, and everyone bedded down for the night. Cruikshank had a fitful sleep, the studs burning worse than if her eyebrows had been covered with acid. She hadn't even been able to smoke a cigar to get a moment of relief—they had all been taken from her. It would have been too much to hope that they would allow their prisoners to smoke in peace.

When the lights came on, Cruikshank blinked blearily. Everyone got up in a slow, sullen shuffle. There were about ten other machinists, all Azyrian, all with holes at their eyebrows. They looked tired and resigned, plodding over to the submersible. Food was brought—a simple curry, but Cruikshank devoured her portion, feeling ravenous.

She waited until she and Kadelta were at a workbench, alone, to finally talk to him. "What is on the studs? They burn like crazy."

"Some kind of alchemical treatment," Kadelta replied. "It's to stop the skin from closing and scarring after they remove them. It takes a few weeks, and the burning goes down gradually. Eventually, they will remove the studs, and you'll be left with holes like mine."

Cruickshank nodded but didn't reply. That made sense—they were marking her as a slave. She also knew she wouldn't be here in a few weeks' time. Either she'd escape, or she'd have completed her valve, after which she would cease to have value. In fact, she would become a liability, because so long as she was a prisoner at the palace, there was the possibility of word getting back to the Marchioness of Damsport. She had no illusions that the moment she stopped being of use to the Seneschal, she would be made to disappear, and quickly.

"Tell me about your submersible," she said.

There might be something in the work area to help them make their way out. And Cruikshank had to admit that in spite of the bleakness of her situation, she was curious. Nobody had ever managed to build a true submersible, a ship that could sail beneath the seas. The problem of boilers requiring steady air supply and exhausts had so far been impossible to solve, and she wanted to see how Kadelta had managed it.

Kadelta led her to a nearby workbench, cleared the surface, and spread out a long roll of paper. He held the four corners in place using a mixture of paperweights and tools. The delicate lines of a blueprint weaved across the paper, and Cruikshank's eyes scanned them with interest.

She moved her finger along the plans as she took it all in. They were as she would have expected until she reached the boiler exhaust. It connected to what appeared to be some sort of complex filter, the other end of the filter connecting back into the tube that should have fed oxygen into the fires.

"Tell me about this," she said, tapping on the filter.

A glint of pride lit up Kadelta's sunken eyes. "You remember when I left Damsport."

Cruickshank nodded, thinking it best not to remind him of his disgrace after the disaster of his last prototype. The explosion had almost ended another young machinist's life, and though it had been an accident, Kadelta had fled the city in disgrace.

"I came here," Kadelta said, "because I had heard an Azyrian had created an alchemical filter that purified air. It was quite a simple thing. I took the basics of the filter and expanded on it. It was long, gruelling work, and I had to learn a lot of alchemy, but I finally managed to make something that converted the carbon in the boiler emissions to oxygen. It works similarly to what plants do, just much quicker and in a larger volume. And of course, once I had that filter, I no longer needed an exhaust or air-supply pipe."

A note of pride rang through Kadelta's voice, and with reason. It was a fantastic achievement, a real piece of creativity. Cruikshank had a hundred questions, but the pain at her eyebrows was a good reminder that now wasn't the time to get excited about new technology. Now was the time to strategise and find a way out.

"The problem I'm having," Kadelta said, "is actually controlling the oxygen supply. It's too unstable."

Cruikshank nodded. "Meaning your boiler could overheat and explode or run too low to power the submersible."

"Exactly. Which is where your valve would come in. It could be linked to an oxygen reader to automatically control how much oxygen is let into the boiler. I've tried so many different things, but so far as I can see, your valve is the only solution that would work."

"I see." Cruikshank mulled this over, studying the blueprint. Something occurred to her then. "How were you taken? How did you go from working on your project to being a slave at the palace?"

Kadelta's face twisted with shame. "You have to know, I never agreed with slavery, never. I also never agreed with... with the social issues of this city. But I was broke, I was a disgrace, a pariah in my profession."

Cruikshank crossed her arms, trying and failing to hide the coldness that she was feeling. She hated excuses, especially ones put forward to justify behaviour lacking in integrity.

"The Seneschal heard of my work," Kadelta continued, "and he heard that I was struggling financially. You know how it was. Nobody would touch me back then. I couldn't get any funding. I used up all my money, then I worked my way through all the money my family would lend me. I was reaching the point of being flat broke, and I didn't know how I would be able to live, let alone work on the submersible. That was when the Seneschal offered me funding as an advance on the purchase of my submersible once it was completed." He took Cruikshank's arms, his eyes feverish. "You have to understand that for years people laughed at me, called me a dreamer, a fool, even an idiot for thinking I could make this work. To have someone take me seriously was like... being given water after crawling through the desert. I drank it all up." Kadelta's voice grew bitter. He let go of Cruikshank. "I was so desperate and so passionate about seeing my life's work come to fruition that I took the Seneschal's offer. The condition was that I would work in the palace. He gave me this workshop." Kadelta lifted his arms to encompass the space around them. "He gave me people to work for me."

"Slaves?" Cruikshank asked coldly.

Kadelta nodded miserably. "I treated them well," he whispered.

Cruikshank didn't answer, her mouth a thin line.

"Anyway, eventually, the Seneschal found a way to frame me for stealing money from the Prelate. It was stupid, and I should have caught on, but I was so involved with my work, so consumed, I... I was arrested, tried, and found guilty. My sentence was enslavement, as per Azyrian law. They've kept me here ever since then, forcing me to complete my submersible for them."

Cruikshank listened in silence. No matter what she thought or felt about the whole thing, she could see how little it would achieve to lecture Kadelta on his lack of ethics and morals. He had been more than punished for his foolishness.

She sighed, softening and feeling sorry for him. While he was a gifted machinist, he had also made some huge mistakes that had cost him enormously. She looked down at his broken, badly set little finger and gaunt, haggard appearance. She hoped she would be able to get the two of them out of the mess he had created.

Cruikshank looked over the plans again. What Kadelta had said about the valve meant she had value, but not for long. Still, she'd be able to delay the completion of it for a time. Long enough, maybe, to find a way out.

CHAPTER

47

Rory held her cards, feeling the slippery smoothness beneath her fingers, in contrast to the fuzziness of the table felt. She clutched them tightly, creasing them. Reheeme stood at the table, taking the place of the dealer. Next to Rory were Oma and Terrell. Rory had her back to the private room's entrance, but she knew Rafe and Urzo were in position on either side of the curtain. They had doused the light by the entrance, so the only remaining alchemical globe hung above the card table.

Rory waited, all her senses strained towards the curtain behind her. She tensed at every sound, convinced it was a member of the Watch entering.

She heard voices muffled by the curtain, then they grew abruptly louder, underscored by footsteps as the Watchmen pushed the curtain aside and entered.

"Inspec—"

Rory turned around.

Rafe had been so fast that the two Watchmen were already collapsing among gurgling sounds, their throats cut. Neither had had the time to shout a warning.

"Lights," Rafe hissed.

Rory leapt to her feet, snatched the alchemical globe overhead, and shoved the divider in. The divider was a slice of metal, each side alchemically treated to repel one of the two alchemical solutions inside the globe. The mixing of the solutions created the light, and when the divider came down, the solutions separated, the reaction dying so that the room went dark.

Rory heard Rafe and Urzo dragging the guards away.

"Quickly now," Rafe whispered.

Rory felt her way in the darkness to help them strip one of the Watchmen while the other was dragged to the back of the room.

Urzo quickly put the uniform and armour on. Reheeme searched the other Watchman for cuffs then put a pair on and passed the other to Rory. Rafe took another pair from the Watchman he and Urzo had stripped down.

The cuffs were a simple loop of chain with a telescoping tube around the middle that could be extended and locked into place to create tight-fitting handcuffs. They all kept the tubes extended but unlocked so it would be easy to slip off the cuffs.

Rory kept her wrists far enough apart to keep the tension in the chain.

"Let's go," Rafe whispered.

"No," Urzo whispered back. "I need to swap studs."

"There's no time," Rafe said impatiently.

"If anyone see his studs," Oma whispered, "they'll know he's not really Watch and his uniform will count for nothing."

Rafe cursed softly, and Rory heard him pad away. She saw the faintest twitch at the curtain.

"Hurry up, then," Rafe murmured. "So far, nobody seems to have noticed that two Watchmen disappeared."

Waiting for Urzo to swap studs was an agony. All it would take was for one Watchman to walk in and make enough noise to catch the attention of the rest.

"Ready," Urzo whispered at last. "Oma, you're sure you'll be alright?"

"I said so, didn't I? Nobody cares about an old woman or a young boy—they're all looking for foreigners and for Reheeme. All of you get out of here, and I'll make my way back to Maksur."

They got into position, Urzo holding Rafe and Rory by the back of their necks, Reheeme following.

"Good luck," Oma rasped.

Urzo shoved Rory and Rafe forward through the curtain and out into the main room.

Rory blinked, feeling horribly exposed. She glanced surreptitiously around her. Had anyone seen them come out?

Urzo dragged them along quickly towards the exit. The Watch were still moving about the tables, checking the players, and a few stopped to look at Urzo and his prisoners. Rory made a show of dragging her feet, staggering and dropping her head as if dazed and injured.

A Watchman a little farther on was hurrying towards them. Urzo put a finger to his lips as soon as the Watchman was close enough to hear.

"There's a third one," Urzo whispered quickly. "In that direction." He gestured with his chin away from the exit they were aiming for. "I wanted to keep it quiet. I don't think he knows I've seen him slip away."

"A third one? Another Damsian?" the Watchman asked.

"Yes."

"I thought there were only two. Thank goodness you saw him. Here, I'll help you with them." The Watchman gestured to Rory.

"No need," Urzo replied. "That one can barely stand."

Rory chose that moment to let her legs go slack, and Urzo grunted, yanking her back up.

"The others have agreed to cooperate," Urzo added. "The Seneschal only wants to talk to them, after all."

Rory winced. They had no idea what orders the Seneschal had given. First rule of a con was to volunteer as little information as possible. For all they knew, the Seneschal had genuinely only ordered the Damsians brought in for questioning, and Urzo's tone hinted at something else.

The Watchman gave a knowing nod. "Ah, yes. Talk. You'd better hurry along. I'll go tell the others to search for the remaining Damsian."

Rory sagged with relief.

"Don't ever say anything you're not completely sure off," she hissed as softly as she could as they walked away.

As Urzo dragged her forward, Rory flicked her gaze towards where the Watchman had left. He had caught up with another, and they were exchanging words, glancing towards Urzo then in the direction of the made-up third Damsian. *Good.*

Rory hoped Oma and Terrell had been able to slip out of the private room. She hadn't heard any warning shouts, which was a good sign.

Urzo continued his brisk march towards the exit. Rory could see a small cluster of the Watch there, and her heart leapt into her mouth. Would Urzo be convincing enough to get past them?

They reached the Watchmen.

"Well, well, what have we here?" one of the Watchmen said.

His studs weren't significantly higher than Urzo's but enough for him to be a supervisor of some kind. He looked Rory, Rafe, and Reheeme over, and his eyes gleamed. "Good work, soldier. I'll take it from here."

"If you don't mind," Urzo said stiffly, "I'm the one who found them, and I'll be the one to bring them to the Seneschal."

The Watchman snorted. "Getting ahead of our station, are we?"

"I just want to get the full credit for the capture," Urzo replied.

A second supervisor—or so Rory guessed from his studs—grinned. "Ambitious, aren't you?" He turned to the first Watchman and shrugged. "He can take them through to the lieutenant. It's only through the incinerator, and it's only fair the lad gets some credit for the capture."

Rory's heart pounded. It wouldn't be easy for Urzo to get past a lieutenant.

The first Watchman frowned, looking ready to argue. But before he could protest, Urzo shoved Rory forward towards the incinerator chamber.

"Fresh recruits getting ahead of themselves," the first Watchman grumbled, but he didn't stop them from going through.

They stepped into the incinerator that connected the gambling room to Petrik's office, and for a heartbeat, Rory felt an irrational terror that it might be activated while they were inside.

Rafe pulled back, forcing them all to stop. "If it goes bad in Petrik's office," he whispered, "we have to find a way to turn on the incinerator, cut off the Watch in the gambling room so they can't come up behind us. Reheeme, do you know how the incinerator operates?"

"No, but I guess the switch will be somewhere around Petrik's desk."

"Right. First sign of trouble, you make for that," Rafe whispered. "We've got to hope there's only a couple of Watchmen in there."

Urzo took hold of Rory and Rafe again, pushing through the second curtain of the incinerator. Rory felt the thick leather against her face.

She felt a little sick from nerves. She didn't think it likely that Urzo could continue to keep control of his three prisoners. She felt a bubble of nervous laughter rise up at the thought that they might have just delivered themselves to the Seneschal on a silver platter, all trussed up with cuffs and ready to go.

The door to Petrik's office was open, and they walked through.

As before, Petrik's men were dotted about the office, while Petrik sat behind his desk. However, the room was now also crowded with a large cluster of Watchmen and - women. The lieutenant was easily recognisable by the thin coils of gold woven into a delicate pattern over his scaled armour at the level of his heart. Rory would have recognised him by his studs alone, which were clearly more precious than those of anyone else in the room—save for Petrik. The two men had been in conversation, the lieutenant sitting across from Petrik, when Rory and the others entered.

Urzo pushed them forward. "I captured all three of them," he told the lieutenant, looking convincingly proud.

Rory counted twelve members of the Watch plus the lieutenant. If fighting broke out, thirteen against four would be a tough match, even with Rafe's fighting abilities. To say nothing if Petrik's muscle got involved, or if Reheeme couldn't activate the incinerator in top to stop more Watch joining.

Then it would be downright slaughter. Which meant they *had* to get out of here without a fight.

The lieutenant stood. "All three of them?" He looked surprised, though fortunately not suspicious. "On your own?"

Urzo nodded. "I told them that the Seneschal would hear of their cooperation if they came peacefully."

The lieutenant gave Urzo a look that Rory couldn't read. He stood opposite Rafe, examining him. "Hmm."

He came to Rory's side and yanked her head up by her hair. Rory kept her gaze down as if she were beaten. Looking pathetic and nonthreatening was her specialty, after all.

She was heavily stained with blood from the Watchman she had helped strip, and without a thorough examination, she knew she looked convincingly injured.

"Hmm," the lieutenant repeated. He gave Reheeme a brief, if disgusted, look before turning back to Urzo. "That does look like the three of them. Why did no one else come with you?"

"Apparently, there's a fourth in the den," Urzo said. "Another Damsian man. I thought it best to slip out with these three."

"A fourth?" the lieutenant asked, frowning.

Urzo nodded.

"Well," the lieutenant said, "if there is another, we will find him. Good work, soldier. We will take it from here."

Urzo placed a proprietary hand on Rory and Rafe's shoulders. "I know I can't bring them to the palace myself, but… could I at least escort them out of the building? I was the one who found them after all, and they can't escape. I—"

The lieutenant skewered him with an icy look. "You will do as you are told," he snapped. "The Watch doesn't trust important prisoners to low studs."

Urzo opened his mouth to protest.

"What regiment did you say you were from?" the lieutenant asked, his eyes narrowing. "Your face isn't familiar."

Rory felt her entire body grow cold. Urzo had no way of knowing which regiment was searching for them.

"Well?" the lieutenant asked.

Sweat broke out on Rory's forehead. She felt a drop run down her temple, tracing a track in the blood. Urzo would have to make a guess and hope that by some miracle he was right.

But instead, Urzo made a fatal mistake. He glanced over at Rafe, his expression unsure, his eyes asking for a clue of what he should do. The lieutenant drew his sword immediately. A rasp of steel against steel ran across the room as all the Watchmen drew their weapons.

Rory's cuffs fell to the ground with a tinkle of chains. Rafe's knives were already out.

Rory's stomach clenched painfully. They couldn't survive the fight.

CHAPTER

48

Cruikshank felt tired, the lack of sleep and lingering effects of the narcotic weighing heavily on her, especially since the work was so intricate and delicate: tiny copper wires and minuscule gears that needed to be handled with tweezers. She didn't have to pretend too much to work at a glacial pace. It had been a couple of hours, she estimated, since they had all been woken up. The other machinists worked with the plodding movements of those worn down by hard work and absence of natural light.

"What time is it?" she asked Kadelta.

The lack of windows was disorientating.

He shrugged. "I've stopped thinking about time. I don't even know if they wake us up when it's dawn outside or just at some random time of day. What I do know is that we have a few hours until the next meal."

Cruikshank nodded. That would have to do.

She turned back to her work, but she found her eyes were struggling to focus. She left her workbench to go look at the furnace. It was impressive in size, and it ran on gas, not coal. Cruikshank nodded as she familiarised herself with the dials. Gas was good. A gas furnace could be made to leak and then explode.

It would be dangerous, probably deadly for some, and it would rip a great hole in the wall. The issue, of course, was that she had no idea what lay beyond the wall and how she would be able to get away from the palace Watch, who would inevitably come rushing over at the explosion.

She would have to find out where in the palace she was, for a start. She wished she had come to the audience with the Prelate. Then she would at least have some clue of the palace layout. Of course, if she had gone to see the Prelate, she'd probably have been taken there and then.

Cruikshank returned to her workbench, mulling it over. She looked back at the submersible hanging over the dark pool of water. The metal gleamed wetly in the alchemical light, and she could see iridescent sheens where oil had been applied.

"Am I disturbing you?" the Seneschal said from behind her.

Cruikshank started and turned around.

"No, what am I saying?" the Seneschal said, voice like honey. "You're not even working."

"I just took a quick break," Cruikshank said. "The lingering effects of the narcotic—"

"Oh, the narcotic…" the Seneschal said. "You'll probably also blame not sleeping enough, the food—what else?"

"The food is fine," Cruikshank said stiffly, "but yes, I haven't slept much."

"You see," the Seneschal said, "the mistake you are making is that you assume I am someone who is willing to tolerate excuses. Someone who is either too weak or stupid to accept subpar work. I am neither of those things. I expect the best at all times."

"And I will give you the best," Cruikshank said. "But I'll remind you that you've drugged me, kidnapped me, put these bloody painful studs on me, and now you're expecting me to work at my usual level of efficacy. You're naive, Seneschal."

Cruikshank heard Kadelta suck in a breath behind her, but she didn't care. The anger she had kept at bay since finding out she had been tricked into coming to Azyr was welling up inside her.

"I am the only one who can complete this machine for you," she continued. "No one else. You can't afford to kill me until the machine is complete. Sure, you might be able to find a machinist who can replicate my work, but certainly no one here, which will mean untold delays. So if you want me to work well, I'd suggest you ensure I'm kept under good conditions. And the first thing for that would be to let me get a breath of fresh air to clear my head. I can't think or focus as it is."

Cruikshank projected far more confidence than she felt. Making demands like that was rash, but she knew she was right about being the only one who could complete the submersible. And if she could use it to her advantage, she might at least be able to orient herself within the palace to plot out some kind of escape route.

"You are making demands?" the Seneschal asked, clearly amused. "You are a fool, Cruikshank. You seem to think I won't realise that you're working slowly on purpose. Of course I know it. Because you see, what *you* don't realise is that I was a machinist before I became Seneschal."

Cruikshank was taken aback.

"I understand what you are building," the Seneschal continued. "I know how long it should take. I know that you're trying to play me for a fool, and I don't appreciate it."

Cruikshank recovered her composure. "Then you must realise that if I make the valve even the slightest bit wrong, you run the risk of the engine exploding midjourney, or if too little oxygen is fed to the engine, it could stop, causing the submersible to sink. So you see, I am precious to you. Very, very precious. And it seems to me that you can't afford not to have my cooperation." Cruikshank took a breath, having thought of something else. "If you were to give me proof that you've released the other four, I could guarantee you a perfectly working submersible."

The tiniest flicker passed over the Seneschal's face. It was almost nothing—the faintest twitch of his lips—but enough to let Cruikshank know that he didn't have them all. Either Rory or Rafe, or hopefully both, had gotten away. For a moment, Cruikshank felt the overwhelming urge to laugh in the man's face. It was an idiotic urge, and she swallowed it quickly.

"I'm afraid," the Seneschal said, his voice suave as velvet, "that you are now a slave. Slaves do not make deals. Slaves do not negotiate." His voice became smoother and smoother until it sounded almost liquid, but his eyes were two chips of flint.

Cruikshank decided not to press on the matter of releasing the others—she knew it would never be granted. The Seneschal would be doing his best to make sure none of them returned to Damsport. She would be better served by aiming for a moment outdoors.

Cruikshank crossed her arms. "But we *are* negotiating. If you want me to work faster, I need fresh air. Simple as that."

The Seneschal regarded her, then he shook his head slowly, looking aggrieved. "This is so disappointing, Cruikshank," he said, his tone regretful. "So very disappointing. I expected so much more from you."

Thick hands grabbed hold of Cruickshank's arms, making her jump. She hadn't seen the two Watchmen coming up behind her.

To her right, Kadelta gave a whimper, and she saw him cringing like a whipped dog. "Please, Your Grace," he whispered, his mouth working.

The Seneschal cocked his head, looking Cruickshank up and down. Cruickshank calmly returned his look, doing her best not to let her fear show.

"If you kill me," she reminded him, "you won't get the valve. You cannot crack my head open and get the calculations in there."

"Oh, my dear," the Seneschal said, "whoever said anything about killing you? That fine speech you gave me just now, that was all theoretical talk. We are dealing in the real world here. And in the real world, just how useful are toes to a machinist?"

Cruickshank's eyes widened, and she felt sick. The Seneschal looked down at her feet thoughtfully as if puzzling out a problem.

"Alright, let me go," Cruickshank said, trying to keep her voice calm. "There's no need for that. I can do without the fresh air."

"Hmm?" the Seneschal asked, looking up from her feet as if he hadn't heard her.

"You heard me. Let me get back to work."

"Oh, that. Yes, of course you'll get back to work," the Seneschal said smoothly, looking back down at her feet. "And fast too. I'm just trying to decide the optimal ratio of pain to ability to work, you see."

Cruikshank caught sight of a Watchman grabbing a heavy hammer from a nearby workbench.

"Enough," she said, her voice cracking loudly against the brick ceiling. "We're not savages. Enough of this nonsense. Let me do my work."

"But, my dear Cruikshank, it is *you* who started this nonsense," the Seneschal said, surprised. "You are my slave, and you dared defy me. You had the nerve to suggest we could negotiate, that you were somehow my equal, when you are just a slave. That kind of behaviour simply cannot go unpunished."

"Wait, wait, wait," Cruikshank said, her eyes following the hammer as the man holding it approached. "Wait. I can't work if I'm in pain. The valves are delicate, complex. I need all my faculties." Words were pouring out of her mouth, and she no longer knew what she was saying, babbling incoherently as she watched the hammer. "There will be no delay. I will get the valve done and quickly."

She had never known such fear before. In a distant part of her head, a voice was telling her that this wasn't real—that someone would come in any minute now and stop it all, and the Seneschal would die of spontaneous combustion.

"My dear Cruikshank, if I don't punish you, what incentive would I be giving you? You need to experience the real-world consequences of your actions to truly understand that your only choice is to obey me in all things." The Seneschal pointed out her right foot. "The big toe."

Cruickshank let out a cry, shouting at the man with the hammer to stop, to wait. She'd do anything, anything at all.

The hammer rose up.

CHAPTER

49

A heartbeat passed. Rory's sword was in one hand—a reassuring presence—her dagger in the other. The Watch surrounded her and the others in Petrik's office, leaving their backs to the incinerator. Not that anyone could escape through there.

Petrik and his men stood well back, out of the way.

There was a moment of stillness as if everyone collectively held their breath. A calm before the storm.

And then it burst like a bubble, everything erupting.

Rafe threw a knife, then another, catching two men in the neck. He shouted and attacked, drawing most of the Watchmen and the lieutenant to him.

Reheeme darted off, and Rory rushed after her, covering her against attack so she might reach the incinerator switch.

That was all she had time to think about—two Watchmen charged her.

She parried and was immediately overwhelmed. There was no space for strategy or planning—only survival. Steel

345

clashed against steel, and it seemed that everywhere, sharp metal was lunging at her, trying to cut her. Blows rained down like a thunderstorm.

Rory stepped back and back again. The swords pressed around her. Sweat dripped down the sides of her face.

She was dimly aware of Rafe beyond, drawing almost all the Watch to him. They crowded him, hiding him from sight.

The lieutenant roared for backup.

Rory looked up in fear.

She missed a parry, only just deflecting enough so that the jab that would have gashed her stomach glanced off her ribs, slicing a neat red line. Fortunately, the wound was shallow, and her ribs protected her.

Five Watchmen ran in through the open door of the incinerator, shouting and drawing their weapons as they entered the room and saw the fighting.

A blow sent Rory's sword skittering out of her hand. She threw herself to the side, only just dodging a jab.

Rafe was surrounded on all sides. Urzo was fighting four Watchmen, backed into the corner nearest the incinerator.

They were losing.

Rory ducked this way and that, deflecting the blows with her dagger. Without her sword, she couldn't retaliate and was forced to stagger farther and farther back.

Another Watchman ran in through the leather curtain of the incinerator, joining the fray. Then a roar erupted in the incinerator, not loud enough to drown out the screaming within the chamber.

A ball of heat swept into the room, a belch of flames whooshing out of the open incinerator door, sending the leather curtain flying.

The shock of the fire had the Watchmen facing Rory pause for a heartbeat.

A man all aflame ran into the room, crashing into the Watchmen fighting Urzo.

In the confusion, several more of the Watchmen caught fire. Urzo took the opportunity, leaping past them. He rolled on the ground, putting out the flames that were nibbling the edges of his uniform.

Rory's legs were suddenly kicked out from under her, and she fell heavily on her back. Her arms shot out to break her fall, her hands slamming into the floor. Her dagger clattered away from her.

Somewhere, Reheeme screamed, and there was the sound of struggling.

A Watchman drew back his sword to strike Rory.

Her guts twisted with fear.

And then a knife sliced across his throat, drawing a gushing red smile.

Petrik's men, who had been standing aside, attacked the Watch in one quick swoop. The fighting didn't take long. In a few heartbeats, the Watch were reduced to a scattering of bleeding bodies. Rafe stood in the middle of his own collection of corpses, panting. He was heavily bloodied but didn't seem badly hurt.

The fire from the incinerator roared on. Beyond, Rory could make out faint shouting.

"What... what was that?" Reheeme gasped at Petrik, pulling herself up. She had taken a wound to her right shoulder but nothing too serious.

Urzo had fared well with his Watch armour.

Petrik smiled, wiping his knife on one of the dead men's uniforms. He had dispatched the lieutenant himself. "That was a good move, turning on my incinerator. It will be a while before the Watch out there can cross back into my office."

"Why did you help us?" Reheeme asked.

"You know very well that I'm a friend to everyone and to no one," he replied. "I betrayed you, and now I betray the Seneschal. I have helped the Seneschal and now I help you. The balance remains. Of course, the Seneschal will hear of how my men tried to stop the dangerous Damsian spies escaping. I believe a few of them died in the fighting along with all the Watch."

He gestured with his chin. Two of his men went to a nearby door, dragging out a corpse. "I think we'll have lost six men tonight." He turned to Urzo. "When the time comes, I expect you and Oma will remember this gesture."

Urzo nodded soberly. "You have my word on that."

"Good," Petrik said. "I'll see to it that she and Terrell make it safely back to Maksur."

"Thank you," Rory added, unable to find a better word to convey how grateful she felt to still be alive.

Petrik nodded, and Rory fetched her sword and dagger.

Petrik pulled out a whistle and smiled as his men finished dragging out the sixth corpse and slipped out through another side door.

"You won't have long," he said to Rory, Rafe, Urzo, and Reheeme as he moved into a crouch.

Rory and the others broke into a run.

***

Urzo led the way through the passages beneath the racecourse. They ran, their footsteps echoing on the stone. Rory's wounded ribs throbbed in rhythm with the beating of her heart.

Urzo took them a different way than they had come in, passing through a series of storage rooms.

Rory's every muscle was taut to the point of snapping as she strained to make out the sounds of pursuit. She thought she heard the shriek of a whistle.

"Petrik," she breathed.

Rafe nodded, his face grim. Reheeme was breathing heavily, struggling to keep up the pace. Her tunic's shoulder was soaked with blood.

They reached a small exit door without coming across anyone. Rory thanked every god she could think of for the luck. Urzo opened the door a touch and pressed his face against the crack, peeking outside.

"We're near the Tarwanese exit," Urzo whispered. "But there's Watch at the doors."

"We can climb over the racecourse walls," Rory whispered back. "Use my grappling hook and line."

She swapped places with Urzo so she could take a look at the courtyard where the various vehicles were parked during the races.

The grey early-morning light was still weak enough that shadows pooled in every corner. The doors where the Watch congregated were quite far to the left. They were calm and didn't yet seem to be on the lookout for anyone.

Rory nodded to herself. She and the others should be able to slip past unnoticed so long as the Watchmen didn't hear any alarm from within the racecourse.

They sneaked out the door quickly, padding over silently to the wall. It was about as high as two Azyrians, and narrow. This wasn't the Dividing Wall, bristling with members of the watch who walked along the top. It simply marked the end of the racecourse courtyard, separating the parking area from the rest of Tarwa.

In a couple of heartbeats, Rory had her grappling hook and line secure. Reheeme was carried on Urzo's back, the injury to her shoulder preventing her from climbing. Rory and Rafe followed quickly after. Rory sighed with relief when she landed on the other side, into the darkened street.

The Watch still stood peacefully by the doors.

Just as Rory retrieved her hook, voices rang out across the courtyard.

"Quick, this way," Reheeme said.

"No," Urzo said. "Come with me."

"We need a place to hide," Reheeme said.

Urzo nodded. "And everywhere you know of is compromised," he said quickly. "I can take us somewhere safe that Jabir, the Seneschal, and the Sons and Daughters know nothing about."

"Urzo's right," Rafe said. "We have to assume any location connected to you is now compromised. Now, come on. We need to get out of here."

Reheeme didn't argue, and they set off, moving at a brisk pace but refraining from running so as not to draw attention.

"Where can you take us that's safe in Tarwa?" she asked Urzo once they had put some distance between them and the racecourse.

"The Risen have a safe house," Urzo replied.

"In Tarwa?" Reheeme said incredulously.

Urzo nodded.

"Why did you never mention this?"

"Because we didn't trust you," Urzo replied.

"And right you were," Rory said, "or Jabir would know of it, and there would be city Watch waiting for us there." She stopped abruptly. "Cruikshank's spider. We have to get it—I left it on that rooftop by the racecourse."

Rafe shook his head. "The spider will be safe enough for now, but we won't be if we go back. They'll be looking for us beyond the racecourse by now."

"And if they find the spider?" Rory said.

Rafe shrugged. "A spider can be remade. The same can't be said about us."

Rory knew he was right, but all the same, she felt like she was abandoning a friend.

***

The safe house of the Risen was in the least wealthy area of Tarwa. The sun had fully risen by the time they arrived, the sky first awash with pinks and oranges then fading back to brilliant blue as the sun lifted itself above the horizon. The house itself was well built but devoid of the more elaborate decorations found in the area close to Reheeme's place.

Inside, it was gloomy, the shuttered windows letting in only thin shafts of light. Waterfalls of dust motes danced in the shafts, never seeming to land anywhere.

"This is a decent house," Reheeme said, looking around the entrance in surprise.

Urzo sneered. "Right. Because you think we're barely more than beggars in Maksur."

"No, I… I just didn't realise you had those kinds of funds," Reheeme replied. "I wasn't trying to give any offence."

Urzo mellowed. "We bought it from a man deeply in debt to Petrik. He lost a big game, and Petrik's thugs would have killed him, but the Risen paid off his debt in exchange for his house."

For a man claiming to be neutral and to betray both sides, Petrik was leaning quite heavily on the side of the Risen. He must have known the implications for the Risen to get this house—giving them a base in Tarwa from which to operate.

Urzo led the way. The place was eerily empty of furniture. Two women briefly appeared, quickly nodding and disappearing as soon as they saw Urzo.

"They keep an eye on the place," Urzo said. "We don't have anyone staying here full-time. We didn't want to risk bringing any attention here."

"I'm assuming there's a kitchen?" Reheeme said.

"Obviously. But we only have the bare minimum. All the furniture was sold when we got the house. We only kept mattresses and a few items for the kitchen."

"I can set myself up in there to make what we need for the diversion at the Eastern Trade Gate."

Rory shook herself. Between the exhaustion from the sleepless night at the races and the pain from the wound at her ribs, she had completely forgotten they had planned for Reheeme to create smoke and small explosions to draw the palace Watch to the Eastern Trade Gate.

"I won't need much in terms of equipment," Reheeme continued. "We can send out for what's missing. The manipulations to make smoke or small explosions are very simple. I'll need a number of ingredients, though. I'll write out a list—could one of the girls go fetch it for me…" She faltered, hands half-raised, and Rory realised she had been about to clap for a slave. "I… I'll need a pen and paper."

"Later," Urzo said. "For now, we all need sleep and bandages. There are rooms upstairs. Each one has water and what you'll need to clean up wounds." He eyed the gash at Rory's side. "That will need stitching."

"I can do it," Rafe said.

The room Urzo took Rory and Rafe to was small, with only a single mattress on the floor. As Urzo had promised, there was a large basin placed on the floor and next to it a jug of water. A wooden box housed clean rags, disinfectant, bandages, and needle and thread.

Rafe poured the water into the basin, wetting one of the rags. He wrung it out.

"Well, sit down," he said to Rory. "It's not going to be practical with you standing over me like that." He made a decent attempt at his usual sardonic grin, but it came out tired. Rory sat down.

The wet cloth felt wonderfully cool as he passed it over her forehead.

"I could do that," she said.

"Without a mirror, you'll do a poor job of it," Rafe said.

He had a point. She let him wipe off the blood from her face, closing her eyes.

"I saw when you fell, back in Petrik's office," Rafe said. "I thought I was going to watch you die."

Rory nodded, opening her eyes. A drop of reddish water fell from her eyebrow down onto her hand. "I thought I were a goner too."

They held each other's gaze for a moment, then Rafe looked away, moving to wipe the blood away from her neck. "Now lift your vest up so I can see the wound on your ribs."

Rory felt a rush of shame at the thought of him seeing just how much her ribs stuck out. She had filled out quite a bit compared to when she'd first met him, but she was still incredibly skinny.

Then she remembered that it didn't matter. Rafe had himself said he had no interest in her. All that was done. She ignored the voice at the back of her mind reminding her that he'd jokingly referred to himself as her love interest.

"Must be your first time stitching up a rake," she quipped, opening the lower part of her vest and lifting the leather up so he could see the wound.

Rafe got the cloth ready. "You shouldn't ever apologise for who you are," he murmured. "You're perfect as is."

Rory fell silent, unsure how to reply to that. Was it a joke?

Rafe dabbed the gash, and Rory sucked air through her teeth at the pain. He prodded gently at the edges of the wound with his fingers. "I'm glad you're not dead," he murmured so low that Rory wasn't sure if she'd heard. "I like the world with you in it."

Rory tried to say something funny in reply, something about being a hard nut to crack, but it died on her lips. All the events of the previous night rushed up to her in a wave. Longinus, Cruikshank, and Adelma being taken, how close she and Rafe had come to being captured, the blood, the fighting in Petrik's office. Her hands started shaking, then her body. An odd strangled sound rose up in her throat.

"Hey, hey," Rafe said gently. "It's alright."

He put the cloth down and then she was in his arms as he held her tight. She found her arms holding tightly back too.

"It's normal to get overwhelmed, when it all stops," Rafe said. "And the shaking too. It's the adrenaline leaving your body."

"But I've killed people before," Rory said against his chest, her voice muffled by his clothing. She felt confused and angry with her body for letting her down. She didn't want to feel like this. Yet at the same time, she found Rafe's heartbeat against her chest soothing.

"It doesn't matter," Rafe said. "It happens. Just wait for it to wash past."

A part of Rory wanted nothing more than to let go of the steely thing inside her, the thing that kept sadness and fear from encroaching. A small part of her, a tiny, shameful part of her, wanted nothing more than to cry and then fall sleep on the mattress in Rafe's arms.

She felt a cold jolt of fear at the thought, and the box of Daria's memories threatened to burst open. She steeled herself at once, shutting everything away. She shifted away from Rafe. "Thank you. I'm alright now."

Rafe gave her a small smile. "Glad to hear it. Now, hold still, and I'll stitch you up. You could take a leaf out of Adelma's book and have a swig." He pointed to the bottle of disinfectant. Rory realised it was the same purplish liquid Adelma had bought when they had first arrived in Azyr. She smiled and let out a cough of laughter, which died at the thought of Adelma being locked in a cell somewhere.

"Worry about it later," Rafe said. "For now, you need to be stitched up, you need to sleep, and it won't hurt you to relax a bit."

"That's normally the kind of thing I'd say to Longinus," Rory said with a wan smile.

"Surprisingly, he's growing on me."

"He has a tendency to do that," Rory said. "Ain't the kind of person you immediately like, but then, once you get to know him well enough…" She choked on the words, thinking of Longinus and where he was.

"Alright," Rafe said, threading a needle. "This is going to hurt a bit."

CHAPTER
50

Longinus's frustration was growing with the passing of the hours. The jailer coming to their cells never carried keys, or if he did, they were muffled in fabric and somehow hidden in his grubby trousers. Adelma and Longinus had discussed attacking the jailer anyway, but they had decided against it. If the man didn't have any keys, they would lose all element of surprise, and he was unlikely to make a decent enough hostage that they could negotiate the opening of their cell against his life.

To add insult to *considerable* injury, not only was the food appalling but he and Adelma were also forced to make use of a chamber pot. A *chamber pot*. He had hoped they would show some respect to his gentleman status and allow him to step out of the cell to relieve nature's calls, but no.

Instead, Longinus had had to suffer the indignity of relieving himself while Adelma turned her back, choking with laughter as she asked him whether he was building up a stock of ammonia.

Worse, she didn't seem to have any concept of modesty, and he was forced to jerk himself around on seeing her begin to undo her leggings, lest his poor retinas be branded with the sight of Adelma squatting.

He and Adelma were sitting at either ends of the cell, dozing, when Longinus started at the sound of footsteps, and more importantly the *jangle of keys*. He looked over at Adelma, and she gave him the tiniest of nods.

She stayed as she was, but Longinus could see the tension in her body, as if she was ready to spring. She was closest to the door, and she carefully shuffled closer, still keeping her casual lean against the wall.

More footsteps rang out, a large number of them. Longinus's heart sank. Adelma leaned sideways, getting a better look down the passageway.

"Watch," she said. "Dozen of them."

She gave a tiny shake of the head, and Longinus grimaced with disappointment. Any hope of overpowering the jailer vanished like cheap perfume on a gust of wind.

The man who opened the cell door wasn't their usual jailer, and he was flanked by the complement of Watchmen. The thick lock clanged loudly open, the rusty hinges squeaking as the door opened.

"Good luck," the prisoner from the opposite cell called.

"For what?" Adelma asked, getting up.

Longinus got up with her.

"You don't need luck," the jailer grumbled. "No need for luck when there's only one possible outcome."

"We facing a lizard, or we fighting?" Adelma asked.

The jailer grunted and shoved her forward. It felt utterly wrong to see Adelma get shoved by a man so much smaller than her and, more importantly, not to see her knock several of his teeth out in response.

Longinus stepped out of the cell. He kept his right hand in his pocket where he had put the poison capsules he'd removed from his clothes. He fell into step with Adelma.

"Don't panic," Adelma muttered. "We'll survive this bugger. We survive the lizard, and we work the rest out later."

Longinus nodded, gulping painfully, feeling as though he were swallowing a coin through a space as narrow as a pea. As they walked past the long row of cells, some prisoners cheered, some hooted, and some laughed. Most, though, watched them go past with blank expressions and dark eyes.

"We survive this," Adelma repeated, staring fixedly ahead. She spoke with an intensity Longinus hadn't heard before, and he realised with a start that for the first time since he had known her, Adelma was afraid. It was such a startling thought that for a moment, he forgot all about his own fear.

Adelma's face was grim, her neck so tense the tendons stood out like rope, and she stared at the door at the end of the corridor as if something there would tell her about the outcome of their battle with the lizard.

To Longinus's surprise, her fear didn't communicate itself to him. Instead, a calmness descended over him. He was the Viper, after all. He had faced Myran, the person he feared most in the world, and he had not only survived but beaten her in combat as well. If he could do that, he could do anything. Vipers, after all, could take on lizards, even large, aggressive ones.

They reached the end of the passage, and one of the Watchmen opened the heavy iron door, letting them out.

***

Beyond was the staging area. It was a huge space cut through overhead with heavy iron beams. Light streamed through slats in the ceiling, falling in slanted white shafts. There were people everywhere: heavily battle-scarred men and women, blacksmiths, animal trainers, and those who, like Longinus, looked like they had been freshly plucked from the city.

The air stank of fear and dung and soot. Blacksmiths worked on weapons, their hammers ringing out loudly against the metal. Their forge belched out sparks and black smoke that was sucked up by a wide exhaust. Longinus could feel the heat from the forge, and the whole staging area felt like some kind of hell.

A man was shaking with fear as he waited at the bottom of a long ramp leading up to a wide wooden door. Bright sunlight streamed through the gaps between the boards. Beyond, he could just about hear music, a hectic rhythm of drums and some kind of nasal flutelike instrument.

If this was hell, what was beyond the door was unlikely to be heaven.

At the sight of the trembling man, Longinus straightened up. If Longinus was going to die, he certainly wasn't going to die like that, trembling and soiling himself when facing his opponent. Whatever happened, he would meet his fate with elegance and equanimity. If nothing else, when his death was reported—and he had no doubt that the Viper's death would be *widely* reported—he would cut a dashing figure until the very last. And Lady Martha would hear of it.

"This way." The jailer led Adelma and Longinus to a set of trestle tables laden with haphazard piles of weapons. "Take your pick."

The weapons were crude, heavy things, some still spattered with rust-coloured flecks of old blood. Longinus kept a step away, breathing slowly. He couldn't smell the dried blood on the weapons, of course, but the knowledge that it was there still threatened to make him feel ill.

He took another slow, deep breath.

Adelma rummaged through the weapons like a housewife rummaging through a table of clothing at a market. She held up one weapon after another, inspecting them. Some were so rusty and notched as to be as lethal as toothpicks. Eventually, she settled for an axe and a mean-looking morning star. Both weapons were in very good condition.

Longinus heard a cry and looked up. Three men were walking up the ramp towards the arena. One of them was the terrified man he had noticed before, the one who was trembling. He was protesting, dragged forward by the other two. He begged them to release him, to let him die there in peace.

They stopped outside the door for a moment.

Then the door opened, letting in a flood of bright light and music. The drums played a rapid rhythm underscored by a wailing melody as if already bemoaning the deaths of the three men.

Two of the men let out a cry, running forward, dragging the third between them as he screamed with fright. The bright sunlight engulfed them.

The music was loud, but not loud enough to drown out the hiss followed by more screaming.

The door closed, returning the staging area to its gloom and clanging.

Longinus's calm from earlier slipped away like water through his fingers. He felt sick. He swayed, extending a hand to prop himself up against the table. Soon he would be out there. There would be blood. And once that happened, he would be as useless as a baby, leaving Adelma alone to face whatever the Prelate had in store for them.

"Don't go funny on me now." Adelma grabbed him with a thick hand and gave him a little, not unkind shake. "You know, there's a reason I like you as much as I do. Most people, when they meet me, practically piss themselves. They go all funny, they stammer, or they go the other way and try to give me all that bravado and attitude, like they want to hide that I make them uncomfortable. Once people know me better, they relax a bit, but it takes a while. But you, you didn't care when we first met. You weren't intimidated or nothing." She gripped his shoulder hard enough to crack bones.

"Careful," he protested. "If I go in there minus a shoulder, I'll be even less than useless."

Adelma snorted. "Well, then, bring my friend back—the one what's a fearless assassin. Whoever this is right now, this pansy leaning against a table, he ain't no use to either of us, alright?"

Longinus was so taken aback by the mention of him being Adelma's friend that he momentarily forgot himself.

He did think of her with a certain fondness, that was true, but until then, he had only really thought of Rory as his friend—and maybe Cruikshank.

To hear friendship declared in such an open, casual way was utterly alien to him. He hadn't had much experience with friendship until Rory.

Adelma must have read something in his face, because she released his shoulder and gave an awkward shrug. "Anyway, you keep that to yourself, right? I got a reputation and all that—don't want people hearing I'm going soft or nothing." She clapped him on the back hard enough to force a cough out of him.

"You're next," the jailer called.

Longinus's heart pounded. He looked up at Adelma, exchanging a silent look. He selected a sword that was entirely out of place among the rest of the heavy weapons. He wouldn't go as far as to call it delicate, but it certainly had some refinement to it. He tried a couple of moves, testing its balance. It wasn't bad.

"Off you go," the jailer said, pointing towards the ramp leading up to the door.

Longinus grabbed a long dagger and slipped it into his belt. He would need a free hand for his poisons, but having a secondary weapon could only be an advantage.

As they walked towards the ramp, the calm from earlier descended on him once again. What would be, would be. He thought of Rory briefly, wondering if he would see her again. He hoped that at least she was free. That thought cheered him somewhat. He pictured her up on some Azyrian roof, giving the palace the finger, and he chuckled.

"What?" Adelma asked.

Longinus told her.

"Ha," Adelma snorted. "She would and all. Good girl, that one."

Longinus nodded. "We shouldn't charge out," he said suddenly, reminded of the three men from earlier. "At the races, the slaves always ran out, and the lizard chased after them. The lizard's vision might work on movement. We might be able to buy ourselves some time by standing still at first."

Adelma nodded. "Running blind into something is for the foolish and the frightened, and we are neither."

"Exactly."

"I reckon we do a two-pronged attack. I'll go first, get its attention on me, get it snapping its jaws. You get the poison in its mouth somehow. And mind you use as much of it as you can."

Longinus frowned. "Normally, I wouldn't be comfortable with a woman taking the risks in this situation. But I have been trying and trying to determine whether you actually *do* qualify as a woman, and I came to the conclusion that you're just... Adelma. You're undefinable."

Adelma grinned. "That's one of the nicest compliments I've ever received. And that's exactly right."

They reached the door. Longinus could feel the sun's heat through the wooden slats. The music had grown louder, the drums beating a rhythm as fast as the beating of his heart.

He closed his right hand tighter around his sword. "If I die," he said, looking straight ahead, "it would have been an honour—"

"None of that nonsense. What did I tell you? We're surviving that lizard, alright?"

Longinus swallowed. "Right."

With a loud creak, the wooden door was pulled back. Longinus blinked as his vision was flooded with hot white light.

CHAPTER
51

The most disturbing part of Cruickshank's ordeal was the care and gentleness with which her smashed toe was attended to. A small Azyrian woman was called for, and she arrived with all manner of bandages and potions to set the broken bone and address the pain. The two Watchmen who had earlier held Cruikshank back now gently helped her to a chair.

The woman carefully removed Cruikshank's boot. Cruikshank gritted her teeth, but the pain of the boot coming off her foot was such that she couldn't help but cry out. It galled her to show vulnerability in front of the Seneschal and give him satisfaction. He hovered behind the nurse, his black robes making him look like a bird of bad omen.

The nurse pulled out a small vial topped with a drop measurer. Cruikshank's foot seemed to throb harder in response, as if it had identified the source of more pain.

"Open your mouth," she told Cruikshank. "This is for the pain."

Cruikshank hesitated.

"There is no sense in poisoning you now," the Seneschal said. "As you so eloquently pointed out before, I need you to complete the valve."

Cruikshank gave him a dark look, but she nodded once, ungritting her teeth long enough to open her mouth. The nurse carefully measured out five drops of a thick, bitter liquid. Cruikshank swallowed, grimacing.

The woman tended to Cruikshank's toe, setting the bone and bandaging it with quick, efficient fingers.

The liquid she had given Cruikshank worked with remarkable efficiency. The pain faded back to a muted throbbing, no worse than badly stubbing her toe. It was so quick, the medicine muffling the pain the way a thick cloth muffled sound.

With the pain mostly removed, she found that her head was clear enough to think beyond basic survival and consider moves and countermoves. If the Seneschal was having her tended to, that might mean he wanted to keep her alive longer than for the completion of the valve.

The Seneschal smiled, a smile that didn't reach his eyes. "You're thinking that because I'm having you bandaged up, I have a use for you beyond the valve," he said in that silky, smooth voice of his. "You don't know me well enough yet. You see, I might have a use for you—it's true. But I might just as well not. Or I might change my mind later about how useful you actually are. It's the perversity that I enjoy:

ministering to someone I'm about to execute. There's nothing quite like giving someone hope, only to see the expression in their eyes when I take it away from them."

Cruikshank kept her face perfectly impassive, her eyes cold. "I doubt you'll ever get that satisfaction from me."

"Maybe I will, and maybe I won't." The Seneschal's voice dropped until it was so soft that Cruikshank almost had to strain to hear him. "Let us be absolutely clear. If there are any more delays, if you purposefully build me a faulty valve—in short, if you give anything other than good, swift progress, I will know. And let me remind you that there are many, many parts of you that can be broken before you cease to be able to work. I speak from experience when I say that with the help of the right drugs, a person can continue to function even if their entire lower body is more broken than an old doll's."

Cruikshank kept her face steady, but the mention of broken dolls sent a distant flare of pain up her foot as she remembered the awful moment when the hammer had swung down.

She couldn't believe the Seneschal had once shared her profession. The machinists she'd known had always been pragmatic, down-to-earth people and, on the whole, rather honest and upfront. It went with the work. When you were used to working with the logic of numbers and machines, you tended not to like slippery dealings. She wondered if the Seneschal had always been like this or if he had been corrupted by his proximity to the Prelate and by his abandonment of the work.

The Seneschal gave a tiny smile and touched the tips of his fingers to her forearm. Cruikshank jerked herself away as though he had burned her. His skin was as cold as a lizard's.

"I want my valve," he said, his voice low but harder than diamonds. "And I want it within a day. That, I believe, is a reasonable amount of time for a machinist of your talents." The Seneschal patted her forearm, gave her a little nod as though they had just finished a pleasant conversation, and left.

Once she and Kadelta were alone, Cruikshank tried to stand. Blood rushed to her head, blood laden with the drug, and she swayed dangerously. Kadelta caught her with a steadying hand and helped her to sit back down.

"Give a little time for your body to get accustomed to the drops. They're very effective, and soon you'll even be able to walk on your foot, although you'll probably limp a little. The drops can make it hard to keep the hands steady, and they also make it hard to sleep."

Cruickshank looked up at Kadelta. His appearance made more sense now—the dark rings around his eyes, the limp, the sallow skin. She wondered how long they had spent breaking and patching him up, feeding him the drugs he needed to be able to still function through the pain. If Cruickshank had held any resentment towards the man for the situation they all found themselves in—and she didn't—it would have evaporated. His last few months had to have been a horror.

When she felt a bit steadier, Cruickshank stood up with Kadelta's help and limped back to her workshop. As

Kadelta had said, she could put weight on it, and the pain was manageable. Her foot throbbed, but it didn't overwhelm her. Someone brought her a stool so she could sit with her foot off the ground.

"I've tried stalling," Kadelta murmured. "I've tried it all. It doesn't work. Don't do it to yourself, because eventually, you will cave. I did, but not until after they'd done a lot of damage."

Cruikshank nodded. There was little to be gained in provoking a man without morals or conscience. There was also little to be gained in any further injuries. If she was rendered unable to walk, her chances of escaping the palace would dwindle to less than nothing.

Not that her chances were looking particularly good. The Seneschal had been right with his assessment: a day for her to make the valve would be sufficient. It was a delicate process, but the real work lay in the complex calculations it had taken for her to invent the valve.

Actually building it required dexterity but not a whole lot of time, once she had the engine parameters and all the right formulae.

The problem Cruikshank faced was that once the valve was ready, the submersible could be completed, and her usefulness would come at an end. It was anyone's guess what would happen then. If it came to it and she had no other way out, she would cause the furnace to explode while the Seneschal was in the workshop and hope the blast would kill him.

It might give Rory and Rafe a chance to escape, maybe even with Longinus and Adelma. The thought of Rory and Rafe still free in Azyr bolstered her.

She knew she was unlikely to face a happy ending, but dying in a furnace explosion and taking the Seneschal with her might not be a bad way to go. If nothing else, it meant that she would avoid sinking into decrepit old age, her joints swollen with arthritis and her mind doddering. Cruikshank feared that fate a lot more than a good, clean death. She'd had a good run at life, really—a very good run.

Cruikshank resumed her work, casting away her first attempt. Not only had she been purposefully slow, but she had been quite sloppy as well. Clearly, the Seneschal knew what he was about, and she didn't want to risk getting caught working on a poorly built valve.

Her hand drifted to her stomach to the incomplete tattoo there. She felt a pang of sadness at the thought that it probably would never get completed.

CHAPTER 52

Longinus blinked, unable to make make out much in the painfully bright light. The heat felt like the inside of an oven. The loud music—the hectic mix of drums twinned with the odd, nasal flute—added to his initial confusion. It took him a moment to realise that there was no cheering, no shouting, no sound of voices at all alongside the music.

They were in the Prelate's private fighting pit. It was a long oval no more than thirty yards in diameter. The floor was covered in sand, and the walls were stone, much like at the races. Looking up, Longinus saw the Prelate and, next to him, the Seneschal. There were other Azyrians around them, courtiers with the elaborate headdresses Longinus had seen back in the throne room. They looked menacing now, the fan-shaped headdresses swaying with each movement of their heads. They looked like carrion creatures waiting for Longinus and Adelma to die.

The Prelate was spread atop a large ebony litter. He stood out starkly in his brilliant white clothing, the diamonds at his eyebrows and fingers winking garishly as they caught the light. White silk awnings were stretched out over him, and he was attended by a large retinue of slaves, who fanned him, mopped his face, and fed him sweets.

The Seneschal looked unchanged. Tall, thin, and as black as a crow, he stood next to the throne, watching.

Straight ahead of Longinus and Adelma, the lizard was waiting, also watching—except that it was nothing like the lizards Longinus had seen at the races or like the ones Rory had described. This was a monster. Everything about it was massive. Large feet and thick legs kept it propped up above the ground. Its skin was beaded, shimmering hard in the sun so that it almost looked like armour.

Its head was bright blue with a thick red stripe running from its jaw down to its neck. Beyond the neck, its body was the colour of sand so that it looked like it had sprouted up from the ground.

There were red knobs on its head and forelegs, like barnacles clinging to the body of a whale. Thick folds of skin hung from the lizard's neck, and its massive head was flat and wide, its small eyes quick and cold. A fiery red crest of spikes ran along its spine.

Each of its feet was five fingered with long, curving claws. They were red like the crest on its back, as though hinting at the blood they would soon spill. Behind, its tail stretched out at least two yards long and thick as a small tree. It curled back at the end.

The beast looked like armour brought to life.

Sweat ran down from Longinus's temples. Behind him, the wooden door thudded closed with a sound that felt as heavy and final as a tombstone.

Longinus could feel the heat rising up from the sand, radiating from the walls. He licked his dry lips, wishing for water.

The music stopped abruptly, replaced by a single, strident blare of a trumpet. The beast moved its head, as if listening, before returning to its examination of Longinus and Adelma.

"We split up," Adelma said in a low voice. "Follow the original plan."

Longinus nodded.

"Don't mess up your aim," she added with a wink that lacked some of her usual carefree confidence. "I want to see my Tommy again." Her hands were perfectly steady. "Second you see an opportunity, you poison that bloody lizard."

"Start, start!" the Prelate called out shrilly. His voice was unnaturally loud, echoing against the high stone walls. "Seneschal, what are these useless spies you got me? My best new lizard is waiting to be blooded, and they stand around like fools!"

"Do not worry, Your Radiance," the Seneschal replied in his smooth voice. "They will be killed presently."

As if agreeing, the creature let its forked tongue slither out of its mouth, tasting the air.

"Well, then," the Prelate cried, "start!"

Celine Jeanjean

Adelma gave Longinus a nod, and she slowly stepped sideways, edging towards the creature's side. As she moved, she swung her axe slowly in a figure of eight, her morning star strong and secure in her left hand. The lizard followed her with its beady black eyes. A shiver ran down its spine, its spiky red crest standing to attention.

It knew the attack was coming.

Longinus stayed where he was, swapping his sword to his left hand. Like any decent swordsman, he could wield a sword perfectly well with either hand, but he had a better throwing aim with his right one. He fingered the poison capsules in his pocket and selected two, closing his fist around them.

Adelma continued her careful progress. The creature looked at her then flicked its eyes at Longinus.

The Prelate laughed, the sound high-pitched. "Look at them. Look at how they try to confuse him, but he's too clever—he's not falling for it."

When the Prelate wasn't speaking, the silence was almost deafening. Adelma moved again, the sand crunching beneath her boots. Longinus could hear his own breathing, and when the lizard slipped its tongue out and in, he heard the soft, slippery sound it made.

Without warning, Adelma launched herself at the beast. It dodged and hissed, moving with surprising speed given its size. The thickness of its limbs and heaviness of its armour-like skin clearly didn't slow it down.

It turned to Adelma, who lunged again, swinging her morning star. The beast dodged the blow and retaliated with

376

a swipe of its massive claws. They missed Adelma by barely an inch.

Longinus crept forward slowly, his eyes riveted on the lizard's mouth, ready for the first opportunity to throw the poison in.

The creature watched Adelma. The tip of its tail flicked back and forth like a cat considering its prey. It shot forward. Adelma flung herself sideways. Her axe swung in a wide arc.

One of the beast's claws caught her thigh, carving out a long red streak. The axe caught its target, but it glanced harmlessly off the skin.

The Prelate giggled and clapped like a demented child. "Again, again!"

Adelma rolled, quickly regaining her feet.

Longinus flung his sword aside. If Adelma's axe couldn't pierce the skin, then his sword was useless. His dagger was thicker, with a stronger blade, and he pulled it out, readying it in his left hand. The poison capsules remained in his right hand. The beast still hadn't opened its mouth.

Adelma and the creature circled each other slowly, each watching the other. Longinus waited, breathing heavily. He kept his eyes fixated on the creature's mouth, doing his best to ignore the red streak at Adelma's thigh.

It's purple, it's purple, it's purple, it's purple…

Longinus repeated the phrase to himself with the intensity of a drowning man finding a life raft. He couldn't afford to lose precision or concentration, let alone faint.

Purple, it's purple…

"Come on, you fat, stupid gecko," Adelma called.

"It's a red-crested desert dragon, you fool," the Prelate shouted, leaning forward in his litter and craning his enormous neck forward. "Seneschal, tell her. Tell her she's a fool! A gecko, indeed. What *are* these spies you got me?"

"I'm sure she will find out for herself just how foolish that statement was," the Seneschal replied. "Let your new lizard teach her a lesson."

"Ha!" Adelma snorted. "A dragon that don't even breathe fire. Couldn't afford a real one?"

"Red-crested desert dragons don't breathe fire—they kill with poison, you imbecile," the Prelate screamed from his box. "See how long you last once it sinks its teeth into you. It takes one bite, just one bite." He gave a squeal of anticipation.

Longinus cast Adelma a worried glance. He had nothing on him to deal with a venomous bite—no antivenom of any kind. If the creature bit into Adelma, the fight would be over.

Adelma swung her axe and her morning star lazily, as though she wasn't approaching a monstrous lizard with a deadly, poisonous bite. If she felt any nerves, she didn't show it.

Longinus crept closer, moving slowly enough not to attract the creature's attention.

It charged, heavy feet thudding against the sand. Adelma spun out of its way, swinging her axe. The heavy blade caught it along the cheek, this time making a long tear in the beaded skin as the lizard's momentum helped to increase the strength of the blow.

The beast shrieked in pain, opening its mouth. Longinus threw the capsules.

Too slow.

The creature hadn't stopped moving, and the capsules bounced harmlessly off the side of its mouth.

To Longinus's surprise, the creature turned away. A thick flap of beaded skin hung from its face, exposing sharp, filthy teeth. It headed to a wooden palisade that Longinus guessed was a way out of the arena.

Men with steam guns had appeared at the top of the wall, and they blasted the lizard as it tried to get to the palisade. The lizard shrieked and hissed and immediately backed away from them. They blasted it some more until it was beyond their range.

The lizard stood still, watching them, making an odd clicking sound in its throat.

"Seneschal, Seneschal," the Prelate whined. "Make it kill the Damsians! What is it *doing*?"

Longinus felt a stab of pity for the monstrous creature. It clearly hadn't chosen to be here any more than he had. A fight to the death had no more appeal for it than it did for Longinus.

The moment of pity was fleeting at best. After a few more bursts of steam from the guards on the wall, the lizard turned back to face Adelma. It flicked its tail, watching her.

Longinus thought he could see calculation in the beast's eyes.

Maybe it understands that it needs to kill us to get out of the arena.

The creature charged, massive legs moving at impossible speed given their size. Adelma stood ready. She swung at the lizard, but it feinted, changing its course at the last possible second and spinning around, whipping its massive tail. It caught Adelma squarely, sending her flying across the sandy pit like a rag doll. She tumbled, losing her morning star, kicking up a cloud of sand.

The Prelate squealed and clapped his hands.

The creature charged after Adelma. She rose up, but the lizard was faster. It pushed itself up onto its hind legs, hurling its full weight at her. They fell back to the sand together.

Longinus rushed after the creature, no longer able to see Adelma in the writhing mass.

He reached its side. Adelma was screaming. Both weapons were on the ground. Her arms held onto the beast's lower jaw, her muscles straining to keep the razor-sharp teeth away from her. The creature hissed, swinging its head from side to side, trying to shake her off. Its claws scrabbled, shredding Adelma's skin.

Longinus didn't pause to think. He threw himself at the beast's side, stabbing it under the right foreleg, in the armpit. The resistance he felt from the thick skin was almost enough to deflect the blow, but the dagger was sharp, the blade sinking in.

The creature shrieked again, wrenching itself and the dagger out of Longinus's grasp.

He flung two more capsules at the open mouth. Again, they bounced harmlessly away, falling to the sand.

The creature snarled, hissing as it moved its injured foreleg back and forth. The dagger was still embedded in the armpit. It reached down, bending its neck until its mouth was level with the knife's hilt. It yanked the blade out with its teeth.

Longinus backed away, right hand grabbing the last fistful of poison capsules.

Behind the creature, Adelma was rising, heavily cut and bloodied. There was nothing Longinus could do to prevent the rise of nausea, the patchy black lights creeping across his vision. He knew the signs, and soon he would faint.

Longinus ran towards the beast, shouting, poison capsules in his right hand.

He had time for one move only before his faculties left him. It was the move he had wanted to teach Rory back on the ship, what seemed like a lifetime ago. It had been his sister Myran's signature move, and he spent countless hours as a young boy practicing until he had mastered it perfectly.

Time seemed to slow.

The dizzy nausea washed over him. His vision grew narrow and blurry. His heartbeat was loud in his ears. Somewhere overhead, the Prelate was clapping.

And then Longinus launched himself forward, feet first, sending out a spray of sand. He aimed just to the left of the beast.

He skidded past.

The beast opened its mouth to snap at him.

Longinus punched his fist into its mouth, flinging the capsules. And the world went black.

A massive impact jerked Longinus back to consciousness, and he felt himself careening through the sand, tumbling over and over again. He came to a stop, his right arm crumpled beneath him like a broken wing. He couldn't draw a full breath to fill his winded lungs.

He gasped, desperately trying to inhale, as he slowly rolled onto his back.

Adelma stepped into his field of vision, standing between him and the lizard. She had found her morning star, and her axe was in her other hand. She stood solidly in front of Longinus, both feet planted on the ground. He closed his eyes, feeling nausea rise up again.

"I think I did it," he wheezed. He prayed the creature hadn't spat the capsules back out.

"Good," Adelma said.

She broke into a run towards the right, and the beast hissed, charging at her. Longinus felt a flicker of hope as he thought the creature was maybe a little slower than before.

Adelma dodged easily. She hacked with her axe, following with a swing of her morning star. Both found their mark. The creature hissed in pain and abruptly retreated. It watched Adelma with wary eyes.

Longinus scrambled to his feet, swaying dangerously. His vision was patchy, and he felt dizzy. The lizard hesitated, looking back at the men with the steam guns, and again, Longinus felt a surge of pity for it.

The creature attacked Adelma. This time, it didn't charge right at her. Instead, it kept her at arm's length, snapping its mouth full of teeth at her weapons. Its movements were less precise than before, less deadly. It had started to die.

Longinus was no stranger to death. He would take the death of the lizard over harm done to Adelma any day, but all the same... he felt an odd sadness for the beast. It hadn't yet realised that its fate had been written.

"Just give it time," Longinus croaked. "Don't take risks."

Adelma grunted as she swiped the axe and morning star to keep the teeth away from her. The lizard's movement got slower, clumsier. It shook its head as though trying to clear it. A low, clicking sound rose up from its throat. It hesitated, swinging its massive head left and right. When it tried again to turn toward the exit, the steam guns blasted it, and it stumbled clumsily back.

The lizard collapsed into the sand. Its massive tail still twitched, and its tongue slipped in and out of its mouth as though tasting the air for the last time.

And then it was still.

The arena was eerily silent.

Longinus watched with detached befuddlement. He was vaguely aware of the Prelate screeching something about the spies owing him a new lizard, but the sound was distant, as if coming to Longinus through water. He felt light, as if his head was floating above his body.

Only then did he realise his phobia of blood wasn't taking over. He raised his right hand, the one that had punched into the beast's mouth to throw the poison capsules. For the first time in his life, he wasn't overwhelmed by the sight of his blood. He took in blankly the long red cuts that the creature's razor-sharp teeth had raked along his hand.

Sand had stuck to the blood, turning it to a reddish paste.

The words of the Prelate came back to him. All it would take was one bite.

The blackness at the edges of Longinus's consciousness rose up like a wave. He was still observing his hand when the blackness crashed over him, the sand rushing up to meet him.

CHAPTER
53

Time seemed to both fly and crawl past as Rory helped get everything ready for the night's expedition. She had caught a few hours of fitful sleep, her eyes flying open every half an hour or so. Every time she woke up, she found Rafe still asleep on the floor a few feet from her.

Rory hadn't felt comfortable sleeping on the mattress, so Rafe had declared he would also sleep the floor. Try as she might, Rory couldn't think of the gesture as ridiculous. She knew Rafe was being chivalrous, a concept that had always seemed stupid to her, yet now she was oddly touched.

Once they had all snatched a few hours of sleep, they began to prepare for smuggling themselves into the palace. Rory had gone to the kitchen to help Reheeme get everything ready for the diversion that would draw the Watch away from the rebel force.

Rafe, meanwhile, was in the front of house, explaining how Cruikshank's drills worked. The drills would isolate the Dividing Wall and the Great Gate at the top of the cliffs from the palace so that neither could send warning of an attack. Once the Dividing Wall and the Great Gate were down, the Lower Azyrians and the Maksurians would be free to sweep through Tarwa, hitting the palace.

Rory and Rafe would be among the group smuggled into the palace, looking to open one of the palace gates to let the rebel force in. The diversion, meanwhile, would be set up near the Eastern Trade Gate, where the Watch were likely to be expecting an attack.

Much as Rory and Rafe wanted to help the rebellion, their priority was to find Longinus, Cruikshank, and Adelma. She and Rafe would therefore split from he rebel force to go looking for their friends.

Rory no longer cared whether they rescued Kadelta. So long as the other three were in danger, they took full priority. Once they were safe and sound, then she would consider what do to about the Damsian inventor and his machine.

More and more Risen were gradually joining the safe house, and it was now quite full. Urzo was there to organise them all, sending the ones who would join the smuggling mission to the kitchen. They drifted in, each one showing shock at Reheeme's presence, before slinking to the side of the room to join the other Risen.

Reheeme worked with complete intensity, muttering to herself as she moved, and she seemed unaware of the confusion and hostility she was causing.

The Risen stood on the edge of the kitchen, muttering amongst themselves and glaring at her.

"How is it all going?" Urzo asked, walking in.

Reheeme looked up at him. "I should be ready in a couple of hours."

"Good. That gives us plenty of time. We'll head off at nightfall. I heard from Oma, by the way. She and Terrell made it out of the racecourse fine."

Reheeme nodded, obviously distracted. "I'm making the various compounds I'll need, but I'll have to mix them together at the time of activation to get the reactions we need."

Rory frowned. "Wait, that ain't gonna give us close to enough time to get away before we draw the Watch's attention."

"Well, obviously, I'll be staying behind while you go on to the new location," Reheeme said.

"No," Urzo said. "We don't leave anyone behind."

"Oh, don't give me theatrics and grand speeches," Reheeme said crossly. "We need the distraction. In order to achieve that, I need to be there when the distraction happens. There's nothing much to it. I have my studs, and when they find me, they'll take me to the Seneschal. So long as the rebellion happens, you'll get to me before they can arrange my execution."

"But the risk you'd be taking..." Urzo said.

"Is my business," Reheeme snapped.

Rory snorted. "This ain't made you any more pleasant, has it?"

Reheeme shrugged and returned to her work. "Pleasant doesn't achieve anything. I do what I have to do."

"Or are you trying to stay behind on your own so that you can tell the Watch where we'll really be going?" a woman asked. She stepped forward. "The whole plan depends on us getting into the palace unnoticed so we can open a gate and let the main force in. If the Watch finds out where we are really coming out, the whole thing will fall apart. Everyone will get slaughtered at the palace walls. We can't take the palace straight on—you all know that. We *need* that gate opened."

"And we can't trust anyone from the Sons and Daughters," a man said, also stepping forward. "They showed their true colours, turning to the Seneschal. What makes *her* any different?"

"Oh, for crying out loud," Reheeme snapped. "We don't have time for this. I need to get ready. I was down at the racecourse with the Damsians, with Oma and Urzo. I've been working towards this rebellion my whole life. I'm *nothing* like those other cowards who ran before the Seneschal."

Urzo, who had listened in silence, stepped forward, facing the Risen. "I understand your mistrust. I didn't trust Reheeme either at first. But I do genuinely think she's on our side. And we need help. We need someone to pull off that diversion. If we leave one of you behind to be caught by the Watch, you'll likely get executed on the spot. Using Reheeme is our best bet."

"Oh, really?" the woman said. "And what if she's like her husband, trying to make a deal with the Seneschal? I mean, look at her. We're going down into the sewers, and she's wearing silk! That's not someone preparing to see battle."

Rory bit her lip. She could completely understand the woman's distrust, but at the same time, Reheeme had the right of it. They couldn't afford to waste time arguing.

"I'm wearing silks," Reheeme said, her tone dangerous, "because I haven't had a chance to change. And because I'm not going to be fighting—I'm going to be the diversion. *And* because I'll be staying behind to get arrested, and I've got a better chance of surviving if I look like this."

The woman smirked triumphantly, crossing her arms. "There. She wants the Watch to find her, and she wants them to know she's a good, loyal Tarwanese, not one of us filthy Risen."

"You want me not to look Tarwanese? Fine." Reheeme unscrewed the studs at her eyebrows, removing them one by one.

The room fell silent as everyone gaped. Urzo looked shocked, as if she'd just stripped naked. Even Rory had to admit she felt uncomfortable seeing the gaping holes at Reheeme's eyebrows.

"There. Now I look no different than a slave," Reheeme said.

Still, no one spoke, stunned.

Reheeme looked around at them all. "You know," she said, the anger gone from her voice. "This is the way we should be storming the palace. Not wearing studs that are an integral part of the repression of Azyr. So long as there are studs, there can be those who are studless and therefore not free. There can be Lower studs and Higher studs. So long as there are studs in Azyr, things won't ever really change." She looked down at her studs, wonder on her face. "I didn't understand that until right now."

The kitchen felt so charged with energy that Rory half expected the air to crackle with it. The Risen were staring intently at Reheeme.

"No more studs," Urzo said with wonder. He slowly unscrewed his own studs.

"No more studs," voices shouted around the kitchen. Rory saw more and more hands unscrewing studs. Excitement mounted. "No more studs!"

"We make ourselves the same as those who have been taken into slavery," Urzo said eagerly. "No one is superior to anyone else anymore."

"The Tarwanese will never accept this," someone said.

"So what?" Urzo replied. "When the revolution has come, they won't have a choice. We'll build a new Azyr, and they can either join or get left behind."

Urzo scanned the faces of the Risen, his eyes burning. "Get the word out. Anyone in support of our rebellion fights without studs on." He raised his fist in which he held his studs. "This is the symbol of our rebellion. This."

The kitchen erupted in cheering.

Urzo turned to Reheeme. "That was inspired."

CHAPTER

54

Longinus awoke to find himself in the cell once more. He was laid on the floor, the stone cool against his skin. The rest of his body burned with fever, perspiration rolling off his forehead.

He turned his head slowly, wincing at the stiffness in his neck. His gaze fell on his right hand. It was swollen, angry red tracks crawling up his forearm. He was surprised to notice that once again, the sight of his own blood had no effect on him.

In fact, if not for the cool feeling of the stone against his skin, he would have felt like he wasn't actually in the cell. It was as though he were watching the scene from a distance.

"You're awake!" Adelma said, hurrying to his side. She crouched down next to him. "I tried to suck the poison out, but I didn't know what I were doing. I don't know if it helped. There was so much sand all over it—"

"Don't worry." Longinus's voice was little more than a croak. "Too long had passed—the venom would have entered my bloodstream no matter what you did. And if you had ingested some it, then we'd be in an even worse position than we already are."

Adelma gripped his good wrist. "I'm getting you out of here one way or another," she said through gritted teeth.

Longinus nodded, finding the interaction exhausting. His body began shivering as an abrupt chill settled over him. "How long was I unconscious?"

"A few hours. I carried you back to the cell on my shoulder." Adelma winked. "The Prelate was angry, let me tell you. He was practically spitting with rage. Thought he might strangle himself from all his spluttering, but no luck."

Longinus gave her a slow, tired smile. "Good, good. Can you prop my back up?"

Adelma immediately sprang to action, sitting against the wall and picking up Longinus more gently than he would have thought possible, given her thick hands, then propping him against her bent knees. The movement sent a mad dizziness coursing through him, and he closed his eyes against it.

"Like this?" Adelma asked.

"Yes. I need to keep my hand lower than my heart. And my heartbeat needs to stay as low as possible. It's a slow-acting venom, clearly, so we need to hamper its progression as much as possible. I've taken measures for years to build up my body's tolerance to poison, so it will affect me slower than a normal person."

"Yes, yes, good. Anything you can think of to help. What about that narcotic business?" she asked pointing at his sleeve, where, hidden in the piping, was his special narcotic powder.

"More jokes about micturition?" Longinus asked.

"I can joke about piss till I'm blue in the face, but right now, I'd rather know whether it can help."

"Sadly not. I need an antivenom."

"Then we'll get you one," Adelma replied. Her lips pressed together in a grim line.

"Sure, sure," Longinus replied.

He felt exhausted. His head was growing heavy. It felt too big, too full of his heartbeat, and his eyes were hot. He let his lids close. There was no point disabusing Adelma of her illusion. Longinus guessed from the way he felt that he probably had a few hours left.

If he was lucky.

The chance of them getting out in that time without weapons or poisons was nonexistent. And as much as Longinus wanted to cling to the hope that Rory was out there, mounting a rescue mission, she had no idea where he was. The palace was huge, easily big enough that sneaking around unseen would be possible, but it would also likely involve her getting lost. Not only that, but if Jabir had betrayed the rebellion, it would be in complete disarray. Rory might not even be able to get into the palace.

No, there really was only one outcome. Longinus was going to die in this cell, propped up against Adelma's knees.

His thoughts strayed to Lady Martha, and a wave of sadness washed over him. He would never tell her how he felt. All this time, he had been so careful to be subtle, not to betray his feelings in any kind of obvious way, and yet now he found that not being more obvious was his biggest regret. He didn't regret much else, but this—yes, he regretted it.

Longinus's throat tightened. It was an odd feeling to be contemplating one's death like this. He would never see Rory again or Cruikshank.

At least he was leaving people behind who cared about him. His sister had hated him since the day he was born, his mother had died in some faraway place, and everyone had laughed at him growing up because of his peculiarities, so he had matured into a man who lived life alone, on the margin. Friendship had never come naturally to him, and now he realised that he had three good friends. Even Rafe wasn't too bad.

"It will have been a pleasure fighting alongside you," Longinus croaked to Adelma.

"Shut it. I ain't sitting here and listening to none of that defeatist talk. And don't talk. Waste of your energy to be saying that sappy nonsense. Priority number one is to keep you alive." She fussed with him, shifting him so that he rested slightly differently against her knees. As he moved, Longinus's head lolled as if he had lost consciousness.

"Longinus?" Adelma asked, voice thick with worry.

"Still here." A smile quirked on Longinus's lips as he wondered whether Adelma would cry at his funeral. Now, that would be a sight. Almost worth returning as a ghost for. He wondered if he could mess with her, make it his dying wish that she should wail at his funeral like a mourner for hire. The thought almost made him chuckle.

The sound of the door at the end of the passage squeaking open made him open his eyes.

"Put him in that one," a voice said. Longinus recognised it as the Seneschal's.

"Your Grace, I can still be of help. I know how they think, how they operate. I-I know—"

Jabir's plea was cut short, and Longinus heard a cell door slam. The thought of Jabir was enough to stir him out this torpor, and he felt a vicious sense of justice at the man being locked in a cell.

It occurred to him that if Jabir was being punished, it was because he had done something very wrong—and what could be more wrong than allowing Rory and Rafe to escape? Longinus felt a spark of hope.

"You will be very useful," the Seneschal said soothingly. "His Radiance's lizards need feeding."

The Seneschal then appeared at Longinus and Adelma's cell door. He watched them calmly.

"I have to admit, I didn't think you'd survive that," he said softly. "You Damsians are harder to crack than I expected."

"Damn right," Adelma growled.

"Not to worry. It won't take me long. It took me no time at all with Cruikshank."

Longinus pushed himself up. "Cruikshank?" he croaked. "What about her?"

Celine Jeanjean

"You'll see her soon." The Seneschal produced a small vial from a pocket in his robes and sighed, examining it. "And to think that if I gave you this dose of antivenom, you would recover in a couple of hours."

"Give it to him," Adelma urged. "Give it to him. We can fight again and entertain the Prelate. Or you can use me as muscle for hire and him as an alchemist. It's just daft wasting us like that."

"Hmm," the Seneschal said. "You could potentially have some value, I suppose." He shook his head. "But the most value you have to me is dead. I'm in no rush. I don't mind letting nature take its course. I've removed all antivenom from this part of the palace too. Don't think about trying to force anyone to get it for you." He turned to Adelma. "Once he's dead, you can go back out in the arena. I'll have to come up with some better adversaries for you to face. Or maybe I'll wait until your ship has been found and sunk— see how well you fight with the knowledge that you are the last one left alive." The Seneschal smiled, although it was more of a baring of his teeth. "It will depend on the will of His Radiance."

"That fat fool is insane," Adelma growled.

"That is the first time I've heard anyone say those words out loud." He lowered his voice. "You're right, of course. Which makes it so much more fun to manipulate him—I never quite know which way he'll go. I'd best be off. Enjoy the end of your stay in Azyr," he added to Longinus.

"Bugger off to hell," Adelma snapped.

Longinus heard the diminishing sound of the Seneschal's footsteps, followed by the rusty squeak of the door at the end of the passage.

Then the door slammed shut with echoing finality.

He looked up at Adelma. "Your ship…"

"He ain't never finding the *Eel* if she don't want to be found," Adelma scoffed. "Best smuggling ship manned by the best crew, each one trained by me. No chance in hell. My Tommy is safe, and word *will* get back to Damsport if we disappear and my crew don't get my signal."

Longinus nodded. There was some comfort in that—although it would do little to improve his current situation. "What the Seneschal said about Cruikshank—do you think it means she's dead?"

Adelma didn't answer, but she looked bleak.

"He said nothing about Rory and Rafe, though," Longinus said. "And if Jabir is locked up…"

"That means they must have gotten away." Adelma grinned. "Come over here—let's find out."

She picked Longinus up and carried him to the cell doors. Across from the corridor, to the left, was Jabir. He sat against a wall, looking wretched. His expensive clothing was rumpled and torn, and he had lost his hat. He still had his studs and his bracelets, but he looked a world away from the confident, wealthy man Longinus and the others had met when they'd first arrived.

"You didn't get Rory or Rafe," Longinus croaked gleefully. "That's why you're in here. You didn't get them."

Adelma crowed with laughter. "You failed. And you know what? You ain't seen the end of us Damsians."

Jabir glared balefully at them, and he got up to go sit farther into his cell, out of sight.

Longinus chuckled, feeling revived. Rory and Rafe were free.

"They might make it to us in time," Adelma said, bringing him back to his original position against the wall. "Rory and Rafe. They might get here in time. And that Reheeme's an alchemist, right, so she can make an antivenom for you."

Longinus smiled so as not to disillusion her. Unless Rory and the others made it here in the next couple of hours, all the alchemy in the world wouldn't revive him.

CHAPTER 55

The sewers were only just about tall enough for a person to stand in, and Rory stretched up a hand to brush her fingers against the dirty orange stone. A fine dust tickled her face. The tunnel was rounded, stretching forward like the gullet of an enormous beast.

Stinking water ran along the floor, a murky brown that Rory did her best not to think about. She breathed through her mouth to keep the stench at bay. How did Urzo bear working down here? She whispered a silent apology to Daria for the damage to her boots, before catching herself. Memories of Daria were coming back to her far more often since that night on the ship, and she didn't like it. The box of memories was shut, it had to stay shut. Now more than ever she couldn't afford to get distracted.

Around her, the Risen were muttering balefully about the waste of water. For them, water was for drinking, for surviving, so to see it used to wash away sewage must have felt sacrilegious.

Rory could feel their anger rising as they progressed.

She was walking roughly in the middle of the procession, between Rafe and Reheeme, the group of rebels stretching out in a long, single file. Urzo was at the front, a little ahead, wearing his uniform disguise in case any Watchmen were waiting for them.

The alchemical globes the little procession carried made quivering patterns on the walls as the light reflected on the filthy water. The long tunnels distorted sounds so that the whispers at the start of the procession drifted down as ghostly moans. Rats squeaked, darting past through pipes that opened out onto the main tunnel.

Rory nearly stepped on one, and she cursed, kicking it and missing, sending a spray of foul water on Rafe.

"Hey!" he protested. "I think I stink enough as it is."

The procession moved mostly in silence other than whispered communications up ahead to check that the coast was clear. As they had hoped, the focus hadn't been on placing the Watch in the sewers themselves, since there were far too many tunnels and branches to cover all of it. Instead, Watchmen would have hopefully been posted at all the sewer openings near the Eastern Trade Gate. Even if they hadn't, Reheeme's explosions would draw them there.

Up ahead, Rory heard a fresh wave of ghostly moans, signifying a message being relayed.

"We're reaching the eastern stop-off point," those in front whispered.

Everyone fell silent, as agreed. The tunnel changed, widening to make space for a narrow orange-brick walkway to the left. They all climbed up, one after the other, footsteps ringing out on the brick despite everyone's best efforts.

Urzo had stopped, leaving the others to go ahead. "This is it," he whispered to Reheeme.

She nodded. Rory had to admire the woman. There was no fear on her features, no hesitation. She pulled out her studs and put them back on. When she was found and taken by the Watch, her studs would ensure she was taken prisoner rather than killed. Those who had been carrying packs, including Rory, undid the straps, carefully lowering the jars to the ground. Reheeme checked over each one, setting them up in clusters. She also had some empty beakers, and she lined those up.

She stood up, her face betraying nothing. "I'm ready."

"Will you be alright?" Rafe asked. "Here, take—" He'd pulled out a knife, but Reheeme waved him away.

"I don't know my way with weapons. My best defence will be my studs. I will be immediately identified by my status and treated accordingly. I'm trusting all of you to get to me once the gate is open." She gave them a meaningful look. "So don't go around giving your knives away," she added to Rafe. "Now, go."

And that was that. She turned away and got to work. Rory was impressed. It took some serious steel not betray any nerves.

"Take my alchemical globe," Rory said. "In case the other one stops working." She placed it on the ground.

Reheeme nodded but didn't look at her as she busied herself with her compounds. "Well?" she said, finally looking up at them. "Go! You have things to do."

As they walked away, Rory turned back to look at Reheeme. She was crouched down in the middle of a yellow circle of light amid perfect darkness. The farther away they got, the smaller Reheeme looked and the more insignificant her light.

"I'm growing to like her," Rory whispered to Rafe. "Didn't think I'd ever say that."

"You're telling me," Rafe replied. "But I agree. Not many people would have it in them to stay back alone."

Rory hoped they'd succeed in opening the gate and Reheeme's bravery would have been for something.

***

Rory and the others reached their exit from the sewers without any trouble. Urzo climbed out first.

"Clear," he whispered.

Just as Rory reached the top of the ladder, she heard the first explosion. She froze, head stuck out of the hole, while everyone at the surface dropped to a crouch. Shouts rang out farther ahead, and she heard footsteps against stone.

Thick smoke rose up in the distance.

Rory hoped Reheeme was alright. So far, though, their plan seemed to be working. There was no great concentration of Watch at this part of the palace, and with any luck, they would all be charging towards Reheeme.

Rory pulled herself out, joining the others in the shadows. The palace looked blue in the night, and it gleamed softly, reflecting the moonlight. It was far more beautiful now, not as harsh and blindingly bright as during the day. This part of the palace looked less like one structure and more like a conglomerate of smaller structures and outbuildings.

Once they were all out of the sewers, Urzo and Rafe pulled the heavy iron cover back across the hole.

"The gate is the other side of that building, there," Urzo whispered.

"Do we know if there are any Watch inside?" Rafe asked.

Urzo shook his head. "No way to know."

Rafe nodded and pulled out his helmet from his bag. He put it on. It gleamed darkly, the slick black ponytail moving fluidly with each of his steps. He gathered up the end and carefully unsheathed each of the knives hidden in the long horsehair. He then released the ponytail gently. The knives were razor sharp, and the slightest mistake would have meant a cut, but Rafe handled the ponytail carefully, making it obvious how much he cared for it, and how much he'd missed wearing his helmet since coming to Azyr.

"Everyone keep well clear of me," he whispered. "And if there's trouble, stay back and let me go first."

Urzo led them to a nearby door. He paused, his ear against it, and then opened it silently.

The shadows were thicker inside. They were in some sort of long storage room, and at the end was another door. A line of light bled out from under the wood. Rafe padded across, removed his helmet, gesturing for everyone to stay back, and he pressed his ear to the door.

"There's quite a few out there," he whispered once he had stepped away from the door and put his helmet back on. "Ten, or probably more, but it's hard to tell."

Urzo looked worried, glancing back at the group of rebels. The Risen would have limited fighting experience, and their weapons were inferior to those of the Watch. A skirmish now could cost them dear.

"Any way around?" Rafe asked.

Urzo shook his head. "Not without taking a massive detour which increases our chances of coming across more Watch."

"Alright, well in that case, let me go in first," Rafe replied. "Don't get too close."

Urzo nodded.

Rafe stepped back. He took a deep breath, slowly drawing his matched set of long daggers. Then he launched himself forward, bursting through the door. He'd been right about underestimating the numbers. There were about twenty members of the Watch sitting, playing cards, plus a good handful of regular workers.

Rafe ran amongst the Watch, and they leapt to their feet, knocking the tables over and scattering the cards. For a minute, Rory forgot herself, mesmerised by the sight of a Varanguard in full fight. Rafe didn't just swing the ponytail around him in a circle—he was a blur of continuous motion. He used his arms to interrupt the ponytail's swings, smacking it out in a sharp dart so that the knives slashed and stabbed and retreated too fast for anyone to react. The ponytail was so accurate it seemed animated of its own will.

Rafe spun and kicked and slashed with his twin daggers, like a black tornado with teeth unleashed among the Watch. And yet his every movement was so controlled that there was a hypnotic grace to his deadly efficacy. It was both beautiful and horrifying, and Rory realised just how inadequate a fighter she was by comparison.

Then the fighting was everywhere, and there was no more time to think. Rafe could only engage so many at a time, and the rest of the men rushed at Rory and the other rebels. Rory found herself fighting a large worker who looked like he might work in the stables or something of the sort. His chest was bare, a thick mat of wiry hair reaching down to his bulging belly. He was strong, hefting a piece of heavy steelwood studded with mean spikes.

Rory was immediately on the back foot. The man was large for an Azyrian, broad-shouldered and muscular despite his belly, and his black skin glistened with sweat. Rory ducked and retreated away from his cudgel, her sword inadequate against such a heavy weapon.

She parried one of his blows with her sword, wincing as her wrist absorbed the force of the impact.

Again, she blocked a blow with her sword, but she lacked the strength in her right arm, and this time, her weapon went clattering to the floor. She jumped nimbly back, only just dodging another blow. The truth of Rafe's words became obvious: the sword wasn't the weapon for her.

She looked desperately around for anything she could use as a weapon or a defence.

Her heart pounded. The man stood between her and the rest of the fighting, cutting her off.

He swung his cudgel at her head, and she dropped to a crouch, feeling the wind of it as it passed. She sprung back up, grabbing a stool, and hurled it at him. He ducked left, and the stool leg only clipped his shoulder.

He grinned. "Foreign rebel scum."

Rory dodged another swing of the cudgel, and it buried itself into a table, cracking the wood and sending splinters flying. As she ducked, she grabbed something heavy, made of metal, and threw it.

It caught the man square on the temple, splitting the skin at his eyebrow.

He snarled, increasing the violence and speed of his blows. Rory ducked and weaved, realising that he was forcing her into a corner.

Her back foot caught on something, and she went sprawling to the ground. She felt the handle of a whip on the floor beneath her fingers, and she grabbed it, quickly rolling away before the cudgel smashed into the ground where her head had been.

She jumped up to her feet, cracking the whip. She didn't pause to think. The movement felt completely natural, like loosing her grappling hook.

One crack of the plaited leather, and an ugly welt appeared on the man's neck.

He roared and ran for her, hefting his full weight behind his cudgel.

Rory threw herself sideways, tucking herself and rolling into a ball then springing back up. The cudgel made splinters of a stool.

She cracked the whip again and again, forcing the man back, the whip licking his face and arms. The whip felt alive in her hand, easy. It felt like the extension of her arm that the sword should have been.

The worker raised his cudgel, and Rory aimed for it. The whip wrapped around it lightning quick, and Rory yanked it out of the jailer's hand. Too heavy to go far, it rolled just behind Rory.

She felt a grim satisfaction—the tables had turned at last. The jailer watched her, obviously unsure of his next move.

She cracked the whip, this time aiming for the jailer's neck.

He put out his arm, interrupting the whip and nearly catching a hold of it. Rory snatched it back just in time. An angry welt raised the skin on his arm where the plaited leather had lashed against it.

The worker picked up a piece of the table he had smashed. As he threw it, Rory dodged sideways, rolled forward, and sprung up at the man's side. She unleashed the whip, and this time, it curled around the jailer's neck.

She immediately pulled, jerking the jailer off balance. She coiled the whip up until she was a couple of feet behind him, too far for him to reach, but close enough that she could pull on the plaited leather and strangle him.

He scrabbled with his hands, trying to loosen the whip. He jerked back and forth, but Rory was far away enough that he didn't destabilise her.

The worker choked, the fight draining out of him.

"Enough." Rafe stepped to the man's side, pointing a knife at the man's throat. He was breathing heavily, spattered with blood.

The worker fell still, but he continued to choke. Rory loosened the whip. He leaned forward immediately, hands rubbing his throat, coughing and spluttering. She felt something wet at her nose and wiped it with her hand, her fingers coming back bloody. She wiped her bloody nose again on her forearm, sniffing.

Rory glanced around her. Every one of the Watchmen was dead. She felt a pang as she saw that twelve rebels had also fallen. A third of the force. Rory recognised among them a couple who had spoken out against Reheeme back in the kitchen.

Urzo seemed unhurt, but he grimaced as he took stock of their losses. "This is bad." He rubbed both hands over his face. "Really bad. If we face a large group of Watch at the gate we won't be able to overpower them."

Rory and Rafe exchanged a glance. What now?

Urzo turned to the worker who had been fighting Rory. "You. Can you take us to the Prelate's fighting pit?"

The man looked around him, licking his lips. He gave a jerky nod.

"'Adelma," Rory breathed. "She might have gotten sent to the fighting pit. It would be the most logical place for her."

"And more importantly," Urzo said, "we could free the pit fighting slaves and see if they'll join us. We need to swell our numbers—I just don't think we'll have enough as it is. Your keys there," he asked the worker. "Will they get us access to the cells?"

Rory realised that she'd been so focused on the fighting, she hadn't even noticed the set of keys jangling from the worker's waist.

The man licked his lips again. "Please, they'll kill me if I do that."

"And we'll kill you if you don't," Urzo replied darkly.

The worker looked from Urzo to Rafe and then nodded. "I work at the pit. I have keys for the fighters and the lizards."

"Good," Urzo said curtly. He looked once again at all the bodies littering the room, his worry written all over his face. "Let's hope we can convince enough of the pit fighters to help us," he murmured.

The rebels were passionate and did their best, but the reality was that they weren't good fighters, and against highly trained Watch, they couldn't hold up well. Urzo caught Rory's eye.

Neither of them said what was on their minds: if they weren't able to open the gate, it would all be over.

The jailer caused no trouble, leading them to the pit fighters. They walked through another courtyard and entered a set of lizard stables, and Rory was hit with the heavy smell of animals, dung, and sweat. The jailer had no light with him, so the stables remained thick with shadows.

"Keep clear of the cages," the jailer murmured.

Something hissed in the dark. Rory shuddered, thinking of the monsters from the races.

The group moved forward cautiously. They were at one end of a long passage lined with iron-barred cages. As they passed the first one, Rory heard a low clicking sound coming from the shadows, but it was too dark to make out what was inside the cage.

More hisses and clicks rang out, the lizards vaguely visible in the gloom. Some even made a kind of growling sound. Each one reacted to the group's passage.

They reached a door at the other end, which the jailer unlocked with one of the keys that hung from the metal loop at his waist. Beyond was a small room from which several led several other heavy iron doors.

"Some of the pit fighters are there." He pointed at a door. "And behind those other doors, there." He pointed the doors out then set about unlocking the one in front of them.

The door swung open on creaking hinges.

Beyond was a long, narrow corridor lined with barred cells. Here and there, arms stuck out, and hands were wrapped around bars.

"Open them all," Rory ordered.

The man stepped forward and was about to obey when a voice cut through the silence. "Rory?"

Rory's heart leapt up into her mouth. "Adelma? Adelma!"

She snatched the keys from the jailer's hands and rushed down the passageway. "Adelma!"

"Over here!" Adelma's thick forearm stuck out of a cell almost at the bottom of the corridor.

Rory ran, her boots ringing on the stone. As she passed other prisoners, they shouted for her to open their cells. She ignored them until she reached Adelma's cell. What she saw turned her insides to water.

Longinus lay on the ground, eyes closed. His breathing was laboured, his normally brown skin pale and waxy and shiny with sweat. Dark rings circled his eyes, and angry red lines snaked up from his scab-covered, swollen right hand.

"What—what happened?" Rory's hands shook as she fumbled for the right key to open the cell door, and she almost dropped the set.

Rafe arrived beside her, sucking in air as he caught sight of Longinus. "What happened?"

"We got set to fight against a lizard," Adelma replied grimly. "Longinus killed it, but it was poisonous, and it got him."

"Someone get antipoison," Rory shouted over her shoulder as she opened the cell door.

Rory rushed inside the cell and knelt down by Longinus, brushing a sticky strand of hair from his forehead. His skin burned with fever. He stirred.

"It's me," Rory said. "Longinus, it's Rory. Don't worry. It'll be fine. We'll get you antipoison, and it'll all be fine."

Longinus's cracked lips stretched a fraction. "You're... late." His voice was like the tearing of dry paper. "And it's antivenom...not antipoison... If you bite it and you die...it's poison... If it bites you and you die, it's...venom."

Rory snorted, and her breath caught in her throat. Only Longinus could be pedantic at a time like this.

"There ain't no antivenom left but with the Seneschal," Adelma said. "Bastard came to gloat before."

Urzo joined them, dragging the jailer with him. He shoved the man forward, down on his knees and pressed the tip of a blade at his neck. "It this true? Is there antivenom anywhere near here?"

"It's true, it's true," the jailer said breathlessly. "The Seneschal has always been the only one to control the antivenom."

"You must have some here for yourself," Urzo growled. "Where is it?"

"I don't... we don't have any, I swear! Disobeying the Seneschal is... is... madness. I swear on my life there's nothing here."

Urzo nodded and withdrew his blade. The jailer sagged with relief.

Rory wanted to kick the wall. "Reheeme," she said through gritted teeth. "If we hadn't left Reheeme behind, she could make him something." She took a breath. "Alright, so we go find the Seneschal." She turned to Adelma. "What about Cruikshank? Where did they take her?"

"I got no idea," Adelma replied. "I woke up here, and I ain't seen her since. The Seneschal mentioned that he had her... that he managed to... crack her. I don't know what that means."

Rory gave a grim nod. Whatever it meant, it wasn't good. "We need to go after her."

"Longinus also got some sleeping stuff in his sleeves," Adelma said. "There in the piping. Apparently, you can activate it by pissing on it or mixing it with ammonia, whatever that is. But apparently, that can't help him with the poison."

"Well, it seems to me like things are pretty clear," Rafe said. "We need to find the Seneschal fast and get the antivenom and Cruikshank's location from him."

Urzo shook his head. "The Seneschal has a large complement of personal guards. To go after him without proper backup would be suicide. You should wait until the gate has been opened and the palace is under attack. Then we can help you find the Seneschal."

"That's too long!" Rory shouted. "Longinus can't wait that long. Look at him! He needs antivenom *now*."

She was only just managing to keep calm. The thought of a world without Longinus made her feel sick and dizzy. He had to get the antivenom. He had to.

Urzo shook his head again, his face grim. "I'm sorry. I really am. You've helped us with our cause, and we are very grateful to you, but I'm not jeopardising the attack on the palace to save your friend. If we go to the Seneschal now, we jeopardise the entire rebellion. We'll have to hope Longinus can last until the palace is secured."

He picked up the keys from the ground where Rory had dropped them, and he threw them to a woman. "Free the fighters, and ask them if they'll join us."

The other prisoners clamoured, hands reaching out between bars.

Rory gently let Longinus's head rest on the ground once more. "Then tell me where the Seneschal is," she said to Urzo. "I'm going to find him."

"Don't be ridiculous," Urzo said. "He will have his personal guard with him as well as members of the Watch. You'd have no chance alone against them all."

"But she's not alone, is she?" Rafe said, stepping next to Rory.

"No," Adelma said, "she ain't. So give us the damned directions now so we can be on our way."

"I can help you with that," a voice said.

Rory started and turned.

Adelma grimaced. "Jabir," she spat. "The Seneschal brought him here."

"I can take you to the Seneschal," Jabir said. "And I know where Cruikshank is being kept."

Rory's fists clenched. She wanted to tear Jabir limb from limb—Longinus was on the brink of death because of him.

"Should I let him out?" the rebel with the keys asked.

"If you want to see a grown man ripped apart, go ahead," Adelma growled.

"No, I can help you," Jabir said. "I've been locked up here same as you. Why would I have any loyalty left to the Seneschal? I want to get myself out of here, same as you."

"You put us in here," Adelma said, stalking over to his cell.

"Wait, wait," Rafe said. "Adelma, wait. Come back." He gestured for everyone to come closer so they could talk.

"You can't seriously consider trusting him," Rory said incredulously. "He betrayed us. We should leave him here to rot."

Rafe turned to Urzo. "Do you know where they might be keeping Cruikshank? Or where the Seneschal might be?"

Urzo shook his head. "I know roughly what wing his rooms are supposed to be, but it's huge."

"Or what about the submersible?" Rafe asked.

Again, Urzo shook his head. "I've got no idea."

"Then I don't see that we have a choice," Rafe said. "Cruikshank could be in as bad a state as Longinus. If we set off alone, with no direction, we'll get lost, and we could take up more time than Longinus has left."

Rory winced as if from a blow at the mention of how little time Longinus had left. "You're right, you're right. All that matters is that Longinus gets the antivenom."

Adelma cracked her knuckles. "I'll make it clear to Jabir how important it is that he don't mess with us." She walked out of the cell. "Open Jabir's cell," she said to the woman with the keys.

"No, wait, wait," Jabir said, backing away. "I said I would help you. I can be useful to you. I can take you straight to the Seneschal's rooms without passing his personal guards. And I can take you to Cruikshank too. She's being held close to his quarters."

The cell lock clunked open, and Adelma savagely pulled the door open.

"Wait," Jabir said, scrambling away, his voice shrill. "I can show you—"

"I heard you the first time," Adelma growled marching on him. "Just want to make sure you fully understand the consequences if you try to screw with us again."

***

They left the long row of cells as the pit fighters were all being freed. The slaves cheered, marvelling at the rebels' lack of studs.

Adelma carried Longinus slung over one shoulder so that his upper body, head, and arms swayed in rhythm with her steps. His eyes were closed, his breathing laboured. The red marks snaking up from his right hand looked as if they were trying to climb up his arm.

"Hold on, Longinus," Rory murmured, raising her hand to touch his arm. She stopped herself, not knowing if the red marks were painful.

Rafe walked close to Jabir, a knife at the ready. Adelma hadn't beaten Jabir too badly, just enough to break his nose and give him a black eye. The man deserved far worse.

Jabir directed them back the way they had come. They reached the door to the lizard stables.

"I'll go ahead," Rory told the others. "See if there's trouble." She gave Jabir a warning look.

"I swear this is the right way," Jabir protested. His voice sounded nasal, as though he had a cold. His nose was swollen where Adelma had hit him.

Rory cautiously opened the door to the lizard stables. The area beyond it was dark, the cage bars just about visible. She could smell the lizards—a thick, acrid, animal smell—and she heard their low hisses and clicks.

She nodded at Rafe and Adelma. "Clear."

"I told you it was safe," Jabir said.

Adelma raised a hand at him, and he quickly fell silent, glaring at her.

They slipped into the lizard stables, Rafe keeping Jabir in line. When they reached the door at the other end, Rafe opened it a crack and glanced out.

"Shit," he whispered, silently closing the door. "Men with steam guns. Maybe six of them."

"Shit," Rory echoed. Their weapons would be useless against the steam guns. No matter how good a fighter Rafe was, his knives couldn't cut steam.

"We go another way," Rafe said.

"It will take longer," Jabir said.

"Are you hoping we'll go out there and die?" Adelma asked.

Jabir cringed away from her.

Rory hesitated. They couldn't afford to waste time, given Longinus's condition, and yet stepping out that door would be pure suicide.

"Let... the... lizards... out," Longinus croaked.

Rory started at the sound of his voice, hurrying around Adelma. He lifted his head weakly and let it drop again. Rory pushed a sticky strand of hair from his forehead. "The lizards?" Rory prompted him gently.

"The lizards... afraid of the steam guns... see them as threat... they'll attack."

"That's a good idea," Rafe said. "We can hide back in the previous room and wait for the lizards to make their way outside."

"Yes, yes," Rory said eagerly. "Quick. Come on."

"I'll take Longinus and that one back," Adelma said, grabbing Jabir by the collar. "I could beat you even blacker and bluer with only one hand. So no funny business." She dragged him along without waiting for an answer.

Rory opened the door that led outside first, by a tiny fraction. It opened outwards, so the lizards would be able to nudge it open and get out. She paused, waiting to see if the

418

men with the steam guns had noticed, but they were facing the other way.

"All good," she whispered.

Rory and Rafe then started with the cages nearest the door. The dead bolts were loud, each one clunking open as it was pulled back. Rory hoped the noise wouldn't carry outside to the men with the steam guns.

They threw back each cage door, moving quickly. They were halfway down when the first lizard cautiously nudged past its cell door. It froze when it caught sight of Rory and Rafe.

"Forget about opening the doors," Rafe said. "Just do the bolts."

They moved quicker, and by the time they finished, several more lizards were crawling out. The first one was examining the outside door. Rory and Rafe slipped back out, joining Adelma and the others.

"All done," Rory whispered. She crouched down by Longinus's side. Adelma had propped him up against the wall. "You alright?"

Longinus didn't reply, but he opened one eye a touch.

"That were a good plan," Adelma said in a low voice. "Good to see that poison ain't turned you into a fool quite yet."

Longinus kept his eyes closed, but the corners of his mouth stretched a fraction in an approximation of a smile before falling slack again.

Adelma turned serious. "You better not die on me now."

"I'd be... a most... elegant ghost."

"No," Rory said, unable to stop her voice from rising. "I ain't hearing no nonsense about ghosts." She didn't add that he already looked like a ghost, his skin sickly and pale, his eyes darkly ringed. Rory had no idea how much time he had, but she knew that it wasn't long.

Longinus didn't reply.

Rafe was still at the door, and he opened it a touch before closing it again. "Lizards are opening the outer door," he whispered.

A moment later, a shout rang out. Rory came to Rafe's side to peek out at the scene. The outer door had been pushed fully open, and a large cloud of steam sent a lizard shrieking and racing off to the side and out of sight.

The lizards poured out of their cages then, streaming out of the door, making hissing and clicking noises that almost sounded like they were communicating.

The first scream tore through the night. Rafe closed the door silently. "Not a good way to go," he whispered.

"They don't deserve any better," Rory said stubbornly. She found herself hoping the lizards would make it back out to the desert—and that they wouldn't attack any of the rebels on their way.

CHAPTER
57

Jabir ached all over. His nose was an agony, as was his jaw, and his eye throbbed. He hated the big smuggler as he had never hated anyone. She had made him cower in fear, and he loathed the fact that she had made him feel small.

It was all he could do not to glare his hatred at her while the Damsians waited for the right moment to head out. But now wasn't the time to blunder about, seeking retribution. Now was the time to carefully plan. Jabir knew he potentially had a lifesaving opportunity in front of him. He still couldn't quite believe his luck that the Seneschal had put him in a cell right next to the Damsians and that they themselves had then freed him. But he was also aware that if he played this card wrong, he still stood to lose everything.

"Alright," Rafe whispered. "It's been quiet for long enough. I'll go check if it's safe to go ahead." He slipped out the door.

Adelma cuffed Jabir on the back of the head. "Don't think that's an opportunity to do nothing shifty."

"I said I would help you, and I'll be true to my word," Jabir said.

"Right," Rory grated. "Because you've been *so* trustworthy until now."

Jabir let his face crumple. "I'm so sorry. I had no choice, I—"

"Shut it," Adelma grunted. "We don't want none of your rubbish here."

Jabir fell silent. If he'd had any faith in the rebellion succeeding, he would have helped the Damsians in the hopes of making up for his previous actions and winning back his life and his freedom. But he knew for a fact that the Sons and the Daughters of the Elephant had pulled their support away. All that was left was an untrained forced of disorganised paupers, without proper weapons or proper leadership.

The Risen would rise up and crash against the palace Watch, dying in their thousands, whether the gate was open or not. But in their determination to have their rebellion, they had given Jabir a priceless opportunity to bring the Damsians back to the Seneschal.

Jabir briefly wondered where his wife was. He wondered if she had continued on her mad obsession to rebel against the Seneschal or if she had realised how futile it was and retreated. Not that it mattered. Once the Risen were dealt with, Reheeme would be found and arrested as a traitor. Jabir wouldn't have the influence to stop her execution, nor would he be prepared to jeopardise his position with the Seneschal by trying.

All the same, Jabir felt a brief pang at the notion that he might never see Reheeme again. He had always pictured having her at his side when he emerged victorious, ensuring that she was left chastised, meek, and happy to do his bidding. That would never happen now.

Rafe reappeared, and Jabir pushed aside all thoughts of Reheeme. For now, he had to focus on ensuring that he led the Damsians straight to their capture.

"We can go," Rafe said. "They're all dead out there, and the lizards are gone."

The Damsians slipped out, and Jabir followed, docile as a lamb. Every lizard cage in the stables was empty, and beyond, through the outer door, he could just make out part of a mangled body, the leather armour ripped away like it was no thicker than skin.

He shuddered at how close he had come to meeting a similar end. Well, better them than him.

Jabir and the Damsians stepped out into the courtyard, now littered with torn bodies. He mentally ran over the different ways he could take them to the Seneschal, trying to figure out which way would most likely have them run into the Seneschal's personal guards.

He would have to play things very, very cautiously. He couldn't have Rafe slicing his throat before the Seneschal's guards could get to him. Still, Jabir was feeling more and more confident that he would find a way out of this mess.

***

As they threaded their way through the courtyard, stepping over the mangled bodies, Rory found herself hypnotised by the horror of the torn limbs and black pools of blood reflecting the moonlight. So much death. How many had died so far, and how many more would die before this was done?

"Wait," Rafe whispered harshly to Jabir, yanking him back. "Stay here."

He crouched down by a body and wrestled with the straps that held the steam gun tied to the man—or what was left of him. Rory understood what he was about, and she went to help him, giving Jabir a warning look as she walked past him.

"We can't trust Jabir," she whispered to Rafe.

"Of course not," Rafe whispered back. "But he will be wanting the same thing as us: to get us to the Seneschal. He's the only way we have of getting there quickly. And I've got a plan. After this, I'll go ahead with him while you and Adelma stay far back enough that if there's any sign of trouble, you can slip away and find another way to the Seneschal. Jabir will be taking us in the right direction but probably a way where we're likely to bump into the palace Watch. I can hold them back while you find the Seneschal."

Rory didn't like that plan. "There might be too many Watchmen for you."

Rafe grinned. "I can take on quite a lot. Don't worry about me."

They had freed the steam gun, and Rafe hefted it, strapping it to his back. Rory helped him.

"I ain't happy with leaving you behind," she said, again glancing to where Jabir was standing. He was looking warily at Adelma.

"It's not up for debate." Rafe winked. "You're not the only one who can be stubborn. And anyway, you're not leaving me behind. It's only if we run into trouble, and then I will act as a diversion to allow you to get Longinus the antivenom in time. But the Watch has no idea we're here. They'll either be focused on the Eastern Trade Gate or on the rebels. If we run into anyone, there won't be many of them, and I might be able to dispatch them all quickly."

Rory frowned, still not quite convinced.

"And I'll have this," Rafe said, gesturing with the steam-gun nozzle. "I'll do quite a bit of damage with it."

That mollified Rory somewhat. He'd be able to kill a whole bunch of the palace Watch before any of them could get to him. And he was a Varanguard, after all. He would be a better fighter than any of the Watch.

Rafe finished fussing with the straps holding the tank of pressurised steam in place. It was heavy, but he seemed to bear it without strain. The long copper nozzle gleamed hard in the moonlight.

It took Rafe a couple of tries before he managed to let out a powerful burst of steam.

Rory retrieved a pair of thick leather gloves for him before struggling with the straps of another steam gun. Best to take as many weapons as possible, she figured.

She glanced over at Jabir again. His face seemed blank, yet she felt sure she saw the faintest look of concern there, probably because with two steam guns, they'd be able to hold back any assault from the palace Watch.

If Jabir hadn't been their only way to get to the Seneschal and the antivenom, Rory would have thought nothing of dousing him in steam then and there. He was to blame for Longinus getting poisoned, and the man was slimier than a slug—he deserved nothing better.

"Hold on," Adelma said, gently placing Longinus down. In no time, she had released the steam gun Rory was struggling with. "Strap it on me."

Rory shook her head. "You're carrying Longinus. I'll take it."

Adelma snorted. "Rory, you're about as strong as a stick insect. You strap that on your back, and you'll keel over like an overladen skiff."

"And you'll probably struggle to fire it," Rafe added. "The recoil on that thing is pretty strong."

"I can fire it," Rory replied, stung. She grabbed the nozzle of the steam gun, careful to place her hands on the leather grips, and she fiddled with the trigger, removing the safety until a powerful jet of steam burst out. The force of it sent her staggering back a step, jerking her arms upwards and sending the spray of steam completely off mark.

As soon as the steam had stopped, Adelma snatched the nozzle away from her.

"You need to keep one arm to hold Longinus," Rory protested.

Adelma raised an eyebrow. Looking at Rory deliberately, she aimed the nozzle, holding it with one arm, and fired.

The steam came out straight, her arm barely moving from the force of the recoil.

"I'm taking it," Adelma said. "Now, stop wasting time, and strap this to my back."

Reluctantly, Rory did as she was told. "Careful you don't bang Longinus's head against the tank." She placed her palms on the copper to make sure it wouldn't burn him if he touched it. The metal felt warm, but the inside was obviously well enough insulated to keep the scalding heat contained.

Once the steam gun was strapped to Adelma's back, she gave Rory the nozzle before crouching down and carefully picking up Longinus. His eyes remained closed, and his head lolled back.

"We need to hurry," Rory said. "He's getting worse."

Adelma slung him on her left shoulder, holding him in place with her left arm. With the nozzle in her right hand, she looked like a cross between a thug ready to kill and a firefighter rescuing a burn victim.

"Let's go," Rafe said to Jabir. He grabbed the Azyrian by the arm, holding the point of his knife a finger's width from Jabir's throat. "We come across any trouble, and it'll be trouble for you."

"I can't help all the Watch crawling over the palace," Jabir whined.

"Then you'll have to take us where there ain't no palace Watch," Rory snapped back.

"Of course, of course I will," Jabir replied. "But I can't help—ah…"

He fell silent when Rafe pressed the knife against the skin of his throat.

"That way there. Yes, I'm sure we won't come across any Watch," Jabir said after a moment of thought.

"You better hope that's right," Adelma said darkly.

Rafe led the way with Jabir close to him. Rory and Adelma followed at a distance, as agreed, and they entered the palace.

***

They made their way through darkened corridors, moving quietly. Jabir did nothing to try to give their presence away. He couldn't afford to arouse the Damsians' suspicion, certainly not with Rafe's knife hovering so close to his throat.

He was also frustrated by the latest setback: not only did the Damsians now have two steam guns, but he and Rafe were also walking far ahead enough that even if he led them straight to the Seneschal's personal guards, Adelma and Rory could conceivably get away—especially given that Adelma had a steam gun.

Jabir knew far better than to underestimate the infuriating foreigners. And he also knew better than to hope the Seneschal would be happy with only getting Rafe captured.

Rafe paused at the end of each corridor, peering cautiously around and waiting for Rory and Adelma to catch sight of him and for Jabir to see the direction they were headed.

They passed a window, and Jabir saw fighting. He frowned. It looked like pit fighters against palace Watch.

The Risen were almost at the Barraba gate, no doubt the one they planned to open. That would be why the corridors were empty of Watchmen—they were all outside fighting the rebels. A stroke of luck to add to the Damsians' account, then.

As Jabir watched, a large lizard ran down a wall outside and snatched a Watchman. It spun around and, with a flick of its massive tail, sent a nearby rebel flying.

In the distance, near the Eastern Trade Gate, was a thick column of smoke. Jabir cursed. All the Watchmen would be concentrated over there, especially if there was a fire. Still, he hoped the Seneschal's personal guards would be keeping close to their master.

And then he had an idea—the perfect plan to ensure that Rory and Adelma couldn't get away.

He was careful to keep his face neutral, despite the glee he felt. He could still turn his fortunes around.

***

Rory and Adelma followed Rafe and Jabir cautiously. The two men moved awkwardly up ahead, Rafe holding Jabir like a hostage at the tip of his knife. Rory's heart pounded loudly. They hadn't come cross any Watchmen yet, and that made her nervous. She knew Jabir would betray them—knew it in her bones. But as Rafe said, they didn't have much choice other than to trust that he wanted them to get to the Seneschal as much as they did and to hope they would manage to avoid whatever trap he tried to set for them.

Adelma had her steam-gun nozzle ready. Rory walked with her newfound whip in her right hand, her dagger ready in her left. If there was to be an ambush, they would be ready.

They reached a fork, each passage a long, narrow corridor without windows. Rafe and Jabir were in the right one. Rory and Adelma followed cautiously. The two men stopped near the top of the passage, Rafe pulling Jabir back. His knife was still at Jabir's throat.

Rory and Adelma stopped too.

The silence was heavy. There were no windows in this part of the palace, so the only sound that broke the stillness was that of their footsteps as they headed deeper into the palace.

Rafe peered around the corner then stepped forward, dragging Jabir with him. Rory and Adelma followed.

They turned into another narrow, windowless corridor with a single door at the end.

Rory's skin crawled as she walked. Something was wrong, although she couldn't have said exactly what. She was opening her mouth to whisper that they should turn back when Jabir collapsed on the ground.

Except that he didn't collapse. The fall was fake—Rory had faked falls enough times to be able to distinguish a real faint from a false one.

Jabir made noise as he hit the ground, his bracelets ringing against the stone. It was a trap.

Rafe stepped back, pulling out his steam-gun nozzle. "Back," he called in a harsh whisper.

Rory had already yanked Adelma around, and they hurried away. She heard the ring of footsteps, no doubt summoned by the clatter of Jabir falling.

Before they could reach the corner, five Watchmen were running over, blocking the way.

"Damsians," one shouted. "Damsians have escaped!"

Adelma swung her steam-gun nozzle. The burst of steam caught the first Watchman. He collapsed, screeching in pain. The air filled with the stench of boiled meat.

Shouts rang out back from where Rafe was. More footsteps echoed, and more Watchmen joined the fray in front of Adelma and Rory.

Rory glanced back to see that Rafe was also sending out bursts of steam, holding back a number of Watchmen who were crowding the corridor at his end. They were trapped.

The Watchmen she and Adelma were facing had retreated beyond the limit of the steam gun's range, and they glowered at the two Damsian women.

"Stay back or I'll turn you into boiled ham," Adelma warned, still pointing the nozzle at them.

More footsteps. More Watchmen. Rory again turned back to see that the Watchmen were swelling in numbers at Rafe's end too.

"Do we push forward your side or ours?" she called to him.

"Way we came."

Adelma gestured with her nozzle towards the Watch. "Move."

She let out a burst of steam before stepping forward. The Watchmen stepped back alertly, keeping exactly beyond the steam gun's range. They kept their eyes trained on Rory and Adelma.

Rory and Adelma edged forward carefully, Rafe following behind them, keeping the Watch on his side at bay. He moved quicker, closing the gap. Rory stepped over the dead Watchman, doing her best to look away, sickened by the sight of his boiled flesh.

Soon they were all back in the first long, windowless passage, which was now clogged with the Watch at each end. Rory, Adelma, and Rafe were hemmed in closely on both sides by Watchmen.

She wracked her brain, going back over the last few passages they had been through, searching for a way to get out of this impasse.

When a Watchman tried to reduce the distance a little between him and Adelma, she immediately unleashed a burst of steam, catching him head-on.

Rory covered her mouth and looked away as the man died screaming. The rest of the Watchmen hurriedly took a few more steps back.

"Keep moving forward," Rafe whispered.

One member of the Watch stumbled towards Adelma as if he had been pushed. Adelma reacted at once, sending a burst of steam.

To Rory's dismay, the burst finished in a faint mist. She checked the gauge on the back of Adelma's tank. It read Empty.

"Rafe," she said in a low voice. She tapped Adelma's tank. Rafe understood at once, shifting so he could point his nozzle back and forth between both clusters of Watchmen without catching Rory or Adelma.

The guards on Rory and Adelma's side took the opportunity to press closer. Rory cracked her whip, catching two in the face. Ugly red welts appeared, but still, they pressed forward.

Rafe issued a warning burst of steam.

Rory could feel sweat dripping down her back. The air was close from all the bodies crammed into a small space and roasting hot from all the steam. There was no way out of this. Rafe's steam would run out eventually, and they would be left fighting an entire horde of palace Watch—far too many to beat, even with Rafe and Adelma's fighting skills.

Adelma must have had the same thought. She gently placed Longinus on the ground. Then she unstrapped the heavy steam canister and flung it at the Watchmen. There was no space to dodge, and the first row crumpled backwards as the tank hit them.

Angry shouts rang out, and a number tried to push past to attack.

Rafe let out a burst of steam.

It had only a tiny amount of pressure, and it didn't even reach the Watch before petering out.

His tank was empty.

One of the Watchmen facing Rory gave a predatory smile. "Kill them."

Adelma pulled out her battle-axes.

CHAPTER
58

Cruickshank listened to the sounds of the night as everyone slept in the workshop. They had all bedded down a couple of hours earlier, but there was no way she could sleep. The pain in her foot was flaring up again, like a flower slowly blooming. The nurse had given her more drops earlier, but their effects were starting to fade. The silver lining was that it was easier to think without the painkilling haze.

Back at the door, the two Watchmen were still in position, but they looked bored and sleepy, their eyes glassy.

The workshop was dark save for the soft glow of the single vapour lamp close to the furnace. There were no windows, no moonlight that could filter through, and the only way Cruickshank could determine the passing of the hours was by how tired she felt.

The furnace had been turned off, and it ticked softly as the metal began to cool. Cruickshank was the one who had switched it off, but she had only cut the ignition at first, leaving the gas to flow into the furnace's chamber. Once the chamber was full, she had turned the gas off.

She would easily be able to blow the whole thing up, including the gas supply, if she wanted. The explosion would be strong enough to tear a serious hole through the wall.

Cruikshank turned her head left, and she saw that Kadelta was also awake. She remembered what he had said about the drugs making it hard to sleep. Not that she wanted to sleep.

Now was the time to plan, to work out her next move. The problem was that Cruikshank was totally and utterly at a loss for what to do. The valve was completed, which meant that while not perfect, the submersible was operational. There were small adjustments to be made come morning, but essentially, the submersible could be operated without risking a boiler explosion due to too much oxygen.

Which meant that Cruikshank had gone from valuable machinist to inconvenient piece of evidence.

Cruikshank could blow the furnace up now, but then what? With her foot, she couldn't run, at least not fast enough to get away from her captors. She had no weapons beyond the tools at the workbench, and she had no idea how to make her way out of the palace. Not only that, but if anyone saw her out and about, she was sure to be immediately arrested and brought back.

She chewed the inside of her cheek. Blowing up the furnace was the one card she had to play, and maybe she should save it to take out the Seneschal—a final gesture of defiance rather than a doomed escape attempt.

Cruikshank froze when she heard footsteps ringing out beyond the wall. She strained to listen. There were voices, then a scream, amidst an odd hissing.

Her heart pounded. What was going on out there?

The guards had heard too, and one of them turned to open the door. Cruikshank saw nothing other than an empty passage through the open door, but a second hiss rang out, and this time, she knew what it the sound was: steam guns.

Her heart pounded. If the rebels had made it into the palace, they wouldn't stand a chance against steam guns.

More footsteps—reinforcements joining the fray.

More hissing and screams.

Suddenly, the card she had to play, blowing up the furnace, took on a whole other dimension. If there were rebels out there, blowing up the wall might kill the Watchmen and help the rebels, also giving her an escape.

The problem was that she had no way of knowing where the rebels were in relation to the Watch. If she blew up the furnace, and it was next to the rebels, she would kill them. Maybe if she got closer to the wall, she could hear better and figure it out.

She sat up but froze as the guard shouted, "Get back down!"

Cruikshank hesitated then obeyed. She couldn't risk being restrained. She needed to be able to blow up that furnace.

She strained to listen to the fighting beyond, trying to glean some clue from the muffled sounds.

***

It was a bloodbath.

Watchmen pressed on either side, Adelma holding them back at one end with her battle-axes, Rafe at the other with big swings of his ponytail. Rory stood between them, over Longinus, cracking her whip when she saw an opportunity to help Adelma.

The Watchmen swarmed beyond, their white armour gleaming, like a swarm of shiny insects clogging up a drain. The white was dotted with the Seneschal's personal guards in their black uniforms.

The dead were being dragged away in an attempt to make space, but it was clumsy, and the press of bodies meant only two members of the Watch at a time could engage either Adelma or Rafe. Adelma and Rafe were both drenched in blood, but already, Adelma was starting to step back. She had caught a nasty blow to her hip, and it bled freely.

Rafe was still going strong, killing with disturbing efficiency. The Watchmen were struggling to move the dead away without getting caught by his deadly ponytail.

Whenever she could, Rory cracked her whip at the Watchmen facing Adelma, snatching weapons away or disrupting blows. Rafe moved too much for her to get anywhere near him, and she didn't want to risk catching his ponytail. Between them all, Longinus laid on the ground, unconscious, his chest barely fluttering with each breath.

Rory glanced about her, desperate for anything that could get them out. There was no way for them to keep this up for much longer, and there seemed to be no end to the number of Watchmen pouring into the corridors.

But everything around her was smooth stone. There was no way out.

***

Cruickshank continued to hesitate. She feared making the wrong move and killing the rebels along with her only chance of escape. She could hear shouts, angry roars, and the clash of weapons. What was going on out there?

She looked at the furnace again. Nothing gave her any clue as to the rebels' position. If she blew it up and killed the rebels, it was all over. If she did nothing, it would be all over for her. But then again, if she killed the wrong people...

Cruikshank looked over at the remaining guard. The other guard had gone outside, so did that mean the Watchmen were level with the door? Or had he gone to attack the rebels?

There was simply no way of knowing. All she could do was either blow up or not blow up the furnace without knowing which was the right decision. It would come down to pure luck.

Cruikshank hesitated.

***

Adelma cried out and staggered back as a blade stuck her in the shoulder. Rory threw her whip aside, pulled out her

438

sword, and jumped in front of Adelma, barely parrying a blow that would have caught the smuggler on the neck.

Rory only just managed to keep hold of her sword as she absorbed the impact of the blow.

If they were reduced to counting on her to hold back the horde of Watchmen, it was all over.

Adelma rallied, hacking with her one good arm and dispatching two more Watchmen.

There was a brief scuffle in the Watch ranks as the next guards struggled to get past the dead, and Adelma sagged against the wall. Rory grabbed hold of her whip, cracking it over and over again, but it wasn't enough, and the Watch charged Adelma again.

The smuggler only raised her right axe, her left arm hanging uselessly at her side.

Rory heard a shout, and she turned to see Rafe staggering back. He was so drenched in blood that she couldn't tell where he was wounded.

He launched an attack again, but his movements didn't have their usual grace.

Rory blinked away the sweat that poured from her forehead. They were failing. The Watchmen were pressing in, and soon Adelma would fall, then Rafe.

And then the world exploded.

Rory was thrown back in a spray of rubble, slamming against a wall. Something hard flew past her cheekbone, cutting the skin. Plaster rained down.

Rory coughed and moved slowly, her head throbbing painfully where she had hit the wall. Her ears were ringing. She coughed some more, her mouth and nose full of dust.

She scrambled clumsily on all fours, dazed and confused. Blood trickled down her cheek.

Somewhere, someone was screaming.

The dust was so thick that Rory could barely see. Her eyes alighted on a hand that was no longer attached to a body. For a moment, she didn't understand what she was seeing, then her head cleared enough for the last few moments to come rushing back. She got to her feet and scrabbled manically to find Longinus.

She tripped over him, falling, one of her hands catching painfully on a broken brick. She scrambled back to him. He was still lying as before, still unconscious. She pushed her ear to his chest and was flooded with relief to hear a faint, hectic heartbeat.

"Here, lovey."

Rory stared in shock as a familiar thick-jointed hand extended down, a tattoo she knew all too well covering the wrist. She looked up, half wondering if she was concussed and hallucinating. "Cruikshank?"

The machinist hauled her to her feet. Her hand felt thick and solid.

"Cruikshank!" Rory flung herself at the older woman, hugging her tight. The relief at finding Cruikshank alive was so overwhelming, after what had just happened, that she almost began to cry.

Then she remembered the Watch and turned back and forth to see how many were left.

Beyond where Adelma had been fighting was a huge, ragged hole in the wall. In front of it were the mangled bodies of the men who had just a moment earlier been attacking.

Adelma was finishing off one who was still alive. She stood up, moving slowly, obviously in pain. She was also caked with plaster dust, her hair dusted white, her wounds bleeding tracks into the powder.

Rory turned back. There were dead bodies on Rafe's side too, but not torn apart like the ones at the site of the explosion. The Watch seemed to have disappeared, along with Rafe.

"Look at that hole," Adelma said, limping over to Cruikshank. "You nearly blew us halfway to hell." She grinned and clapped Cruickshank on the shoulder. "I can't believe I'm saying this, but I'm seriously glad to see you."

"I second that," Cruickshank gave a grin, but her face turned serious as she caught sight of Longinus. "Did the blast catch him?" she asked, her face twisting with concern.

Rory shook her head and quickly explained what had happened. As she was speaking, Rafe appeared, materialising out of the dust like a mirage. He too was caked in plaster, and he had received a few more cuts from flying rubble.

"We need to go now," he said grimly after a quick nod to Cruikshank. "There's no—"

He pulled out his twin knives in a flash.

"Stop!" Cruikshank shouted. "That's Kadelta. This is the man we came here to rescue."

Kadelta stood frozen, having stopped in the middle of crossing the hole into the corridor. More like a ghost than a man, he was painfully thin, his eyes sunken and ringed with dark, his skin the same colour as Longinus's.

Adelma limped over to him, still menacing in spite of her injuries, and she grabbed his thin tunic. "You've caused us a whole lot of trouble," she growled.

Behind him, Azyrian slaves were fearfully looking out through the hole in the wall.

"Don't harm them," Cruikshank said to Adelma. "They were working on the submersible with us."

"Can you tell us where the Seneschal's quarters are?" Rafe asked.

"Very c-close," one of the slaves answered. "C-Continue that way, and then turn right."

"You can go," Rory told them. "There's a rebellion going on. Maksurian rebels should be storming the palace by now to free all the slaves."

The slaves exchanged glances, and Rory could see wonder and mistrust in their eyes. They quickly scrambled through the hole and ran away.

Adelma grabbed Kadelta once more. "Listen here," she growled. "My friend there is close to dying because we came here for you. So you follow and do as you're told. You give us any trouble, and I mean *any* trouble, and I'll kill you myself and report back that the Azyrians executed you, you hear me?"

Kadelta nodded shakily.

It was odd to see him standing there. At first, all their efforts had been aimed towards rescuing him, but things had changed so much that his rescue seemed irrelevant. Rory only cared whether Longinus lived or died.

"We need to go, now," Rafe said. "For some reason, there are no Watch left—the ones that survived disappeared. Jabir has also gone. I don't know why they've all gone, but we're not wasting this opportunity. We need to move *now*."

"I can carry Longinus," Cruikshank said.

"I'll help," Kadelta said quickly.

Cruikshank shook her head. "You're too weak, and I don't want to risk dropping him. Someone help get him on my back."

Rafe helped her pick him up and sling him over her shoulder. They set off.

"That don't seem right about the Watch," Rory said to Rafe in a low voice.

"I know," he replied. "I don't understand it, which means I don't trust it. But at the same time, if they do come back, then we're all done for. So best we move now. Keep an eye out."

Rory nodded. She caught sight of Cruikshank taking a step and wincing with pain. "You hurt?"

"My foot," Cruikshank replied. "I'll be fine. Better I go slower carrying Longinus with you three able to fight. Machines are my specialty—I was never much good with weapons."

Rory checked on Longinus's breathing again. His breath was so faint she thought it had stopped. But no—it was faint and laboured and rattling, but it was there. Rory gave his arm a squeeze in case he was able to feel it from within the depths of his unconscious. She had never felt so useless.

"Not long now," she whispered to him.

As Cruikshank walked, his head bobbed a little as if he was agreeing.

CHAPTER 59

It didn't take long for them all to reach the Seneschal's quarters. It wasn't far, as the slave had said. They were at the start of a corridor, and farther down were ornate wooden double doors that were thrown open, as though the Seneschal was expecting guests. There were no guards outside the doors, which was odd. There would be guards inside, though—there was no way it would be that easy to get to the Seneschal. In fact, Rory found it odd that they hadn't been stopped or attacked again.

She and the others moved slowly, edging towards the door.

"It's a trap, it's a trap," Rory muttered to herself.

Longinus was clinging to life by his fingertips, and they had no choice but to go forward.

When they got close to the doors, Rafe gestured for them to stop. He inched forward alone and peered quickly into the room beyond.

"Ah, finally. Welcome," the Seneschal's voice rang out. "Please come join us. Don't be afraid. My guards have strict orders not to harm you."

Rafe turned back to exchange a glance with Rory and the others. That sounded decidedly like the guards had been ordered to kill them all.

"And I have Longinus's antivenom," the Seneschal added.

That decided Rory. Not caring about whether it was a trap, she stepped forward quickly, entering the Seneschal's office.

The room was luxuriously furnished, and on one wall was a painting that looked eerily similar to the one in Reheeme's office. The Seneschal sat with Reheeme on one side and Jabir on the other. Reheeme looked tired and dirty and a good deal roughened up but unhurt. Her face was the picture of cold fury.

Across from her, Jabir looked triumphant. Behind them were just three of the Seneschal's personal guards. Rory heard Rafe and the others join her.

The Seneschal stood up. "Congratulations," he said with that silk-soft voice of his. "You made it. I had to call off the Watch when I heard that Cruikshank had exploded the furnace. It turns out, my dear"—he turned to Cruikshank— "that you still are of value to me."

A throwing knife had materialised in Rafe's hand, but the Seneschal made a tutting noise. He held up a glass vial.

"The antivenom Longinus needs so desperately," he said with a small smile. "Kill me, and I'll drop it, smashing it onto the floor and rendering it useless."

The floor was stone, and the vial was made of delicate glass.

"Where's the rest of the antivenom?" Rory asked.

"When I heard the pit fighters had been released, I had it all destroyed."

"You must have kept some back for yourself," Rory said.

"Yes. This vial right here." The Seneschal seemed to be enjoying himself.

"Reheeme, can you make more antivenom?" Rory asked.

The Seneschal shook his head, the smile spreading on his face like oil on water. "For Reheeme to make more antivenom, she needs access to the lizard that creates the venom. I heard that you took the liberty of releasing all the Prelate's lizards." He shook his head, smiling widely. "What a shame. Now, if you want that vial, you will have to do exactly as I say."

Rory gritted her teeth. "What do you want?"

"It seems I made a mistake. I assumed the rebellion would be taken care of when I swept away all support from Tarwa. I wasn't expecting Maksur to mobilise in such an organised and effective fashion."

The Seneschal looked casual, but Rory picked up a hint of tension. She felt a stab of pride—she might not have been from Azyr, but she was from a similar background to the Maksurians, and to hear that their revolution was succeeding almost brought a smile to her face.

"It seems this *revolution*"—the Seneschal spoke the word as though it tasted bad—"will win out. My city is lost, and I have to resign myself to that."

Jabir had paled. "What?" he stammered.

The Seneschal threw an annoyed glance at him, as though Jabir was an ant crawling up his robes. "As I understand it, my submersible is now operational, if in need of some fine-tuning. I will therefore get away in it, with Kadelta and Cruikshank on board."

Adelma spluttered. "Anything else? Why not demand that we pummel your back for you while you're at it?"

"Nothing could give me less pleasure," the Seneschal replied coldly.

"Then I'll gladly pummel away," Adelma growled.

The Seneschal made a threatening gesture with the vial.

"Adelma," Rory warned.

Adelma clenched her teeth but nodded.

"If you want to get away, fine, get away," Rafe said. "Give us the vial, and we will ensure that the Risen do not pursue you." Reheeme began to protest, but Rafe put his hand up. "Longinus is more important. The rebellion is what matters, not revenge on the Seneschal." He turned back to the Seneschal. "You don't need Cruikshank and Kadelta on board with you."

"You're a machinist," Cruikshank added. "You'll know enough to get yourself out of Azyr in one piece. And you can get the submersible out via the underground river, so the Risen won't be able to stop you. Just give us the vial, and we'll step aside."

The Seneschal gave a small laugh. "Step aside? You're in no position to make demands. Your friend will die before we reach an agreement."

"And how long will it be until the Risen get here?" Rafe asked. "When they do, they're unlikely to be willing to negotiate. You're also running out of time. Give us the vial, and you can leave now."

The Seneschal shook his head slowly. "I want to replicate the submersible to sell it. I need both Cruikshank and Kadelta for that."

"Longinus don't have time," Rory shouted, unable to contain herself. "He needs the antivenom *now.*"

"Then it's a shame you're wasting his time, isn't it?" the Seneschal replied with infuriating calm.

"Fine, I'll go," Kadelta said abruptly. "This mess is of my creation, and I won't have others paying further for my mistakes."

"I'll go too," Cruikshank said shakily. "I'll go. Just give Longinus the antivenom."

"I will," the Seneschal said, "just as soon as I'm in the submersible with you both. Now, drop your weapons and come with me. And remember: any sudden movements, I drop the vial."

Jabir stood up, still looking bewildered. "And me? Will I be coming in the submersible?"

"There will be no space," the Seneschal said coldly. "I need the three guards with me to make Kadelta and Cruikshank obey."

"But… but…" Jabir looked around him, cringing when he made eye contact with Adelma. "But Your Grace, I could be of use. I could help—"

"Shut up," Reheeme hissed.

Jabir shrank away from her.

Rory couldn't care less what happened to him. "Let's go, let's go."

"First, you must surrender your weapons," the Seneschal said.

"Fine, fine," Rory snapped, throwing her sword, dagger, and whip to the ground. She would have done anything to get him moving and to get Longinus closer to the antivenom. She could feel every second trickle past, each one a little more life leeching out of Longinus.

Rafe surrendered his helmet and his knives, and Adelma placed her axes on the floor with obvious reluctance.

"Now, you remember the way to the workshop, I assume?" the Seneschal asked. "You will all go ahead so I can keep an eye on you."

They all headed off, with the guards bringing up the rear behind the Seneschal. Jabir trotted behind them, keeping back by a few careful paces.

"Any of you do anything that makes me uncomfortable, I smash the vial, and Longinus dies," the Seneschal reminded them. "He doesn't have long now. In fact, it's a miracle he made it this far."

"Your Grace," Jabir called from behind the guards. "Could I be of service? I could perhaps restrain one of the Damsians or—"

"Quiet," the Seneschal snapped.

Adelma stopped walking so abruptly that Rory almost walked straight into her. "Wait. Longinus needs more space to breathe." She sounded panicked. "He needs to breathe. Help me take his shirt off. Quick."

Rory understood at once. Longinus's sleeping powder was in the sleeve piping. She went to help Adelma, who could only use her right arm and was bleeding all over Longinus.

"What are you doing?" the Seneschal asked.

"Freeing Longinus so he can breathe better," Rory said. "Buying him some more time."

She and Cruikshank carefully lowered Longinus to the ground. Cruikshank looked a little confused but fortunately didn't say anything.

"Reheeme," Rory called. "Please help us."

As Reheeme helped them remove Longinus's shirt, Rory told her about the powder in a few quick whispers.

"Find a way to get an alchemical globe," Reheeme whispered back, "and smash it open."

They finished removing Longinus's shirt.

"That's better. See, he breathes better," Adelma said.

Rory actually caught herself checking his breath to see if it was true. In fact, Longinus had never looked so fragile. His breath was as weak as a bird's, and he no longer looked like himself, stripped to the waist and spattered with Adelma's blood. Rory's throat tightened. They had to get him the antivenom in time. They had to.

"Are you done now?" the Seneschal asked impatiently.

"If you'd give him the antivenom, we'd go much quicker," Rory said angrily.

She gave Reheeme the shirt to carry, and they all set off again.

There were alchemical globes in sconces on the wall, but Rory could hardly snatch one without arousing suspicion, especially after the kerfuffle over removing Longinus's shirt. If the Seneschal got wind of anything, he would smash the vial, and with it would go Longinus's chance of survival.

And then Rory was given the perfect opportunity. A lizard appeared farther down the corridor, crawling along the wall. It was one of the smaller ones, and it froze on seeing them. It made a clicking sound, and a bright green frill of spikes appeared around its neck.

"Back," Rafe called. "That's one of the poisonous ones."

There was a brief moment of confusion as everyone tried to back away from it without making sudden movements.

Rory snatched an alchemical globe from its sconce and threw it at the lizard. It smashed harmlessly against the wall, but the lizard scampered away quickly, out of sight.

"Good work, Rory," Adelma said.

"Onward," the Seneschal ordered. He looked a little worried—no doubt because the lizards were a completely random element, beyond his control. They would be in the palace, and there was no telling who they would attack.

They reached the shattered glass from the alchemical globe. "Such a mess," Reheeme said, bending down and wiping the floor with Longinus's shirt, careful to wipe the sleeve piping into the spilt liquid. "Everyone is always having to clean up your messes, Seneschal."

"Stop that at once," the Seneschal warned, "or I'll break the vial."

Reheeme stopped and straightened, shaking out the shirt so it was clear nothing was hidden within it. "You think I was trying to gather the smashed glass?" she said scornfully. "What it is to be so paranoid as to be frightened of an unarmed woman holding a shirt. That's why you murdered my parents, isn't it? Because you were scared of their ideas, as scared as you are now of me with my empty shirt."

As she spoke, she walked towards him, still shaking out the shirt.

"I wasn't scared of your parents," the Seneschal said. "They were as irrelevant to me as ants—but when you come across ants trying to make a nest in your home, you stamp them out and pour boiling water on their nest. And that's what I did."

Reheeme stopped, giving him a look of pure disdain and hatred. A very faint white mist was rising from the shirt. Rory hovered behind Reheeme, not wanting to get too close and inhale the sleeping draught.

Reheeme and the Seneschal locked eyes, staring at each other with pure loathing. "You will pay for what you did," Reheeme said through clenched teeth.

The Seneschal sneered. "No, they will pay *me* for the submersible."

The white mist was continuing to rise from the shirt, but it was faint, and the Seneschal was so focused on Reheeme that he didn't seem to notice.

Rory's every muscle was coiled, waiting for the right moment.

Then the Seneschal frowned, his expression growing confused. Rory took her chance.

She leapt forward. The Seneschal cried out and lifted his arm to smash the vial, but his movements were slow. Rory crashed into him, aiming for the vial with both hands.

His guards shouted, but the one closest to him collapsed in a gurgling sound as a small knife flew into his throat.

Before Rory had even wrestled the Seneschal for the vial, Rafe had vaulted over. But one of the remaining guards was faster than him, yanking the knife from his collapsed colleague so that Rafe was left weaponless.

"You… will… pay," the Seneschal said, struggling against Rory, but his movements were clumsy and ineffective as the narcotic took effect.

Adelma bellowed, charging in at Rafe's side. She dodged a blow from a halberd and let out an almighty kick that caught the guard at his side and sent him stumbling back.

Rory sent her forehead crashing into the Seneschal's nose, feeling it break. She yanked the vial away as the Seneschal collapsed. Her momentum sent her stumbling back. She felt herself fall, the vial in her hand, and her stomach leapt up to her throat.

A hand caught her just enough to steady her back on her feet. Reheeme's face was slack from the narcotic. "Needs…

to be… injected…" Reheeme stumbled back and collapsed from the narcotic she had inhaled.

"Lovey, quick," Cruikshank said, hurrying away from the fighting, holding Longinus.

Rory ran after her and Kadelta, hearing Adelma grunt as she and Rafe fought the guards, unarmed.

"Here, help me lower him," Cruikshank said as soon as they had rounded the corner.

Kadelta and Rory both grabbed Longinus and gently lowered him to the ground.

"He's not breathing," Rory shouted, panic rising. She clenched her fist on the vial. "He's not breathing."

The vial stopper doubled as a syringe. Rory pulled the plunger back with shaking hands.

"Where? Where should I inject?" She stared at Longinus's unmoving chest, feeling hysterical.

"There," Cruikshank said, pointing at the base of his neck. "The artery, there."

Rory plunged the needle in at once, depressing the plunger. "Come on, come on," she pleaded, eyes riveted on Longinus. "What should be happening?" she asked no one in particular.

Nobody answered.

The silence was deafening.

Beyond, Rory could hear Rafe and Adelma still fighting the Seneschal's guards. Her eyes filled with tears. Longinus still wasn't breathing.

And then he let out a slow, shuddering breath.

"He's breathing!" Rory shouted. "He's breathing! Did you see, did you see?"

She looked up at Cruikshank, too happy and overwhelmed for words.

"He's breathing," Cruikshank confirmed. "And better than before."

Longinus's chest rose and fell, although he was still unconscious.

"What happened?" Rafe said behind them.

Rory turned back.

Adelma and Rafe were limping over, Rafe leaning heavily against Adelma. A strip of fabric had been bound tightly over his thigh, blood already seeping through. That had to be a bad wound. He was so covered in blood she couldn't tell how much of it came from his injuries, but it clearly had been a close fight against the Seneschal's guards. Adelma looked in a similarly bad shape.

"You need help," Cruikshank said, rising.

"We're fine," Adelma replied. "Few scratches. What about Longinus?"

"He's breathing again." Rory felt like all the weight of the world had suddenly been lifted from her shoulders when she spoke the words, and she sagged to the floor, overcome.

"We need to get him out of here," Cruikshank said. "And we need to wake Reheeme up. He will need more tending to."

Rory nodded, but she couldn't speak.

"You alright, lovey?" Cruikshank asked.

Rory nodded again. The tears that had welled up in her eyes spilled down her cheeks. She had come so close to losing Longinus.

"Come on," Rafe said gently, squeezing her shoulder and extending his hand to help her up.

"I'll carry Reheeme," Adelma said. "What about Jabir and the Seneschal? Both are still alive, although I knocked Jabir out as deeply as the Seneschal."

"We'll tie them up and tell the rebels where they are," Rafe said. "Our first priority is to get Longinus back so he can be tended to, and then you and I are going to need some stitching up."

Rory looked at him, brimming with gratitude that he had said Longinus was the first priority. "Thank you," she whispered.

CHAPTER

60

Rory remained glued to Longinus's bedside, refusing to let anyone relieve her. Reheeme brought liquids for him to drink and things to inject him with. She had doctors brought over, in spite of the fighting that still went on in the streets. Rory could hear it from the window. All of Azyr teemed, the streets and palace roiling with the rage of the Lower Azyrians and the Maksurians.

Mechanised elephants had been stolen and were used to tear down the palace walls. Tarwanese wearing studs were dragged into the streets and often killed. The scene was chaos.

Reheeme's house had been marked as a friend of the Risen, so nobody stormed the place, but it would take time for the outside world to die down.

None of that mattered to Rory, though, as much as the fact that Longinus would live. Reheeme said his lungs might have been permanently damaged, and he might suffer from shortness of breath. Throughout his recovery, he sweated and struggled, his body doing its best to purge itself of the poison, helped by Reheeme and the doctors.

The irony that the most talented poisoner, and therefore the best person to treat the poison, was the one struggling with it wasn't lost on Rory.

Finally, after a couple of days, he opened his eyes. Rory grinned at him, happy beyond words.

"From the state of your hair, I deduce that I have not died and gone to a better world," he croaked, a smile tugging at his mouth.

Rory burst out laughing. "Good to have you back," she said affectionately, squeezing his arm.

"The day hasn't yet come when poison will best me. Not the Viper."

Reheeme bustled in efficiently, snapping at Rory to be quiet and forcing Longinus to drink some liquids before ordering him to rest.

She had to be the least warm or friendly nurse, but she was curing Longinus, and that was all that mattered.

The following day, they were all summoned to the palace by Oma to attend the first meeting since the Prelate and the Seneschal had been toppled.

Longinus stayed behind, still too weak to be up and about.

The meeting was held in what had been a disused part of the palace, close to the Eastern Trading Gate, the place the rebels should have originally attacked.

Everyone gathered in an old audience chamber. Paintings, wall hangings, rugs—any form of decoration—

had been removed so that all that was left was a large white marble room with huge windows that looked out onto the manicured gardens below.

It was crowded with people, their voices a constant hum. Looking around, Rory could see that they were mostly from Maksur. She spotted a couple of Tarwanese in simple garb without their studs. They were conspicuous because of the quality of their clothes and their obvious discomfort, but it was encouraging that they had come.

Reheeme threaded her way through the crowd. There were some angry mutters as she passed, but she ignored them, walking with her head held high. As with every other Azyrian in the room, she had removed her studs. The sight of so many people without studs was startling, and Rory could only imagine how shocking and liberating it would be for people who had lived under that shadow for their whole lives.

Oma sat on a small chair beneath the throne, which remained significantly empty. Urzo stood behind her, his right arm in a sling, part of his face swollen into an ugly bruise. Rory gave him a nod, and he nodded back then broke into a full grin.

"Look at Terrell," Rafe whispered.

Rory looked over to where he was pointing. Terrell stood to the side, his hands clasped behind him. He had smart clothing on, and he looked a world away from the shy slave who had washed Rory's feet when they had first arrived in Azyr. His face was serious, yet he radiated pride.

Rory gave him a wave and a wink, and he gave her a half smile before quickly settling back into his serious position.

"Someone doesn't want to appear like a child anymore," Rafe whispered, looking amused.

Rory nodded. "Boy's done well for himself. I'm happy for him."

"Me too."

Urzo called for the room to quiet, and a hush fell at once.

"As you know," Oma rasped, making no effort to project her voice so everyone had to be perfectly quiet to hear her, "we are holding both the Prelate and the Seneschal captive. The Prelate was taken when the rebel force stormed the palace, thanks to Urzo and his team opening one of the gates to let them in."

A roar ran through the room and fists punched into the air as the Azyrians celebrated their victory. They chanted Urzo's name, and he gave a tiny smile before waving for the shouting to die down.

"The Seneschal," Oma continued, "was taken by the Damsians and Reheeme."

A surprised murmur ran through the room. People turned to look at Reheeme, who stood next to Rory and the others.

"On behalf of all of Azyr," Oma said to Reheeme, Rory, and the others, "thank you."

"It's our pleasure," Adelma replied. Her hip and shoulder were bandaged, and she still bore other minor marks and cuts from the fighting. "Myself, I would have killed the

Seneschal even if it weren't for your revolution. Never met a nastier man."

The Azyrians hooted their approval.

"What will happen to them?" someone shouted.

"They will be tried once we have selected suitable judges," Oma replied. "And they will be given a fair punishment."

"Have them killed!" another voice called out.

"Feed them to their precious lizards!"

The room erupted with shouts and calls for the Prelate and Seneschal's lives. Oma stayed silent, watching the crowd with a stern face.

"Quiet!" Urzo roared. "Quiet!"

When the noise had died down, Oma spoke again. "We will not begin this new chapter of Azyr by acting like the Prelate or the Seneschal," she rasped calmly. "Judges will be appointed, their crimes will be examined, and a sentence will be passed. It will be a fair process, though one that won't give them any particular leniency."

Some grumbled at this, while others cheered and shouted that Azyr was now a city of fairness.

"The current Council has been dissolved," Oma continued, "their members allowed to remain free and alive so long as they cooperate. We will need to establish a new Council…" She paused as a mutter ran about the room.

"We are not executing half the city," Urzo snapped. "Everyone is to be given one chance to realise the error of their ways and join us as we forge the future. We didn't liberate Azyr to instigate mass killings like when the Seneschal came into power."

Everyone fell silent when Urzo's spoke, and Rory realised that he was now considered a hero for having led the team who opened the palace gate. The Tarwanese in the crowd were keeping very quiet, and the one nearest to Rory was sweating noticeably.

"As to the Damsians," Oma rasped, "they have brought assurances from their Marchioness that trade deals will be negotiated between Azyr and Damsport."

An interested murmur ran through the room.

"The trade deals are conditioned upon Maksur having full water access and slavery being abolished," Oma added.

At this, another cheer ran through the room.

"The Damsians also came to liberate one of their own who had been forced into slavery," Oma continued. "Kadelta was tortured and forced to complete a machine for the Seneschal. As a token of our appreciation to the Damsians for their role in capturing the Seneschal and to begin our new relationship with Damsport on the best possible terms, they will be taking back Kadelta's machine along with Kadelta."

"That submersible could bring significant revenue into Azyr," a man called. He was dressed well and had the look of a reasonably successful merchant.

"As would the trade deal with Damsport," Urzo replied. "In any case, Kadelta was forced under torture to create that machine for the Seneschal. Since we want no part in slavery or torture, we aren't going to now try to profit from the Seneschal's disgusting practices."

The merchant stepped back, suitably chastised.

Oma continued, explaining plans for a system to elect the new Council members.

Reheeme stepped forward. "For the new Council, my parents had devised a system for electing—"

"We don't want a system from Tarwa!" a voice shouted.

"If it wasn't for Reheeme," Oma said, "there wouldn't have been a revolution. She was instrumental in getting my grandson and his team into the palace, which allowed us to carry out our attack. As I said before, we owe her a debt of gratitude. If she has something of use to suggest, we would do well to listen and then evaluate whether it will suit us to follow her advice."

At Oma's bidding, Reheeme gave a brief explanation of her parents' system.

"It's gonna be quite the job, ruling this city," Rory whispered to Cruikshank.

"You can't wipe centuries of hatred and mistrust in a few days, even with a revolution," Cruikshank murmured back. "It will take time for Maksur to accept anything coming from Tarwa, and vice versa."

Rory nodded. She didn't bother listening to the intricacies of the system to elect new Council members. Instead, she looked around the room, not quite believing that they had pulled off the mission. Longinus was alive, Kadelta had been rescued, and his machine would be going back with them to Damsport, which would ensure the city's trade

464

dominance as well as preventing any chance of the slave trade spreading—although Rory had to admit that this new Azyrian government seemed likely to succeed in completely eradicating it.

She grinned to herself. Not so long ago, she'd been a filthy urchin, scratching a survival on the streets, and now she'd been on a proper adventure and not only survived but succeeded in a difficult mission. She felt a swell of pride.

She supposed she hadn't been an urchin for a while. All that was quite far behind her, almost growing distant. And if she wasn't an urchin any more, what did that mean for her boots? For Daria's boots?

She wigged her toes. The boots were too big, even with the newspaper she stuffed them with. They would probably always be too big. Daria had been tall.

Rory could feel the box inside her, the box with the memories of her time with Daria. She was moving on, she was moving further and further away from those memories.

Maybe it was time to let go of the past.

CHAPTER

61

After the meeting, Oma asked Cruikshank, Reheeme, and the others to come back to her office with her. Cruikshank noticed that the older woman had very easily slipped into the role of leader. She wouldn't be surprised if Oma became the first elected member of the Council. Leadership suited her, as stylish clothes suited Longinus.

Like the audience chamber, Oma's new office had been stripped of all decoration. It wasn't the Seneschal's former basement room, with its adjacent torture cells but, instead, must have been the office of some senior official or Council member. It was hard to tell, given the bare walls and lack of furnishings.

All that was left were a desk and chair and, leaning against the desk, a painting of Azyr that Cruikshank recognised from the Seneschal's office.

"Oh," Reheeme said, catching sight of it.

Oma smiled. "I heard it used to belong to your parents."

Reheeme nodded, still looking at the painting with a mixture of sadness and hope.

"Then you should have it back," Oma said. "Your parents were good people. They didn't deserve what was done to them."

"Thank you," Reheeme said, her voice thick with emotion.

Oma nodded. "And then there's the matter of Jabir." She called out, and two guards entered, dragging Jabir in. "We thought you would want to be involved in deciding his sentence," Oma said. "And of course, in the Seneschal's trial too, given your history and the fact that you were instrumental in capturing him."

Reheeme looked her husband over as though he were a cockroach, which wasn't much of a stretch, given his recent behaviour.

"Just tell me why," Reheeme said. "Was it money? Power?"

"Did you really expect me to put up with your condescension, your superiority and lack of respect, without taking matters into my own hands?" Jabir replied.

"This is what you call taking matters into your own hands?" Reheeme asked incredulously. "Betraying the rebellion to the Seneschal and giving him the Damsians?"

"That is what *you* drove me to," Jabir said. He turned to Oma and Cruikshank. "She has tormented me, treated me worse than a dog—she drove me to the edge of my sanity! I didn't feel like I had a choice—it seemed like the only way to escape. The Seneschal had lied to me about his intentions too. I hadn't realised the use he meant to make of the Damsians, and he told me he planned to improve the situation in the Lower and in Maksur. He claimed that Reheeme was simply power-hungry and ambitious. It seemed like a good decision to side with him, for me and for Azyr. A way to free myself from my wife's oppression while joining what seemed to be a good cause that would benefit Azyr without causing bloodshed."

He looked down, his face a mask of contrition. "I realise now how wrong I was," he said in a low voice. "I was taken in by well-crafted lies, and in that, I made huge mistakes. It is my heartfelt wish to repent and attempt to right the wrongs I created. The rebellion is the ushering in of a new era, one that will benefit all of Azyr and not just Tarwa. I want to help craft this new world, in any way I can. Please allow me to help you—I know I could be useful to you, and I so deeply wish to make amends."

Cruikshank had to admit that he was an excellent actor, but she was staggered that he thought anyone would believe his little show. Was there really no dignity or integrity in the man?

Reheeme shook her head, her disgust plain to see. "Do what you want with him," she said to Oma. "Have him tried by the Risen. Whatever seems appropriate to you. I'm washing my hands of him. And as to the Seneschal, I don't want to be involved in his trial. He needs to be tried by Maksurians and Lower Azyrians—by the slaves he made and the people he tortured—not me. None of this was ever about me."

Oma looked wary. "I don't want to give Jabir a trial. The Maksurians are clamouring for blood, and it's going to be hard enough to keep the Seneschal and the Prelate alive and unharmed until a trial can be arranged. If I announce Jabir's sentence, it might help appease them all enough to get the trial together."

Jabir paled. "You can't execute me without a trial. I'm innocent. This wasn't my fault! I… I was forced. I was tricked! The Seneschal—"

"You betrayed us at the palace when no one was forcing you," Rory pointed out coldly.

Jabir turned to Reheeme. "You wouldn't let them execute your own husband?" he whined. "In the name of the love we once bore each other, have them spare me."

Reheeme looked incredulous. "The love we bore each other? Are you delusional?"

"Cruikshank," Jabir said, turning to her. He tried to touch her arm, but she snatched it away. "Surely you aren't going to let them execute me without a fair hearing?"

"Oh, I would," Adelma said. "Even better, I volunteer myself as executioner." She smiled nastily. "Got a battle-ax right here, and my right arm's still good enough to take off a head."

Jabir looked frantically from one person to the next, backing away from Adelma. "Someone please stop this madwoman. Don't let her kill me. Surely some recognition must be given for the fact that it was I who arranged for the Damsians to come here with trade deals? And if not for them, communications between the palace and the Dividing Wall would have stood, and the attack on the palace would have been much harder. I was indirectly responsible for that—surely you must recognise it!"

Jabir was wringing his hands, scanning each face in turn, his voice bordering on shrill.

"I have another idea," Cruikshank said slowly. "I'm not sure that I agree with an execution."

"Oh, thank you, thank you," Jabir said. "I knew you were fair."

Cruikshank looked away from him, disgusted by his snivelling and his utter lack of integrity. Because of him, she'd been taken by the Seneschal, had her toe broken by a hammer, and had her eyebrows pierced against her will. Luckily, regarding her eyebrows, the alchemically treated studs hadn't been in long enough, and the holes would close in time.

"Since Jabir betrayed the rebellion," Cruikshank said, "he obviously thought the lives of the Lower Azyrians as they used to be were suitable—working in the mines, living in the slum of the Lower. So I suggest he live out his days just like that, living in Azyr the Lower and working at the mines. Since he thought that was good enough for the Lower Azyrians, it must be good enough for him."

Adelma let out a bark of laughter. "Excellent idea."

Jabir gave Cruikshank a look of pure venom.

"Don't look at her like that," Rafe said. "She's suggesting you keep your life, so I'd be grateful if I were you."

"There must be some other way I can be of service," Jabir said to Oma, ignoring Rafe. "I could help you. I could advise you on how to rebuild—"

Oma gave a small smile. "You can help by being an example of what happens to those who betray us, while showing the feasibility of avoiding mass executions to all those who opposed us, so the Maksurians won't be so bloodthirsty."

She gestured to the guards, who grabbed Jabir and dragged him away, ignoring his shouted protests.

Oma turned to Cruikshank and the others. "Glad that's done. Now, how long do you think you'll want to remain in Azyr before heading back to Damsport?"

"Only as long as it takes for Longinus to get better," Rory said at once.

"And I need to signal my crew to return with my ship," Adelma said.

Oma nodded. "Whatever you need for the journey back, send word to me, and I'll get it arranged."

"Thank you," Cruikshank said. "I have no doubt the Marchioness of Damsport will be appreciative of the way you have treated us."

"Good. We'll be looking forward to negotiating the trade deals and alliances once we have sorted out our city," Oma replied. "For these next few days, though, enjoy Azyr. You've deserved some rest."

Cruikshank smiled. Rest would be good. She absentmindedly scratched at the unfinished tattoo on her stomach. She was looking forward to getting it completed. Adding it to her collection had been tricky, and she felt a real sense of accomplishment. She would enjoy telling Liv about what it represented.

CHAPTER

62

It was a couple of weeks before they were ready to leave. By the time they descended the long staircase that snaked down the cliff, Rory was stunned by the changes that had taken place. The staircase itself was unchanged, with the same stalls and rush of traffic up and down, but the Great Gate and the walls on either side of it had been torn away. The sellers were different, too, cheerful as they called out rather than presenting the hard, fake smiles that Rory had seen on the way up.

But nowhere was the difference more obvious than in Azyr the Lower.

Tarwa had been forced to supply the Lower Azyrians with paint in every possible colour, and they had been painting their ghetto with obvious relish. Every door, wall, and roof bright, so the staircase seemed to lead down to a rainbow town. Patches of grey still remained, but the happy colours were slowly swallowing them up.

As Rory reached the bottom, she noticed that even the last few steps had been painted so that they all cheerfully clashed with each other.

People smiled, chattered, and even sang as they painted. Children drew on the walls of their houses and ran in the streets, as though everyone had been given a new lease on life. It was such a joy to see that Rory couldn't help but grin.

The mines had been brought to a halt, too, the pistons now still, the great booming heartbeat silent. The mine machinery still looked like a monstrous insect but a dead and harmless one. The dust had settled and been swept away so that the air was clean and no grey remained to mar the pretty paint.

Rory noticed that a few people still toiled away at the mines. She frowned, but before she could speak her confusion, Reheeme spoke up. "Oma thought this was an excellent alternative to having a bloodbath similar to the one during the Seneschal's rise to power. She wants this new era of Azyr to be as different from the past as can be, so all those who would normally be sentenced to death are sent to work the mines."

"And the actual miners?" Rafe asked.

"We are looking for a safer and better way to mine Beranthium," Reheeme replied. "Using better, more modern machinery. All the liberated machinists will be working on this. I imagine some input from Damsport's Head Machinist later in the design process might be a great help."

"I'd be delighted," Cruikshank said. "They are welcome to write to me for advice at any time."

"Thank you."

By the time they were in Azyr the Lower proper, Adelma couldn't hold her impatience any longer. "You milksops all walk too slow. I'm off to my ship and my Tommy." She hurried off, barging people out of her way in her eagerness.

Rory and the others arrived at the port at a more leisurely pace. It bustled with activity as the sailors made ready to leave. Cargo was being loaded, while farther back, at the cliff, Kadelta's machine was being lowered under his supervision. Adelma stood in the middle of the *Slippery Eel*'s deck, balancing Tommy on a hip and bellowing orders with a huge grin on her face. In between each order, she turned and said something to Tommy in a low voice, and each time, he laughed.

"I'll go check all is well with the dockmaster," Reheeme said, stepping away.

Longinus took a deep breath as he reached the side of the ship. He stepped onto the gangplank. "I never thought I'd say this," he said, reaching the deck, "but I'm glad to be back on the ship."

"Same," Cruikshank said, following more clumsily with her cane and injured foot.

Longinus took another deep breath, smiling as he looked around. Rory was relieved to find that the shallowness of breath Reheeme had predicted wasn't too bad. She had been worried when he'd struggled a little with the stairs, but he seemed fine now. She joined him on deck.

"We are going back to Damsport as heroes," he said, smiling. "Our mission is a roaring a success. Lady Martha will hear of it." His smile widened until he looked positively jubilant. "I don't even think it's a problem that I was unconscious for the end. I have plenty to work with, between my heroic victory in the Prelate's fighting pit and my idea that we liberate the lizards to attack those men with the steam guns. Yes, I will begin to write my report the moment we set sail."

He turned to Rory and lowered his voice. By that point, Rafe and Cruikshank had stepped away to attend to their things as they we were being loaded.

"Would you mind if I said I was the one who unlocked the lizard cages?" Longinus asked Rory. "Of course, I'll also need to check with Rafe. But it will sound more heroic. I think I could really use this report to get Lady Martha to notice me. She would be impressed, wouldn't she?"

Rory grinned. "I got no idea if she'll be impressed, but sure, you can tell her you opened the cages."

Longinus nodded, then he cocked his head, examining her. "I'm not complaining, but I'm finding your lack of sarcasm and general niceness unsettling. I hope that by the time we get to Damsport, you'll be back to your usual irritating self."

Rory laughed. "I'll do my best."

Adelma stomped past at that moment, shouting an order. Tommy was still balanced on her hip, and as she walked past the main mast, she lovingly ran a hand along it, looking like someone freshly reunited with a long-lost lover.

"Adelma," Cruikshank called. She hobbled over with her cane. "I thought we should toast our departure from Azyr and celebrate the success of our mission." She handed over a bottle of liquid so dark it looked like ink.

Adelma's eyes lit up. She put Tommy down and uncorked the bottle with her teeth.

"Ooh, that one smells strong," Tommy said.

"Indeed it does, Tommy-Boy. Cruikshank got me some good stuff there." Adelma winked. "We'll give it a try once we're out at sea, though. We should never be drunk when manoeuvring," she said deliberately to Tommy, who nodded wisely.

Adelma took another sniff of the bottle. "Oof," she said to Cruikshank. "I got a feeling this here is gonna knock us off our feet."

"Can I try some?" Tommy asked.

Adelma laughed. "That's my boy. But not till you're older. When you got hair on your chin, you can drink."

Tommy frowned, rubbing a hand on his smooth chin.

"Now, hurry up with that mainsail," Adelma shouted. "I want to be back on the sea in quick time!"

Rory leaned back against the rail, watching the scene with a feeling of peace and contentment. Longinus had gone to make sure his writing materials were on board so he could begin writing his report for Lady Martha. Cruikshank was talking to Tommy while Adelma stomped around the deck, bellowing orders and insults with a grin that made them more like endearments.

Rafe came and leaned against the railing next to Rory. They exchanged a smile. Rory enjoyed how comfortable she felt around Rafe. No more nerves, no more jolting stomach. Things were so, so much better this way.

She nudged him with her shoulder. "You did good."

He nudged her back. "So did you."

"Your fighting skills could use a little work, though," she said, grinning. "If you need help practicing, just let me know, and I'll show you."

"A property magnate, a sword-fighting instructor—is there no end to your talents?" Rafe asked with a quirked eyebrow. "Is modesty one of your many virtues?"

"As Longinus informed us before, modesty is for amateurs," Rory said, laughing. "And I ain't nothing but a pro."

"You know, we make a good team," she said, looking back at the deck, where Longinus had settled himself to begin writing, unable to look Rafe in the eye.

"We really do," he replied, and Rory felt his shoulder and arm against hers.

***

Once the cargo was all loaded and Kadelta's machine securely tethered behind the ship, they got ready to cast off. Reheeme, Oma, Urzo, and Terrell all stood on the dock, seeing them off.

"You will be welcome here anytime you want to return," Oma said.

"You'd better come back," Reheeme added.

"And thank you," Urzo said.

"I wouldn't say it was a pleasure," Cruikshank replied, "but you're welcome."

Adelma called out her orders, and the ship edged away. Rory waved goodbye with her whole arm. Terrell had stood soberly next to the others, but when Rory waved, he broke into a grin, waving back with just as much enthusiasm.

The *Slippery Eel* gathered speed, slicing gracefully through the sea.

Rory watched as the four figures on the dock grew smaller, until finally they were small specks among Azyr the Lower, then gradually the city began to dwindle from sight as well.

She stood at the railing, remembering how it had felt when they had arrived. She'd been excited to start her first adventure overseas, but at the same time there'd been that one night of sadness, thinking of Daria.

The boots, her only remaining link to Daria, felt bulky and cumbersome on her feet. She wanted to take them off and crawl up and down the rigging, feeling the freedom of the wind in her hair.

She wasn't an urchin any more. She had money, now. She could buy boots that would fit her, and she could even get steel caps added, if she wanted.

Holding onto the boots no longer really made sense. And neither did dragging an old loss around with her. Rory remembered the jolt of fear she'd felt, back at the safehouse with Rafe. Much as she worked hard to keep thoughts of Daria locked away, they were still holding her back. And she couldn't let her past still control her, not when she had come so far.

"Daria," she whispered.

Rory took off her boots. She felt a quick, sharp stab of pain deep in her stomach, as if a plaster had been ripped off from her insides. She hugged the boots tightly for a long moment, breathing in the smell of the leather, feeling its cracked, roughened surface beneath her fingers.

She threw the boots into the sea in one quick, smooth movement without pausing to think about it. They splashed in the water and sank immediately. The wind blew Rory's hair, lifting some of the smaller segments. The ship rolled softly beneath her feet, the wood of the deck warmed by the sun.

Rory touched her right hand to the whip she'd kept from her time in the palace. Rafe had had the right of it—the sword was a remnant of her past. She still wasn't prepared to give up on sword fighting, but she was looking forward to experimenting with the whip and broadening her fighting repertoire.

"What was that about?" Rafe asked, coming to stand next to her. "You threw your boots away?"

"Letting go of the past," Rory replied, staring out into the distance.

Rafe smiled. "That's good. That's very good."

Rory gave him a small smile.

Longinus rushed to their side. "Oh no," he moaned. "No, no, no! No! *No!*"

He gripped the railing with white knuckles.

"You alright?" Rory asked with a frown.

Longinus nodded, looking dejected. "It's nothing I haven't experienced before, after all," he said miserably. "I'd just hoped things would be different on the journey back."

"Ah," Rory said, understanding. She patted his back. "Well, at least it's got a nice symmetry to it, ain't it? You start off sick, and you end sick. And you're a man what appreciates a good symmetry, ain't you?"

Before Longinus could reply, whatever he'd eaten earlier that day popped up for a revisit.

Celine Jeanjean

The Adventure Continues...

Revolution in the streets
A deadly weapon stolen
A wardrobe too wide to fit up the stairs

All is most definitely not well back in Damsport

Go to **celinejeanjean.com/dollmaker**
to grab *The Doll Maker* now

PS: leaving a review is like giving an author cake.
Did I mention that I love cake?

WANT TO FIND OUT WHO DARIA WAS AND WHY SHE HAD SUCH AN IMPACT ON RORY?

Then *The Pickpocket* is for you. You can get this book for free, exclusively, by going to:

http://celinejeanjean.com/The-Pickpocket

Made in the USA
Middletown, DE
08 February 2020

84406440R00291